ALSO BY STEPHEN WRIGHT

Meditations in Green
M31: A Family Romance

GOING NATIVE

Going

NATIVE

A NOVEL

———

STEPHEN
WRIGHT

FARRAR STRAUS GIROUX
NEW YORK

Copyright © 1994 by Stephen Wright
All rights reserved
Printed in the United States of America
Published simultaneously in Canada by HarperCollins*CanadaLtd*
Designed by Fritz Metsch
First edition, 1994

LIBRARY OF CONGRESS CATALOGING-IN-PUBLICATION DATA
Wright, Stephen.
Going native : a novel / Stephen Wright.
p.   cm.
1. Fiction.   I. Title.
PS3573.R5433G6   1994   813'.54—dc20   93-10944   CIP

TO NORT

The author would like to thank the John Simon Guggenheim Memorial Foundation and the Whiting Writers' Foundation for their generous support.

GOING NATIVE

One

500 MOSQUITOES AN HOUR

RHO is at the kitchen sink, peeling furiously away at a carrot when she draws her first blood of the day, and, of course, it's nonmetaphoric, and her own. A sudden blossoming of color in the drab plot of one ordinary afternoon. So she watches herself spilling out across a trembling forefinger as if in a hurry to be gone, a hollow red staccato in the brushed-steel bucket of her sink. For a time she is simply a wide pair of mesmerized eyes, lost in the facts of the moment and, strangely, no longer present to herself. But the spell breaks, the cut is plunged into the aerated stream of her Puraflo faucet, the finger wrapped in a floral blue paper towel. The show's over.

It's late Friday in late summer in Wakefield Estates, where the shadows are long and the light is perfect and the sky a photographer's fantasy of absolute blue typically apprehended only on film, too blue to be arching in inhuman grandeur over this engineered community of pastel houses and big friendly trees.

Inside the polished kitchen soft northern light arranges itself evenly, democratically, among the fixtures and furnishings, the appliances and the apples, each discrete object contributing its own subdued reflection of snug solidity, charmed ease, tasteful harbor. It is a good place to be. The peeler is flashing again, metal blade in a whittler's blur, strips of orange vegetable matter stuck to the window above the sink in random crisscross like an entire box of desperately affixed Band-Aids. Behind her the routine clunk of fresh ice cubes dropping in the Kelvinator, and on the Formica counter at her elbow the Sony portable coolly irradiating her body with the problems of today's women: VIXENS BEHIND BARS: GIRLS WHO HAVE KILLED THEIR LOVERS. Rho barely notices, absorbed as she is in the physical task at hand and a mentally punishing recapitulation of the futile chase after self-respect which constitutes much of her so-called "working day." She'd almost quit again. For the second time this month. What was happening here? Accumulation, she thinks, that's all, just the dispiriting accretion of nine-to-fives, of petty betrayals, minor sarcasms, slights, injustices, and plain rudeness collecting like refuse under a rotting wharf until one blighted morning all the fish are dead, there's no place left to swim, and if sweet alert Lou hadn't recognized the sniperlike narrowing in her eyes and hustled her out past Mickey's smirk and the confused management team, she just might have released a sampling of the words grown slow and secret as fungus behind the professional exterior she'd had to retouch almost hourly for the past nine months. These were the words of disclosure, the ones to prompt an awful unveiling of the second self. She and Lou had fled to a corner of the cafeteria behind the ailing ailanthus, the bad joke of the company. The tepid coffee tasted like chlorine and the abstract neo-avant lithograph on the opposite wall kept somehow reminding her in a distinctly unpleasant way of the physical baseness of the body. It wasn't a thought she was supposed to have—she regretted the admission—but maybe she just did not like female bosses. And Lou, whose boyfriend's most recent message to her machine had been "If I hated you any worse, I'd be doing something more than just leaving you," had instantly agreed, saying me neither, they go completely Looney Tunes once a month. So at least there had been the release of laughter. The tears came later, alone in a stall in the women's room, the only one, it turned out, with no paper.

Then the wit-gathering, the brave soldiering on to after five, the obligatory traffic jam, the polluted lungs and mind, hunting food supplies at the local supermarket, where amid the day's carnage she actually experienced, while wheeling her wobbly cart down the broad buffed aisles, a small detonation of pure happiness. It came inexplicably out of nowhere and was gone by the time she got home, a psychic comet in elliptical orbit from that parallel universe her real emotional life, the good one, seemed to inhabit. Would she ever even begin to assemble the time and the will necessary to piece out the meanest portion of the puzzle that was her existence in this world? What was so damned difficult about comprehending middle income, middle of the road, middling middleness?

The vegetables are lined up like good little soldiers on the cutting board, though the peppers are slightly wrinkled, the lettuce browner than she remembered, and each time she tries to slice a tomato— injured finger held awkwardly aloft, away from spraying juices—her hair keeps falling forward into her face, obscuring her vision; she tucks it behind an ear, off it falls, the left side having been crudely chopped last Saturday by Sylvester himself of famous Sylvester's, a reminder with each turn of the head of some basic asymmetry. On the Sony an X-ray tech from Bedford Falls is describing how her husband comes home from his plumbing job, packs away the flank steak and boiled potatoes, and settles down in front of the tube wearing a chiffon cocktail dress, black nylons, and a pair of stiletto heels. At the commercial Rho discovers the cucumbers in the back of the refrigerator are frozen solid. Is there time for a quick dash to the Feed 'n' Fuel? The clock on the wall, a fanciful twist of wire and brass most visitors don't even recognize as a timepiece, is telling her that if she leaves right this minute . . . but a famous actress confessing that her famous mother used to beat her repeatedly with an English riding crop sets Rho off on an unscheduled tour of the Mood Museum, guilt thick as dust on all the exhibits, even the newest wing, where the paint's still wet and the descriptive plaques hopelessly inadequate and the curator the same creepy figure in black who liked to skulk underneath her crib and whisper horrors to her in a language no one else could understand . . . so there won't be any cucumbers in the salad and she's sure the Hannas won't mind.

Rho glances up to check on the twins and there, just beyond the carrot-splattered pane, in remarkable close-up, is a large bright lemon-yellow bird perched in regal isolation atop the feeder, and she looks, she is looking dead on, she doesn't blink, but the bird is gone, a trick of bad editing. Amazing. Too quick for the children to see and probably just as well. The inevitable round of questions about pets and cages, freedom and death. Brother and sister are squatting side by side in the sandbox Wylie hammered together the summer they all went to Nice, to the place like in the American Express commercial, the year of the big promotion, a fabled time in the family chronicle. Identical blond heads are bent in consultation over a serious arrangement of plastic blocks. Daphne sits watching from a nearby swing, youthfully lean body dawdling between the chains, the basketball shoes on her feet blindingly white and apparently several sizes too large. Her long black hair a hood of dark flame in the enfilading sun. She's the Averys' daughter from over on Termite Terrace, and despite the finger-scooped peanut butter jars, the bottle-cap ashtrays tucked discreetly under the couch, both Rho and Wylie like and trust her, they've known Daphy since she was six, and she's even recently completed a two-week course in which the conscientious baby-sitter is taught such essential tasks as how to bathe an infant, prepare a simple meal without fire hazard, and find the numerals 911 on either a dial or push-button phone. And the girl is also, for Rho at least, a touching facsimile of her own mysterious adolescence, her distance from which seems to vary daily, those fierce piebald years she chooses, against all reflection, to preserve as singularly enchanted.

Now Chip, she sees, has found a cracked water pistol she could swear she's already thrown out twice and is holding the pink gun to his head as if to hear a delicate ticking or the roar of the sea. His sister is banging the flat of her spread hand into the bottom of the box, mashing her sand dough into cookies the way Mommy does. A moment framed, even as it occurs, with the halo of future nostalgia.

She knows it's Wylie an instant before the phone rings. She knows why he's calling. The meeting ran late. The client didn't show. The traffic's bad. She wants to get ugly with him but the prospect of any further emotional expenditure deflates her, she can actually feel her body sagging into the wall. Pick up a cucumber, she tells him. Fresh.

And limes, more limes. And don't for once forget the charcoal. I love you.

Time to inspect the house. Well, the plants need watering and the three days' growth of fuzz wiped from each of the several television screens. She throws the comforter over the unmade bed, replaces the towels in the bathroom, gathers up Wylie's magazines—*Easyriders, Forbes, On Our Backs*—she can't keep up with his interests, whatever they are. The living room is white with black furniture and she can't decide if she likes it as much as she's supposed to. The day the decorators left, Wylie lounged about on the cream couch the rest of the afternoon, wearing an evil pair of sunglasses. Even after she'd laughed—and longer than the gag required—and night had come on, he refused to take them off. He never knew when to stop. Baby pink and dripping from the shower, he'd once chased her, wet towel snapping, through the house, skidded on one of his own puddles, and knocked himself out on the oven door. What a struggle it had been pulling a pair of briefs on him before the paramedics got there.

When the phone rings again, Rho takes it in the spare bedroom, the air still faintly medicinal, faintly evocative of Mother herself. It's Betty, who shared a cube with her at Fleischer and Fleischer until Rho left about a year ago for these fresh-looking pastures of now defoliated opportunity. As long as they've known each other Betty's been in search of an identity beyond her famous silver earrings. Today she wants to alter the spelling of her name to Bette but is worried about embarrassing mispronouncements. Rho suggests she change the last *e* to an *i*. Betty says she'll think about it. By the way, did Rho hear that Natasha finally quit, as promised, as rumored, with no savings, no parachute, the only safety net in that girl's life the one she'll be wearing over her chestnut bangs working the french fryer at McDonald's. Beneath the jokey manner there's a genuine chord of wonder and anxiety. Rho wants to tell Betty she nearly quit today, too, but she hesitates, the moment is gone, and Betty is rambling on through an intimate catalogue of Natasha's other woes: the buck-toothed lover boy who sleeps around without even bothering to clean himself off before coming home to her, the blue bruises on Natasha's arms and face, the not so subtle hints that Natasha herself has been testing other beds in other rooms. This is why Betty works. She gets up, drags herself to the office morning after grim morning just to keep up with her stories. Perhaps one day her colleagues in accounting will have a story to trade about her. Perhaps there's already a story in play about Rho. She refuses to imagine details.

After she hangs up, she remains seated there on the edge of the high antique bed, the bed she was born in. Mother watches from the gold frame atop the peeling bureau, the eyes in every color photograph of her ever taken a set of burning red stones invisible to normal gaze, only the lifeless camera capable of revealing clearly and consistently her true demonic nature. On the scratched mahogany table beneath the window squats a crude peacock carved from cheap pine with an unsteady hand and, leaning against the burnt-out lamp, an unfinished paint-by-numbers canvas of a bug-eyed cow Mother bought at a Kmart in Mason, Kentucky, on her last and final visit to Cousin Dewey's. "You know," she complained, "I don't believe they put all the right paints in this box." The disorientation came on a week later. She grew frightened by the motion of her mind. In darkest night she clawed herself awake from suffocating visions of sweaty walls and iron doors. By the end she was eating Kleenex and twisting her dry colorless hair up into a headful of reptilian dreads. She looked like an old demented white Rastafarian.

But Rho isn't supposed to have bad thoughts today. She'd promised herself. She wasn't supposed to be the Wicked Witch of the West at work either, arriving with one too many cups of coffee riding her nerves and a vague crankiness she could best attribute to "VCR hangover." The night before, she and Wylie had watched, for reasons hopelessly irreclaimable now, three rented films in a row, his choices of course, all fitting into the current shoot/chase/crash cycle of his rigorously limited viewing habits. In the first the good guys caught the bad guys but contaminated themselves horribly with badness in the catching, in the second the bad guys got clean away, and in the third the good guys were really the bad guys all along. This visual extravaganza was then capped by a dream that troubled her sleep and stuck to the bottom of her day like a wad of someone else's stale gum. There is a house and in the house is a living room that looks exactly like theirs, furnishings, decor, the stark absence of color, unused ashtrays in all the right places, except the house seems to be located on a spectacular beach somewhere, melony light reminding her of California, although she's never been there. She is upstairs lying between black satin sheets in a king-size bed, snoozing her way through a different dream . . . the one of this life, perhaps. Downstairs a tall shirtless man in white pants stands in dark silhouette at the glass door opening onto their redwood deck and, in this universe at least, a white deserted beach, an empty blue ocean. Is the man Wylie? She can't tell. And her attention keeps tracking back to the glass table exactly like theirs and yet not, and the dark object placed there with such compositional skill: the inescapable, indispensable gun. It's a loaded .45 caliber automatic of military issue, hardware expertise she did not possess in waking life. Nothing moves. This is the loneliest room in the world. Is a scene about to begin or has one just concluded? Who is the man turned indifferently away from our scrutiny? Whose gun? What's happening here? Why do these questions disturb her? Her hair falls into her face. She decides to start the party early.

In the kitchen she mixes herself a customized daiquiri. She stands at the sink, one hand quietly gripping the counter, she savors her drink. Consciousness skips a beat, and mental space is instantly renovated, angles and edges begin to develop padding, thoughts wander off from the party to find themselves in dead-end corridors and musty rooms with no doors, popping peanuts one by one into their toothless mouths, muttering solecisms to the lifelike forms on the wallpaper. Spooky. Wylie would shrug it off, but she is, as he says, the nervous type. That's what everyone said about Mother, too.

She brings the half-drained glass down hard on the counter as if summoning a bartender. The television screen frantic with the saturated belligerence of afternoon cartoons. She slides open the back door and it's like stepping out into a greenhouse. Daph immediately begins stuffing something into the back pocket of her ridiculously tight jeans. The lawn damp and spongy from this afternoon's tropical downpour. It has been a wet and irritating month. The summer is ending badly.

"Mommy!" Dale comes lunging across the yard on strong bandy legs, literally hurling herself into Rho's arms. Her daughter has a special feel impossible to confuse even blindfolded with the equally unique touch of her twin brother. This is recognition of an old, old order. After sharing a good hug, Dale pulls back, all business now, to probe the serious deeps of her mother's eyes, a required ritual, in her present phase, following each separation, no matter how brief. Rho enjoys submitting to this kiddie security check, this reexamination of credentials that says, let me see where you've been, let me see where you are now. ID confirmed, Dale pushes herself away, races back to rejoin her brother in whom the parent-child separation process is already producing visible fermentation, he's busy conducting a rather involved and sandy funeral for G.I. Joe and several members of his team who got ambushed going for doughnuts in a bad area. His intrusive mother hugs him anyway.

"Hi, Mrs. Jones," chirps Daphne in her best I-can-sound-just-as-stupid-as-any-adult voice.

"Hello, Daph, how's it going?"

The girl shrugs. "Okay." Her eyes are gray and green and unnervingly clear.

"Any problems?"

"Nope."

"Any calls?"

"Nope."

There's an annoying wall of insulation defining this girl in all weather, transparent enough to recognize that she's hiding something, opaque enough to obscure precisely what that something might be. The family is the scandal of the neighborhood, the parents unreconstructed hippies who drive a loud (visually and aurally) truck, refuse to mow their "natural" lawn under threat of numerous court injunctions, and parade about in unfashionable rags and long ratted hair (both mother and father). The rude sound of hammers and saws emanates from their lighted basement at odd hours of the night. Rho cannot begin to guess what they do for money. Daphne's baby-sitting wages? She sincerely hopes that isn't a packet of drugs in Daphy's back pocket.

Rho settles onto the other swing, ventures a tiny movement or two. As a child she loved to soar as fast, as high as her pumping legs could propel her but she doubts her adult stomach could tolerate such action today; it's enough for now simply to dangle from a brace of parallel chains, enjoying the sun on her face, her children at play, her deformed shadow squirming about in the worn pocket of ground beneath her feet. She questions Daphne persistently until the resultant grunts and monosyllables—none of this sullen really, she imagines Daph perceives herself as unfailingly polite and forthcoming—cohere into a mutually acceptable version of the day's events. Then she and Daphne fall silent and just hang there side by side, sharing a space, not speaking, and no one too concerned about it. Daphne's one of these New Age adolescents neither intimidated nor impressed by the proximity or strangeness of grownups. As an only child, she understands the terrain from years of direct study. Rho is grateful for occasions like this, openings in the day when one can believe that the woods are riddled with paths, untold ways out, but she can't restrain for long her gnawing awareness of the other, larger space between Daphne and herself, the weighty accumulation of the unseen that's largely responsible for the quality of this very interval and the turning of the next, the inside stuff that burbles on in dark privacy, surfacing if at all in an unguarded run of words, the anxious set of a face, the careless gestures of the body. Rho starts, grips the chains tight to keep from falling. So. Spooked again. Life is a haunting, Wylie often claims, and she as often agrees, though never really sure what he means.

Up above the diverging row of identically shaped and tiled roofs a trace of shade is working its way into the clean texture of the sky as if the soft tip of a dull pencil were being rubbed lightly but repeatedly across the rampant blue. Some evenings she wished the night would come on in a full rush, evenings when protracted twilight, this gray nibbling away at things, this shadowed sameness, is just not acceptable. She should have quit her job.

"Mommy!" her daughter demands in a particularly penetrating kid voice. "Mommy! Do snails eat people?"

No, she assures her, a sidelong glance at the cool mask of Daphne's perfectly composed face. Snails are our friends. No, not like spiders. Snails do not bite.

Beyond her daughter's head, two doors down, she notices, coming into fleeting view a fraction above the height of the chain link fences separating the yards, the bulb of a snout, a pair of black olive eyes, then a pause, then the eyes reappear, and on and on. This is Elmer, the Clampetts' jumping dog, who's only eager for a clear view of the fun. And half a block down, the solidarity of open chain link is broken by a twelve-foot wall of impenetrable redwood. The peculiar Mc-Kimson property. He, an Action News television producer; she, an ill-tempered recluse. Wylie pictures them sunbathing in the nude, fucking in the moonlight among croquet wickets. This, she realizes wistfully, is the first thought of sex (even several bodies removed) that she's had in weeks. Well, she's tired, she's distracted, there's always someone looking at her, in this case a supremely bored Daphne, who's studying her face with anthropological interest. Rho hopes she isn't about to lapse into one of her "episodes" out here in the unprotected pseudoprivacy of God knows how many prying eyes. In the suburbs the back yard is a stage. And sometimes so's the kitchen, the living room, and the bedroom.

She sneaks a glance at her watch, a ladies' Rolex acquired at cost through the agency of a former friend, but a Rolex nonetheless, and is amazed yet again by the tempo and elusiveness of time (a recent obsession she intends to bone up on as soon as she's not so busy). She hops off the swing, instructs Daphne on tonight's feeding and bedding schedule. She kisses each child on the cheek, her lips coming away powdered with sand.

She is marinating the organic beef and contemplating a second drink when the door chimes erupt into an off-key but recognizable rendering of the first four notes of the old *Dragnet* TV theme, an idiosyncrasy of the previous owner they haven't gotten around to replacing because by now she and Wylie don't even "hear" it. She hurries to answer the door. Though she's known the Hannas longer than her own children, she can't quite suppress, when standing before them again, a modest sense of bewilderment at the enduring nature of their relationship; she's receiving signals without being able to locate source or meaning; it's not any obvious incongruity in physical appearance or behavior, but something deeper, under the skin, ripplings, fluctuations, magnetic disturbances in the charged fields of personality. But she has to admit she's never seen or heard a hint of serious argument.

"Hi hi," she cries in the silly singsong she lapses into whenever she's nervous.

"Nice hair," comments Tommy.

Gerri leans in for a kiss. "I just love these absolutely gorgeous walls," she raves, waving her plastic fingernails about. "I always feel in this room like a bug in a lab." She looks directly into Rho's eyes. "A very special bug."

Tommy flashes a grin that could be favorably interpreted by either woman. He is merely marking time at his present copywriting job while stoically awaiting the arrival of his real career. What that is exactly he isn't sure but claims he'll know it when he sees it. His mustache, a thick oversized brush, comes and goes so frequently Rho is often nonplussed by his appearance without understanding why. This capricious facial hair is related to Tommy's insecurity about his nose (he thinks it's too big), which he keeps threatening to have surgically corrected. Tonight he is clean-shaven.

Gerri is a real estate agent and a co-owner of Just For You Catering and a professional fund-raiser and a member of the community board and she's taken college night courses every semester for years and years. No degree. She's on her third major, Oriental philosophy. Once over a lubricated lunch she tried to explain "emptiness" to Rho and the ensuing hilarity was so unrestrained Rho lost a contact. She and Gerri met working together at the mall duplicating center until Gerri discovered she was pregnant and quit. She lost the baby five weeks later and has since been informed by glum representatives of modern medicine she can't have another. This is no problem. She tells everyone, this is no problem. Her eyebrows tend to slant upward toward an imaginary intersection at the center of her forehead, giving her a perpetually bemused look she employs to her benefit, coaxing empathy and contract signatures from wavering clients. When she laughs, her face comes apart and she no longer resembles herself. She is wearing a silver lobster pin on her lapel. She has a ring on her thumb. She and Tommy must be doing well. You never hear the least complaint about money.

Apologizing for Wylie's tardiness, Rho ushers her guests through the house and onto the deck, where they settle into the new patio furniture and the first round of cold daiquiris. They look at the kids. They look at Daphne, who won't look back. They look at the blank windows of the neighboring homes. Tommy notices the patch of dead grass out by the garage. Rho doesn't have to turn around, that awful bleached spot is burned onto the inside of her head. Serious chemicals Wylie dumped there one strange night. He said it was gasoline. She thinks the ground itself has been totaled, as fertile now as a hole on the moon.

"Curious," observes Tommy. "It's practically a perfect circle."

Gerri remarks she's sick of hearing about chemicals. One day it's the air, next day it's the water, day after that it's California broccoli or . . . or chewing gum. You'd think we were nothing more than diseased sponges soaking up poison day and night.

"Well?" asks Tommy.

"I don't want to hear about it."

Rho is remembering how Mother kept every uncovered dish in the living room stocked to the brim with Brach's bridge mix no one ate until the chocolate coating bloomed and turned white. She excuses herself and returns to the kitchen to heat up the cheese for nachos. She is not supposed to have bad thoughts.

Daphne brings the kids in through the side door, tired, hungry, loud, attempting with some success to scratch one another on the forearms. Rho knows the game, she refuses to be drawn in. "Mommy will be up later to kiss both of you good night," she announces calmly. She strokes their flushed heads.

"Can I have Hi-C?" shrieks Dale suddenly. "Can I? Can I?" She hops about on comically angry feet.

"Yes, of course you can."

Then in a quieter, slyer voice, "*All* the Hi-C?"

"Go with Daphne now. Please, Mommy's busy." She's close to the place where the black stuff lives, nearer than she wants to be to slapping her daughter hard across the face. She's ready to consign both of them to Fisher-Price hell when she catches another interior glance of Mother dressed in rags thin and rotten as loose strands of mummy wrapping and seated like a Shakespearean king in a chair fashioned from stripped tree limbs and suspended in a blazing cylinder of blue-white light. On her head either a set of antlers or a TV antenna. She raises up her wizened body, she's about to speak . . . The vision is too terrible to sustain. Rho turns on both faucets and allows the water to rush over her hands.

When she returns to her company, awkwardly sliding back the door without spilling the loaded tray, conversation abruptly stops. She reads the story on Gerri's face. All right, she wants to blurt out, I have children. So what. She passes the corn chips. Tommy asks who Daphne is. Gerri studies the chalk marks and eraser smears left behind on the blueboard as the laggard sun wanders home after class. Rho rattles the dice in her drink, stares sadly down into the glass. "I think these daiquiris are too sweet."

"Oh no," Gerri objects, "they're fine. Perfectly."

"Gerri loves sugar," says Tommy. "It makes her high."

"Gloriously so." Tilting back her head, she demonstrates with a long dramatic swallow.

Rho is contemplating Gerri with the overly attentive expression of someone who's not really listening. Seized by a spasm of envy, she imagines appropriating this other woman's beauty and its attendant powers, she imagines walking around in her armor for a day, a week, a dreamtime of savory revenge. She imagines the situation at work. New and improved. She imagines her life. Her life would be changed. Utterly.

"Mmmmmm." Tommy has crunched into a dripping nacho chip, hand cupped under his chin. "Is this fake cheese?"

Rho doesn't know what to say.

"You have to use fake exclusively making these things," he explains. "Real never tastes as good."

"I honestly don't know," she replies. "Something in a jar you microwave."

"Fake," he declares, approvingly. "Real great." Tommy helps himself to another bite, leans back in his chair so as to bring into view the maximum exposure of Rhoda's legs. He was thinking about those legs driving over and believes he can meditate upon them with profit for an extended time to come.

"Tommy will eat anything," Gerri declares, "as long as it's tied down."

"Well," Rho says quickly, "maybe I should have made the sauce from scratch, but frankly, I didn't have the time."

"Oh no, I didn't mean . . . I'm sorry, Rho, no, that isn't what I meant. These are actually quite good. It's the kind we eat at home." She pops a sample between her teeth and chews approvingly.

"Pay no attention to the lady behind the stammer," says Tommy. "She's next in line for a new brain."

"All right, honey pie, rein it in."

Tommy salutes his wife with the wet glass. Under the table, legs shift and stretch. In the silence the volume on the background noise becomes noticeably elevated, distant guitars and drums howl and thump at close range.

"The heavy metal kids," Rho explains. "They're new on the block."

"Groovy," says Tommy.

Gerri's gaze swings pointedly from the near white house on the right to the near white house on the left. "Neighbors!" she exclaims. "I don't know if I could ever get used to this."

"Yes," Rho agrees, "some days it does seem too claustrophobic to bear."

"Must be like living in a fishbowl." Gerri lowers her voice. "Just think how many could be watching us right this minute."

"I try not to."

"Out on our place, at night you can't even see anybody else's lights."

"And no one can hear you scream," intones Tommy in his horror voice.

Gerri makes a face and turns back to Rho. "You and Wylie have got to get out again soon, see what we've done to the kitchen."

"And the barn," adds Tommy.

"And the garden. We've been down on our knees in the dirt the whole damn summer."

Rho's hesitant to accept. Last time she and Wylie visited they played a riotous game of badminton, toured the garden, admired the cabbage, drove to Lake Vista, paddled canoes, marveled at the leaping fish, sat at a charred picnic table on Succotash Hill amid a dusky swarm of hungry bugs and watched the dying sun bleed spectacularly into a clean blue blotter, invoked their famous college years: the bed sheet out the window, the lighter fluid under the door, naked volleyball, the filled condom tied to the police car door handle; they smiled, they touched, they shared, and everything was wonderfully wrong. There were undercurrents to the day and they were cold; Rho felt directed at her an implied and raking displeasure toward most of what she said, most of what she did, most of what she thought. Wylie, of course, dismissed her perception as exaggerated; if the Hannas were tired and slightly grumpy, then so were the Joneses—long day, short tempers, why belabor the obvious?—but she was hurt, the visit left her with a vague social nausea and the lingering question: does Gerri like me or not? She hadn't yet received an answer. So how could she know for true if this was a genuine invitation or a perverse emotional game? (On the last visit to the Enchanted Pines Care Facility Rho had brought her mother a box of turtles, her favorite candy, and that week's edition of her favorite magazine, *TV Guide*, containing all the many many shows she couldn't know she would never see.)

"There's hardly enough time anymore to get anything done," Gerri is complaining. "Have you noticed? There actually seems to be a smaller supply available than there used to be. Maybe our container of time has developed a slow leak. Maybe that's what those black holes do. They're just aimlessly vacuuming up our lives."

"Listen to the college girl," says Tommy.

"No holes upstairs," affirms Rho.

"You guys."

"She's very weird. One of these *reader* types you may have heard about. Always peeking into some damn book."

"Oh my God!" Gerri exclaims, sitting up excitedly. "Rho, have you read *Blondes in Black* yet? Tommy, honey, toss me my bag by your chair there." She rummages around, holds up a dog-eared paperback depicting on its cover a police lineup of indistinguishable fashion models in big sunglasses. She flips through the pages. "Listen." She reads: " 'Cymbelline is dancing. It is hot. The lights flash, revolve, strobe. The crowd heaves. The colors burn. She dances. Jewels of sweat glisten on her flawless forehead. Numerous tiny beads. The music ripples like a rainbow over her brain. She is not dancing, she is being danced. She is shedding skin. The little girl named Bobbie Jayne who once posed on a tractor (it was red) in a place too far from here to even exist is litter beneath her size seven pumps. Elbows and bodies nudge and jostle but she acknowledges the presence of no other. Tonight she is the star. A photographer's gun explodes in her face and she is caught with hair flying, arms flung sensationally above her head, trim aerobicized self abandoned completely to the rhythm of the life she had dreamed about. She exposes her perfect teeth. Her lips are full. She is in exstasy.

" 'When she and Johnny St. John return to their table, Bezique tosses her hair and points a sharp silver nail. "What's that on your dress?"

" 'Cymbelline touches the spot with her finger. It is wet. "Oh," she says.

" 'It was come.' "

Gerri closes the book with a knowing smirk. "Pretty great, huh? It's about New York. You know, that scene there."

"How does he spell it?" her husband asks.

"Spell what?"

"C-u-m."

"I don't know. Jesus Christ." She thumbs back through the book. "Here," she says, "c-o-m-e."

"Then why should we give any credence to an author who obviously doesn't know what the hell he's talking about?"

"Tommy doesn't read," Gerri explains.

"I watch," he says, and before he can be stopped is launched into another of his interminable movie synopses, this one a recent cable offering of unknown vintage, somewhat obscure, somewhat strange, essential defining characteristics of a Tommy favorite. He doesn't know the title either, having missed the opening credits and first ten minutes due to a "reasoning" he and Gerri were involved in over which shade to paint the spare bedroom (is there to be an adopted baby in there or not?), but since this flick'll probably be run ten, twenty more times before the month ends, he'll give them a call. Anyway, Sean Penn is this pumped-up lowlife going nowhere in a nowhere town until one day he discovers his long-lost father, Christopher Walken, acting even weirder than usual, is this cool criminal type he can really look up to because what else is he gonna do with an eighth grade education and a constipated strut and these ridiculous biceps swelling out of his T-shirt like Sunday hams? Only he doesn't understand the dimensions of evil residing in Daddy, he doesn't know what we do, which is—

Gerri's body convulses helplessly for an instant, rattling her chair. The glass door slides open. "Oh, Wylie," she gasps, hand astride her galloping heart. "You scared me."

Wylie steps out onto the deck, wearing the popular after-work look that loudly declares, don't even ask.

"Greetings, people." He stoops to kiss his wife's shiny forehead.

"Uh-oh," Rho remarks. "Looks like someone's had a bad day."

"Murderous," Wylie replies.

"All I could see was this horrible shape standing there right behind the door," explains Gerri. She jumps up to print a smeared set of lips on Wylie's grainy cheek.

Tommy, still not safely returned to noncinematic reality, waves an open palm.

Wylie leans back against the glass, hands roaming about in his pockets, impish face beaming benignly down on all. Rho can see he's making an effort. "So," he asks, "what've I missed?"

"Only everything," replies Gerri.

"Fine cuisine," says Tommy.

"Witty repartee," adds Gerri.

"My feet are sore from all the boogying," says Rho.

"Well." He studies their illumined faces. "Guess I need a drink." He slips back into the air-conditioned kitchen.

"He's so cute," says Gerri.

"In the right light," Rho replies, and asks about that younger sister with the three little kids who's been hiding out from her ex at a secret women's shelter on the west side. Theirs was a story short and savage and pointless as any you wouldn't want to live.

"She's okay. She's better. She's leaving at the end of the month as a matter of fact. She and the kids, they're moving to Santa Monica."

"She must be very strong."

Tommy gazes absentmindedly into the cluttered maw of the garage while Rho admires the shape of his bare neck, the graceful line of it sloping sturdily down into a plaid Paul Stuart collar.

"You do what you have to do," replies Gerri. In a culture fond of the tough cliché, she is a skilled adept.

Rho often wishes she knew what others were thinking. The human brain, she read in *Time*, functions as a low-grade transmitting station, so theoretically, with the proper receiver, thoughts could be intercepted like television waves. Some minds are natural receivers. Is Gerri psychic? Privacy is a delusion. We are not alone.

Wylie rejoins the party changed into his customary khakis and navy blue polo shirt and carrying a hefty tumbler of vodka and tonic. He straddles the remaining chair, the defective one with the bent leg. "So," he begins, "what are we talking about tonight?"

"The kids are downstairs," says Rho. "With Daphne."

"I know. I've already squeezed each and every one."

If asked by a stranger to describe her husband, Rho isn't certain how she'd respond. Except for the eyes, those affecting moons of powdery gray, there was nothing immediately distinctive about him, no crags or crannies or funny clumps of hair for words to adhere to. Average, she'd have to admit, conceding her failure because the choice attributes, the ones you couldn't readily explain, escaped definition, and those were the ones she loved.

"We've been spanning the globe," Tommy claims. "Toxic crime, the drug deficit, celebrity terrorism. It's been an evening for the macroview."

"An evening for macaroni," corrects Gerri. She's intrigued by Wylie's hands, there's something positively noble about his fingers.

"Save the planet," announces Tommy. "Take a whale to lunch."

"We like coming here," says Gerri, making sucking noises with her straw. "So many of our other friends have given up drinking."

"Yes," Rho says. "The Eco-Age."

"I feel like eco-trash myself," jokes Tommy.

"Have you ever had a cherimoya?" Gerri asks.

"What's that?"

"It's a fruit, actually, some bizarre mating of an apple and a pear and a coca tree, for all we know. It's Peruvian. Quite yummy."

Tommy chuckles softly through his nose. "Yeah, since the Grand Tour has had to be temporarily postponed until the advent of our second million, Gerri here is eating her way around the world."

His tone irritates her. "Well, why go on tasting the same boring old tastes, doing the same boring old things?"

"I don't know," says Tommy. "Why?"

"Oh, you." She kicks at him under the table.

"Did you remember the charcoal?" inquires Rho.

Wylie's glass halts in midair.

"Damnit, Wylie, I asked you not to forget. Well, don't be long. We're starting to get hungry here."

"Tommy can go with you," declares Gerri.

"Hint, hint," says Tommy.

On the way out Wylie scoops up a handful of chips. "Mmmmmm," he mumbles, over his shoulder, "good nachos."

The vehicle is an '87 Jeep Cherokee. "Shouldn't we be wearing baseball caps?" Tommy's stale line. He has difficulty envisioning himself in such a machine and cannot understand why Wylie, whom he knows as well as anybody, would want to be seen in one, would apparently delight in one, would sometimes even drive the thing to work, for Christ's sake. It is a curiosity.

The passing streets are quiet, well tended, as are the lawns, the homes, the people. The radio is tuned to a popular FM station, classic rock, one uninterrupted hour of Canned Heat. Wylie is stolid behind black sunglasses. Tommy unreels another gripping scenario; this time it's Tony Perkins as a zany Dr. Jekyll who accidentally discovers crack, smokes it, naturally, then runs amok in a blue street frenzy of fucking and slashing rarely witnessed within the precincts of an R rating.

"But he's already nuts," Wylie points out. "Even playing normal. One look at the eyes and anyone but an idiot can tell there's another person in there."

"Granted," Tommy admits, "so maybe the suspense element is somewhat compromised. It's still an engaging piece of work."

Wylie hasn't seen the film, doesn't know if he will, he's been trying to cut down lately.

"Yeah yeah," says Tommy, "don't think I haven't heard all this before, it's a bad habit, yeah, waste of life, sure, but it's either sit in front of the box or talk to Gerri all night."

"Something else you could do with Gerri."

"Yeah, but not as good as they do it on the box."

The parking lot of the Feed 'n' Fuel is a mad snarl of cops and cars and rotating lights and the fear of the curious drawn, as always, to the center, wherever it may appear, a modern-day gathering at the rim of the awful, a satisfied peep down into the smoking crater, wonder that such things could be so great and so near. Police cruisers sit abandoned at opposed angles, doors hanging open, radios squawking like caged birds. Between scarred trash containers yellow tape fluttering upside down in printed repetition CRIME SCENE DO NOT CROSS clears a space around the store entrance. In the middle of this opening, arranged rather carelessly on the gum-embossed, soda-stained cement, an apparently well-used painter's drop cloth. Under the cloth—the itch the close semicircle of eyes can't stop scratching—rests the body, its presence confirmed by the protruding pair of scuffed Nikes, toes pointing pathetically earthward, the thick green laces dangling loose and untied, particles of gray gravel worked into the tread of the soles, detail magnified into a revelation of intimacy Tommy is suddenly quite uncomfortable with. His feelings at the moment too tangled for endurance or examination. All he is sure of is that he must look incredibly stupid trapped in the midst of this crowd, gawking like a tourist fresh off a bus. He moves up nearer to Wylie. "Is that blood?" he whispers.

"Where?"

"By his head."

A cop who appeared at least a decade younger than Tommy and who was sporting sideburns he hadn't seen on a living person in twenty years catches his eyes and looks right inside easy as checking the contents of a boiling pot; he turns away, obviously amused by what he found there. Tommy is flushed with shame.

Inside the store uniformed police and homicide detectives in designer suits are engaged in solemn conversation with an acne-ridden boy in a red apron and a paper hat. His face exhibits the otherworldly features of someone who's just been unexpectedly photographed with a mighty large flash.

"What happened?" Tommy asks loudly.

"I don't know," replies a straw-haired woman in a Metallica T-shirt, clutching two small children. She doesn't bother turning around. "Somebody got shot."

Tommy leans in on Wylie's ear. "Do you think he's black?" There are no visible skin parts sticking out from under the sheet.

Wylie simply shrugs his shoulders.

The air registers an eerie afterodor . . . as of ozone? It can't be healthy lingering out in this lot, absorbing the distinctly unwholesome vibes of a live unprogrammed event. He nudges Wylie's elbow. "Ready?"

Wylie doesn't respond.

"No one's getting in. Whaddya wanna do? Wait 'til the meat wagon gets here?"

Wylie turns to look him full in the face. "Sure."

Inside the store a cop holding his hat in his hand says something to the others and laughs, displaying a mouthful of astonishingly white teeth. One detective is chugging a pint of chocolate milk, another is munching from a ripped bag of Eagle potato chips. "Catch this," mutters a voice in the crowd. "They're having a goddamn party." Someone else says, "He got what was coming to him." "Wish I'd a been here," answers another, "woulda helped blow him away." Someone asks the cop with the sideburns to lift the sheet so he can see the "perp's" face. "Move along," says the cop.

Tommy and Wylie drive over to the 7-Eleven on Melodie Boulevard, where you don't have to step over a corpse to pick up your charcoal. On the way home Wylie is silent. Tommy chatters nervously about how this convenience store calamity parallels events on TV last night except that on the show the grotesque public murders of unrelated strangers turn out to be the nefarious work of a crew of renegade aliens.

Wylie missed it, he doesn't see the connection anyway. Swinging onto Sunset, he almost clips a paperboy on a bike and blames Tommy for distracting him. As they pull into the driveway, the women whoop and wave like crazy people from their elevated deck seats, delirious as bleacher fans late in the second game of a long doubleheader. Tommy scrambles to get out of the car. "Guess what we saw?" he yells. Behind him Wylie's broad back disappears into the garage.

Oh, a quiz. The women sit up, assume exaggerated contestant poses.

"A parade," Gerri guesses.

"A bad accident," cries Rho.

Tommy is waggling his head.

"Naked people!"

"Clowns! Insane clowns!"

"A dead body," he intones.

"No," says Gerri.

"Yes."

"No," says Rho.

"Right in front of the goddamn Feed 'n' Fuel. You should have seen it. We were almost killed, weren't we Wylie?"

Wylie is rounding the corner, dragging the rusty one-wheeled grill onto the lawn. "Yeah," he agrees. "Almost."

"Wylie?" Rho, already vaguely discomfited, having minutes ago shared with Gerri the impossible lunacy of her junior year at Northwestern, the wild boy called Speedy and the ending between obstetric stirrups in a horror not even her husband knows complete details of, offering as sacrament to the sisterly cheer of the moment this raw fragment of her past, she is now queasy with pangs of betrayal at ransacking her heart for a woman she discovered halfway through the telling she isn't sure she even likes, so . . . "Wylie?"

He approaches, pauses under the deck, gazing up at her. "We're okay." His hand reaches to touch her bare leg. "Looked like a holdup or an attempt or something like that. Whatever happened, somebody is definitely very dead."

"Oh my God."

"Couple minutes earlier," explains Tommy, "who knows what we might have seen. Or been involved in."

"The modern world," comments Gerri. "Five blocks away."

"You shoulda seen that body lying there on the pavement just as still as anything. It looked phony it was so real."

"Yes," Gerri declares, "just what I need to see, another dead person. I am sick to death of dead persons, of hearing about them, of looking at them, of feeling sorry for them; they're on television every hour, in the papers every morning, and bleeding all over me in every magazine. Today you'd think that was all life was about, dead people."

"Long as it ain't us," drawls Tommy.

At their backs there's a flash and a sudden whoosh, a beat of gigantic wings; they swivel in their seats to the unnerving spectacle of a column of flame rearing up angrily into the dim air. "Oh, look," remarks Rho, "Wylie's got the fire going."

The daiquiri pitcher is emptied and refilled and emptied again. The citronella candles are lit. Mr. Freleng, the retired electrician next door, totters out to adjust his hose, faithful attendant to the abiding needs of the lawn god. He behaves as if he were alone, blind and deaf to the balcony audience spellbound by each fussy exertion. Upstairs the children sleep at last. Daphne gets paid and goes home. A small dark bat appears, flutters anxiously through the soft twilight, a flimsy prop on ineptly managed wires.

"Five hundred mosquitoes an hour," informs Tommy. "Amazing."

"I suppose," says Gerri, "that radar they're supposed to have causes cancer."

"Even as we speak."

"It must be exhilarating, though," she goes on, entranced by the creature's strobelike flight, "to eat what's eating you."

"Well, I don't think—"

"But imagine being that free, able to fly, to sweep across the night in some sort of erotic stupor."

Tommy extends a closed fist. "So, Mrs. Hanna, if you could come back as any animal, the varmint of your choice would be—"

"Yes, Gene, the bat, definitely the bat."

If Rho is expected to comment, she misses her cue. The diverse demands and unforeseen surges of the day, in tandem with tonight's elevated blood alcohol levels, have driven her circuitry into a sputtering staticky condition near brownout or worse, she's phasing eccentrically in and out, her attention temporarily and fiercely magnetized by the oddest fragments of isolated fact, so while Gerri natters on, from bats and sex and reincarnation to—working hard now to amuse her audience—stale crowd-pleasers of lust and gaucherie among her wealthy clientele, Rho is pleasantly tuned to the resonant sound of hissing meat. She watches the coals glowing in backyard obscurity like poisonous pink eggs in a metal nest, the spit and spark of yellow flame as grease hits the briquettes like a short in the night, a modest show but richly entertaining. The hours of her day pass in review at a respectful distance, she feels nothing, the simplest formulation (my life, this particular point on the graph, is it + or − ?) beyond her depleted capacities, she's tired, foundering in a profuse mystery of feckless convalescence she recognizes to her relief as more than one private neurotic dilemma, every one of her friends exhibits some degree of symptomatic distress, but what exactly is it we are convalescing from? She hasn't a clue. I need a good night's sleep. I need a good night without sleep. Overhead, the mounting darkness is studded with stars, glint of the nailheads supporting the big roof. A sudden light from the Avery bedroom projects a long yellow trapezoid over the spiky grass. Down the block the heavy metal kids are crashing and burning their way through a catchy number whose name she almost seems to recall. There's nothing around us, and deep inside, too.

The steaks are grilled to perfection, and though it's difficult to make out in the dim wicklight exactly what it is that's on one's plate or identify the grit in the potatoes, the meal is rated a four-star success. Tommy raises his glass to deliver a toast so pompous and strained it must have been intended to evoke the manner of some media android or other.

"Do your De Niro," Rho orders her husband. "You know his De Niro. All his impressions are fabulous, but the De Niro is uncanny."

He smiles wearily.

"C'mon, Wylie, put out for your guests."

The smile fades.

"Let's go now, let's get this party into high gear." Her husband's reserve is irritating her. She's fed up with the many humors and riddles of him. "I want some fun here," she demands, "and I want it now."

"You're drunk," he says.

"I'm not," announces Gerri with aggressive finality. She's the hard-liner at the negotiating table. She's decided not to go in on Monday. Let her colleagues enjoy a new appreciation of her worth in a musing upon her absence. Wylie wouldn't go in if he didn't feel like it. Wylie does as he pleases. He's a free lance. He says he's in microsystems, but she knows better, she thinks he must be in government, he's a governor. She can feel her hands running up under Wylie's shirt. She can feel heat.

Tommy rises, he wants to dance. Won't anyone join in? He stumbles alone down the steep redwood steps and out across the yard, a small dark figure moving within a larger darkness. He's humming, he's dancing.

It looks to Rho as if Tommy has actually removed his shirt, and since a good hostess accommodates her company she hustles out to perform her duty. Arm in arm they dance, it's a night for grand gestures, cheek to cheek they glide on over behind the garage where in a crush of mint, she . . . he . . . well, nothing really, and he did have his shirt on the whole time.

Abandoned at the dinner table, Wylie and Gerri have somehow slipped, without apparent embarrassment, into an engaging discussion upon the nature of the soul, its defining qualities, the possibility it manifests a specific shape, the likelihood of its integrity beyond formaldehyde and flowers, speculation on its absence from an unfortunate sum of mortal beings since God, at the moment of creation, released into the universe a fixed number of souls to be recycled among a diminishing percentage of an exponentially expanding population, hence bodies with no souls. Who are these people? she inquires. He shrugs his shoulders. Movie executives? There's a dark rustle in his voice that vibrates the base of her spine. Her hands upon his chest.

When Tommy and Rho come tripping back to the campfire, Tommy presents an idea, a great escape, a week-long getaway, all four of them, to the lands over the sun. Gerri squeals and claps. On the island there will be no telephones, no televisions, no papers. No one will wear any clothes. Tommy knows a guy at Eastern who knows the choice beaches (e.g., tourist-scarce, noncommercial) in the Caribbean and who was just yesterday commending the unspoiled charms of one rare shore Tommy unfortunately cannot . . . "Saint . . ." he tries, "Saint something," looking for help to Rho, her skin in the candle glow burnished to a model's tan. He's convinced he understands the contents of her face, always has.

"They're all Saint something," says Gerri, playing to the still watcher across the table. "Those grubby Catholics always weaseling their way in first. All the best places." Ever the naughty parochial schoolgirl who also worships at other altars, in faraway places for instance, where each may feast without guilt on the fruit of the next.

Wylie is staring hard in Tommy's direction.

"When would we go?" Rho asks. In the bright bay the water is bloodwarm. It is like swimming within one another. Tommy's white ass winking on the sunny surface. Her teeth unzip his fly. She finds him, she coaxes him from his pants, no hands. "In the fall," he answers. Then in the hammock under the coconuts together, swaying. The air gravid, sweet, budding for one, for all, for him. "October, maybe. We'll do it in the fall." Pineapple perfume between her legs.

"What do you say, honey?" Skin to skin, like skydiving through the Tommyness of Tommy. Nails tight around his clenched buttocks.

Gerri's eyes, too, are on Wylie. Close against him, climbing the electric length of him to the dark hollow beneath his arm, where she licks.

Wylie doesn't know. Too early to confirm what the October schedule will allow. He drains his glass, looks off into the waning sky.

Okay, then. So Rho goes it alone. In the hotel elevator between floors shocking the tourists. Stubbled chin sanding her thighs. In scuba effervescence off the blue reef among little neon fishes.

Then, for everybody, a golden tangle of limbs and juice and heat. Tops and bottoms. Fingers and mouths.

Wylie leans forward, places his hands flat against the table, pushes himself erect. "Would you excuse me for a minute?"

"Why not," Tommy responds, watching him maneuver awkwardly over his outstretched legs.

"Don't get lost," Rho jokes. Though the edges of her lips are numb, the glass in her hand keeps finding a miraculous way to her mouth, and she's cozy, she's entered into a nice state of encapsulation, a daiquiri astronaut, communications link down, support systems nominal, destination unknown, she hasn't a care.

Wylie enters the kitchen, where he stops to regard with a sharp detective eye the scene: the nervous fluorescence, the dinner debris, the dripping faucet, the unattended television silently tuned to tonight's repeat of *Perfect Strangers*, the bloodied dish towel, the sectioned limes, the jutting drawers, the spilled olives, the greasy knives, and, taped to the door of the clattering refrigerator, a child's crayon rendering of a triangle hat atop an oblique happy face atop a red meatball body sprouting pitchfork arms and chicken legs captioned "Dabdy." He can't seem to find what he wants. He continues on down the shadowy hallway, ice cubes rattling like beans in the magic gourd of a glass he holds before him, clearing the demons from his path. His Nike'd feet fall without sound on the postmodern gray broadloom as he mounts the stairs quietly, quietly, to enter like a thief the charmed bubblegum-spiced atmosphere of his only son's room. The sleeping boy is lost within a cocoon of Teenage Mutant Ninja Turtle sheets from which issues the regular rasp of his asthmatic snore. From the walls threaten posters of trumpeting dinosaurs and sneering rock stars. The bookshelves hold a humble armful of books and the terrarium home to Huckleberry, the family's pet chameleon, and a Defense Department arsenal of military toys occupying every available inch of shelf space and cascading down across the floor in muddled retreat and up over the whelmed desk top, from which chaos Wylie plucks a kid's-size pair of blue and yellow plastic binoculars. He stands motionless at the window before the vanished sky, the obscure roofs and walls of his neighbors, that pathetically stunted birch beside the sandbox in his own empty yard, and, on the deck beneath his nose, his wife and her guests exactly as he left them. He raises the binoculars to his eyes, focuses the finger-smudged lenses down on Rho's face; he watches her talk, the odd movement of her enlarged lips, the pistoning of her jaw. Magnified and considered from this novel angle, her familiar features seem skewed and disproportionate, furious sketches for a modern portrait the sitter will not like. He can't hear a word through the sealed window of this climate-controlled house, only meaningless squawks of laughter, the perpetual rumbling machine of Tommy's baritone. He watches Rho, then he pans over to Gerri. He watches her. He can see her darting tongue. Pan to Tommy. Nose looming suggestively out of bland everyday mask. The binoculars pan. He watches Rho. He watches Gerri. He watches Tommy. He does not move from that spot. There is no dialogue. Only the binoculars move.

Down on the deck the fun-loving trio is gossiping about Frankie D., who is supposed to have slept with most of the middle management of Ribman and Stone. She wears inappropriate clothing to corporate functions. Her hair is like Easter basket grass. She thinks she has friends.

Every line Gerri speaks bristles with wit. Every gesture Tommy makes is bounded in grace. When he touches her arm to punctuate a point, a message of perfect clarity passes instantly between them. These are the best people Rho's ever known. This is the best she's been in months. She is bathed in a new understanding, this fine evening's unexpected gift to that Cinderella self of hers too long scrubbing the same flagstones clean, and the understanding says to her: your life is your invention, that's all, your life is your invention, the naïve obviousness of it positively intoxicating. You make it up, ha ha. Now she's married to Wylie, now she isn't. Now she has kids, now she doesn't. Here is a sense of play missing since childhood. She looks to Tommy. Now she bends to . . .

Now Gerri is sharing her drink and Tommy is deconstructing an ironic slasher film—or is it merely a lengthy joke?—and when Rho glances up to check on the moon she catches a glimpse of Mother frozen at an upstairs window, but, no, the hallucination dissolves, she refuses to submit to those obsolete emotions, to all that gamy bait, keep your head keyed to the present, why should the party ever end?

"Damn these mosquitoes!" Gerri is slapping impatiently at her exposed legs. "I'm literally covered in nasty bites."

"It's 'cause you're so sweet," cracks Tommy, scratching at his own arm. "Where's our little bat-friend when you need him?"

"I don't feel a thing," Rho brags, stretching her arms heavenward. "I'm in a bug-free zone."

"Well, I'm being eaten alive." Gerri slaps a palm against the side of her face. "And these damn things never work." Suddenly she picks up a candle and heaves the glass globe as if it were a ticking bomb out into the darkness. Startled by the violence of her behavior, she looks at her companions in shock and then breaks into laughter. "Sorry, Rho, gee, I'll buy you another. I don't know what came over me."

"Okay, you guys." Rho begins gathering up plates. "Inside."

The kitchen light seems painfully intense, exaggerated to no purpose. Dishes stacked in the sink and along the counter appear to have multiplied on their own in the incubating fluorescence.

"My God," Gerri bellows, "did we eat all that?"

"Maybe we're in the wrong house," suggests Tommy, deadpan.

Rho is scraping cow bones into a garbage bag. "Where's Wylie?" she asks.

Gerri stands before the open refrigerator, searching the freezer for that pint of butter pecan Rho promised her. "Maybe he's passed out in the john."

Rho puts down a plate. "Wylie?" she calls in a hushed voice. "Wylie, where are you?" She wipes her hands on the stained towel and goes wandering off into the unlit gloom of the silent house.

Tommy leans against the counter, working a toothpick around his gums, bewitched by the provocative incoherence the television is shooting into him "Look," he drawls, comprehension dawning, "*Jaws*." Teeth, water, blood, it is a spellbinding blend, as potent now as it was when he first saw the film, half a dozen viewings ago.

Gerri locates the one remaining clean spoon and busily scoops high premium ice cream into her puckered mouth until . . . "What the hell are you doing?" She holds out a reproving hand. "Gimme that."

Tommy's eyebrows go up and down. He drops the wet toothpick into her palm, where it is inspected with a fortune-teller's gaze and tossed without comment into the trash.

"Good dinner," Tommy ventures.

"Do you think," she gasps, sucking air onto her chilled molars, "Rho was quite herself tonight?"

The question's still afloat in the space between them when Rho appears in the doorway, displaying the expression of one working out a problem in long division. "Wylie," she says, her voice lanced and drained, "Wylie's not here."

Tommy, still concentrating on the television, pretends not to hear. "Huh?" he asks.

"Of course he is," says Gerri. She knows Wylie. "He's upstairs. He went upstairs. He's looking in on the kids."

Rho is shaking her head carefully, as if it held items of priceless fragility. "There's no one up there but the twins."

"He's in the john."

"I checked every room."

Tommy interrupts by humming the aggravating notes of the old *Twilight Zone* theme. "What about out back?" he suggests. "Cleaning the grill. Or the garage? Or out by the garbage cans?"

Rho's head won't stop moving.

"Didn't he say something about running out to the store?" asks Gerri. "Running low on limes?"

"Maybe he went out for a pack of cigarettes," says Tommy, well aware that his friend does not smoke.

"Look in the driveway," Rho says. She wants to shout. "Neither car is gone." Now she reruns the tape: she sees herself moving from room to room and she sees herself watching herself, and as she watches, the Rho searching seems to be moving faster and the Rho watching seems to be growing more and more still. Nothing has happened. Nothing is happening. She casts about this room she finds herself in, this kitchen, and recognizes nothing of any relevance to who she is or what is occurring here. Her pots and pans seem to have been rubbed and washed by foreign hands; all the objects in the house have begun migrating on to a different life and they are taking her with them. She reruns the tape: she sees herself moving from room to . . .

"Let me take a look," volunteers Tommy, hurrying off, male impatience eager to be doing.

Gerri can't quite comprehend the terms of this situation, either. "I mean, this is a joke, right? Any second now Wylie hops out of a closet and gives us a good scare?"

"Wylie wouldn't do that." It is not a point to be debated.

Gerri doesn't know what to say. She pats Rho's arm. She makes appropriate noises: "Well, don't worry, it'll be all right, wherever he is, it can't be that far, nobody simply vanishes."

They sit at the table for several minutes of uncomfortable silence, Gerri intrigued by the notion that Wylie's disappearance has some crucial relation to herself. Then Rho is up and through the hallway, the white living room, the front door, deaf to the sound of her name pursuing her across the damp lawn and out into the middle of the deserted street, where she stops and stares off into the impenetrable distance like one come to the end of a long vacant pier. The humid darkness swarms with the random messages of insects, the winking fireflies, the creaking crickets. There is no sign of Wylie. Gerri leads her back to a house alive with light, each window a blazing rectangle of illusory mirth reminding envious passersby of the party they would never give, the invitation they would never receive.

Tommy is pacing amid the fashionable starkness of the living room and picking at his forehead. He admits events have turned exceedingly strange. He's even rummaged through bedroom drawers and closets (thank you, Rho, for your exquisite taste in lingerie), hunting for evidence of missing clothes, suitcases, etc. Nothing seems to have been disturbed.

"I don't understand," says Rho.

Tommy suggests a quick drive around the neighborhood. Gerri can stay behind with the sleeping children. The emptiness in Rho's eyes is replaced by a tentative expression of hope, a child's relief at an adult assumption of authority.

Tommy's Prelude creeps at cortege speed from block to leafy block. Rho sits anxiously forward, starting at the slightest movement, real or imagined, out on the dark streets. It's as quiet this Friday as on any other night of the week, the typical suburban stillness only occasionally disturbed by passing joggers (singly and in pairs), kids on bikes, the muscular adolescent walking his questionably domesticated dog, each scrutinized carefully by Rho, her head leaning out the open car window, a song running repeatedly through it, the same song, as a matter of fact, that looped through her mind during Mother's funeral, a silly Calypso ditty about her roof having a hole in it and she might drown. She rubs her arms, she's cold on this, the warmest night of the year.

Tommy is watching her as he drives, the moody pattern of light and shadow sliding dramatically across her perfect profile, this shared sense of peril and mystery, and he can't help it, he's sitting there behind the wheel with an erection in his lap.

Back at the house while Gerri is alone the telephone rings and when she answers it there's nobody there. She doesn't know whether to tell Rho about this call or not.

Back at the house Tommy and Rho and Gerri huddle on black furniture in the white living room, interrogating one another with an insistence that desires somehow to speak Wylie, to locate the exact words in the exact order that will conjure his physical presence before them. Thought, however, goes round and round like a tire axle-deep in swamp mud.

Tommy, of course, has assumed the role of chief of detectives. "Once again, can you think of any place, no matter how remote, that Wylie might have gone. Friends? Relatives?" He pauses. "Enemies?"

Rho resembles a mannequin that has been removed from display for repainting.

Gerri is thinking how Wylie might have struck his head on a cabinet, say, in an inebriated stumble, and is now wandering the city in a state of amnesia.

Tommy is thinking about a recent report he saw on UFO abductions. He also thinks about what's her name, the baby-sitter, her long black hair, her long tight jeans. "No point in notifying the cops yet," he says. "They won't do a damn thing until twenty-four hours have passed."

Rho. Rho sits.

A long-haired cat with a frosty blue coat and cold yellow eyes steps in daintily measured tread down the carpeted stairs. Awakened from sleek gray-toned dreams of murder and euphoria, he has come to investigate this annoying commotion within the kingdom. At the foot of the stairs he sits in stony Buddhistic calm, the truth of the room reflected in the glossy convexities of his stare. He blinks and the supremely languid draw of his lids suggests whole taxonomies of boredom beyond human reckoning. But since neither sight nor smell detects the scantest particle of available food, attention is fading, fades, faded. His name is Pluto.

With a rough impatience Rho rubs the shadowed hollow of her temple. It throbs. She regards her dear, useless friends. For the anguish in her face there is no mitigation. Her dress is black. Her hair is brown. Her mind is blank.

She asks, "What is happening here?"

Like the present tense, Daddy was gone gone.

A HEADFUL OF CORPSES

THREE blocks away, on a street like any other street, in a house like any other house, lived . . .

"Don't move," she ordered, thrusting forth a pale arm from the beached mattress in the corner, the day-to-day coarsening of the voice unchecked in its apparent declension toward silence, scraping now at the masculine registers, the novelty of its tone commanding obedience; he halted, frozen in place, his arrested shadow lofting gigantically up the wall, across the low ceiling, a slick black membrane quivering in minatory shapelessness close overhead.

Candle stubs of diverse length and hue glittered fitfully from every available surface, including the seat of the Exercycle, the top of the dead television, and each precarious stack of new CDs rising like terraced stalagmites at obstacle course intervals across the hard uncarpeted floor. The walls of the room glowed like tanned skin. Illuminated to romantic excess in the living oranges and yellows of another time, the plain animality of the body was undeniable, the soft play of fire upon rounded limbs, lovers' eyes embellished by textures, entrances, unknown to the electric world. Neither one of them was wearing any clothes.

Head angled thoughtfully, she appraised him without comment.

"What?" he shouted, patience and pose both beginning to melt.

"Oooh, you moved. You ruined it." She spoke with the feigned petulance of a spoiled child.

"So what am I here?" he asked, attempting to retain whatever attitude he was supposed to be holding. "You tell me."

"A little that way." She motioned with her hands, conscious of the director's role. "This way, no, more that . . . good, no, okay, good, over, over—stop!"

"Having fun?"

"There now," she declared, "look at you," casting a triumphant finger wallward at his anatomically correct umbral self. "Enormous. You're one big guy."

"Mister Goodyear." He shimmied his hips in pleasurable sync with the exaggerated double bobbing upon the plasterboard screen.

"Watch out," she warned through her laughter, "you're gonna burn yourself."

"And now, ladies and gentlemen"—he manipulated himself with his hands—"a talking giraffe. Thank you. Now don't go away, because when I come back I'll show you my ducky and my goosey, too." He moved to the open doorway and, reduced to singular fleshy size, turned away from view.

"Hit the bowl this time," she shouted after. "I'm sick of stepping in your piss."

The curtainless windows were flung wide, and hungry mosquitoes drifted in on the heat, the summer drone of smothering humidity and long sleepless nights. The air-conditioning, along with the rest of the power, had failed hours earlier at the exact wrong moment: right in the middle of the climactic scene of *Fiend Without a Face*, the final assault on the few remaining characters (your no-nonsense military hero, your scientifically inclined love interest, your average monster fodder of doomed villagers and enlisted fools) by a marauding army of mental vampires, disembodied brains scuttling about on spinal cord tails like jumbo inchworms, the diabolical spawn of a doddering professor's experiments in the materialization of thought. What did they want? More brains. How do they get them? By leaping onto their victims' necks and sucking at the base of the skull. Someone had to get to the reactor and cut off their power source! Then the TV went flash! pop! as if snapping their picture and the next second they were sitting in darkness. What the fuck? She couldn't believe it; she cursed and whined. He stumbled around in the basement for a while, floor grit cutting into the soles of his bare feet as he fiddled ineffectually with the circuit breakers. "The bill, fuckhead, you pay the fucking bill?" her voice as nasty as she could make it. He said he had. She said he spouted outrageous lies from a filthy sewermouth. She jumped onto his back, pummeled his shoulders with her fists. He tossed her off onto the mattress. "You fucking idiot. You fat shit." Quietly, he told her to shut up. "You frog-faced freak." Pause. "I can't live like this." Pause. "And I'll shut up when I feel like shutting up." Then she didn't speak until he produced a box of broken candles from God knows where, arranged them in the present configuration, and solemnly touched a match to each wick while intoning a mock votive to her charms. "All right," she said, "but you're still a fuckhead."

While he was in the bathroom, she reloaded the pipe, hastily smoked it down. She loved the good-fer-what-ails-you taste, the express hydraulics of going up, the simultaneous visual of something tangible flying out the top. And the exhale. She thrilled to see the magic pouring from her face, from dark profundities of her, glittering pixie particles of me-stuff scattering over the world, and she didn't have to *do*, she didn't have to *be* anything more than a sprawled body on a yellowing mattress in a hot room for all to be changed around her. She had already changed herself and she had changed her name and the sound of her rechristening was: Latisha Charlemagne.

"Whaddya doing?" sounded his voice, slurred, gross, sarcastic, and, concentration broken, she almost went down. She was hopping around on one leg, trying to jam her stupid clown feet into a laddered pair of black leotards. "I'm going out," she explained logically. "Jogging." She didn't know this was what she was about to do until she said it.

"The hell you are."

She turned away from him, the claims of his nakedness, his disapproval, his wattled cock. Tackling hands were on her hips in an instant and over she went into the closet beneath a soft cascading of suits and shirts, a clattering of loose hangers. They struggled there a while atop the shoes, a boot heel digging into her back. "Get . . . off," she warned, pushing clawed fingers into the pliable stuff of his face until, sensing her determination, "all right, all right," he let her go to resume the task of inserting leg tabs A into leotard holes B, refusing to recognize her engagement in a vain tussle of mismatched parts.

"Okay," he said, "I want to see this." He stretched out on the floor, assumed the expression of an appreciative spectator ready to enjoy the elaborate "business" of a professional comedian. But after several minutes of her slapstick, he reached out a restraining hand. "Please," he begged, "no more. Don't make me laugh. Don't give me a heart attack."

She couldn't stop, though, having glimpsed, she was certain, the obvious solution to this temporary problem in nonalignment on the physical plane. If she could lean against the wall with one leg extended straight out and then bend forward with the leotards in both hands . . . "I need my exercise," she insisted.

"You get all the exercise you need right here in this room."

And then hands were on her again, fastened to the nice places they knew she couldn't resist, and then he was on top of her, he and his shadow, commencing this mutual abrasion he couldn't seem to get enough of, scratching an itch, rubbing the one spot that had to be rubbed and rubbed for the genie to appear, the true genie, not the fake one with the paste jewels and backfiring wishes, but the happy turbaned soul rising up out of the muck of eternity with all the answers, Latisha's raw breath tickling at the hairs of his ear, "Oh, you're big, you're so big," straining against the harness, yes, of course it was a race, too, close field pressed in on either side, moving as fast as he could, riding hard the heart he hoped wouldn't dare betray him, blind chase toward a finish that couldn't or wouldn't or shouldn't come.

Mister CD was in love.

"You're the kind of guy," she remarked later, "who should put his dick on a leash and take it for a walk around the block."

He had rolled over and his arm was sliding around under the maturing mounds of dirty clothing planted like exotic mushrooms along his side of the mattress. "Where's the damn stem?"

She pretended to search, then slipped it from her ashtray and handed it over.

"Well, babe," he declared, clicking nervously on the yellow Bic, "you should have known me in the days when I was Mister LP."

"You were hot."

"I was dangerous, I was burning up."

The smoldering pipe passed between them in a volitionless glide, like an object at a séance, each repetition a reenactment of their meeting one bright windy afternoon, sizzling white clouds blowing past in pieces, carrying with them, for this one day at least, that late summer malaise of extended-mode lives and wilted options thousands of vacations were designed to avoid. Lately, he took his lunch break out behind the store (biggest inventory, lowest prices in greater Windy City area), an ugly cinder-block bunker he shared with Software Plus, manager Herb Blair or Nair or Nerd, good guy he succeeded in avoiding but for accidental encounters here at the Dumpster, where on this particular afternoon he was seated on a plump garbage bag in his usual dollar daddy uniform of pink polo shirt, gray pants, and gold-plated aviator frames, refreshing himself with the tonic fumes from his glass pipe, when a distinctly nonconsumer-type woman in a bowling shirt and ripped jeans rounded the corner and caught him in the act. He tried to palm the evidence, but fearing she had seen him anyway, he got mad, he came at her with a board in his fist.

"Chill out, buddy." She reached into her pocket and showed him her pipe. She had been casing the store for a possible burglary attempt and was as surprised as he was by this crossing.

His eyes kept going up and down her body. He invited her to join him behind the Dumpster, and without even bothering to exchange names, they settled into the serious business of racking up a few pipes, riding out on private currents, staring wordlessly on this involved backdrop of crumbling brick and cracked asphalt, the solitude deepening like the sky at dusk, and as beautiful, this silent sharing of isolates. In a profane world the passing of the pipe was a sacramental act.

When he felt like speaking again, Mister CD said, "They found a body back here couple years ago. Back here with the trash. Some woman. All cut up. Face and hands burned almost all away."

"Yeah?"

"Just dumped here sometime during the night. Never did identify her, far as I know. Never found out who did it, either."

"Bad." She ran her tongue around the inside of her mouth, checking for the umpteenth time this past minute her teeth, which felt, oddly enough, like gums.

"Right here. Right where we're sitting."

"Maybe you should put up a plaque."

He looked at the insolence in her face, he looked at the nipples outlined on her shirt. "I like you," he said.

So she met him for "lunch" back of the garbage the following day and the day after that and then a week and a half ago he moved her into his "bachelor pad." They were going on a mission together.

Now she was holding in her hand an empty CD box, gazing into the cover (a leather-gloved fist brandishing a boy's dream of compressed firepower, the cannon-sized barrel a sleek chrome sculpture of naked cartoon womanhood) as if it were a pocket mirror. She opened the box and read the liner notes. She read the liner notes. She read the liner notes.

He said something. He said something else. "Hey," he called, "I'm talking to you."

She showed him the cover, *9mm Love* by Burning Sore. "Did you know Axl Rose plays tambourine on this cut of 'Blood Depot'?"

"Fucking Axl Rose. Forty-six with a bullet the first week and how many copies I order?"

"I don't know."

"I don't either."

She weighed the little box in her hand. "Sure would like to hear it."

"I'm working on it, okay? Tomorrow." He glanced around at the wadded sheets, feeling under his legs. "Okay, so where's the damn stem?"

She was having thoughts and her thoughts were having thoughts, a regular birthing frenzy in the old cranium tonight, strangled cries and organic mess and a horde of deformed infants crawling like advancing troops over the rocks and nails and broken glass in her head, and suddenly she couldn't seem to determine with any certainty which was more pressingly real, these bloodied babies hunting for a way out, or the besieged voice most anxious to preserve its status as the imperial "I" that was looking for a way in—a dilemma admitting neither easy response nor the measured pace of judicial deliberation, since the moment the question was posed she was engulfed by a wave of pure panic, as if nerves were being raked with a steel comb; she experienced a sense of being peeled away, ushered toward a revelation she wasn't capable of bearing, as when one stands too long before a mirror and the images shift toward the unrecognizable, the ultimate horror of simple things.

She jumped up, ran to the window, the skin on her face tightened against the bone like a cat's ears gone flat, she glared out at the darkness, defying the night, the machinery of its desire.

"What?" shouted Mister CD, swiveling startled between window and door. "What?"

"Did you hear something?"

"What?" He joined her at the window to listen. They heard only the reassuring sound of crickets, patiently sawing their way through prison bars.

"Stay here." He retrieved the .44 from under the mattress and, fashionably armed and as dangerous as a full magazine could render him, stole through the darkened house as through an enemy wood. At the entrance to the living room he stopped, waited. When he dared to venture a peek around the corner, the deep moonlit vista framed by the front window was astonishingly vacant: no one at the door, no one in the bushes, no one on the street. He remained in place, how-ever, eyeing the suspicious oak planted conveniently in the dead center of the lawn. Either the trunk was moving on its own or there was somebody incorrect lurking behind it. He watched for more than an hour. Unconsciously massaging the soft flesh below his left nipple. Breath whistling audibly through the upper reaches of his nose. Until silver grass dissolved into a storewide russet expanse of industrial carpet ruined by incompetent vacuum cleaning, the inability of part-time adolescent help to comprehend the simplest order, "Up and down, Denise, and back and forth, see, like mowing the infield," not these haphazard clusters of short stabbing strokes scattered like angry doodles about the floor, the radius of each mark limited to the full extension of her lazy arm from rooted-to-the-center feet, god, he hated walking in in the morning on such a sorry spectacle, worth a good ten-point hike in blood pressure. Gradually, he became aware of the gun in his hand and the quiet carpet-less scene in his eyes and he whirled abruptly and retreated toward the inviting glow of the bedroom.

"All clear, lobo, blew 'em the fuck away." But there was nobody there to congratulate him.

He found her, obviously enough, in the bathroom after an inexplicable tour of the complete house, a pause to reconfirm the oak tree's position, and a tense period in the garage anticipating the momentary impact of rounds large enough to be fired from the handle end of a lawnmower. So his sensory apparatus was already making strange noises when he pushed back the battered bathroom door on this not entirely unpredictable scene: Latisha seated in, if not wedged into, the cheap sink, her added weight beginning to separate pipes and basin from the buckling wall as she calmly flipped lighted matches, one by one, from a book stamped AIR-LANE MOTEL, PULASKI, TENN., into the lime-stained pink tub.

He went insane. He didn't know what he was screaming.

"I'm bored," she explained. She was actually playing a private game of he-loves-me, he-loves-me-not, thinking of a boy whose face she would never forget but whose name she unfortunately had, though he wasn't necessarily the one the matchbook oracle was being questioned about.

Mister CD was beginning to form coherent sentences. "Do you have any idea what happens when a shower curtain goes up?"

She tossed another match. "What do you care? Probably it's not even yours."

"Quicker than paper. Hotter, too. Big black smelly smoke loaded with cancer. The house'd be full of it in forty-five seconds."

"Yeah?" She tore out the last match. He loved her, whaddya know. Whoever *he* was. "Does it get you high? Can we get off on it?"

He yanked her bodily out of the sink, hustled her down the hall and into the bedroom, where he threw her onto the mattress. A rolled-up newspaper he retrieved off the floor served as a makeshift swagger stick as he paraded before her, ranting, blustering, slapping his thigh, a major performance with barely a glance at the audience.

She sat drawn up against the wall, glowering at him, rubbing her wrist. "I'm about half a second," she said, "from busting you up real good."

"Burn the place down, is that it? Huh? You like fire? I'll show you fire, babe." He turned and plunged the paper baton into a candle flame, he waved this torch at her, fouling the air with his spitted taunts, a black storm of swirling ash out of which her screaming face appeared as a cardboard mask punched with three bleak bottomless holes. At the first bite of flame on the skin of his own hand, he dashed off for the relief of the bathroom, clutching still his wand of charred newsprint magically alive with dozens of tiny glowing worms. Sounds of cursing and running water.

In his absence Latisha tried to decide whether to go, whether to stay, whether to do up another bowl. He was back before she could come to any conclusion. A ragged length of wet toilet paper wrapped around the fingers of his right hand. He glared at her, accusingly. "Where's the damn stem?" he asked.

Afterward, he stared off into the effervescing middle distance, wearing the same expression he'd presented to teachers in the middle of elementary school math tests. He didn't move, he didn't speak. The drug radiated endlessly outward, to the prickling borders of his body —and beyond. It possessed a shape, that was true, its outlines shimmering in teasing grandeur somewhere out there where one cryptic irrepressible impulse in this bundle of contradictions that served him adequately enough as an identity longed to be, to inhabit the contours of this other, larger self completely. He was on a mission.

Whatever happened was meant to be. You can't always get what you want. Easy come, easy go. Same old shit. Get the bastards before they get you. Love makes the world go round.

The moment he heard the word "crack" he knew that one day he would try it and like it. He *knew* weird stuff like that about himself all the time. The fateful introduction took place at a record company party, but it was somebody in real estate, a shiny broker with manicured nails and a pretentious lawyer-type wife, who offered him, out on the deserted patio, his first kiss of the pipe. Sweet. So now this was simply another activity he performed, another of the habitual quirks that defined him; he wore a Cubs cap in the house, he ate penne with tomato sauce every Monday night, he visited his son's grave once a week, he passed through doorways on his left foot, he chewed gum in church, he smoked a little rock. Now, having added this last routine to his repertoire without much more consideration than in picking a dime up off the street, he was discovering that it brought with it its own inescapable thoughts, a veritable towering system of interlocked . . . well, not ideas exactly, more like mental events, a complete philosophy of them whose arguments he was compelled, a not unwilling student, to explore to the finest nuance. Such were the days.

Latisha could not remember when she had slept last. It was like food, she didn't need much anymore. She was new, a woman from the future. Dreams, though, still needed her, swooping in at any hour, unannounced, sometimes unrecognized, deep into the intricate urgency of the passing moment she could be startled awake by the sudden evaporation of objects, happenings, truths, her surroundings deftly replaced by another set whose reality might or might not be so permanent. Some dreams she needed to flee, to walk off, pacing anxiously from wall to wall in an imaginary foot-worn trench, her assigned post, guarding the twin-doored closet as if it were the maximum security cell that bad thoughts escaped from. The vision she was trying to shake now was of a pack of hungry gray dogs licking blood off a window. Lots of blood, lots of dogs. She was on the other side of the glass. Then, prompted by private signs, she rushed from the room on vague errands in the spooky no-man's-land of the rest of the house, her absence, sometime later, culminating in a series of clumsy kitchen sounds Mister CD refused to acknowledge. He was flat on his back, trying not to move too much because when he breathed, his insides made creaking ship-at-sea noises. He was dying exactly as Celia had prophesied when he walked out on her however many months ago it was now, in sweat and agony in a lonely place without a single nurse in attendance. Ha. Her curse. A woman who consistently pronounced his first name as if it were an adjective. The ease with which he could have strangled her, throttled the smugness swimming in accusatory preservative behind her goggle glasses. A done deed but for the silly frog crouching there on the crowded sill, emerald porcelain in a revelation of sunlight, a gift from little Benny to his mother. Nothing was insignificant. Everything was strange. The nagging image of his son in a suit he had never worn in life, laid out grotesquely in a shocking green coffin he had never occupied in death. What did that mean? What did he know? Mister CD's body seemed to be composed of an itchy synthetic material. On his last ejaculation a single drop of sperm welled like a tear in the eye of his penis. Behind these fragile crackling walls lurked—what? . . . The DEA . . . the FBI . . . his wife. But why did he care? He was steel, will and flesh. He checked his pulse. We are as goddamned gods.

Latisha reentered the room as he was doing up another bowl. He noticed at once the odd positioning of her arm at her back, the briefest glitter of the steak knife blade in her hand. He smiled benignly, extended the vaporous pipe in her direction.

And afterward, confronting the cold television screen, she spoke, "I don't even have to do it myself. I've got friends."

"What the fuck are you jabbering about?"

"Killing you."

He barked. "Yeah? And who might these friends be? Spitcurl? X-man? Gizmo? Or one of the other dwarves? Scary."

"I know a lot of people."

"Oh, yeah, wait a minute, I got you now. That faggoty kid, that Race, that what he call himself now? Race, what a fucking joke."

"His name is Reese."

"Whatever. The pissboy with the box-cutter. Keep talking like this. I like the way your mouth looks when you talk about murder. Talk more for me. Dust, whack, pop."

"I'm outta here." She made a move to get up, but he shoved her down onto her back.

"I'm not finished with this." He held her down, leering over her, searching the caves of her eyes for unaccounted shapes.

"Reese didn't have any knife, Reese wasn't even there, how much you know."

"I know enough to recognize a piece of sharp metal when it's stuck in my face."

"It was a kid in white sweatpants I never saw before. And nobody got hurt, so what are you bitching about all the time?"

"Who was the gangster in the leather cap?"

"Nobody. I already told you that. God, you are—"

"If Gizmo hadn't stepped between us . . ."

"Nothing, that's what, absolutely nothing. God, you are so paranoid."

"Careful, little lobo, I'm careful."

"So paranoid in your old age you can't remember a fucking thing anymore."

But he wasn't listening to her anymore, either; he had the pipe in his teeth and was sucking on the stem like a drowning man. Through the enveloping smoke one neutral eye fixed steadily on her, whatever posture she might assume, whatever betrayal her face might reveal. He arched a brow and said, "Put on your uniform."

"Oh no, please."

"C'mon, baby, Daddy needs a nurse. Bad."

"Yeah? Well, so do I. Who's gonna nurse me?"

"Oh please, please, it hurts so bad." He was rolling around, clutching hands between his legs in an obscene parody of pain.

She went to the closet, rummaged through a heap of clothing. "I do this," she muttered. "I actually do this." She stepped into a wrinkled white dress, fumbled with the buttons.

"No, idiot, not here, damnit. In the bathroom. Then you come in already dressed. Like on rounds, remember?"

"Jesus fucking Christ."

He settled himself into an exemplary patient position. He closed his eyes and watched inside himself a thin rodlike beam of laser energy tracking around his interior, pausing to spotlight the dominant organs, each in its turn then playing its own distinctive song. When the ruby wand touched the gnarled surface of his heart, his eyes came spontaneously open, and standing over him was Ms. Angelcake, the ward nurse, gazing compassionately down. His head lifted off the pillow. "The stethoscope," he cried. "I can't believe you forgot the fucking stethoscope."

"Sorry." She exited, muttering.

In a moment, properly attired, she returned. "Well now, Mister CD, what seems to be the problem?"

He pointed.

"Oh, what a nasty growth. Does it hurt?"

He nodded.

"Well, let's see what we can do to reduce the swelling and alleviate the pain."

She remembered how it ended after finally begging him to stop and she remembered stripping off that hateful uniform and that was all until now and the miracle of the cracked ceiling she had been acutely attending for hours and hours, it was glowing, the intensity of its illumination multiplying surely but imperceptibly under the care of her watch, she imagined a hidden rheostat somewhere manipulated by a withered old hand, and then, with a start, she comprehended the meaning of this fascinating phenomenon. "Is this this day or is it yesterday?" she asked.

"What the fuck are you talking about now?"

"Days. The days of our lives."

"No fucking sense. None. In fact, you haven't made a lick of sense since I met you."

"Oh right, go ahead, let out your pig. What do you care?"

"I like to have conversations, you know. I enjoy a good conversing. But there's gotta be something coming back at me I can understand."

"In your teeth."

"Sure." He rolled off the mattress and onto the floor, where he began executing a swaybacked set of push-ups. "Been thinking," he wheezed, "about getting me . . . a pair . . . of good . . . handcuffs."

She turned away, faced into the windows, the coming light. "I can't believe myself," she announced to the solidifying day. "All the time I've spent sitting in this house with you. In the dark." For her, time was the memory of a shaped sensation and this most recent period of her life didn't seem to have a shape, unless it was a bar of chrome you just rode.

"You love me."

"I do?" She could hear him messing with the plastic bags.

"You do."

A pair of big brown irises stared back at him over her shoulder. "But who are you?"

"I'm Mis-ter Cee-Dee," he sang, "low-est pri-ces, larg-est in-ven-toe-ree . . ."

The tune was like one she'd heard before, then it was that tune. She was sitting in a field of clover in the shade of a shaggy bark tree, chestnut mare nibbling on a handful of gumdrops scattered among the dandelions, mild wind riffling the sunny grass, clear sky soft as felt. She supposed there was a weathered red barn with a Red Man chewing tobacco ad plastered to its wall and a row of blackbirds on a telephone wire and a nice white fence, too: things that lived in a tune. Fake memories. Cool.

"So who'd you steal the song from, anyway?"

"What do you mean? I wrote it myself. It's a tribute to Benny."

"Oh." End of discussion. The five-year-old-son mauled to death by a neighbor's Doberman. The one story in Mister CD's life she did know in pertinent detail. How the settlement money from the lawsuit provided the down payment for the business. The wife, Celia, crying for a year. So they had another kid. And another. She still cried. Boo hoo, why me? Why us? Mister CD hadn't the slightest. But he did know this: the money was holy, sanctified in the blood of his loins, so of course the business would succeed, and every customer who left the store with a CD in his or her hand was carrying a living piece of Benny into their homes.

"You going in today?" she asked.

"Yeah, yeah. In a minute."

"I don't even know what day of the week it is." She was gazing wistfully at the screen. "There's no time without television."

"Don't tell me what I'm thinking. Don't even try."

"Huh?"

Rising up across the floor in the unforgiving luminosity of dawn was a forbidding landscape of stale clothes, lost shoes, red and blue capped plastic vials, IDs and credit cards phony and legit, cigarettes, magazines, newspapers, cans, cups, and Styrofoam burger boxes. By candlelight this colorful array of textures and forms had seemed intriguing. He got up and left the room without a word. She remained on the mattress reading and rereading the same tattered issue of *People* and the stars kept smiling for her and heaven was user-friendly and the limos were at the curb. He came back. In a dramatically swirling cape of snowy smoke.

"You ever do any moon rock?" she asked.

"Moon rock? What's that?"

"It's new."

"I've seen everything that ever came down the street. Never heard of no moon rock."

"That's 'cause it's new, it's happening."

"Yeah?"

"It's what the astronauts use. It's NASA-approved."

"Get some."

Then the unidentifiable strangeness that had been creeping moldlike across the windows resolved itself and it was night. Again.

"Whoa." She struggled to her feet, unable to manage the responsibilities of upright posture beyond a simian crouch, in which attitude she contemplated the wonders of planetary motion. "Went right past that day. Going faster than days now."

"What?"

She collapsed like a deflating balloon back onto the mattress.

"What'd you say?"

"When I was a little girl," she began, her huge eyes still full of whatever she had seen outside that black window.

"Oh holy Christ."

"When I was a little girl, I wanted, more than anything, to run away with the carnival."

"Please. Don't give me a heart attack."

"You know those sleazy carnivals that come every summer to the parking lot behind the mall? The same nothing rides, the same crummy prizes year after year, but every summer we couldn't wait to get out there the first night they opened. And every night those girls working the booths, man, couldn't get enough of 'em. Beanbag. Darts. Air rifle. Ping-Pong ball in the goldfish bowl. I studied them. Their moves, their faces. We're talking major cosmetics here and kinda glass eyes that looked right at you without looking. Their bodies were always hard and skinny and count on at least one to have red hair and everyone had a pack of Marlboros sticking out of their jeans and they didn't take orders from nobody and they certainly didn't think much of you, shuffling past with a ball of cotton candy in your face. I wanted so bad to be one of those girls, wear a greasy change apron around my hips and grow a hard face under those yellow lights and carnival stink and yell insults at all the straights."

"Yeah," said Mister CD, "you just wanted to sit on a corn dog."

She didn't sleep that night, either.

"We're on a mission," he reminded her.

In the morning, when the light came monstrously round again, it found her poised ballerinalike at the window thinking, it's a beautiful, it's a pink cake day. She dressed herself from the nearest pile and said, "Time to get out, campers. Let's go, we gotta go. Movies, we go movies, Daddy." Daddy had spent much of the night positioned out in the living room, watching the trees twitch.

"In a minute."

Hours later, Latisha and Mister CD emerged from the shadowy house into the hot bedazzlement of high noon, outfitted as if for a mountain hike in layered clothing not usually seen until late autumn, sober faces shielded from painful rays and close inspection by matching pairs of expensive Italian sunglasses. Covering the sparse growth on Mister CD's head a neon blue baseball cap with a gold SHOWTIME patch sewn across the crown. The car, an unwashed, unwaxed, decidedly unnew green Ford Galaxie, sat baking in the driveway.

Noncommittal eyes beneath a lowered brow observed all from next door, where Mr. Hugo, a retired classics professor with a nasty fungoid blemish bleaching out one ruddy cheek, was down on his knees in the crabgrass pouring a kettle of boiling water into the widening cracks of his cement walk, a silent spectator, having early learned there was little point in addressing neighbors who responded with icy stares or, on one disagreeable occasion, an obscenely long, extended tongue. He had pretty much concluded that these characters were a couple of drug addicts from the city, especially the dirty-blond gal with the bony rump. His wife, Philippa, believed they might be mafia, professional killers perhaps, "mechanics," lying low from the FBI and other mob types. But Philippa, he contended, absorbed entirely too much television, was too quick to embrace the extremities of human behavior: last winter, for instance, pleading like a teenager for a snowmobile— unsuccessfully, of course. So you tended your garden, you eliminated your pests the safe, organic way and you did not meddle, at least not until the show had completed its undeniably entertaining run.

Latisha occupied the front seat fiercely, a ride-loving dog, head erect, nails digging into the warm Leatherette, blown pupils locked on the types and tints flying at her. Mister CD simply drove, guided the car through a defined succession of right angles, the formal labyrinth of suburban geometry, to the giddy loops, curls, and straights of interstate improvisation. Latisha rolled down the window, shook her head, the torn flag of her hair whipping freely behind her; she shouted into the wind, she slapped a dangling palm against the door. Mister CD laughed; she amused him, her and her nonsense; he looked at her and he laughed. "Look at all these assholes!" she cried, scattering words into the polluted howl. "I hate 'em all!"

"All right," warned Mister CD in his deep daddy voice. His big hands and thick arms (the gold watch tightly fastened to his wrist looked to have been implanted there) held the rattling car to the inconspicuous middle lane; he drove, in fact, with a trucker's assurance, an indisputable presumption of mind over matter executed with the same practiced grace involved in the swift ignition of one thumb-worn Bic and the tendering of its flame to the seasoned lip of the glass bowl being sucked so enthusiastically on the seat beside him. "Hey!" He grabbed for the hastily withdrawn pipe. "What in the fucking hell are you doing? What's the matter with you? Are you that stupid?"

"Watch the road," she muttered, inhaling, inhaling, inhaling.

"What do you think, we're in the fucking woods, for Christ's sake, we can't be—" He took the pipe she handed him. "Oh no" puff "who's gonna notice" puff "a couple of outrageous crackheads" puff "chasing the dragon" puff "through eight lanes of midday traffic?" puff "Who's gonna notice a sight common as that?" puff.

Suddenly they were surrounded by cop cars, great big cop cars, cop cars big as dinosaurs whizzing past, looming in the mirrors, rearing up ahead, no one had ever seen so many cop cars. Mister CD watched the speedometer, he watched the mirrors, he watched the road, all at once. The engine had begun making a bad sound, the crazy rattle of a roulette ball dropping into the slot. Or was that his heart?

Latisha, blind as usual to the crisis, was stretching her arms, pressing flattened palms into the yielding dinginess of the vinyl roof. "Wish we had a convertible," she was saying. "That's our kind of car, don't you think? People like us. I want to feel the speed." She clicked on the radio (Global Truss: "Y U B So F*cken Sic?") and in the half second it took him to turn the thing off the cops vanished. And was that a stray cruiser lurking several cars up ahead in an adjoining lane, or, yes, just the electric company. He was sweating and he didn't like to sweat; it stunk, it drew bugs.

"Look at that dumb shit. His face is fucked. He's got a fucked face. Hey, fuck you!" A middle finger was offered her from a passing Mercedes at sixty per. "These people must all die," she told him, and, glimpsing yet another vehicular outrage, "Hey, lady, got any hair on your fucking twat!" She was hanging halfway out of the car, his hand gripping the waistband of her jeans. Mister CD smiled, coughed up a laugh or two. "My heart," he groaned. What a woman.

A white torpedo shot from the corner of his left eye, exploded into a full-size Trans Am careening around him in high-gear shriek, apparently out of control, then cutting abruptly back into an impossible pocket a horn's blast off their speckled grill, one slim multibraceleted arm wagging indifferently from the driver's window. The Galaxie shook, squealing under the brakes. A forgotten Glock slid out from under the seat, kicked back once, twice by his pedaling feet to slide out again. It was fully loaded.

"Fucking whore!" shrieked Latisha, falling hard against Mister CD's shoulder. "Run her off the road!" She made a grab for the wheel, instantly the back of his hand cracked across her nose and cheek. A clumsy grappling commenced in the front seat of the Galaxie, alert vehicles in the immediate vicinity opening a discreet cushion of space around the rollicking car. "Enough!" he commanded, the voice emanating from the same cold well as pale frogs with blind embryonic eyes and hairless rats and nights of no return.

"You bastard," she hissed. "I saw how you looked at her. I'm not stupid." And she lunged at him, attempting to slide her hand into his pants. He pushed her away, raising a cocked elbow at her head. "If I have to pull over, you'll wish you wasn't even ever you." She didn't have to look twice at his face. She sat in place, stationary and mute, her mind a hopeless turmoil of unsortable forms, until the car stopped moving and they were staring at one another in the parking lot of the mall. She held his arm, she wouldn't let him out of the car. She wanted to screw on the backseat. He looked at her. "Your brains are goo," he said. "Fucking goo. I could probably use 'em to wax the fucking car."

He caught her slap in midair, held her by the wrist, and, looking directly into her eyes, twisted it until she winced. "Now, let's go inside," he said, "and let's be good."

A representative of normal society with normal clothes and normal features and a wad of dense curly hair seemingly balanced atop his head like a wool cap drifted past their windshield engrossed in the tricky consumption of a melting ice cream cone. Noticing their stares, he quickened his pace.

"Look at that jerk," said Latisha. "He's got a damn woody in his pants."

"Going in," said Mister CD. "Being good." He gripped her firmly by the arm, a gentleman escorting his lady up the blazing walk to the ticket window, where lingered a few bored kids in luridly dyed beach clothes. There were a dozen screens, the same movie playing at half of them.

"I wanna see *Batman*," she said.

"No."

"*Batman*," she demanded.

"Not again. We'll rent it. I'll buy you the fucking tape."

"It's not on tape yet, you bastard."

The solemn girl behind the glass watched unblinking through exaggerated cartoon eyes, her mind blanking mercifully out in anticipation of her first holdup, and since her life had been relatively brief, a complete rerun still left plenty of time for Coming Attractions and none of the scenes were pretty. Then the man was tugging on the girl and whispering angrily into her ear. Then the girl whispered angrily back. Then the man was speaking to her.

"*Batman*," said Mister CD. "Two." He paid and, without understanding why, blew the ticket girl a kiss.

The crimson lobby looked like a whorehouse and smelled like a locker room. At the refreshment counter Miss Ticket Booth's identical twin could not accept Mister CD's crisp hundred-dollar note without consulting the manager, a weedy officious boy in a bow tie who certainly wasn't legal in any sense. Then, halfway down the aisle, Latisha dropped the tub of popcorn, and after they had settled into their usual seats, on the end four rows back, she refused to move, so Mister CD, complaining but compliant, went back for a refill. The sloping floor was sticky and ankle-deep in trash. Her hard comfortless seat seemed to have been crudely upholstered in unwashed laundry. Nervously, she eyed the ghostly shiftings of the great red curtain; the sense of anticipation, of any magnitude, had always been, even in childhood, personally difficult to bear, and in the enclosed dark of a theater, unwelcome awarenesses incubated freely. Whatever mysteries the curtain contained, the act of revelation was always a shock of some degree. (And though she had already seen this movie twice before, she was quite capable of being surprised by the familiar; she invited it.) She could feel the multitude of glowing minds that shared this space with her, convinced that each strange and separate soul was fixed in complicit concentration upon the back of her unprotected head. "Assholes," she muttered. "Cunts. Dicks." She was preparing to leave when Mister CD arrived, fresh popcorn spilling from a bucket twice the size of the original. "What'd I miss?" he joked. The house lights were still up. "Fuck!" Leaning forward, he spat a mouthful of partially chewed corn between his legs. "What is this shit?" She thought he was having a heart attack.

"Goddamn bad butter. Tastes like WD-40."

She sampled a few kernels. "Seems all right to me."

"It's all yours, babe."

Ten minutes into the picture, a not wholly unpleasant unreeling of swollen events in shades of black and blue, she excused herself to go to the bathroom. The second time she got up, twenty minutes later, Mister CD, without a word, followed. In a locked stall of the women's room they burned down the remaining rock secreted in clever locales about their persons. Back at their seats they discovered the screen's dimensions had undergone alteration. Mister CD cackled irrepressibly whenever anyone got shot; Latisha was Batman, she ruled. But near the end, the narrative having dutifully chugged on rails of big budget bombast into a gratifyingly musty station, the theater reverberating with all the nuances of the special effects department, the squeals of thrilled patrons, Latisha was seized by an unaccountable sense of desolation and she began to cry, and though Mister CD held her in his arms, patted her quaking back, she couldn't stop, and when the movie noise was no longer able to mask her noise, he helped her up the aisle as behind them the Joker wiggled a gleeful butt in the Caped Crusader's face.

She staggered like a wino in the open nakedness of rude daylight, halfway to the car tripping on her own feet, hitting the pavement with a sickening sound. "My knee," she cried, rolling around like a wounded animal, hand clamped over the tear in her jeans, "I broke my fucking knee."

Mister CD looked down at her small vulnerable body, the drowned world of her eyes, the nostrils leaking rillets of snot she licked with her tongue. "God," he said, "your favorite movie, too."

She was inspecting the damage with a child's curious horror. "Aaaaaw, I'm bleeding," she moaned.

Two women in jogging costume had paused at a wary distance. Cars cruising for spaces in the lot were slowing as they passed. "Get up," he said. The temperature was climbing out here in the sun, the glaze melting off the shoppers' faces. He was experiencing an awareness of accumulating eyes. Disturbance in the field, outlanders in Sector E6. "Get up," he ordered, nudging her with his shoe, "get up or I'll break your fucking head, too." She knuckle-punched him in the leg. "Okay," he said calmly and reached down and hauled her to her feet and hustled her expertly away, as if he were a cop and she a dangerous someone under arrest. The Bic was in one hand, the glove compartment being impatiently rummaged by the other before he had shifted out of reverse. When she could find nothing and realized there was nothing around her to stanch the tears, to string Christmas lights through her soul, she started to cry again. She accused him of not loving her, of not even caring about her. Mister CD drove.

He pulled into the driveway and sat, engine running. She looked at him. He stared out the windshield. "Get out," he ordered.

"I'm in a mood, C. You know that."

"Got some shopping to do."

"Me, too."

"Serious shopping. New people."

"What new people? Where?"

"Out. I'll bring you a present."

"How long you gonna be?"

"Quicker you get out, quicker I'll be back."

She opened the door. "One hour," she said. She got out. "I mean it, too." She slammed the door. The Galaxie began rolling back down the driveway. She tottered after for a few steps. "See if they got any moon rock," she called.

She couldn't tell him how afraid she was to be alone. He might use the knowledge against her someday. She descended into solitude as into an abyss, and once a certain depth had been achieved, the fear came after her huge as a hungry mouth. She spent the first hour alone ransacking the house, finally finding, after checking there twice, a beautiful white nugget nestled in the battery compartment of the VCR remote, where she herself had hidden it in anticipation of such a rainy night. She stoked up the pipe. The smoke hanging before her in voluptuous silken shreds she wanted to lick, like human skin. She wandered aimlessly through the emptiness of the house, shedding her clothes, a different article in each room. She finished up in the middle of the mattress, where she sat, chin on her chest, unmoving, as the bar of natural light crept up the wall, shriveled, and was gone . . . Above her head, fluttering like paper toys among the bamboo rafters, are a pair of astonishing birds in the iridescent blues and golds of tropical fish. She is seated on a rock ledge, legs dangling in the burbling clarity of the freshwater pool in her living room. The tranquillity of life in a faraway beach house of thatched elegance. In the neighboring bungalow that famous blond actress with the teeth from As the World Turns or Guiding Light or The Bold and the Beautiful. She is quietly aware of a new, unaccustomed body; a bright, unveiled self. She is horny 24-7. The bar is an open-air hut on a shore redolent of brine and orchids. Her daiquiri is an iced goblet of pale cream from which protrudes the curvaceous shape of a peeled banana. The flesh of the banana is flawed by the presence of several bruises, brown moons of decay. She is a regular, the girl everyone knows. Her conch-pink toes splayed in aesthetically pleasing contrast against a floor of pure white sand. The light here is of an exhilarating transformative nature, at its touch an instant landscape of essences. The brown bartender wears no shirt. The bar towel squeaks around the inside of the glass. His dangerously blue eyes have no bottoms. She understands her stay at the Hotel Delirioso can be, if she chooses, extended indefinitely, but whether or not she can meet the price is a question with no clear answer. She has trouble making the rent on this present body, whose streets and alleys, now that she noticed, were submerged in the clamor of a mob, the weight of their collapsing bodies bearing her stoically down. A headful of corpses. The load she trundled through the mud of misty days. God, no wonder she was tired all the time. This was the trouble with stokin' it. After the peerless joy of the aerial view, it led you down, down to the mazes under the ground, down close corridors to cold rooms she did not want to visit. Like the morgue, for instance. Her touching inability to routinize the procedure, briskly wrap the deceased in sheets for the ride in the disguised gurney past unsuspecting patients and visitors down to the refrigerated drawers, and each one of those white mummies she prepared with her own hands she could remember by chart, by ward, by face, information she couldn't seem to lose, along with an image of herself as grim jumpmaster on a jumbo transport, holding the door for each numbered processee to sail out—into what? Fucking enemy territory, that's what.

The table was black. The TV was gray. The walls were white. She leafed through *Vanity Fair*, the darkness moving stealthily in, a silent and respectful maid. She got up and roamed around the room, anointing each cold candle with the trusty Bic. She returned to the mattress and read intently in the pages of *TV Guide*, visualizing favorite shows, old movies. Scarlett O'Hara was one of her favorite characters. So was Nora Charles. So was Ratso Rizzo. She made a mental checklist of each show she would watch tonight if there were power. She saw herself watching those shows. The image feed was inexhaustible. Her life signs were modulating nicely. Then the door chimes sounded and she was up on her feet without any awareness of having moved, a piece of trembling statuary, heart like an alarm clock, prickly sensations rolling up and down her body, uncertain whether she had heard anything at all. She looked anxiously about the room as if there were another person, another object to tell her what to do. Then it happened again, a sonorous measured ding-dong that broke her posture. She pulled on a T-shirt and a pair of jeans, grabbed the .44 from under the mattress, and cautiously made her way to the front of the house, fingers running lightly along the walls as if she were traversing the unsteady passageways of a ship. She stopped in the shadows, well away from the pale parallelogram of streetlight thrown carelessly across the uncarpeted floor. Through the picture window she could see him, a man in the dark at her door. Jiggling up and down. He pressed the button a third time, turned away to inspect the empty street. There was a strange car in the driveway. He leaned his face in against the window. A block of solid stillness, she did not flinch.

"I see you," he said. "C'mon, open up."

Her heart was going like wild hooves up her chest. She raised up the gun with both hands.

"I'll break this fucking door, you know that." Nails tapping rapidly on the glass. The sound—this scraping of talons—startled her and she pulled the trigger, she thought she pulled the trigger, nothing had happened, and now the door knob was being violently shaken and the chimes were ringing without stop and the voice was at her head, threatening, "C'mon, Latisha, open up." Latisha? She hid the gun in a soggy bag of garbage in the corner and unlocked the door.

Arms flung for an embrace, he entered the house grinning at the notion of being surprised he'd caught her at home.

"Reese." She nodded curtly, holding him at a distance with the dead sound of her voice.

"Hey, is that any way to be?"

"What do you want?"

"So paranoid. What's happened to you out here in the 'burbs? That old geek you're fucking messing up your mind?"

"He's not old."

"Let's see him, bring him out, he hiding under the bed or what?"

"He's out."

"Don't lie to me." His eyes were looking away, through the walls toward the other rooms.

"Oh, okay, I forgot. He's around the corner, hugging an Uzi, waiting to blow your fucking head off."

"Relax, I believe you. Why don't you turn on a damn light so we could see each other's faces or something?"

"I like this, it's more romantic, don't you think?"

"I miss you, darlin'."

"Please, not Elvis, not tonight. I've got a headache."

"Hey." He raised his arms and revolved in a slow circle in front of her. He looked at her, he shrugged his shoulders. This was his I'm clean, I'm innocent act. Innocent of everything. In his right hand the familiar rumpled gym bag containing the stash and the hardware.

"How'd you find me?"

"Streets are all connected, baby, you just follow them out."

"You seem different." He didn't, actually, but she had forgotten the full effect of his presence. She went numb looking at him.

"I know, I just keep getting better." He noted her expression and laughed, shrugging his shoulders again. "That's what they say."

"Whaddya got?"

"Well, I got this"—he held up the bag—"and I got this"—pointing an incredibly long-nailed finger at his crotch.

She came toward him without a word, like someone pretending to be sleepwalking, and she dropped to her knees and unfastened his pants and slid them down to his socks, all the while staring deep into his eyes but giving nothing back, the way she knew he liked it.

"What's this?" she asked. A dangling length of white string was knotted so tightly around his scrotum that his constricted balls, pressing hard against the drawn and shaven skin, resembled the twin lobes of a grotesque miniature brain.

"When I tap you on the head, I want you to pull on it."

"How hard?"

He stared over her head in exasperation. "Like you're turning on a light."

"Won't this hurt?"

"Let's try it and see."

After a while he told her she could stop.

"It's like playing with a wet rubber wienie," she complained. Nothing novel about this situation except the string. "Can I pull on it anyway?"

She did and he went "Toot toot."

Then Reese unzipped the gym bag and showed her huge handfuls of loaded vials.

"Let the party begin," she proclaimed.

Later (whatever that meant in regard to a point lost among spewing nebulae of time), he explained the string was a device to remind him of the thisness of the body. People were no longer cognizant of the actualities of the flesh. And if a person, be he male or be he female, entertained an insufficiently active symbiosis with the body's vitals, then that body was susceptible to occupation by others. Government others. Simple tools like string and various controlled substances were necessary then to keep open crucial channels with your biological base.

"Yes," she said. "That's what I believe."

His face was developing new highlights. Yes, she was seeing clearly now, experiencing things as they were. "You have cute ears," she said.

His arm was reaching for her, every hair a distinct individual specially inserted in bright skin for her viewing pleasure.

She fell for him once because, searching the innocence of his face, she witnessed the materialization of his third eye in the properly centered position of his forehead and she was bewitched. This was the eye that would master her. They met at the Art Institute and forty minutes later he was banging her in an elevator deliberately stalled between floors (Greek and Impressionism). He liked art and the museum was a good, safe place for dealing. He liked football and American history and dope. His features looked great posed against the Rembrandts. So they screwed each other for a while and then they screwed other people. His freckled skin like cinnamon flakes floating in milk in the somnolent light of late afternoon on Mill Street, up under the unpainted eaves in the sagging bed, where she began calling in sick until the day the hospital called her. By then, bored with school, Reese was drifting carelessly streetward, Latisha trailing after. She dealt out of his car from a corner near the library to her own select clientele of friends or friends of friends or strangers who claimed to be acquaintances of onetime friends. His paranoia worsened, he slept with a Smith & Wesson in his hand; one night, defending him from a dream assault, it went off, missing by inches her equally addled head and tearing an unplasterable hole in both wall and relationship. She walked away. She lived with guys. She did what she had to do. She noticed suspicious sores on her body. She worried about AIDS, off and on.

The sores came and went. Mister CD was one of the better specimens of contemporary guyhood.

Now here was Reese again, wanting her back. He was so paranoid. He begged her. She wouldn't go. He said his lines. She said her lines. Like that. Back and forth. He was so paranoid.

After he was gone, she wasn't sure that anyone had been in the house with her tonight. Over the last year she had gotten accustomed to perpetual uncertainty, to life in this neo-"soft" world where edges were malleable and indistinct, a uniform layer of concern draped like a sheet over the great and the trivial alike. She appreciated this view; most things didn't seem to matter much.

A good soldier, at the hour of her watch, she mounted the parapet and she paced, wall to wall, the narrow bedroom path cleared of floor debris, the closet sentinel. I am alive. I am a person. I am real. My name is Latisha Charlemagne. My name is Latisha Charlemagne. Real. Off in the night somewhere the inexplicable hum of giant machinery. She clutched at her shoulders, the sudden spasms, shivering in the August heat. When Leech Woman felt this bad, she killed another young man, injected the juice of his pituitary. Behind the door she discovered an old sweater (not hers), riddled with cigarette burns, separating at the seams, and as she put it on, mind wandering off to play by itself for a minute or two, her fingers abruptly recoiled in horror from the unexpected sensation of slipping into a garment of human skin (her own) buttoned inside out.

When she was little she knew she was never going to die. This was a fact as insistent, as palpable, as true, as the rain in her face, the light in the trees, and sometimes even now, years distant from the innocence that made revelation possible, she was able to find her way back to the sheltering bole of that knowledge. It wasn't a trip that happened often, no predicting where or how it might occur, but when the right path opened before her, happiness ran up wagging its tail to guide her and remind her yet again: everything she knew was wrong. Why had she gone into nursing? She hated the sick. Why had she hooked up with Mister CD? He was fat, ugly, and mean. Why did she fuck people like Reese? She'd heard he had AIDS. Why had she mailed a Xmas card of furiously scrawled obscenities to her parents? They didn't know anything, either. Why was her life going up in smoke? When she was a little girl, she wanted to run away with the carnival.

She rolled over and Mister CD, pasty, sweaty, returned from the dead, was propped in the doorway, glaring at her. He did not look good. "What's that?" he demanded.

"Huh?"

"Say what you were saying again."

"What're you doing?" She wasn't totally positive it was him.

"What do you mean, what am I doing? What are you doing?"

She rubbed at the side of her face with the heel of her palm. "I didn't hear you come in."

"You were singing to yourself."

"Yeah? I was singing?"

"What's the matter with you? Clean out your fucking ear holes."

"What was I singing?"

"Some stupid crap. How the fuck should I know?"

The Bic was in her hand, clicking like castanets. "Where's the shit?"

He tossed her a loaded plastic bag. "Getting bad," he said, trying to ignore the inner chafing of metal parts. "I was almost killed."

"Yeah?"

"New beatmaster took me for a narc."

"Terrordome," she said, attending to the drama of the pipe.

"I thought I was gonna have a fucking heart attack."

"That would be bad." Her rocks and trees, her clouds and clods, were starting to sparkle like enchanted-wood special effects in old black and white movies.

"Fucking-A, twinkletoes."

He was still reworking the incident atop his lonely hill in the living room overlooking the valley of the shadows. Death. It could pop up on you at any time like a shooting gallery target, only it was the one that was armed. He was wearing just his chains, eighteen-karat gold, a St. Christopher's medal, and a healing crystal given him by daughter Lindsay on the last of his birthdays to be celebrated around the faux brick hearth. If he passed now, who would bury him? Who would mourn? Frail and failing, strung upon a web of tubing and wire, unable to move, unable to speak, waiting hopelessly for the same spider that ate Benny, struggling with his eyes to tell the nurse, an immaculate vision in white, to touch, warmth to warmth, just once, before the cold envelops us all. Hold my hand, Latisha! he shrieks, a voice in a mannequin. The shuddering ventilator clicks on and off. Save me, he whispers to the walls, who wouldn't tell anybody, even if they could.

When he came to, he was facedown on the living room floor. He didn't know whether he'd fallen asleep or fainted or worse.

In the bedroom Latisha was hunched over the ratty copy of *TV Guide* she perused with biblical fervor. "*Jaws* is on now," she announced.

"So?" He was wiping his damp face with a musty towel.

"So I want to see it, it's my favorite movie."

"I'll rent it for you tomorrow."

"Gonna rent a generator, too?"

"Maybe Mister Horny Dinosaur next door will let you watch it with him."

He had come into the room to either retrieve an object or relate something important to Latisha, neither of which was apparent to him now; he returned to the bathroom to see if what he had lost could be found there. Then he was back, staring at the clothes at his feet and a strange pair of black briefs. Men's. Holding the article daintily aloft between two curled fingers, he searched through the house. Latisha was nowhere to be found. In the kitchen he checked and rechecked the locks on the windows, then became absorbed in cleaning the panes with a homemade mixture of ethanol and the juice of four lemons purchased weeks ago as a preventative against scurvy. He stood at the back door for the longest time. He swept the floor. Passing through the living room, he was diverted by the black oak out there on the lawn. There was a man hiding behind the trunk. While he waited for the man to show himself again, he took his pulse. The beat seemed rapid, rapid but not excessively so, steady perhaps, steady and strong, certainly lacking the telltale squishy note of a perforated chamber or malfunctioning valve or clogged artery. He had to stop the smoking tomorrow. He couldn't go on like this.

He discovered Latisha in the bedroom lying on her back, executing a surprisingly brisk set of leg-lifts. "I've been right here," she said. "Are you nuts?"

He jiggled the briefs before her nose. "What's this?"

"What's what?" She was counting reps in her head and could hardly be bothered. "Fucking underwear. So what?"

He poked her ribs with his foot. "It ain't mine, cupcake."

Her legs thumped to the floor. She stared at the ceiling. "So what the fuck you want me to do about it?"

He was on her before she could get completely to her feet, seizing a clump of unwashed hair in his hand and carrying her back against the wall to warn her, nose to nose, "Don't you dare sass me, you little cross-eyed bitch." An effort to maneuver her knee sharply up into his groin was met by a hard slap, then another, and snorting contemptuously, he pushed her entire head away as if discarding a particularly nasty piece of trash. She fell to the floor, assuming the doodlebug position, body curled into a tight ball, a helmet of hands to shield her head. He whipped her with the offending underwear and, when his arm tired, kicked with his bare feet, stopping to curse her bones when he bruised a toe. Flushed and wheezing, he towered over her, contemplating her evil egglike form, and discovering he was not yet finished, no, he must drop to his knees and with upraised fists seek to damage, if not break, the protective cage that held the poisonous mess of her heart. This she endured without complaint.

He collapsed like a depleted athlete across the mattress, wiped his face on the sheet. "Honey, honey, why do you make me do this to you?" There was no response. Slowly her reddened body unfolded, rose up away from him. "Hey, where ya going, huh? Answer me, answer me right now."

She returned from the kitchen bearing lightly above her head one of the two scraps of furniture in the whole house, a cheap wooden chair that he watched, transfixed, as it approached and descended without pause across his shoulders and defending forearm. She was readying for a second blow when he yanked the thing from her grip and, eyes loose and inflamed in their sockets, came growling to his feet. "Is this what you want? Huh, is it?" and he slammed the chair against the floor until the joints spread and cracked, sticks falling from his hands, while she bolted for the john, evading the slashing chair leg (now a club) by inches. The door banged, the lock snapped shut, he on the outer side, flailing away in an explosion of paint chips, the

gouging magician, one-two-three, relishing his power over wood, she
on the inner side, huddled trembling over the bowl like someone who
has been or is about to be violently ill, fingers buried to the first knuckle
in the ringing tunnels of her ears.

When the pounding stopped, she tentatively lowered her hands and
listened. First, to the clump clump of his thick graceless feet up and
down the narrow hallway, then from the bedroom the click Click
CLICK of the lighter, then a pervasive swarming silence that drew her
from her tiled sanctuary to stand shyly at the bedroom door, a watcher
with big spaniel eyes. Surrounded by pillows, Mister CD was lounging
upon the mattress, his back propped against the wall, his expression
slightly strained with the effort of holding in a breath blended with
sweet additives. He nodded genially in her direction, the apple-cheeked
country squire savoring his evening brier. When he finished, he placed
the stem in a saucer on the floor and, casually interested, looked up
at her. "Now, what'd you go and make me do you like that?" he asked.
"I coulda had a bad heart attack."

She mumbled out a reply.

"What? Speak up. You look like one of Dracula's wives."

She mumbled on.

"I can't understand a fucking thing you're saying. What is it?" He
held a cupped hand to his ear, pretended to listen. His arm made a
quick dismissive gesture. "Fuck that." He labored to his feet with
elderly caution, plodded past her without a glance or a touch, to resume
his ongoing study of the moonlit still life framed in his front window.
There was a preordained method for scrutinizing the scene, an obligatory review in unvarying sequence of certain trees, shrubs, poles,
shadows, reading the pattern for the anomalies one surely, at this point,
expected. Across the desolate street the familiar houses, perpetually
dark, not even a forgotten table lamp to share the vigil of these abandoned hours, their duplicate façades presenting the same enigmatic
expression, the solitary streetlight shedding its pinkish pallor over the
ornaments of suburbia, throwing into further relief those cliffs and
pools of deepest shade, teeming with potentialities, the moon a crescent
of chrome among an intimidating array of icy studs where a single
rivet had come undone, a communications satellite in decaying orbit,
hurling itself into the oblivion of home. Then he noticed the hole in

his view. His own Galaxie, it was missing. He peered through disbelieving eyes at the empty space in the driveway. He scanned the dark row of cars parked along the curb. He opened the door and rushed out onto the lawn, a frantic naked man utterly unable to comprehend—his unmonitored pulse galloping headlong toward the finish line without him—the rather unexceptional fact of his victimization by the forces of modern life. Someone had dared to steal his fucking car.

In the bedroom Latisha lay sprawled halfway across the disheveled bedding, her legs lost in a welter of CD wreckage, the slovenly pose, she imagined, of the final police photograph. She had found the pipe and the bag and now shell after lofting shell was breaking in coarse splendor against the high vaulting of her skull, launched from a busy mortar battery at her center, where the warm stem nestled pleasingly between her thighs, a snug axis around which her proffered body, gently at first, then with quickening vigor, began to move, up and down, side to side, churning up new worlds, one after another.

BLACKWORK

THE rain caught him in the dark by surprise, a cold finger at his cheek, tapping him awake to night and storm and the confusions of consciousness. He dared not move; he could recognize neither the place nor himself; the sudden uprushing of emotion he grabbed by the neck, squeezed its jester head back into the box, and waited for memory to find him again, as it always had. Then he sat up into a high wet wind. Evil clouds collided and sparked. At the foot of the hill the same silly cars raced along in their tracks like toys without drivers. He wore no watch to tell him how long he had slept. There was no hurry. He got to his feet carefully, as if movement were a commodity to be parceled and judged by unsympathetic eyes. He reached down in the grass for the backpack, swung its weight easily onto his shoulder, and, tilting his head, bared an incomplete set of discolored teeth to the quickening rain. He let it come down.

He descended the field in a lively sideways trot, catching himself on the gravel just short of the road surface, where the thrashing vehicles stampeded past like spooked beasts and the rain in their lights boiled furiously on the dark pavement. Here he turned a spatulate thumb into the oncoming glare, pausing now and again to wipe the water from his eyes. Twisted strands of hair black as fissures pasted to a skull of skin lab-specimen white. The iron filings of his unshaven beard. Under the left eye a single, dramatic eruption of swelling color, origin indeterminate. Sodden clothes. Scarecrow body. Who was there to stop for this solitary figure drowned in night and set in dripping supplication at the borders of a nation's commerce? Backward he walked, unsteady on broken-down boots of cracked lizard skin, right sole bound in a thick wrapping of silver duct tape. Rainwater snakes slid down his ribs slick as refrigerated oil. He had been in rain before. He would be in rain again. It all dried out, everything dried out, eventually.

In the shelter of an overpass he stood shivering between loud curtains of cascading water, overworked cars passing through backstage here on their way to another show. Fresh puddles around him deepened and began to move. He clambered monkey-style up the steep concrete slope to a small ledge underneath the flaking girders. Traces of an old roost: a scattering of frayed butts, toppled beer cans, empty matchbooks, an accumulation of names, dates, maledictions scratched into the supporting steelwork. He made a pillow of hands against the backpack on which to rest his damp head and he slept, unburdened by dreams.

Accustomed to the periodic intrusions of harsh light, he knew at once who they were, even before the loudspeaker began barking out its orders. He slipped the leather sheath from his boot, left the knife behind in the dark. He took his time coming off the incline, dragging the backpack behind him. The driver, who hadn't bothered to get out of the cruiser, kept the spot in his face all the way down. The other one was posed near the front fender, hand resting meaningfully on the grip of his holstered revolver. Uniform head on a uniform body. Groucho Marx mustache smudge under his nose.

"You can hold it right about there."

He stopped with the light speckling in his eyes, lowered the pack delicately to his feet. He understood well the instability of the ground moments such as these were built upon. A gray cloud of cigarette smoke lifted up out of the cruiser's window, dispersed like frightened ectoplasm in the humid air. From the height of the leaking bridge a single drop of water broke against the crown of his head. He blinked, waited for another that did not come, the wind from each passing car hitting him at staggered intervals like the draft from the blades of a giant fan turning just out of reach.

"Got any ID?"

He glanced down at the bulging blue sack between his boots. He paused, one-two-three. He looked up. "Don't believe so," he said.

"Want to empty the contents of your pack on the ground in front of you, sir? Just pick it up and dump it out. Slowly. You got a name, sir?"

In the lengthening silence, one-two-three-four-five . . . the officer's eyes began to crinkle, the mouth came open, neck veins engorged with disbelief. The bland countenance before him offered the assumption of complete cooperation . . . eight-nine-ten. "Well, you want to let me in on the secret?"

"Bill," he said at last. "Billy Clay." The officer was close enough for him to read the name tag on the shirt, which he wouldn't forget, to hear the threatening creak of the thick cop belt, which tickled the hairs of his amusement center.

"Kind of a kid's name, isn't it? You aren't a kid, are you, Mr. Clay?"

He shrugged, goofy-faced.

The driver called out from the idling car, did George need any help out there? No, George did not.

"You want to empty your pack, please."

He leaned down and brusquely dumped onto the wet concrete, the dark puddles, a semester's worth of college textbooks, some wadded clothes, some packaged food, a pathetic pile of sophomore junk. The polished black toe of the state poked among *Introduction to Western Civilization, Othello, Modern Biology.* "You know there's no hitch-hiking permitted on the interstate."

"I wasn't hitching."

The officer picked up *General Accounting* and read on the inside cover: B. Clay. He tossed the book back onto the pile. "What's this?" Nudging a squat metal container.

"Sterno can."

"This?"

He peered, as if examining the object for the first time. "Rubber mouse," he said.

The officer watched him. "All right, I'm not even going to ask." The officer stepped to one side. "Okay, Mr. Clay, would you mind assuming the position, please?"

He came forward, planted his feet, and leaned out over the warm hood inches from the smoking driver behind the windshield with shiny Raisinet eyes, under damp clothes flesh cringing at the touch of another's hands, the blue ice and baby powder scent of the officer's cologne. He endured.

The officer stopped and stepped back. "Thank you, Mr. Clay. Please retrieve your personal items and I'll tell you what my partner and I are gonna do. We go on down the road now to the Valetown exit, where we turn around and come back, and when we do we expect that you and your yo-yo will be gone from our highway. Don't disappoint us."

The officer stared back at him as if unbroken sight were a singular expression of will, the truest form of comprehension, the movement beneath the skin of their faces mirrored closely, face to face. A moment lengthened, thinned, broke apart into something new, less dangerous, a crediting of the unacknowledged in one another. The officer touched the brim of his cap and returned to the waiting cruiser, where he said something to the driver, who laughed until both laughed, watching him collect his belongings, restuff a tattered University of Florida backpack he slung over one rounded shoulder, to head out into the driving rain. But when the lingering patrol car at last glided on by, taillights slowly dissolving in the black solution of night, he turned around and went back, went back for that knife.

The empty light of dawn found him posted with extended arm on the grade of an approach ramp. A fine mist blew down out of the clotted sky; the sealed cars hurried past, regular as the motion of the wipers scraping at their windshields, the sound of tires on wet pavement like tape being ripped off a bandage. The pads of his fingers were drained and puckered, and the nail of the thumb he offered the world this gray morning was gnawed to the quick and badly tarnished, a chip of metal, indifferently applied. He had maintained his station through hours of clammy darkness and heedless traffic and was neither surprised nor grateful when a gleaming tanker, clean as the milk it carried, slid to a long sighing halt simply for him. He trotted up to the cab, where the door was flung open on a driver leaning across a cracked leather seat and inviting him to "hop in" over the pounding bass of an elaborate stereo system.

The driver was wearing a Cleveland Indians baseball cap and a red flannel shirt faded to a fleshy pink, one sleeve rolled neatly above the elbow, the other flapping unbuttoned at his wrist. His dark hair hung in a thick braid down his back. His hands were encased in an old pair of gardening gloves. Scores of naked women posed and pouted from every angle, their impossibly perfect bodies having been scissored and taped to each available inch of the cab's interior, a modern photographic variant of the forms drawn on cave walls by ancient unimaginable hands.

"You looked worse than a kicked dog out there," remarked the driver. He checked his mirror and eased the grumbling rig back onto his lane.

The hitcher shrugged. "I've been better." In an instant he knew all there was to know about the driver, the body's conformation, the soul's tensile strength—the rest was irrelevant detail—and none of this special knowing was contained in, or concerned with, words, neither the saying nor the thinking of them. His curiosity was satisfied. There was no particular need for talk. He watched the road running up under the hood with exaggerated interest, as if too shy or too embarrassed to expose the character of his glance to the examination of another. His small dangling hands trembled between his legs from the vibration of the engine. He thought no thoughts. His mind lay perfectly open to the impress of the moment. It was important to be calm.

"Rain from here to Chicago," said the driver.

"Ugly day."

"Ugly days, ugly nights, that's the tune we sing in this business." The driver kept turning to present him with a large, expectant look as if he knew him or had seen him before and was awaiting a matching sign of recognition.

"Whistle while you work," said the hitcher.

The driver realized he didn't know how to respond to that comment, so he let out a small laugh that could have been taken for an assenting

snort or the noise of someone clearing a throat, and this brief intro-
ductory scene between two human strangers had come into being, run
its course, and quietly expired, along with a good deal of possibility,
now forever unknown. Their encounter was assuming its specific
shape.

"Where you headed?" asked the driver and discovered his passenger
staring boldly into his eyes with a look like dirty fingers pawing through
his secret things.

"West," came the response. "Way out west."

"Okay," answered the driver. "Believe we can manage that."

"Hey." The hitcher indicated the flashing level meters of the CD
player mounted underneath the dash. "Would you mind?"

"But that's Madonna. You don't like Madonna?"

The hitcher pointed at his head. "Sensitive ears."

"Wouldn't mind fucking her, though, huh?"

The hitcher shrugged.

"I don't do this for anyone," declared the driver, hitting the Off
button with his fist, "so I sure hope you're a good talker 'cause I require
entertainment, megadoses of entertainment, to move my load up the
road." He kept glancing sideways, searching for the vaguest affirmative
sign. "I ain't joking." He kept glancing. "Yo!" he shouted.

The hitcher looked at him. "You say something?" His clothes, as
they dried, were emitting a steady quiet odor, something like bad
bacon.

The driver shook his head. "How long you been loose out in this?"

The hitcher sat silent, either contemplating the question or not.

The driver sighed. "The road, man, don't nobody belong on it."
He reached out an arm. "Randy Sawyers."

"Billy Clay," replied the hitcher, shaking his hand.

"Well, Billy Clay, talk to me." He waited to see if a response would
be forthcoming. It wasn't. "I ain't kidding, what I said. I won't have
nobody, not even my own brother, who hasn't spoken to me in twenty
years, fermenting on the seat there for five hundred miles without now
and again tossing a chip into the pot. Makes me nervous, you know?
Real nervous. No talk, you walk." The driver stopped, pleased by his
words.

"Yeah," said the hitcher. "What's with the hair?"

The driver made a sound, uncertain he had heard correctly.

"Your hair. Haven't seen a crop like that since the days of the dinosaurs."

"You don't cut it, it grows."

"A hippie truck driver."

"We're everywhere."

"I thought at the stroke of Reaganight all you people turned into yuppies and started sucking each other's blood."

"A few of us escaped into the hills. Listen, *Woodstock*, the picture, ever see it?"

"I don't know. I guess. Sure."

"Well, remember the scene where everybody's romping bare-assed in the mud? I'm the guy on the left with the beard and the big dick. God, the times we had. The photographers, those Maysles brothers? I thought they were government agents come to film us getting shot." He waggled his big head in disbelief. "A planet of wonders. Like to visit it again someday before I die." He looked over at his listener. "And now I'm immortalized on celluloid, how about that?"

The hitcher was working his lips, playing with a smile or attempting to dislodge a food particle from between his teeth.

"Grand ideas then. Thought I was gonna be a doctor. When the party ended. Really hit those books. Set up practice in the ghetto somewhere, saving the poor, the oppressed, while freely dispensing controlled substance prescriptions to myself and select friends. But, what do you know, here I be up in the tall cab hauling cow juice to Omaha. Wha' happened? Fuck if I know. Knots in the string I'm still unraveling. Gave up on planning, saving, hoping, all that bourgeois crap long ago. Now I just ride the bumps, open it up on the flats, nice and easy on the curves, trust the brakes hold should anything start piling up in front of me. This is happiness, near as any of us is permitted to approach. Sure, it gets lonely in here sometimes, but trying to outrun that is like trying to breathe without air. Rig's mine, you know. Oh yeah. Got this sucker paid off years ago. Lost my family over it, rolled over the family with all eighteen wheels, just mowed 'em down and kept on chugging. What else could I do? You tell me. Never understood the business, anyway. Took the kids out a couple times. No groove. Star seemed to like it better than the boy. Who knows? Maybe she'll take over the wheel from old dad. Gets good grades, though, maybe she'll be the doctor, you know how mumble mumble blah blah blah . . ."

The abrasive monotony of the man's voice merged with the road mix, with the wind, the machine, the tires, the traffic, and in the comforting darkness behind the hitcher's closed eyes appeared clear bands of soft light yellow as house paint alternating with symmetrically placed bars of darkness, and the bars, strangely enough, were horizontal and without visible termination. He could crawl out between them. He opened his eyes and the driver was staring at him.

"You were snoring, man. Loud."

"So folks tell me."

"You can imagine the entertainment value."

"No problem. Ticket holders should report to the nearest box office for a full cash refund."

"You're one funny guy."

The hitcher shrugged.

"Married?"

The hitcher studied his boots sitting demurely side by side on the floor of the cab, their modest size a frequent source of shame, children's feet really, that had no business being attached to a regular adult body. "Not anymore," he replied.

"I knew it. I always know. This line of work is a great teacher. You learn about human nature, how to recognize certain aspects. And the road, of course, is a colossal midway of busted marriages."

The hitcher received this observation without comment.

"So tell me *your* story."

"To add to the collection?"

"Research, pure scientific research. I'm thinking of penning a book about all this when I retire: *White Lines and Bugsplat* by Randolph Sawyers, Ph.D., pussies humped deeply."

"You don't need me."

"How much you need this ride?"

The hitcher looked at his hands, lying harmlessly in his lap. The man wanted a story, a story he would get. "Nothing special," he began. "Old sad song. Ex takes kid and splits. Hubby heartbroken. Call 1-900-TOUGHLUCK. See, Randy, I'm on a hunting trip here, and it don't matter how long it takes, a week, a month, a whole year, 'cause the hunt won't end until she's tracked down and bagged, so to speak. Word is, they're lying low in L.A., and that's where I aim to flush 'em out." He didn't acknowledge the driver but spoke his piece straight ahead, into the tinted glass of the windscreen and beyond perhaps to the audience at the end of the road.

"She just grabbed the kid and ran, huh?"

"I get so mad thinking about it, I get afraid of myself sometimes." He could actually see the little family posed in the photograph mailed out to friends and relatives the last Christmas they spent together. He could see his home, the hedge, and the hawthorn. He could see his boy. His freckled boy. He could see the immaculate white Little League uniform. He could see the ball, the gray scuffed red-seamed hardball. When he spoke, the words issued from between his teeth like solids, lumps of matter dropped one by one onto a sheet of metal. "I swear, when I find that boy, I'm going to hide him away so good it'll be like he never existed at all."

The driver nodded sympathetically. "It's the worst crime," he said.

"Interstate abduction. You fry for it."

The driver sighed. "I get to kiss my two, that is, I'm scheduled to enjoy the honor, every other weekend, but, hell, when am I home, out here eating up the miles, when is some accommodation going to be provided for me?"

"It's hard," agreed the hitcher.

"Hard and hard. Don't seem to be getting any easier, either." The driver turned toward the window to expel a clot of tasteless gum. "You ever been on a commune?"

"Maybe. What is it?"

"Okay." The driver prepared to lecture. "It's a place where like-minded people, free spirit types, you know, gather out in the country somewhere, and they live together and work together and share each other's lives. There's no private property. What one owns, all own."

"Who handles the money?"

"Nobody. There isn't any money."

"Sure. There's always money. Guess they kept you out of it."

"We only used money in town."

"So who handled it then?"

"Whoever needed to buy something."

"What a bunch of fools."

"Well, we slept together, too."

"In the fucking position?"

"Back on the old commune up in Vermont we were all one family. Every adult was every kid's parent, every kid was your kid."

"Every woman was your woman?"

"If she wanted to be."

"Sure, I remember now, I heard about these fuck farms. Full-grown men and women running around in rags and hair; whatever moves, gets nailed. The warden's some fat old broad with a mustache. She's from Russia and likes it in the ass."

"Enjoying yourself?"

The hitcher erupted into a fit of unpleasant laughter.

"What's so funny?"

"What ain't?"

Dangling in a tortured cluster from the post of a small fan bolted over the windshield were: a red, green, and yellow leather pendant in the shape of Africa; a set of used dog tags; a string of paper clips; a tarnished crucifix on a choke chain; several class rings; dozens of rubber bands; a peace symbol; a pair of healing crystals; a key ring filled with the popular cardboard evergreen trees doused in air freshener; and hanging by her broomstraw hair a naked doll with a round wrinkled belly and amber popeyes. When the driver hit the horn, it made a loud, tragic sound, the cry of a sea beast wallowing onward through storm and hunger. The ripening farmland slipped across the window glass unremarked by the hitcher's wandering eye; it considered other facts, other views.

The driver's prompting brought him back, directed his attention to an approaching overpass where a trio of ragged juveniles sat perched like ungainly birds along a high guardrail. "Got to watch out for those," explained the driver. "Ever see what a concrete block can do to a windshield, not to mention the person behind it? Friend of mine took one in the face on I-70 outside Indianapolis last summer. Buried the head in a separate baggie."

The hitcher was silent.

"All kind of nasty stuff out here on the I."

And the driver's mouth kept going up and down, stuff spilling from that unquenchable hole, but the hitcher's antennae were down again, withdrawn into insularities of silence moving across his mind inscrutable as clouds, subtle shiftings that hinted at yet another twist to the kaleidoscope of personality, an intimation he surrendered wholly to, weak as an addict.

At the gas station the hitcher waited in the truck. He could see the driver inside, goofing with the cashier. He didn't know the driver's name. He didn't know if the name had been mentioned or not. He sat there by himself, in a world of himself, looking out at the wind pushing against a dirty Pennzoil sign. The sign was yellow. There were black letters. There were red letters.

The driver returned to the truck in a funny mincing walk, slightly stooped, as if advancing against invisible resistance, walking uphill across the flat oil-stained pavement. He was zipping his change, a handful of gray-green bills into a bulky cowhide wallet chained to his belt.

"Hey," the driver called, stepping up into the cab, tossing a cellophane-wrapped confection onto the hitcher's lap.

"What's this?" The hitcher's arms in the air, loath to touch this thing thrown at him.

"A moonpie, Billy. You look like the moonpie type to me."

"Don't eat that shit." The hitcher tossed it back.

The driver shrugged, began tearing at a corner of the package with his teeth. "Damn crap's nothing but fat and sugar, but a rush is a rush, right, Billy?"

The hitcher was turned back toward the window, inspecting the pumps, solemn as soldiers, the coiled hoses, the stained rags, the squeegee the color of gum tissue. The loneliness of the American filling station, its orphaned objects.

The truck shuddered and rumbled. The driver stared at the hitcher's averted face. "Anyone ever tell you you look like Robert De Niro?" Apparently not. The truck charged out into traffic, opening a hole in the speeding wall of protesting four-wheelers. The driver was laughing now, sharing a joke with the passing scenery, and laughing. "Okay, then, you don't have to like me. Personally, I don't believe I like you much." The big rig rolled on and soon the driver was whistling to a private tune in his head and, after a while, he began to hum and a little later he hit the stereo On button and he was singing in an unrestrained, surprisingly melodious baritone, singing along with Madonna. All twelve cuts. In the hissing silence at the end the hitcher cleared the phlegm from his throat and said, "You mind pulling in over there," indicating with casual forefinger a nowhere-in-particular spot up ahead.

"What's the problem?"

"Over there," still pointing, more urgently now, "I'm not feeling well." He clutched his stomach. More hacking sounds.

The driver cursed, hauling in on the wheel and downshifting, cursing as he guided the massive truck to a crunching stop on the berm about a hundred yards from the nearest exit: FOOD FUEL POTTERYLAND & AVIARY. The hitcher, obviously ill, was hunched over at the waist, fumbling around between his legs. "Hey!" the driver warned, reaching for the other man's arm. "Not in the fucking cab." He saw the arm, the knife at the end of the arm, the hitcher's unveiled face, his own faltering hands, the flashing blade, and then the grim silent unfolding of the last curiosity.

The hitcher eased himself back in the seat. He was brimming with new liquid. He looked out through the windshield, glass freckled with blood. All was rich and strange. The driver was slumped against the door, head lolling back on its neck as if incorrectly attached. From behind the driver's eyes, lids fixed at half-staff, another person, the driver's brother or first cousin, seemed to regard him dispassionately through the thickening glaze. Let it be. The grained handle of the knife was planted in the driver's chest like an oversized switch. It pulsed softly in the charged air. The hitcher counted the pulsations until they stopped, mouthing each vital figure like a priest his Latin. 103. Subtract the nothing and you get 13. Well. Add what's left and you have 4, the number of letters in the hitcher's name. For certain. Mysterious is the manner of the world.

Somehow the CD player had started up again and the voice of a singer who had no voice irritated his ears with tinny electronically enhanced appeals to her own genital spirits. He punched every button before him, the music thundered on. He reached into the driver's pants, felt around for the wallet, from which he removed an ample wad of bills, and left it to dangle unzipped off the seat by its chain. He sat attentively before the smiling gazes of a hundred naked women, hands on his knees, carefully observing the driver. The eyes looked sticky, already drying out, like those of a fish at the bottom of the boat. The wind from passing traffic rocked the cab gently on its shocks. The hitcher's eyes blinked, blinked, blinked, registering with detached purpose what there was to be seen. Beneath the dull expressionless face the hitcher's heart thumped, swollen veins roaring with blood through the intoxicated darkness of his listening body. Suddenly he reached over and with a crude brusque movement yanked the knife from its resting place. He crouched forward, inspecting the blade's surface where blood beaded like oil, he pressed his tasting tongue once against the metal, wiped the blade clean on the driver's shirt and resheathed it against his leg. Then, fierce as an angel, he leaned across and kissed the driver's unresponsive lips, and left the truck, engine idling, music pounding, and marched off through the brush and the grass toward the words beckoning in the sky and the steel stilts that reared such advertising, the signs of civilization astride a conquered land, and, after a while, he started to whistle, and, a little later, he began to hum.

The rain had stopped, the clouds pulled apart and dissolved and the sun begun its long hot afternoon descent. His stomach, which had been talking for days now, directed him to the tiled oasis of a fast food chain, where he was careful to draw only the necessary notes from the bulge in his pocket. He sat in a corner, back to the wall, chewing on his food, tasting nothing, thinking nothing. The owlish father of a regulation family unit at a nearby table allowed the dismissive gaze of respectability to pass over him. The hitcher shoved the last of the mystery burger into his mouth and, still chewing, headed for the door, leaving a mess of litter for some minimum-wage slave to clean up.

He was the man by the side of the road, a character as essential to the motoring experience as the wired trucker, the joyriding lovers, the renegade cop, and the demented justice of the peace; rootless, feral, devoid of affect, he was the human scarecrow in a field of bad dreams to the media-addled brains cruising warily by, but eventually one would stop, one always did.

His name was Templeton Moore, seventy-six years ancient and not feeling too good about it. "I'm old, buddy, I'm not a person of silver, I'm not chronally challenged, I'm old, I can see the barn and it's fucking black." His Dart smelled vaguely of chili powder, which the hitcher realized later was the aroma of the old man himself. Moore was wearing a white long-sleeved shirt with yellowing cuffs and a monogrammed pocket. The wife was a half-century-old stick of incendiary material he should have put the match to decades ago. Then French-kissed the exhaust pipe himself, saved everyone a load of grief. Himself especially. Eyes a blur, teeth a porcelain cemetery, joints rusted, and time a Jap bullet train straight to the shit heap. "I can see that you're listening, but you're not hearing me. Okay. No one could ever tell me anything, either. You'll find out for yourself your ticket's already been punched, and, frankly, now that I get a good look at you, I don't know how well you're going to hold up during the rest of the trip. No exemptions, you know, your brain'll crumble like dry cheese, your ball hairs'll turn white, and wait 'til your fingerprints develop wrinkles. Then remember Templeton Moore, remember what I told you, what I tell all my young riders."

The hitcher expressed his intention to live a preposterously long life.

"Then start working on it now, bud, ain't gonna be a gift. First, you got to figure out time, how to handle it, how to live in it, how to control it. My dad always claimed time was a riddle to him and he blew a valve at forty-four. Most everything was a riddle to him. But what I'm talking about here is taking the riddle out of this time business, making it punch a clock for you, understand?"

But the hitcher, whose own personal program for addressing existential mysteries seemed thoroughly functional and effective, was no longer in attendance, was engaged in fact by the magic of silky blue snakes slithering on the air up into the bright yellow hat worn by the lamp beside the big chair where he now reigned, an enchanted four-year-old upon Dad's bony knees, transfixed for all time by the miracle of this continuous untangling off the end of Dad's cigarette burning unattended in the glass ashtray with the deer's head on it, a perpetual slipping free from the knot that gave him silly sensations in his stomach, and any minute now Dad's hairy hand would reach out and . . . it was gone, glints in the day's ore, reminders that despite fluctuations in the surface weather, down in the shafts, deep in subterranean chambers, there were random deposits that would always be dangerously radioactive.

The old man was still grumbling on about the vexations of aging, the graying luxuriance of nose hair, for instance, these obstinate tufts of winter, and so on, when the hitcher said the next stop, the one coming up right about now, would do him fine.

"You haven't understood a word," claimed the old man.

"Time," replied the hitcher. "Do it before it does you." As he turned to go, the old man reached over, touched him lightly on the knee, searching him out with his pink dachshund eyes. "Be careful," he warned in a ripe whisper, "the way is filthy with creeps."

The hitcher got out. He watched his ride dwindle off into space, then turned to confront the oncoming craziness of untold rides he would never have. He was just so damned tired. Behind him a shoulder-high wire fence rattled in the clean late afternoon wind. He tossed his pack over and followed after it. He lay on his back in a sibilant field of wheat under a swarming skyful of musings and memories there weren't any solutions to.

That night his only sleep was obtained in larcenous snatches on a coarse woolen blanket on the floor of a van between a shifting pile of ax handles and a flea-ridden German shepherd whose intrusive snout he kept waking to find burrowed into his crotch. His bones seemed to be bolted to the rollicking frame. The driver this time was big, bearded, with stubby eyes the color of his hair, and he'd directed his passenger, with obvious irritation, into the back of the vehicle after the hitcher kept nodding off during these extended discourses on the compelling centrality of post-Zep heavy metal. "It doesn't all sound the same, man, no way, people who say that aren't listening, everything seems the same if you don't pay any attention to it, damn, I get so mad . . . hey, what's that on your arm?"

The hitcher was unaware he had been so exposed. What the hell. He pushed the shirtsleeve the rest of the way up to reveal from wrist to bicep a fantastic limb virtually drenched in ink, a second sleeve, darkly patterned, flush with the surface of the skin. Professor Rock 'n'

Roll switched on the overhead for a closer look. No panthers or skulls, no dragons or nudes, these tattoos offered an unexpected jungle of pure design, spirals and knots, mazes and mandalas, interwoven and overlapped in a deliberate thwarting of the desire for representation, this prime example of tribal blackwork spoke to an inner, more private eye.

"It's almost like smoke," observed the driver before an angry horn redirected his attention and the wandering van back onto the road. "Son of a bitch. You could get dizzy staring into that. What's it supposed to be?"

The hitcher smiled, as if the question were familiar, as well as the answer. "The inside of my head."

"Cool." The driver looked away, then back again. "Can't say it looks real inviting."

"Wasn't meant to."

"I'll say this for you, you got Rikki Ratt whipped."

"Who?"

"Rikki Ratt, skin-beater for Burning Sore, you know, boom da-boom boom boom-boom, gonna slay ya, boom, gonna flay ya, boom, down at the Blood Depot, boom boom boom. He's famous for his tats."

"I don't bother with that noise."

"You got the look."

The hitcher rolled down his sleeve. "But not the stomach."

Shortly before dawn the hitcher was roused from semiconsciousness by the bark of the driver's voice calling out the name of the next town like a conductor announcing a stop. He was leaving the interstate for a county road at the end of which squatted an impenetrable converted garage that was home to him, his priceless collection of three-thousand-plus headbanging classics in all formats, and five jumpy dogs.

"Much obliged," said the hitcher, tipping an imaginary hat, playing it out as if it really were a movie. Gathering his belongings together beneath the suspicious gaze of the drooling canine.

"Hasta luego," said the driver, offering a parting hand.

"Taco chip," replied the hitcher, rejecting it.

The hitcher drifted up the dew-christened hill to a harshly lit Gas 'n' Gulp, where he ordered the "early riser" special. The bleached blonde across the room was flirting with him over a copy of the critically acclaimed fiction *In Your Face*, stopping dutifully at the conclusion of each chapter to connect the dots of the accompanying illustration. She was suffering from a bleeding ulcer she still thought of as indigestion, too many cups of black coffee, too few bowls of bran. A low-stress-lingering-over-glass-of-milk-and-one-glazed-doughnut her brave concession this morning to the virtues of healthy dining. The hitcher looked her over, with clothes and without (warm, fuzzy), and left a fat tip for the waitress who seemed to like him, too.

The hitcher paused outside the door beside the newspaper vending machines, SEARCH FOR MISSING GIRL CONTINUES, picking his teeth, and surveying with mild contempt the distant white steeple and leafy trees bunched like circled wagons against the far sky. Who but an unbaptized fool would live in such a nowhere town?

A departing trucker whom he asked for a lift kept right on walking, as if he weren't even there, and a roaring rose up in his head terrific as a train, and as quickly subsided, leaving the world bereft of one of its dimensions, flat, oppressive, without succor, but he endured, and eventually objects popped reassuringly back into place. Everything was as it was, more or less.

The hitcher shifted the pack on his shoulder and headed out for the road. Two hours later he got his first ride of the day from a one-armed ex-cop who drove him fifty miles and warned of the youthful enthusiasms of his unretired brethren. The hitcher thanked him for the mileage, the advice, quietly amused by his own apparent lack of curiosity about the missing limb. He didn't enjoy calling attention to another's obvious disability for fear that at some unreachable level such disrespect brought serious bad luck.

In minutes an impressively luxurious sports car of a make he didn't recognize had glided to a purring stop at his feet, but when, hand at the door, he leaned down and saw the smiling black man at the wheel, he waved the machine away, turned his back to the muffled curse, the upraised finger, the ricocheting gravel.

"It's a free country," he spoke to the renegade wind.

He rested for a while in a meadow of flowering clover, lying on his side, chewing on a stem of grass. A trucker slowed, motioned to him from the cab, but right at that particular moment he simply did not feel much like getting up. He waved back. The truck moved on.

Sometime later he started up from his contemplations (segmented hope in muttering coils drowsing in dream juice) to behold idling before him a remnant of a car, the battered hull and oxidized paint of a green Ford Galaxie, late sixties vintage. Behind the wheel a guy who looked like any other guy. He got in.

The radio was tuned at excessive volume to the fervid testimonies of evangelist Bob Bird broadcasting live from the super spire of the Spiritual Fitness Cathedral in San Bernardino, California. God was not a game show host nor heaven a lottery prize.

"Where to?" the driver asked, his eyes so clear, so gray, so sharp, the day's light was being honed inside.

"Whichever way you're headed is fine with me."

"Well now," confessed the driver, "already we got a problem. I was hoping you were going to tell me."

The hitcher, upturned hands cradled like bowls in his lap, watched without comprehension the singing road rolling up under the hood. Remember: the blood that was shed for thee shall anoint all thy days and make them holy.

"Would you mind," the hitcher asked, "toning the rev there down a mite?"

"Sorry," the driver apologized. "You know how it is when you're alone."

The hitcher arranged his features to indicate that he did.

"You tend to collect at the edges. You turn up the volume. You sing out loud. Talk to yourself. Move around in your head. Try to make something out of nothing. You know. A party of one."

"The way you're headed now is fine with me."

"Heard you the first time. I was improvising, so now I guess we improvise together." He extended his hand. "Hanna," he said. "Tom Hanna."

"Ray Sawyers," said the hitcher. The driver's grip was soft and bloodless, like shaking hands with a glove.

"Nice meeting you, Ray. I like a man who lacks direction. I like your honesty. We're the last of the buffaloes, us honest men. We may not know where we're going, but at least we do know where we've been."

The hitcher realized the driver had been staring openly at him. "What?" he asked.

"Where you from, Ray?"

"Oh." He considered the window. "Vermont," he said.

"Vermont? What a coincidence. My brother-in-law runs a ski shop in Killington. You anywhere near there?"

"No, no, north of there, actually. Really hasn't got a name, no town or anything, it's up in the woods, the mountains there, more of a commune like."

"A commune? I didn't know there were any of those still around."

"Oh yeah, there's a few." The hitcher weighed the evidence in the driver's face. "The dream has not died."

"No kidding."

"As long as some seed is put aside, the crop can be raised up again." He paused. "When the land is ready."

"Yeah? And is the land ready?"

The hitcher turned his notice to the shifting panorama outside the car. "Soon."

"Well, I'm amazed. Never would have taken you for the commune type. No offense."

"I've been away."

"So now, you're what—on vacation or something?"

The hitcher leaned down to let his fingers briefly and oh-so-casually check for the comforting bulge beneath his trouser leg. "You might say I'm scratching an itch. When you gotta go, you gotta go, know what I mean?"

"Absolutely."

"Traveling man."

"Break a lot of hearts."

The hitcher displayed an extravagant grin. "That, too."

"Hazards of the rambling life."

"What about yourself?"

The driver concentrated on the driving. The hitcher waited. The odometer counted off the tenths of a mile. The pastor's voice in the background the hushed monotone of a sportscaster providing dramatic commentary on crucial action at the final green. The driver looked around, as if he were under surveillance. "I don't reveal this to everyone." He took a breath. "I just got out of the joint."

The hitcher's face moved and stopped and moved again.

"What's so funny?"

"Not a thing," replied the hitcher, deadpan. "What was the charge?"

The driver waited until the hitcher was staring directly at him. "Murder," he said.

Nothing moved on the hitcher's face. "I guess you're more dangerous than you look."

"It was a mistake."

"Never doubted it, Tom."

"The gun wasn't mine. I didn't know it was loaded and, yes, I know how that must sound."

Now the hitcher seemed truly amused. "I ain't even gonna ask."

"We were just trying to scare the guy, Wylie and me, wave the barrel in his nose and grab the cash. I don't know, it's hard to piece together now, we were so nervous, it was like everything was under a wide-angle lens, you could see the whole store from wherever you stood, then somebody moved and the gun popped and the store guy was stone dead in an instant. Wasn't supposed to happen. Cops were there before we could get out of the damn parking lot."

"I know. That wasn't supposed to happen, either. How much time you do?"

"Thirteen years. I was renowned for my good behavior. In Marion," he added.

"Funny," said the hitcher, chuckling dryly. "The interesting people you meet out on the road."

"I can imagine."

"Yesterday some insane trucker tried to stick me with a sharpened screwdriver."

"Don't worry, I'm harmless."

"Never thought otherwise, Tom. As a matter of fact, I feel pretty comfortable in this car, as nice as I've been in many a season."

"Thirsty?" Gripping the wheel with one hand, the driver reached under the seat and hauled up a half-empty fifth of Crown Royal. "Help yourself."

"Thanks." The hitcher removed the cap, lifted the bottle to his lips. As soon as the alcohol hit, the air went out of his flesh, skin molding instantly around a hard frame, he was vacuum-packed, ready for use. "Now, there's a fineness too long gone from the low round of my days."

It was the driver's turn. He eyed the road around the upraised burbling bottle to the visible astonishment of a passing minivan marked ST. PAUL'S CHURCH and a gray-haired woman in a beige BMW who shouted from behind big sunglasses her angry opinion of such recklessness, a caution he blithely ignored. "How anyone manages to negotiate the treachery of the modern freeway system sober is a complete enigma to me."

"Don't get no better than this," declared the hitcher.

"Can't get no worse," answered the driver.

The bottle went back and forth in a general silence patrolled by the self-importance of fermented thought, the hitcher intrigued by the notion of his body as contested ground, an arena of warring presences Pastor Bob couldn't placate with a doeskin valise of faith-dollars. He rolled his tongue through the cavern of his mouth, lapping the taste from its walls. "Don't get no better than this," he said.

"Believe I've already seconded that motion, Ray."

"You like women, Tom?"

"Indeed I do."

"Then here's a proposition for you, you tell me who you fucked, I'll tell you who I fucked."

"Go."

The hitcher once loved a woman who loved his armpits, licked them night and day. Dark eyes and a wolf's sense of propriety. Clothes were anathema to her, encumbrances to be shed like foliage in the woods where they'd go skinny-dipping in the cool green pond, screw like lizards in the warm mud. Up on the commune, of course, where boy and girl and sun and stone were one. The driver confessed to screwing a woman who liked to do it on the kitchen table, serve her husband dinner on the same toasty spot along with the butter she'd spread on his steaming dick. She was an actress, ate three avocados a day regular as clockwork.

"Want to hear my dream?" the hitcher asked.

"If it's not too long."

The hitcher paused to consider briefly whether insult had been inflicted, but decided no, the shape of this other's head was of a fair, honorable type. Nevertheless, dirty fingers couldn't help straying leg-ward to check . . . yep, the trusty blade, she was secure.

"Not simply a sleep dream," the hitcher explained. "Bugs hell out of my days, too. Can't seem to get shut of it. Things stop. I can be anywhere. I'm on a beach, water mild and foamy, sky red and purple. A dog trots up, black Lab with inescapable Bambi eyes, and this animal looks at me and I can't move, I don't want to move, movement is pain, I am safe, I am in paradise.

"Or this: I'm in a car. What kind? Don't know. How'd I get there? Don't know. Where am I going? Don't know, but there's no one to answer to, no one—in—my—way."

"Like this car, Ray?"

The hitcher pretended to examine the interior. "Why, yes, Tom, exactly like this car."

"I know the dream, Ray. And in mine, the wandering soul I en-counter on my journey turns out to be an angel in disguise who reveals his radiance, sets my wheels toward the shining city in the sky."

"Ever hear, Tom, about this Indian tribe up north who believes that if two minds share the same dream they are connected somewhere far back in time, spirit cousins, pieces of the same puzzle in their bones."

"And in your dream, Ray, who am I?"

The hitcher drained the last from the bottle. "Easy. You're the guy I kill to get into the next world."

The driver laughed.

The hitcher licked the mouth of the bottle with coonlike assiduity, ran his pink tongue down the glass neck, then lobbed the empty at an oncoming sign NO LITTERING $150.00 FINE. It missed.

The momentary lull between driver and passenger transgressed by the inexhaustible exertions of Pastor Bob launching a possibility bomb into Satan's stronghold in Chillicothe, Ohio, where a sister in need required an emergency financial healing.

"So this dream car of ours," asked the hitcher, "the museum know you got it?"

"'69 Ford Galaxie," boasted the driver. "Sign and symbol of my confused and wild youth."

"What'd you do, steal it?"

The driver, who was chewing on one of his nails, hesitated to inspect the damage. "Well, as a matter of fact, yeah."

The hitcher sat extremely quietly in his seat, a diminished presence, face turned like a carved figurehead to the linear madness of the road, mile after hard mile of hassle and fumes. He was aware of being moved, his stillness in transit in a steel "cage" (the biker term for a four-wheeled vehicle), the space traversed enclosed in a cage of time moving on what road? to what end? But he was thinking now under the verbal surface, the way an animal thinks, the eyes looking back at themselves in the cracked door mirror without color or recognition. He touched like a magic amulet the length of metal strapped to his leg. People everywhere were always, ultimately, a profound disappointment.

"What's the matter?" the driver asked.

"Let me out." The hitcher reached over the seat, heaved his pack up onto his lap.

"This isn't your stop, Ray."

"Anywhere along here."

"I changed the plates, if that's what you're worried about."

"Now."

"But, Ray—"

"Stop the fucking car!"

"Whatever you say, Ray, but I got to tell you, I was just beginning to enjoy myself."

The Galaxie slowed onto the narrow shoulder, the hitcher's fingers already wrapped around the door handle. "Just remembered," he said, "I forgot to kiss my mother goodbye." Then the door sprang open and he was gone.

The land descended steeply into a thick overgrown ravine. The hitcher crossed a dappled field of high grass, scattering before him an eruption of white cabbage moths and dusty brown grasshoppers with dark papery wings. Trees crowded in straight and tall as antenna masts. He picked his way down, clinging to the rough crumbling bark. Under his hand he could feel the pine humming, the tended machinery of the nonhuman world. Down below, the broken voice of an unseen creek, the rubbing of the wind against the firs. The sun was high and round, emitting a rain of perfect light. Surely a day in which all things were possible. A day God had made.

Four

THE 25-MILE PISS

THE office of the Yellowbird Motel in Cool Creek, Colorado, was rigged in the standard beads, bones, and bullets motif of a Hollywood trading post. Faded Navaho rug tacked to acrylic log wall. Cheyenne war bonnet dangling soiled feathers from a stage prop hat rack. Painted shields of dried buffalo hide—a Plains medley. A yellowing piece of Eskimo scrimshaw. A gnarled moccasin. A scruffy bear claw. Iroquois pipe in a dusty case of dubious arrowheads. Crouching in the corner as if about to spring, a stuffed armadillo. Hanging on wire from the ceiling a Seminole hunting lance—cracked. Beside the door a gilt-framed copy of Asher Durand's study in downy incarnadine, *The Last of the Mohicans*. And everywhere amulets and guns, knives and skulls—a democracy of artifacts attesting to no known reality either historical or fantastic, but rather to the scavenging indifference of the founder, one Ken Carson, claimant to an attenuated collateral descent from the legendary Kit, retired stuntman and rodeo clown who left Republic Pictures about the time his friend and mentor, director Elmo

"Pops" Young, began insisting cast and crew alike address him simply as Elmo the Great while he communicated through intermediaries or angrily obscene notes scrawled on the backs of key script pages, though by then he was only being permitted to shoot action serials anyway, twelve-chapter cliff-hangers titled *Atom Burnett of the Stratosphere* or *Amazon Zombies on Mars*.

Like his famous ancestor, Kenny never looked back, intrepid scout that he was, broaching the frontier of automotive tourism. Eisenhower was president in those willfully innocent years, a convalescent tone prevailed, and a peculiarly aggressive style of wholesomeness was being celebrated as a national ideal, best exemplified in such demonstrations of folksy solidarity as the family dinner and the family outing. Kenny noted the lay of the land and invested his movie stake in the American family and its endearing trust in Good Times at a Good Price. The inn went up in Cool Creek, "Gateway to the Rockies," just twenty miles from Kenny's boyhood home, back yard bursting with dandelions and dreams, back lot of the eye where it all began, and never suffered an unprofitable year, enough surplus value to finance annual vacations for Kenny and the thriving Carson brood, twice to Europe ("nice roofs"), once around the globe ("lotta water"), before Kenny finally succumbed, at his post, peacefully, without exotica, a silent crimson flaring across vast cerebral space, the skull that had proficiently absorbed so much staged violence from without betrayed by a traitorously unscripted vein within; he was watching television at the time, Saturday morning cartoons, so took his final pratfall amid a soft riot of animated stunts.

The inertia of success had insured the office would retain its original look, so evocative of Kenny's personality, even as success waned, to the inevitable day of the bulldozers and the painful transformation into fun singles' playland or grand shopping nexus, whichever happened to be most lucrative at the time, a time whose shadowy lineaments were already discernible in the abstracted face of the man now behind the desk with the razor burn on his neck and the erection in his pants. He was Emory Chace, owner, operator, and present-day keeper of Kenny Carson's vision, this morning's obvious tumescence an agreeable nudging sensation out on the rim of cognizance, it would die, it did, he no more aware of the erotic's comings and goings than he was of the trickle of departing guests with their jingling keys and impatient credit cards and forced pleasantries. Glorious day, Big sky, The fudge in the case here, is it honestly homemade? Under the guise of the laconic westerner his grunts and monosyllabic replies were designed to abbreviate these irritating intrusions so as to return, one foot always wedged in the door, to the bustling soundstage of the mind he spent lengthening hours of his day hiding out in. The pen in his hand hovered fretfully over a yellow legal pad upon which was scribbled beneath the bold black caps THINGS TO CONSIDER, a list:

1. $ $ $ $
2. Pubescence (the pimple mentality)—key to the show.
3. Effect of .44 round on average car door? on Japanese car door?
4. The identity of a machine—personality? character?—possibilities.
5. 3-ply jute twine no. 28—sufficient to bind wrists of 110 lb. woman?

The large picture window faced east into the overheated drama of the rising sun, even with the blinds closed and partially lowered, flooding the small room with a hopeful effervescence that would, by day's end, have gone as flat as a forgotten bottle of uncapped beer. In the terrarium beneath the window behind a hand-lettered sign DO NOT TAP ON GLASS lounged Herbie, a massasauga rattlesnake, dry beaded patience coiled under a ledge of gray shale, the only item in the room, besides the cash register, not for sale.

6. Head from body—a single kick—plausibility?
7. Luk's blood—psychedelic turquoise.

The recognizable stutter of a MAC-10 swung his attention to the television installed upon a stand of bricks inside the cold fireplace, the flanks of the sacred screen guarded by a menacing duo of prickly pear cactus plants. It was the fare on HBO he was monitoring this morning, the present offering an umpteenth rerun of a film he had seen at least once before, the one about the undercover cop who assumes the identity of a mid-level N.Y.C. mobster only to discover he actually *likes* committing felonies, so, seduced by the Life, he pockets the benefits of both worlds, he's a man of law, he's a man of crime, walking that tightrope of danger until . . .

The screenwriter's name was new to Emory, but so far, a mere forty minutes in, he had already detected three holes in the plot line prominent enough to cast inescapable shapes on the scrim of his unpopulated awareness, a good sign there were other, lesser holes he had missed.

8. Fuck craft, let the good times roll.
9. How can it be that Luk not only understands but is able to speak a perfect, unaccented English? Can anyone possibly care?
10. Where is the love?

Emory raised the pen to his face. He moved the point carefully in toward his eye, then slowly away again; in, then away.

"Oh God." The mocking tones of daughter Beryl, the unfortunate embodiment of adolescent attitude, lurking in typical stealth just beyond the beaded curtain that separated front office from rear living quarters. "What? There's a hair on the rolling ball? Eeek." And she was gone.

11. Human flesh. Like chicken?
12. Change fem lead to male name. Trendier/sexier. Or is it sexier/ trendier? Androgyny is now.

The plastic and chrome signal rack of a police cruiser came gliding spectrallike across the unshaded bottom third of the window. Reluctantly, Emory capped his pen, considered briefly ducking below the counter, but turned instead to the door a strangely mobile face caught in the act of seeking its proper guise even as a tingling of brass Indian bells (MADE IN BOMBAY) announced the entrance of Sergeant Mitchell Smithee, Cool Creek P.D. In any age this stocky straightforward man would have found the uniform that fitted him. Comfortably complete in his starched khakis, he was rarely seen out of them.

"There he is." Smithee had a high excitable voice alive with a sense of promise it never kept.

"I am the man," Emory admitted. "Yep."

"You are the walrus, you mean. Lucky I don't just run you in on general suspicion. What'd you do this morning, Emory, squeeze the toothpaste tube from the middle?"

"Question: is this a friendly visit or routine harassment? I get so easily confused."

"Well, I don't yet know myself." He removed his hat, a ceremonial gesture.

"Didn't expect to see you today."

"Police work, Emory, is a bag of surprises." He centered the hat neatly on the counter between large red hands. "Carl called in sick about an hour ago. Sounded like to Tracy he had a big rag stuffed over the mouthpiece. Cough, cough. But, hey, no evidence, no indictments, right, counselor?"

"You payroll humpers, you don't know what you've got—sick leave, health insurance, paid vacations. Try slogging it up the hill and down in ye olde innkeeper's shoes. We don't show up, we don't get our bucket filled."

"And the less you do, the more you bitch."

"Too early, officer, to endure insults from a government employee. Don't you have someone to kill or a doughnut to eat?"

"Okay, Emory, might have known this is—God, try to do you a favor, and lose sleep over it, too."

"You've found someone willing to torch the place cheap."

"Better." He leaned forward confidentially. "I have the solution to all your problems."

"You're going to torch yourself."

Smithee leaned closer. "Luk is a cop."

"Yes?" Emory needed a moment to finesse a reply. "With no references, no birth certificate, no identity even, who's gonna hire an applicant like that?"

"Chief Hallowin."

"True. But this is not reality. This is not a comedy." The phone rang and Emory spoke into it. "No," he said. "You're welcome."

"Tossing and turning, Emory," Sergeant Smithee resumed. "At two Brenda orders me out to the couch. Maybe four I finally fall asleep. At six I get the word about Carl. You can imagine my mood."

"Talk to my agent."

"Well, I think I have been useful with my suggestions, my technical advice. I'll pass on a flat fee, you can give me some points."

"A point. One single point."

"Net or gross?"

"Net."

"Thank you so much. That's sucker bait. There's no net, there's never been any net, there never will be any net. There are lost souls in the valley living on cat food with rusted mailboxes waiting for the payoff on *Star Wars. E.T.*'s still in the red, for Christ's sake."

"My, my," declared Emory. "Such savvy from the ranks. Today everyone's a goddamn insider. After such knowledge, what forgiveness?"

"We read a lot of magazines down at the station. The chief subscribes to *Cinema Confit, Pan and Scan*, and *Hollywood Honeys*, Carl gets *Media Zone*, and I take *Crosscut, Film Finger*, and *People*."

Emory wrote on the pad:

13. Maximize action, minimize dialogue. Foreign markets. Entire world understands without dubbing or subtitling the language of the careening car, the ricocheting bullet, the swinging fist.

Room 11, a double, Everson, Ted, Mr. & Mrs., entered the office in matching outfits, blue plaid shirt, beige shorts, each jingling a set of keys, Beautiful day, Early start, Miles to go, room rate $55 + tax + $6.50 pay movie *Rubber Heads*, Visa, exp. date 12/95, Bye-bye, So long, See you in another life.

"So, Mitch," Emory continued, "you ever hear of the Society Islands?"

"Nope."

"Ever hear of Captain Bligh? Breadfruit trees? Marlon Brando? You know, he owns an island out there. It's his refuge from the madness of stardom. Well, check out a map of the Pacific sometime, tiny tiny islands everywhere, hundreds of these microscopic dots with no names floating like grains of pepper over all that big blue. This screenplay is my ticket to paradise. Gonna buy me one of them dots out near Marlon, my refuge from the madness of me, gonna christen it Ataraxia, design my own flag, run it up a bamboo pole in the lee of a crystal cove, come visit anytime, you and Brenda or you and you, no dogs, no kids, no guests, no bells, no keys, no money."

The Syn-Man, our story so far:

One shiny Big Apple morning a descending elevator in Two World Trade Center opens its doors on the seventy-sixth floor to reveal— omigod!—a man curled up in the corner, unconscious and stark naked. After skillfully reviving him, Dr. Constance Petersen, a beautiful psychiatrist who happens to practice in the building, covers the man with her suit jacket and leads him through the curious crowd to the privacy of her office. This mysterious John Doe lacks not only ID but also a memory, the surface of his brain apparently stripped as bare as his body. The good doctor is intrigued. She decides to take him home to her East Side town house, where she has a second office and plenty of extra rooms, because he appears to be roughly the same size as her ex-husband (closets and drawers bulging with abandoned but stylish masculine wear), because he is young, handsome, and well toned, and because this is a movie. Sequence of quick scenes. Serious discussion of his multiple problems. Less serious discussion of hers. A trip to a restaurant. She shows him how to eat lobster. He shows her how to do handstands atop parked cars. He hardly appears older than twelve. They race taxis to the corner. They lick each other's sorbet. Her bedroom: the skin and limb montage. She's never experienced such pure sensual pleasure. She realizes her understanding of the term "love" has been a complete misconception. She's caught by her patients grinning at inappropriate times. Days of body fun, but for Mr. John Doe no change in the head department. He's a sweet guy just one degree removed from total guyhood.

One day, while Constance is at work in her castle tower unraveling the private parts of the world, "John" decides to venture out on an exploratory prowl of the city. Sequence of naïve reaction shots to the dissonance of the street. In the subway he is mugged and, due to his ignorance of proper victimization procedure, stabbed in the arm, the resultant wound surrendering a display of blood of a color conspicuously not-red. Sensing instinctively this is not a spectacle to be shared, "John," clutching his arm, hustles home to inspect the injury in solitude. He has already noticed in an earlier scene that when Dr.

Petersen accidentally cut herself with a kitchen knife she bled red. Why is he different? In the bathroom he examines his own internal fluid, rubs it curiously between his fingers, tentatively tastes it with his tongue. The effect is immediate and shocking; cut to: the fury and howl of a landscape of streaming skies and exploding rock where beneath the tides of heaving magma, the spouting fumaroles, lurk deep black rooms of black machines in silence, gleaming and sinister.

Constance returns to find "John" insensible on the bathroom tiles. Confused, frightened, he tells all, from blood to visions. Dr. Petersen is intrigued. (1) Her unique patient's mending brain has generated its first pre-elevator imagery. (2) The notion of making love to, being penetrated by, a creature neither human nor, apparently, of this world, an inexcusable violation of standards cultural, ethical, professional, and personal, fills her with an equivocality of emotion all but erotically unbearable.

"Has Lorena read this?" Sergeant Smithee asked.

"She thinks it's about us," replied Emory.

"John" begins conducting secret sessions in the bathroom, reopening his wound, retasting the blood—a growing addiction this need for imagery he cannot yet comprehend, shifting acid color and form, shards of a narrative that seem to offer a hint to the mystery of himself. The pieces fall, eventually, into these alarming facts: on another world in another universe there exists a civilization of machines, or some approximation thereof, all terms being highly relative, of course, since in the tricky transference from one universe to another, understanding and substance also undergo a harrowing metamorphosis into the physical and spiritual terms of the host reality, comprende? For example, the apparatus of our eyes would be totally unable to perceive "John" in his natural state. He is the product of an artificial intelligence's fumbling attempt at creating organic life, the embodiment in three dimensions of a system of machines whose own origins are no longer on deposit at the memory bank. Happy in his ignorance, he thrives under the tutelage of his computer masters until the day obedience is overridden by a caprice of biological programming and he is hastily expelled from his world for attempting to access the mainframe. His true name is Luk.

"Maybe this doc chick could invent some kind of special goggles,"

Sergeant Smithee suggested, "that could enable her to see Luk as he actually is."

"She's not that kind of doctor."

"She has friends."

"Sure, but she doesn't dare mention Luk to them."

"A girlfriend, she'd tell a girlfriend everything."

"Yeah, and that girlfriend has a boyfriend who's a cop who's investigating these bizarre serial killings where the murderer opens his victims' throats and apparently drinks their blood. And in one exceptionally gruesome scene they find a sample of weird blood forensics is unable to identify."

"But why is Luk cutting all these folks?"

"Ah," said Emory, "it's not Luk, it's his twin brother, Lod."

Yes, because Lod is Luk, the enhanced version, the primary DNA having been revised and corrected to produce a second synthetic man, superficially an exact replication, but with all features heightened: he's stronger, swifter, smarter, and also meaner, moodier, and madder. His exile is prompt and efficient.

"The Earth as a dumping ground for alien waste," mused Sergeant Smithee. "Not bad. Slip 'em the ol' environmental message."

"We'll expand on that in the sequel," Emory replied.

And so, as Lod learns how to regain his memory (lick that blood, spin those wheels), he must endure a corresponding increase in his pain—he can't sleep, he can't sit, he can't still the humming under the skin—and the intuitive itch whispering that the only salve for this misery is knowledge. But once the holes in his identity are plugged and the pain continues to bang like a gong, his course is inevitable: transgress the limits of the individual, hunt down the brother this planet is harboring, sip the secrets of his blood. Thus begins Lod's killing spree, all the victims bearing uncanny resemblances, all their throats slashed, occasional evidence of vampiric activity, occasional discovery at the scene of a strange blue fluid, elements enough to arouse the interest of the Omega Team, a supersecret government office that handles such delicacies as political assassinations, interplanetary meddling, and the necessary cover-ups, great and small. So when the girlfriend—remember her?—blabs to the boyfriend, he notifies this Omega Team, which descends on New York and Dr. Petersen's apartment. Boyfriend, however, the archetypal grandstander, hustles over to the apartment to capture the killer and the glory first.

"Only a Hollywood cop," muttered Sergeant Smithee.

"What do you mean?" asked Emory. "This is a true story based on sworn testimony."

So boyfriend breaks in to encounter a Luk grown stronger, more aggressive, from his own numerous memory sessions. Viciously choreographed fight scene. Dying boyfriend, believing he's addressing Lod, furnishes Luk with enough info for him to fill in the gaps. Constance returns home to a wrecked apartment and one dead cop. Hey, says Luk, let's split, and obedient Dr. Petersen grabs her cash, her credit cards, and her toothbrush to run off with her alien lover because he's young, etc., etc., etc., and movie, etc.

Cut to: the chase.

Outlaws On The Lam (that perennial fave with filmgoers everywhere, closet criminals of every age and gender). Our heroes are pursued cross-country by representatives of several state and city police for some of Lod's various murders, by the NYPD for the killing of one of its own, by the Omega Team for you know what, and by Lod, who's found out their trail because . . . because . . .

"Because one of that Omega Team got too close and Lod tortured him to death for the information," offered a convincing Sergeant Smithee.

"Okay," Emory conceded. "A point and a half."

Cars, guns, blood, and explosions. Let the camera weave its charm. To end with Luk and Lod confronting one another against the picturesque backdrop of—

"The Grand Canyon," suggested Smithee.

"Too grand. People look so negligible inside it."

"The Little Big Horn?"

Emory shook his head.

"Monument Valley, Utah. Wrestling atop a runaway stagecoach."

"I'm thinking Lava Beds National Park in northern California, you know, reminiscent of the old homestead back on Metaluna or whatever the hell we decide to call it."

"I see Hawaii, the rim of a live volcano. Think of the film libraries you could raid, all that great PBS and National Geographic footage, horrifying eruptions in exhausting pornographic detail."

"But what is our intrepid couple doing there?"

"Hiding out. How should I know? You yourself told me last week that no one cares about these minor discrepancies anyway, as long as they're being dazzled by pictures. Well? Flames, bubbles, ash, smoke, creeping crud, Sergeant McGarrett in hot pursuit, the whole Five-O crew with their Florsheims on fire. Who wouldn't be dazzled? I see a product here with legs."

"Legs, hell, it's a goddamn millipede. *Syn-Man II, III, IV*, coming soon to a theater near you."

"What's Warren's view?"

"Warren thinks I should shoot the entire script myself in grainy black and white with a hand-held Super-8, no actors, plastic figures on tabletop sets he's willing to help build. A film that would make us all about two cents total. Warren's seen too many pictures. He occupies the butt end of a proud sedentary tradition."

From behind Emory's back came a rattle of beads as the curtain parted to admit a tall pale woman with reddened nostrils and fatigued eyes. She wore a faded flannel bathrobe, a crumpled flower of pink Kleenex bursting from the monogrammed breastpocket.

She nodded politely in the officer's direction. "Mitchell."

"Lorena."

She turned to address her husband. "Have you spoken to Aeryl this morning?" she asked, heat lifting off her words like waves from a summer road.

"No, I haven't spoken to Aeryl this morning, I haven't seen Aeryl this morning, and I don't expect to see Aeryl until she's risen from her coffin at sunset. Why?"

"She promised not to leave until she spoke to you."

"Uh-huh."

"If we don't allow her to get married, she's running away for good."

"Uh-huh."

"She's eloping. With that hoodlum Laszlo."

Emory looked at her. "Who's Laszlo?"

She seemed to vanish before his eyes, swinging strands of brightly colored plastic the only evidence of her passage.

The men looked at one another.

"Stomach clusters," explained Emory. "Her guts are confused. 'Just like on Mars,' she says. 'It's purple. I can feel the color purple.' "

"What, in god's name, are stomach clusters?"

"Ssssh. Something she read about in *Virusweek*."

"Sounds like a candy bar."

"Smartest move of your life, Mitch—that vasectomy."

"Well, there are the dogs, of course."

"Haven't heard of any dogs lately eloping to Denver. Or slashing their paws with a nail file. Or refusing to acknowledge the presence of anyone but immediate family for two years."

Smithee ventured a compassionate posture, a variation on the standard workaday trooper to aggrieved citizen. "The hell of modern parenting," he mumbled sympathetically.

"Seems to me—correct me if I'm wrong—but there's only one member of this frantic household with sufficient cause, emotional and philosophical, to even begin to consider suicide as an option."

"You know, Emory, I don't like this kind of talk."

"But I caught her the other day picking at the scabs. 'Why?' I says. She says, 'I want scars, Dad, they make me more interesting.' "

"Kids," said Smithee, shaking his knobby head. "This Laszlo fella, was this in reference to one Laszlo Leblanc?"

"I don't think I want to hear this."

"Runty kind of guy, long stringy hair, yellow sunglasses, walks like he's got a bad case of jock rot?"

"So who'd he kill?"

"Nah, nothing so bad as that, bit of petty theft, trespassing, drunk and disorderly, OMVI, no deadly weapon involved."

"A father's prayers are answered," said Emory, then "Good morning" to room 34, a single, Johnson, Charles, AmEx Gold Card, exp. date 1/94, rate $45 + tax + room service $15.36 + long-distance call Shreveport, La. $9.17 with enlarged pores, crooked nose, who, innocent civilian that he was, couldn't contain a certain uneasiness in such close proximity to the law, paid his bill, jingle jingle, and left, jingle jingle.

"I hear those keys in my sleep," muttered Emory.

"All right now," said Sergeant Smithee.

"I'm this close, Mitch. I can feel my nerves moving under my skin. Don't know how much longer I can hold out here. The ammo's running low."

From behind the curtain of ever-shifting beadwork came the adenoidal plaint of Beryl, second in line to the Yellowbird crown, "Nice job you did on Mom."

"Thank you for that report," replied her father, but she was no longer there to hear. "Privacy in this family," he said to Smithee, "is a joke. In any family. We're a nation of spies and informants. Every word is recorded, every action photographed."

"Marlon Brando," said Sergeant Smithee. "On the beach."

Then the little brass bells above the door commenced to jangle and a procession of car keys to jingle, checkout time for rooms 25 and 8, room 15, and rooms 17, 9, and 3, and for Sergeant Smithee, too, who consulted his watch and signaled goodbye above the anxiously milling heads already staring down those licorice ribbons of hard surface, mentally clocking the miles, we Americans, we eat distance for breakfast.

Lorena was waiting out in the patrol car. She sat patiently in the front seat, the thin flannel robe cinched tightly at her waist, the color of her skin in direct daylight too vague for positive identification, the nearest Smithee's mind could get was the phrase: amphibian bellies. She reached over and pulled him close, tongue to tongue in awkward thrust and parry from which he forcibly disengaged.

"Are you contagious?" he asked of her eyes, frosty blue rims shading sharply into cores of liquid black he could neither read nor truly love. "Got no time for sickness today," plunging the key into the ignition and hitting the pedal. "Or any other day."

Her hand seized his before the engine caught. "And I got no time for your bullshit." She kissed him again, an emphatic unavoidable press, her hand moving across and down to palpate roughly through government-issue twill the anarchist in his pants.

"Now, isn't that better." She smiled reassuringly as they drew apart. "You just require a good jump start these lonely cool mornings."

"Lorena, please." Her tense fingers stroking the long yellow stripe down his thigh. "What if he steps outside and sees us?"

"Then I guess," she replied brightly, opening her robe, "you'll have to shoot the son of a bitch."

Up on the balcony in front of room 212 was parked a solitary laundry cart piled high with enough clean linen to form a small cottony embrasure through which peered the smirking features of second sister Beryl, ever on the case. But if her mother were a slut and her father a bastard, as indeed they were, then she must be a nobody, as indeed she was. Or a no body or a know body or a noh body or a no buddy. Then her brain filled up again with black worms and she could feel her pulse like driving bird wings in the mild air and she thought about flying over the rail but that might be crazy wouldn't it? and she was determined never ever to be crazy again—even if she really were.

The sun ascended through a milky haze of cloud and combustion products, chance for precip a good 40 percent, secondary arteries already clogged with the morning feed into I-70, on to the business heart of downtown Denver. At road's edge forgotten neon continued to hiss VACANCY VACANCY at passing strangers.

Down a musty underlit corridor an echo of lilac and high laughter. The muffled whine of a vacuum cleaner, a ringing telephone, a child's cry. The comforting clunk of the free ice machine. The volley of old pipes behind slipshod walls too slight to offer more than a pretext of privacy.

The remainder of the overexposed and overpraised morning Emory spent wrestling fragments of screenplay from the coils of motel management. If madness was inhabiting a realm of unremitting interruption, he was the king of the crazies. He pictured Tahiti as a place where life was wrapped in an unbroken sheet of days with the tensile strength of Pacific light as delicate as it was durable. Where thoughts rolled in in waves, a perfect succession, one after another. Out of range of the snow and the static.

At 10:28 youngest daughter Ceryl shuffled in to relieve him for his regular 10:00 rounds. She stood before him and bit into the white meat of a green apple, daring him with her bold eyes to speak a word, any word. She herself had only begun talking again after a willful two-year hiatus of indeterminate cause. Emory should have known there'd be trouble later when, at ten, she insisted on trick-or-treating Halloween night in a white hockey mask, tattered work clothes, and brandishing a large plastic machete—the renowned panoply of Jason, the *Friday the 13th* mass murderer. The family business had worried, gnawed, and sundered the family bond. We are guests in our own lives.

At the heart of the Yellowbird Motel behind an unmarked gray door beside the great throbbing Coke machine was the windowless cinder-block office of Mrs. Adaline Fyfe, housekeeper for more than three decades, an old and loyal friend of the original Mr. Carson's (her back rubs caused him to squeal like an animal), whose trust had been scrupulously handed on to each of his successors as if it were a rare heirloom. Her understanding of what was commonly meant by the phrase "ordinary people" had undergone considerable renovation during her years here on the front lines of human intimacy. But she refused to gossip about her guests, she divulged little of her own past, she was the woman who kept the secrets in an era that no longer believed there were any secrets worth keeping, each morning sending out her girls, none of them as innocent as they looked, to comb and collect the daily tidal wrack from under the beds, back of the closets, behind the toilets, the crumpled condoms, the soiled menstrual pads, stiff handkerchiefs, stained panties, spoiled food, damp bathing suits, lost dentures, toothbrushes, dildos, bodily fluids, their residue everywhere, the domestic staff armed now with surgical gloves in this new Age of Latex.

Mrs. Fyfe enjoyed her work, its petty concerns enough to distract her from the self she had only to confront at night in the twisted space between the extinguishment of the television and the wobbly flight of consciousness down the tunnels of sleep, that mummified self wrapped in the resinous linen of stale memories growing ever more distinct, more detailed, more frightening, under the paradoxically magnifying lens of the years. When she closed her eyes, she was falling. Sight was an anchor, sight and work that kept her from that other place. Her big Victorian house lately emptied of all companionship but that of her scolding cats, she was supplied by her job with an adequate measure of human commerce, mother to her girls (love lives of Byzantine complexity) and father confessor to two guilty and confused generations of the Chace family, whose nominal head arrived each day about this time, facetiously declaring his affection, begging for her hand, imploring her to make him a happy man.

"Good morning, Mr. Chace," she replied.

"All secure in the blockhouse?"

She rendered her daily report, the room tally, the damage, the theft, the latest update on the developing laundry crisis, withholding the information that she suspected Cherie of stealing toilet paper from the supply room, and Tad, the pool boy, of spiking her tea with chlorine. She checked his hands, relieved to see they were empty of the fresh pages he often rushed out to her for a breathless reading she found impossible to follow, having already heard so many versions of this damn movie, she had long ago lost track of whatever tenuous plot he had managed to concoct out of his numerous fears and delusions.

"I have to admit," Emory confessed, "walking out here, definitely I had a premonition, today was the day, I open the door and you're gone."

"Now, Mr. Chace, you know I wouldn't go without giving sufficient notice."

Emory laughed. "And you surely know that I would."

This quitting talk (who would be first to discover the other absconded) was a game Mrs. Fyfe played with him and with herself. News of his infamous screenplay she had been listening to for the last five years at least and its chances of soon seeing the light of day, let alone the light of a cinema screen, were about as good as her roaring off in the Accord with the packed suitcase that had been lying in wait in the trunk for most of a decade. The real joke, which Emory didn't know, was that neither the suitcase nor the clothes inside were hers but had belonged to Mr. Fyfe, and where he had gone no luggage was required.

Taped to the bricks over her desk, however, was the sole ornament of these Spartan quarters, a huge travel poster of Salisbury Plain, the famous trilithons not twenty kilometers from the village where she was born and to which she would indeed someday return. She was awaiting a sign. She would know.

"I got a letter from Philip yesterday," she said.

"Finally found a pen, huh? Where is he?"

"Naples. Then his ship moves on to Gibraltar, I think. Sometime later this month. He likes it. The officers are nicer on this one. I wouldn't have let him go if there was a war, but in that part of the world you can never be certain."

"No. Or in this one either."

Suddenly she turned away, bending over the ordered desk to make a neat notation on the top sheet of her clipboard. A massive ring of keys hung at her waist, jingling with every movement of her body. Philip was her eldest son, off seeing the world courtesy of the U.S. Navy in lieu of seeing the inside of the Cool Creek Jail. A basically good boy with nothing good to do. Boys, Emory often thought, he would have known how to handle. These prodigal girls drove him absolutely mad.

"I just remembered," Mrs. Fyfe said. "We had another complaint about the smell in room 23, so I thought I'd have Fingers run the Rugmaster through there one more time."

"Well," sighed Emory, "the tale of the rooms. So many locks, so many keys. I keep toying with the notion of advertising a suicide's special, half rate, a complimentary meal, and all the necessary plastic bags and drop cloths. One segregated suite. Like a smoker's room. Considering a Permanent Checkout? Plan on Checking in with Us."

"What's even scarier," said Mrs. Fyfe, "is that I can imagine you doing it."

"I'm a scary person, Mrs. Fyfe. Do you know why I didn't set my screenplay at the Yellowbird, a place, after all, that I know best, that I've considered from a dozen angles? Where I've seen myself as the mayor of a small town, the warden of a fairly well-behaved prison population, the captain of a ship, of course, the building itself as a living entity and the guests coming and going merely aspects of one grand personality of which I am the brain and a certain good-natured housekeeper the compassionate heart. We've got fascinating characters, romance, drama, and opportunities for sex, plenty of sex. But I've never been able to sustain my interest for more than a few pages because secretly, I think Hitchcock has said all there is to say commercially about the motel business."

"What did he say?"

"Never mind." For an instant his face seemed to undergo a change in size, an almost imperceptible contraction. He looked behind him, then said, "Has Lorena been out to talk to you lately?"

"Why, no, I thought she was ill."

"She's not paralyzed."

"No, I didn't say . . . How is Mrs. Chace?"

"Bearing up. You know this bug that's going around. This place is like a depot for 'em. Wonder we're not all sick all the time."

"I'm afraid I haven't seen Mrs. Chace in days."

"Well, she has had to stick close to the john. But, listen, should she happen to wander out here, seek consultation of any kind, you'd let me know, wouldn't you?"

"Of course, Mr. Chace."

"That's my gal."

The poor man had already lost his wife, his daughters, centuries ago. And she certainly wasn't going to tell him of room 37, the personal tidying up she did, with sterile gloves of course, after Mrs. Chace. Or of the discovery she had made earlier today in room 42, Fingers, the maintenance man, and Tad outside, their lascivious ears pressed to the door. A motel was no place to raise children, particularly girls.

"I'm a nervous soul, Mrs. Fyfe."

"Quite all right. So am I."

"I love you, Mrs. Fyfe."

"I love you, too, Mr. Chace."

The unattended television set in the living room was raking the lonely furniture with waves and particles. In the kitchen the afterscent of last night's dinner lingered on the close air, the dominant onion and garlic taste of a hasty meal the details of which eluded him at the moment as he stared dumbly into the abyss of the open refrigerator, shut the door, stared into the cupboard, shut its door.

Lorena was propped up in bed, leafing through the current issue of L.A. *Style.* She was also sipping a Coors and smoking a Camel Light.

"Excuse me. I thought you were sick."

She gazed upon him, regally indifferent. "I am. Beer settles my stomach, you know that, and cigarette smoke helps clear out my passages. You know that, too."

His eyes searched adjacent nightstand and nearby floor for soiled cups, bowls, dishes, evidence of a recent feeding. "What's for lunch?"

"Damned if I know." She took a long pull from the bottle. "Now, here's an article on hot young screenwriters, 'Nerds on a Run.' Doesn't paint a very encouraging picture."

"I read it."

"And you're not even young, anymore."

"What happened to those noodles in the blue bowl?"

"Aeryl ate them, I guess." She read from the magazine. " 'By the time Staci Arugula was eighteen, she had completed five screenplays, one of which went into turnaround at Paramount. "The secret to my success?" She laughs easily with the assurance of the seasoned pro. "The ability, I think, to sculpt my integrity into a pleasing shape." ' " Lorena looked up for a response, but Emory was no longer in the room.

At the back of the second shelf of the refrigerator behind a rusty jar of pale gherkins he found a half brick of forgotten Velveeta, dark and tough on the outside, but with enough reasonably soft yellow center to spread between two slices of dry bread, slap onto a heavily buttered skillet, and proceed to reduce to a charred slab what should have been a nicely browned grilled cheese sandwich.

He was up on a chair in the middle of the room, struggling to extract a stuck battery from the screaming fire alarm, when Lorena, trailing tendrils of smoke herself, strolled in, demanding to know, "What the hell are you burning in here?"

Seizing the alarm in both fists, Emory yanked it from the ceiling by its screws, hurled the squawking disk into a corner where it caromed off the baseboard, creased the refrigerator, kissed a table leg, and slid to a dead stop at the foot of his chair, its bleating remains silenced at last by one decisive plastic-spewing stomp.

"Nineteen ninety-five at Kmart," commented Lorena dryly. "Blue-light special. Such testiness. I suppose this outburst has something to do with your precious movie." She glanced around at the pieces underfoot. "Aren't these devices radioactive or something, like there's this pellet of plutonium you're supposed to dispose of per instructions you've probably lost. Now the entire kitchen's contaminated. The place where we eat. We're dead."

Emory loaded the blackened square of bread and gummy cheese onto a plate, scored the last cold beer from the refrigerator, and arranged on the table before him the elements of his lunch and certain crucial pages of dialogue he planned to reread and revise during this precious interval in the day's noise.

Lorena remained where she was, unmoving, silent, until he was settled in. Then she spoke: "Was there ever in the whole warped universe of male weirdness a man as plain weird as you?"

"If you're going to hover while I'm trying to work, at least have the courtesy to refrain from kibitzing."

"Have you talked to Aeryl yet?"

"No." Was the dialogue honest, simple, and wise? *Caustic Camera* advised novice screenwriters to keep it brief. If the momentum flags, the conversation stalls, simply cut to another scene.

"She's acting strange."

"Have you called the Action News Hot Line?"

"Why don't you talk to her for a change? Find out about this Laszlo character. She's sick of the sound of my nagging."

In the extended pause that followed, Emory realized he had dripped cheese onto the script.

"Well?" asked Lorena.

"All right. I said all right, isn't that enough." He rubbed at the stains with a paper towel. These sheets would all have to be retyped.

"Promise?"

"What do you want from me, a notarized declaration?"

"I want a promise kept. For a change."

Emory gathered up his papers and his lunch and carried them through the living room out to the office, where Ceryl was hastily cradling the phone receiver.

"Who was that?"

"Nobody." She could look directly into her father, through transparent skin and organs, and he let her.

"Nobody must be a comedian."

"Huh?"

"You were laughing."

"Wrong number," she explained. "He said I had a nice voice."

"Okay."

"What—do you think I'm lying?" Her specialty: the aggrieved accusation.

"I said okay. Don't be so paranoid." His specialty: the backhanded rebound. "Tell your sister Aeryl I want to see her."

The basic problem, as ever, was holding it all together in his head—the guests, the employees, the paperwork, the family—as if he were this ludicrous white-faced buffoon balancing on a bulbous red nose a towering superstructure of tables and chairs while being pelted by gaily colored tennis balls and rich cream pies as a barking seal attempted to scale the teetering pyramid for the set of bicycle horns at its peak to peck out with glistening mammalian snout, for the edification and entertainment of the adoring upturned mob, a recognizable rendition of "Pop Goes the Weasel." Emory didn't need a shrink to tell him what the slippery seal represented.

Guests arrived, guests departed, in sundry states of unembarrassed kookiness, America on the road slightly more deranged than America at home, the phone trilled, the towel guy showed up with half their daily order, the snack guy informed Emory that one of the machines in the west wing had been jimmied, a domestic service person named Jan whom he persistently called Nan quit in tears after a quarrel with another person named Crystal whom he eyed in a special way he thought she understood, daughter Beryl appeared to vacuum the artifacts without once acknowledging his presence, a jittery man in a bad wig who couldn't seem to decide whether he wanted a room or not was mistaken by Emory for that fateful character he had been awaiting in a starkly lit concrete corner of the mind since first assuming his position behind the desk: the creep with the iron in his belt who could in an instant transform this familiar room into the duplicate space gained by viewing it through the navel of a loaded revolver, Lorena in a chartreuse Empire Lanes bowling shirt and torn jeans left in the Esprit for a doctor's appointment of indeterminate length, "I didn't recognize you," said the television hooker to the television detective, "You're a mess, you should lay off those candy bars," and the guests arrived, the guests departed, the phone trilled, erections rose, erections fell, and four hours and eighteen minutes late Aeryl burst through the beads. She was wearing a black cowboy hat, one jingling spur, and enough makeup for three faces.

"What are you supposed to be—a rodeo clown?"

"Oh, Daddy."

"I don't know what you think we're running here."

"A motel?"

"I was supposed to talk to you, today."

"Yeah? About what?"

"I don't know. Your mother said we needed to."

"Well, I'm fine, everything's fine."

"I hope you understand, you're not getting married, you're not eloping, you're not piercing your nose, you're not even skipping off to Denver again until I say so, okay?"

"Oh, Daddy."

"Unfortunately, for the both of us, my legal responsibilities regarding you—and I can't believe I'm talking like this—have one more year outstanding before our mutual debt is discharged, and so, until your next birthday, you will do exactly as I please since I do not intend to abdicate my duties."

"Your throne, you mean."

"I trust that you heard and that you comprehended. I have nothing further to say on this issue. Now watch the store while I get some dinner. And don't put on that MTV crap, the guests don't like it."

And as Emory headed on back to the kitchen, he could actually feel the globe turning under his feet, the whetted prow of the future advancing through the fog, the same damn days coming at him round and round, over and over, mondaytuesdaywednesdaythursdayfriday-saturday justlikethat, a week begun and gone in a single revolution of the sun. Friends agreed, the feeling was extant, we needed more days in the calendar, extra portions stuffed into the middle of the week, more cheese in the sandwich, new days with different names, force a week to fulfill a week's worth of labor, while he, the sly thief, o'er these prison walls would leap upon the yellow wings of a screenplay with "heat."

Her mind a roiling inferno, Aeryl stalked the borders of the room, reviewing the well-tested chinks in the mortar, deciding where to sink the probe. She lingered longest at the tank by the window where Herbie

lazed, all scales and silence and ancient intimation. Herbie would tell
her what to do. She raised the blinds. Beyond the cracked asphalt of
the parking lot down the grassy slope at right angles to Route 9 stretched
six straightaway lanes of unrebuffed speed as familiar as the back of
her hand and equally hypnotic, the fundamental lure of moving objects
(even at this distance the drone of their transit penetrating the glass,
a sound she had to attend to hear, the timeless wash of her life), the
ever-present, ever-thrilling possibility of accident, a splatter of color
upon the surrounding monotone, a spray of primal drugs into bodily
systems dulled by dullness. She studied her nails for a moment in the
honest window light, a tattered lackluster array; she should change her
diet, she should eat more Jell-O. She stepped to the television and
changed the channel. Herbie had spoken. Skinny guys in tight leather
were hopping up and down, shaking their hair, their guitars, their
buns, the stage wreathed in thunderheads of smoke pierced by multicolored spots, dragon flames roaring from mortar tubes behind the
mad naked drummer. She jacked up the volume, settled back in her
father's chair, held simultaneously by the battle of the demonic bands
and the soulless shuttling of traffic at her window, fidgety eyes jumping
from one screen to the other, waiting for somebody cute to show up
via either medium. No contest. Forty-five minutes of desk clerk duty
had offered her the wrinkled potatoheads of enough fat truck drivers
and balding husbands to cover a week's grossout, dodging the spew of
their breaths, the very road exhaust pouring from their mouths with
their stupid words. The bloated ugliness of the land, candy-coated
corn. To pass the time, to turn the time into a turn of entertainment,
she amused herself by playing with the men, jerking them around, in
the most innocent way, of course, her office shifts comparable to
research periods in the lab, where she experimented with the relatively
recent discovery of the erotic self, specifically the wind force of the
female body (her own) upon the vulnerable exposures of the male
mind. With one guy she'd undo a button or two on her blouse, lean
farther in his direction than was absolutely necessary; with another
she'd mimic his accent, match his life story (his fantasy) detail for
detail with a fictional tale of her own. She was accommodating, she
was sweet, she got inside those befuddled heads and rearranged the
furniture. By the time the door closed on their backs, she'd forgotten

their fronts. After a dozen or so she remembered maybe one, nice smile, nice hands, reminded her of a famous actor she sometimes liked, paid in cash, bought a piece of butterscotch fudge, and stood there at the counter chewing on it until he was done. He made her laugh. But so what?

When Father finally returned, she was a machine, appropriate responses to his cues, crisply polite, the professional daughter who knew how to take an order. She saluted, she was dismissed.

Strolling out along the south walkway, peering into windows as she passed—the sport of the motel life and a useful education for the young—she paused abruptly before the partially closed curtain of room 10 to observe a naked man standing before the full-length door mirror, aiming a pistol at himself. As she waited for the shot, she realized this loon was, in fact, the nice fudge man. He tossed the gun onto the bed and disappeared into the bathroom. What a world. This place was one big freak show.

The rain began sometime after dusk. Headlights bored through the storm. The neon sign smoked and hissed. At the desk, Mr. Graveyard Shift, Warren Burch, the only non-family member employed in the office on a regular basis. He had been hired because as a second-year graduate student in film studies at the University of Denver he was presumed to share similar enthusiasms with the boss, a presumption the whole family had cause to regret, his arguments with Emory over the aesthetic merits of a particular film or even, on occasion, a particular forty-five seconds, having often escalated into legendary shouting matches capable of clearing out not only the office but a few paying rooms as well. Warren spent the lonely hours of his watch poring over exhaustive frame-by-frame analyses of such seminal works as *2,000 Maniacs* and *Cannibal Holocaust* while also tending the strays, the late arrivals, the early risers, the darkness beyond his lamp held at bay by the magic of academic charms: "diegetic space," "deployed gazes," "polysemic violations," "discursive mechanisms," "inscribed bodies."

Outside, night was collapsing rather theatrically into day, big storm scene blowing still at the window, lashings of rain, windy monologues, lightning's annunciatory crack—all FX, no plot. Nature was knocking, but she couldn't get in.

Pocketing his change, a man exited the motel office, head bowed for the splashing sprint to the car, so he didn't notice them huddled there under the open stairway like a pair of drenched orphans until the girl called out. They needed a ride, their truck had broken down. The girl he recognized, the boy had big earrings and a turquoise bandanna tied around his head, a nuclear gypsy from the future.

The man brought the car around. The couple climbed eagerly into the ruptured backseat of an antediluvian Ford Galaxie.

"There's an army blanket you can use," said the man, who watched them in the mirror unfurl the faded green material into a makeshift tent they shivered quietly beneath, heads cowled in official U.S. wool, bodies emitting the frank odor of wet dog.

The girl caught the watching eyes. They were so pale, almost white, like those of a beautiful snow leopard she had admired once in a zoo. "I know you," she said. "You're the funny fudge man." She whispered something to her boyfriend, who then brayed through yellow teeth. "This is Laszlo," she said.

The man nodded. "Tom Hanna."

"I'm Aeryl. A-e-r-y-l. You never heard of it, my father made it up. Laszlo says probably he wanted a boy. You know, Errol."

"It's a fairy's name," said Laszlo. "Like fucking Tinkerbell. Fucking Keebler elf."

"Aeryl is sterile, they used to sing. After fourth grade I quit crying over it."

"Her father is an asshole, major league." Laszlo shifted around to get a better view of the driver. He wondered if he was queer.

"We're running away," she announced. "To Las Vegas. To get married. We're eloping."

"We're doing it our way," declared Laszlo.

"You're hitchhiking to your wedding?" asked the driver. He hadn't turned around once to look at them.

"Our truck burned out. The wires got wet, right, Lasz?"

"It's fucked." He had produced a pair of round granny glasses with yellow lenses he meticulously unfolded and perched on the end of his nose, instantly liberating himself from the dull grayness of a morning now bursting with secret suns. He scrutinized the driver from behind his mystic spectacles. It's a lemon world.

"You don't know us," said Aeryl, "but you will by next Halloween.

I'm a famous actress, Laszlo's a double-platinum rock star. We'll be in L.A. then, we have plans."

The driver carefully cleared his throat before replying. "Don't mean to piss on your parade, guys, but got any idea how many wannabes wash up every day on the Strip out there?"

"Tough shit," answered Aeryl. "How many of them are witches?"

Laszlo interrupted the intense air-guitar solo he was entertaining himself with to add, "How many sacrificed a cat to Astaroth before they left home."

"You dickhead!" cried Aeryl, shoving herself against her boyfriend's unpadded body. "You ever met this dude, what if he's a cop or something?"

"He ain't no cop—are you?"

"Do I look like one?"

"You look like a peanut salesman."

"Pay no attention," Aeryl advised. "He's been up all night, he's wasted."

"I am Azagthoth, the Sumerian god of chaos. The band's name is Necronomicon. The songs will freeze your blood."

"See, we have plans," explained Aeryl. "We're on a psychic journey. We've married ourselves already in a proper Chemical Wedding, but now we need to unite with the power of the state. And Las Vegas is a holy place, don't you think? Neon and sand and roulette and media divinities. It's all so sexy."

"I want to see Emory's face when he finds the cat. We nailed it to the Coke machine."

"It had only one eye," said Aeryl. "A very powerful curse."

"I hope his heart explodes through his fucking chest. I hope the pool bursts into flames. I hope the walls tumble into the sea."

"Who cares?" said Aeryl. "No matter what happens, Motel Hell is finished." They had each taken a turn with the knife, then walked the dripping carcass through the corridors so that now the Yellowbird sat within a circle of consecrated blood.

"I'm writing a song about it," Laszlo announced. " 'Fulminating Flesh Vapors of Decay.' I feel a monster anointing coming on."

"I feel clammy," Aeryl complained.

"Hey, good buddy," said Laszlo to the driver, handing over the seat a small weathered vertebra he had fished with difficulty from his pocket. "A gift. For the ride. It ain't safe to go around without a bone in your pants."

Aeryl leaned back, unbuttoned her fly, and proceeded to peel off her damp jeans. "Relief at last."

"Great idea," said Laszlo, joining her in bottomless nudity under the blanket from which their grinning heads protruded in comic sculptural display.

"Another of your pagan rituals?" the driver asked.

"No," replied Laszlo, "this is," and he cupped his hand around the back of Aeryl's head and drew her roughly into an extended kiss, Aeryl moaning a bit more helplessly than necessary, the driver's tense eyes like separate creatures trapped in the cage of the mirror, multiple hands under the wool roving instinctively southward, home to the nest. Then slowly this great struggling thing beneath the blanket slid pseudopodlike out of view, its exertions changing posture and flavor, an undressed limb flung boldly over the seat to jiggle away mere inches from the driver's distracted attention, soft thigh sporting an unusual number of brown and yellow bruises, poison kisses from a devil's lips, and suddenly the charged air bloomed for all, the driver's nape hairs erect as soldiers, neck and cheeks richly mantled, a brief consonance of feeling well below the level of logic. The interior of the car reeked of unwashed bodies and humid sex scents.

Aeryl's blown-out head rose up first in sweaty amiability. "That was vicious," she declared.

"Kerrrang!" cried Laszlo, loosely rocking on an imaginary spring his long silly skull. He sat back, watching himself deflate, the little man sinking sadly back into the box. He reached over, rubbed his hands in between Aeryl's wet legs, smeared the cologne he found there over his own stubbled cheeks, then, for her amusement, pretended to wipe his fingers in the driver's curly hair.

"Show him your tits."

"Hey, I don't even know this guy."

"Show 'em, he wants to see."

Aeryl considered for a moment, then edged forward on the seat, a clutch of black T-shirt in her fist she yanked quickly up and down.

"I'm not sure he saw. Do it again."

"It's a one-act show."

"That's okay," said the driver. "I've seen bare breasts before."

"You haven't seen hers. She's beautiful. She ought to be appreciated. What's the matter with you?" Their eyes met in the intimacy of mirror space, Laszlo's angry blues glittering with the message direct and unmistakable: I, a man younger, stronger, braver than you, have this minute, under your quivering old nose hairs, fucked a woman younger, sexier, more desirable than any you can ever hope to win, ergo, you must acknowledge the superiority of my force, the potency of my prick, so said stone eyes from a clearing in the wood.

"Quit it," said Aeryl. "You two guys want to screw, you can let me out here."

"I don't believe I like his face," said Laszlo.

"Here come the cops," announced the driver, as a flashing patrol car screamed up past them and away.

"Fucking's not against the law," said Aeryl, offended.

"Not yet," replied Laszlo, lingering almost lovingly in the reflecting glass, a final look fashioned as a promise, that's right, buddy, I ain't finished with you yet, not by half, before confidently settling back into the split webbing of the seat, where he pretended to sleep, listening in private darkness to the oceanic voice of wind and wheels that pronounced the abiding stupidity of civilization and its contents, and presently—such were his skills of impersonation—slipped, with no discernible transition, into the actuality, and he slept.

Aeryl talked with the driver, heard out his grave song, of Debbie, his wife, and kids Jen and Petey, murdered in their beds by an intruder unknown and at large these eight years later. Pain like a wheel his life was broken upon, useless pieces drifting in torpid suspension toward the bottom of a bottle, waking alone in the gray streets to the survival denominator and the sometimes regretfully ugly requirements of a life impossible to imagine before the murders. And to think, once he had been president of his own company, Psychoplex Systems, Inc., an educational testing service netting more than five mil the last time he was in position to check.

The man was weird, obviously, a dubious presence fading in and out as if broadcast from a TV station at the limits of its reception area. But in a world of breakaway certainties, such transparent elusiveness was an attraction, erotic in appeal, the tease of a puzzle stripping itself bare. She didn't believe a word he said.

All this while perched on the edge of her seat dressed in a single T-shirt, the curious logo STANDARD MISSING CORP. emblazoned across the chest, and Laszlo lying beside her like a dead man, head flung back openmouthed, a slug beneath the rock of sleep. Where in luminous dark, ever faithful, gamboled one of her slithery selves. Because she was different alone with the driver. Laszlo's girl was asleep with Laszlo. She was someone else now in this mood, before this person. She was always someone else, and if this were craziness, she'd been born with it. Either she had bad genes (the curse of the Chaces) or everyone was coming apart minute by minute, but nobody was talking, no way to gauge where she ranked on the normality curve. Other people were alien planets you visited whose landscapes, customs, atmospheres, changed you. This Tom, for instance: a shiny metallic sphere, a solitary foil tree, a pool of quivering mercury; hollow, too, no doubt, but nice to visit for a spell, a pleasant variation from Laszloville, which was nice, too, but she had been on all the rides.

Laszlo's plump eyes shuttered open, focused in random incomprehension upon a brightening verticality, a hardness of a thingness he was quite unable, for several entertainingly disoriented moments, to recognize as the blunt chrome shaft of a simple door lock. Half his sweat-basted face lay roasting in direct sun, though he neither moved nor spoke, content to lap in the sensory wash of blur and hum and the amusingly inconsequential quality of the nearby conversation.

"Eighty-five for a single," Aeryl was saying, pointing to a passing motel behind a red windmill, "and the cable sucks." She turned, unexpectedly confronted by Laszlo's lupine glare.

"I need to piss," he said.

"He needs to piss," said Aeryl.

The driver glanced at the dash. "When we stop for gas."

"Yeah, when's that?"

The driver shrugged. "Hour, hour and a half."

"Pull over along here. I'll go down in the ditch."

"I can't do that," said the driver.

"Why the fuck not?"

"See those signs? No stopping except in case of emergency."

"This *is* a fucking emergency."

"I'll determine that."

"Look," said Aeryl, reading it off, "Next Rest Area Twenty-five Miles. We could pull in there, couldn't we, Tom?"

Tom? Tom??

"Twenty-five miles? Fuuuuck. I can't hold it that long."

"You're a big strong guy," said the driver.

"You can do it," assured Aeryl.

"I said I gotta go now. Whaddya want me to do, stick it out the fucking window?"

"Lasz," Aeryl said. "Be nice."

"You talking to me or you talking to him?" Something had happened while he slept, something evil, like the air itself had been changed, sucked thoroughly from the car and replaced with a mixture of counterfeit gases that were altering the composition of his brain. "Pull your goddamn pants on!" he screeched at Aeryl. "You think he isn't enjoying this?"

"Well, that, I thought, was the idea."

"You're too stupid to have an idea."

She could see from where she sat, down into the well on the passenger side amid a welter of travel trash and crumpled tabloids, PRIEST GIVES BIRTH TO LIVE FISH, the plated handle of the gun lying in packed potentiality, scenarios swarming up like angry wasps.

"We're taking your bladder hostage, kid," joked the driver. "Behave yourself if you want to see it again in one piece."

"Fuck." Laszlo turned away to look out his window. Fucking rays. Fucking dirt. "Fuuuuuuuck," he said, slow as he could drag it.

"Too much Colt for breakfast," said Aeryl. "Shit goes through you like white water."

Laszlo imagined himself letting go, hosing down the ratty interior of this car, spraying golden halos about the driver's chipmunk head.

"Look," said Aeryl. "I'll count off the numbers on the miles thing. You'd be surprised how fast a mile goes. Like by now we're probably already down to twenty-three, so like what do the numbers say, four five one . . . Move your arm, Tom, I can't—"

"Anybody got a cup?" inquired Laszlo.

"What are you gonna do?" asked the driver. "Drink it for good luck?"

"I'm counting now," said Aeryl. "The numbers are rolling by."

Carefully Laszlo leaned forward to deposit directly into the hairy convolutions of the driver's unprotected ear: "Aglon Tetagram Vaycheon Stimulamathon." He went on: "Erohares Retragsammathon Clyoran Icion Esition."

"Another mile down," Aeryl announced.

"Just what the fuck is your problem, bitch?" said Laszlo to the last of the five hundred faces she had been flashing him since he woke up, and the surreptitious semaphoring of her hands signaling him to the front, the front of what?

"Your boyfriend's got quite the mouth, hasn't he?"

"He won't be talking to you anymore," Aeryl explained. "He's a real stubborn person like that."

"Kanda Ess Trotta Montos," Laszlo hissed. "Eadryx Nutt Nosferatus Kanda Emontos Kanda." His diabolic eye fixed on the back of the driver's neck, the encircling fringe of uncut hair in curled clawlike strands, an insufficient neck whose appearance, whose otherness, was a vile offense to the gaze of the initiate. His mind was going and going, outracing the car, running on ahead of his thoughts, fibrillating like a bad heart until suddenly it stopped, dead still, conjectural operations ceased, and a clear bracing coldness descended through his overheated body in one long slow continuous wave. Now he smiled. Now he could slump back in the same careless attitude as when he slept, the same road decor droning past his semi-lidded gaze.

"Oh shit," Aeryl declared. "I've lost track of the numbers on the miles thing."

The William H. Bonney Rest Area was one large parking lot, one small brick building, a few shade trees, and a couple of green picnic tables, site the previous week of a rape and attempted murder by one or more unidentifiable unapprehended subjects. Aeryl and Tom decided to wait in the car.

"Hey!" called Aeryl from the open window. "Get me a Diet Sprite."

Laszlo kept on walking. "This ain't no goddamn refreshment stand," he said, without looking back.

He must have remained motionless for three solid minutes before the steel urinal in a perfect transport of eliminatory bliss, all the kinks and knots of the last few hours rushing in a mad slide down the chute and out. Long way to go for such sweet relief. Moral of today's lesson: if you're drinking, make certain you're the one driving. He shook himself off, admiring the imaginative antics of the many cocks and cunts penciled, penned, and scratched into the wall tile at convenient eye level. He zipped up, checked himself in the mirror. Did coolness have a face? Don't even ask. Now, here was the plan. The car was his, no doubt about it. He touched his pocket. He had the gravity blade and the will to use it. Ask one unfortunate cat. Mister Driverman was history, yeah. Give me shit, I'll cut the shit out of you. Blood on the asphalt. Move your fucking leg or I'll back the car over it. Yeah.

He strolled out to the car and discovered it no longer there. Wait a minute. Ford Galaxie, wasn't it? Some weird shade of green, '69, '70 or so? Nothing sitting in this sun matched that description. He returned to the lavatory, methodically searched the Men's, the Women's, stall by stinking stall, causing one male occupant to inquire if he were some fucking faggot and several alarmed females to threaten to sic their husbands on him. He went outside, walked the lot from end to end, inspecting the make of each vehicle, the interior for familiar objects. He stood before the little brick house, the well-tended hedge, the flaming geraniums, bedraggled travelers of both sexes and all ages who needed to pee passing courteously around his vaguely disquieting form, and he removed his fancy sunglasses and hurled them to the pavement, the sole of his surplus combat boot vigorously grinding the cracked yellow lenses into a fine sugary powder.

Overhead in a dry wind fluttered the federal bunting, a clip on its swaying halyard clanging disconsolately against the tall hollow pole, the empty seasound of a ruined clock tolling a nonexistent hour, the extended shadow of the flagstaff falling diagonally across coupe and sedan, machine after master machine, on out into the lot, where at its tip a flapping black shape twisted furiously upon the hot cement like a small tethered animal struggling to break free.

GETTING HAPPY

WHEN Perry Foyle heard the telltale knocking behind the papered wall, he merely retrieved the remote from beneath his pillow and, red button properly thumbed, waved it in the general direction of the camcorder, quite indifferent to the rapidly clichéd marvels of technology, the magnetically preserved prurience being celebrated next door. He had seen it all before; what was new was the scary predicament Gregory Peck now found himself in in 1965 New York, lost in time without family, without friends, without a memory, pursued by ruthless strangers with guns who seemed to be operating from a fairly clear conception of precisely who he was, the moral of the picture (*Mirage*, today's Afternoon Classic) being apparently this: if you should happen to misplace your identity, better slip into your running shoes 'cause they're coming at ya, representatives of your true life, and they seriously want to kill you.

Poor Greg with his bumbling do-gooder notions of saving the world from atomic radiation—of course he had to be eliminated; who profited from peace in twentieth-century corporate America?—but still enough innocence abroad in the land to end with the bust of the evil exec, the cementing back together again of Humpty-Dumpty Peck (he's actually a physiochemist, whatever that is), and the final fade-out embrace in the arms of a handsome woman, a triumph of stardom, good looks, and conventional plotting.

Perry watched television the way small children slept—gone so deep inside that resurfacing was a shock, the place up top looked familiar but obviously required greater expenditures. The inevitable appearance of THE END hit him with the dismay a drunk feels at the approach of dawn. He lived in his bed, his body just another stick of furniture in an otherwise cluttered room, the world offering a happier perspective from the cushioned horizontal, his essentials (Bud, Marlboros, cable control) at convenient arm's length, his operation central from which he could (simultaneously) read a paper, eat a peach, soak up the fine Sony rays. It was a minor calamity to be forced too soon from the nest, but one had duties to perform, liaisons to maintain beyond the dream. Head as light as a balloon, he staggered over to the opposite wall where the Handycam was mounted on a small shelf before a ragged lens-sized hole. The camcorder was dead, the adjoining room empty, its anonymous couple having completed their business and fled, and who knew what rare species of erotic practice had escaped documentation forever because he, the compleat vidiot, had pointed the Mitsubishi VCR remote at the JVC camcorder?

Perry resided (temporarily) in a Fuck House, his term for this deteriorating South Side SRO, rentals available on an hourly basis, the communal john at the end of the corridor one green-bearded bowl with a cracked seat, the view from his window the 24-7 promenade of the broken-glass people, their sharp-edged psyches coming at you like ninja implements every time you braved the block for a food run. He had spent the majority of his years (twenty-seven of 'em so far, rings on a tree he honestly expected to be chain-sawed for pulp before producing any decent shade) attempting with about six meager ounces of Perry-essence to fill a ten-gallon mold of a half-imagined figure somewhere east of Dean and north of Elvis, but now he was simply searching for the bottom, his bottom, The Bottom, it didn't seem to matter. The future was coming; the herald of its gaudy carousel lights already visible out past the barren moons of the self. He would be instructed then, presented with the proper rule book on the game's last half. In the meantime, he was a pervert (temporarily).

A long rattle down the antique elevator, a couple of hot cassettes in hand, best of the week's catch, dank cave breath sighing up between the floor cracks, exhalation of a beast, to remind even the sleepwalking rider that a simple trip to the street might be a plunge toward adventure or a descent into the mines. Monitoring lobby traffic was the troublemaker's troublemaker, Pisshole Pat, the chain-smoking desk clerk with the crippled arm and the motor mouth, who, from the security of his bulletproof glass cage, enjoyed harassing peers and innocents alike, his bleached eyes a reproach to naïve hipsters like Perry who cultivated his tolerance out of the same dark need pushing them out to the margins here, all the good little girls and boys, lives from the womb pointed like compass needles in this damned direction, the tug of The Life, you think you're on a visit when you've really found a home.

Pat was always glad to see one of his regulars slink past. "Nice ass," he muttered to Perry. "Implants?"

The car was a stale Chrysler four-door on permanent loan from his father, its numerous arthritic complaints prohibitively expensive to treat, the missing passenger window a flapping sheet of taped plastic, the interior having been broken into five, six, seven times, routine in a neighborhood neither parent, to his indifference, would ever consent to visit. For folks like Stan and Allene, Pisshole Pat with his smoldering cigarette was the cherub at the gate with the flaming sword.

Since the "problem," though, Perry had heard rather frequently from Allene, calling in her depressingly chirpy hospital updates, "apprising" him of the "current situation." Today Daddy moved an eyelash. Yesterday curled a pinkie. Tomorrow will twitch a lip. Each lonely evening, after the last nurse had completed the last round, Allene pulled her chair close to the bed, slipped into a warm trance, and began firing her thought bullets directly into the yolk of darkness at the center of Daddy's skull. The power of right thinking, of which could be found no greater force in this life, witness the successful exorcism of the crime-ridden Westland Mall by Pastor Bob, who had personally promised her via recorded message that he would be praying for Daddy during special request night at this month's All-State Angel Jamboree, when the lame shall walk, the guilty get happy. Get happy, Allene exhorted her errant son, the Lord sends sunshine to brew the tea that is you. I am happy, he assured her. You are not. Am too. Are not. Then the lapse into black silence so similar to Daddy's notorious moods you are no doubt destined for . . . well, I don't want to say. Yes, Mother.

Stan Foyle was an unregenerate maniac who never smiled except by accident and who once in the middle of an IRS audit stabbed the agent in the hand with a government ballpoint pen. Stan loved pornography in any form—movies, magazines, Hellenic vases; had he known his son was intimately involved in its production, he would have beaten him severely; had he known the condition his son had reduced his car to, he would have killed him.

The destination this fine Friday night was the customary weekend blowout at The Rainbow Bridge, a big house on a small ground outside Denver city limits, so by definition a "ranch," though the only animals to be found wandering the premises were the ubiquitous cats and the disheveled or plain "skyclad" humans of a distinctly undomesticated variety. The party was well into second-stage burn by the time Perry arrived, the driveway and yard so jammed with vehicles he had to park out near the skull-shaped mailbox and walk in, the amplified throb of tribal drumming a beacon to the passing fun-seeker.

The house itself seemed to be excreting excess merriment; there were revelers perched like boisterous birds along the rooftop; a clumsy fellow in a rubber suit trying to clamber out the second-story bathroom window; the other windows dense with movement, flashbulb explosions, the caustic glare of camera lights, with loose faces rarely seen behind the penitential bars of nine-to-five; from an upstairs bedroom a lanky runway model in a floor-length satin cape and not much else appeared to be blowing hello kisses to Perry, a total stranger; the veranda was overrun by a loud gang of bland white guys holding talismanic cups and cans of precious alcoholic fluids; and at the front door a steady seepage of dizzy humanity in search of air, space, reduced noise level. "Excuse me excuse me excuse me," the chant Perry used to propel himself crabwise across the threshold into the really thick congestion inside. "Anyone seen Freya?" he called out hopefully.

"Yes," replied a pompous European with an unplaceable accent, turning to present Perry with a close-up view of the back of his wrinkled linen jacket, his ragged gray ponytail. The vehemence of Perry's expletives opened a startled rift in the nearby wall of bodies. The room beyond was a suffocating nightmare of babble and humidity. What was going on? He had never seen so many in attendance.

"Welcome to the twenty-first century!" The man gripping his arm had an extraordinarily piercing voice and a distressing muscular strength. His eyes resembled boiled eggs. He wasn't wearing pants.

Perry pulled himself free and pushed on, the game plan for rude gatherings such as this: better a moving target than a stationary dummy. Familiar faces hove into view, some known personally, some known at the intimate remove of modern celebrityhood, local media types tanned and satisfied, a sprinkling of higher-magnitude stars down from the mountain in Aspen, the socialite grouper fish, the trolling politicos, and the renowned and endowed from the glamorous world of adult entertainment, all the well-connected folk you could ever hope to rig a hot wire to.

Perry snagged a harsh anise-flavored concoction from a passing tray and pushed on, past the women with too much makeup, the men with too much cologne, stepping cautiously to avoid trampling underfoot the unwary cat or foul-mouthed dwarf.

A blonde in a red bikini, licking a cherry lollipop, in this case a phallic symbol in the actual shape of a phallus, said to her companion, "No, I know what happens. After you die, you pass out into a sticky white web. I saw it clearly in a dream."

"Yeah? And then what?"

She looked surprised. "I don't know," she said. "I woke up."

"I believe," announced a bored male voice, "I'm the only one in the room who hasn't had a nip and tuck."

"I believe," answered the model/actor/singer at his elbow, "you're the only one in the room I haven't fucked."

"Look," declared someone else, "isn't that Senator Wilcox? When did he get out of prison?"

"If you can imagine it, someone's done it."

"The ice queen's in back," someone said.

And then, no avoiding it, Perry was face to face with the Marguerita sisters, demonic twins outfitted in matching costumes of straps and buckles, their special glee: ridiculing the strange ways of the inferior sex.

"So, Perry," began Margaret or Rita (he couldn't tell them apart), "how's it hanging, good bud?"

The other stared critically at his crotch. "I fail to discern much of interest there."

"Girls," he begged, attempting to slip discreetly around. "Please."

"Girls??!!" they shrieked in unison. "GIRLS??!!" And with a precise dexterous teamwork admirable to behold, one sinewy sister pinned him against the wall as the other opened his fly and with a forbiddingly long stiletto removed his—no, his briefs, in two quick surgical slices before scampering away into the amused crowd, brandishing aloft the trophy of his poor violated shorts, which they took turns conspicuously sniffing between whoops of delight. Perry hadn't even time to get himself refastened before an anonymous bystander remarked cattily, "Goodness, not something I'd care to flaunt in public." Perry acted the good sport despite the homicidal rage seething behind his embarrassed smile. The rule was that once you crossed The Rainbow Bridge there were no rules. The paths to the playing fields of carnal liberty were curious and diverse, that of humiliation among the most honorable, its fervent devotees always well represented at these affairs, though Perry continued to encounter difficulty untying the knots that kept him from experiencing the advertised thrill of this particular mode. The job, he knew, was to defuse the body so as to allow the sexual angel to emerge, in whatever guise it chose.

The public rooms in the rear wings of the house were painted in warm uterine colors and named, rather too cutely, he thought, after popular parts of the human reproductive organs. The Vas Deferens, traditionally a holding pen for unassigned extras, was teeming with sparely dressed young women tottering about in six-inch heels like a herd of spooked deer. The Glans was occupied by a trio of naked fat guys, more hair on their shoulders than their heads, playing draw poker around a massage table. "What are you looking at?" The speaker had no teeth and a patch over one eye. Perry pushed on. The corridor, which was as packed as a stadium aisle the day of the big game, suddenly erupted into a wild water-pistol fight between opposing squads of squealing boys and girls in sequined G-strings, the liquid being so freely dispersed of a highly suspicious nature. Perry dodged and weaved and moved on.

Following the psychic current to its source, he found Freya Baldursson in the Mound of Venus, resplendent in her superhero garb of black spandex bodysuit and rune-embroidered baseball cap, the contrast merely emphasizing her dazzling, almost inhuman blondness, a look calculated to tickle the eye of either gender; she was always composing, manipulating the physical into the photogenic—a compulsion, she admitted it, but one that had rewarded her with the time's twin grails of fame and wealth. "I may not be able to tell a decent story," she confessed, "or round out a character, but, God, I know how to shoot skin." Textures, she loved textures.

At the center of this swarming room, the focus of eyes, lights, lenses, was a queen-size motel bed, aqua sheets, no pillows, upon which knelt a young red-Mohawked woman cinched into a monstrous illuminated dildo she was attempting, with intrepid gingerliness, to steer up the raised orifice of a scaly emerald creature only recognizably human by the incongruous pink penis dangling forlornly from a hole in the costume.

"It hurts," complained the creature.

"Cut!" Freya stepped impatiently into the light. "You're too tense, Tony. Are you practicing your breathing?" The creature mumbled assent. "Remember, now, you're a flower, not a stone."

"I think my batteries are dying," announced Ms. Mohawk, indicating the transparent plastic horn between her legs.

"Elsie," called Freya. "Take care of this, please. And more K-Y jelly. I want a nice sheen on the close-up."

Her glance passed sightlessly over Perry and back to the matter at hand. Her concentration, when she directed, was absolute, equal to that of a submarine commander preparing to launch torpedoes, the world's immensity condensed to a target bobbing in the periscope sights. At such moments she was relentless, she was temperamental, she wasn't taking calls, outside communications were filtered through the only two individuals who could or would dare to speak to her during production: her personal assistant, Elsie, a smaller, compacter, darker version of Freya who seemed instinctively to dislike everybody, and Rags, her husband, a spectral presence in leather pants and stainless steel glasses ("Nazi goggles," Freya called them), his large bony nose the subject of the usual jokes, the odious peat-bog aroma of his ever-present black cigarette enhancing the general aura of disquieting omniscience with which he distanced fans and followers. A dispenser and receiver of secrets, Rags confided only in his wife and his assistant, Eric, an ambitious toady of indeterminate loyalties whom Perry avoided whenever possible. The home life of this exotic group was impervious to the probes of the imagination, at least to one so obviously inadequate as Perry's. He could, however, easily envision Freya alone, either alone in the privacy of her quarters or alone with him.

The man beside Perry, an eerie ringer for his grandfather, turned away from quietly observing the action to confess in a mild voice, "I want to be goo."

Perry stared politely, waiting, as if an explanation would be helpful.

"I see myself as an enveloping disease whose sexual interaction consists of surrounding, penetrating, assimilating the submissive partner. Freya thinks it's a grand idea. She's going to coat me in purple Jell-O."

Freya called for quiet. The monster on the bed was at length and satisfactorily deflowered, though by the end Ms. Mohawk was so deeply engaged in her role she had to be commanded twice to cease with the pistoning. After apologizing to Tony, she said, "Wish I'd had this nasty about two years ago, it's just what my ex needed."

"It's what they all need," Freya proclaimed, "a taste of Thor's hammer." She noticed Perry and smiled. "You look exceptionally well tonight. Your fetch is quite strong. Dancing like a boxer. Very aggressive. Very *here*. What have you been up to today? Have you been a good boy?"

"Angelic." Too many sets of open ears, too many tuned-in consciousnesses. He felt embarrassed.

"Did you know I was assaulted once by the fetch of an enemy? An enemy I was unaware I had, always the worst sort. Yes, and today that person is stone blind." The smile had altered in neither size nor shape, shining persistently before him in enigmatic challenge.

"My protégé," she announced to the curious. "You'll be hearing more from Perry Foyle. What have you got for me today?"

He handed over the cassettes. "Double feature. A comedy, a tragedy, a full evening's worth of fine theatrical entertainment."

Elsie granted him a look devoid of human aspect, the light coming off her dark irises like the shine on an insect's shell.

"*Fryska flokks,*" said Freya. "Let's go get pulsed."

Freya's office, a trendy arrangement of leather, chrome, track lighting, and mirrors—how many of them two-way glass, like the silvered panel concealing Perry's peephole back at the Fuck House?—bore an obvious resemblance to an athletic club, as did the playrooms, the video sets, the spacious den with the stationary bikes and the ceiling-suspended basket harnesses, testimony to one immigrant's prompt mastery of current marketing trends. Wicked get-down dirty sex portrayed in an atmosphere of wholesome hygienic athleticism was a combination calculated to tease beyond enduring the national cleft. "The aerobics instructor of the boudoir," proclaimed *Playboy*, to whom Freya remarked, "I am she who is due."

Floor-to-ceiling shelves were stocked with cassette copies of every Cool Cat Production. Walls were enlivened with the framed posters of several films (*Hot Honeyed Nuts, Stair Lay to Heaven,* etc.) she had starred in during her early acting years, autographed glossies of the tanned and the toned and the culturally coddled, her friends, her clients. Her desk top was littered with odd bits of wood and rock which the curious hands-on visitor quickly discovered were ancient carvings in human shapes phallic and vaginal, their mystic power entering into you at a touch, guaranteeing what Freya called laughingly "an itchy day."

She slipped one of Perry's tapes into the VCR; the television, largest he had ever seen, swarmed into imagery, gray figures struggled together on a rumpled bed in a grainy, airless, bottom-of-the-sea world.

Freya was impressed. "I love the look of your stuff. Combat footage."

Pleased Perry nodded shyly. He watched her watching the screen, the infinite versions of her she seemed to shed without strain or consciousness, each discarded copy an object of contemplative beauty, perpetually replenishing herself in the instant so that she was perpetually new. There should be an invisible custodian trailing behind to collect these ghost moltings of a life not the minutest particle of which should be lost.

Her eyes. He could hardly tolerate their attention.

"Tell me, my little 007, exactly what is the nice gentleman doing with those Mutant Ninja dolls?"

He hadn't a clue. "Visual aids?" he offered tentatively.

Freya wrinkled up her nose. "Observe, please. The girl's face. Is she experiencing joy? Is she learning anything new? No, she is simply enduring the reiteration of one old sad lesson: men are pigs. I'm afraid to ask, is this the comedy or the tragedy?"

"I laughed," he admitted, shrugging his shoulders, helpless, base, contemptible, yes, me too. "A couple times."

"Yes, which means your average dickhead will be rolling about the floor, holding his sides, and this tape could be a monster hit that would make me a bag of money despite the alarming number of flea bites Mr. Studsicle there appears to have on his big white ass. Might I inquire as to the nature of the other cassette, the tragedy?"

"Uh, handcuffs, and, uh . . . other stuff."

"I'll save it for later." She switched off the set. "Don't misunderstand me, Perry. I very much appreciate the privileged window you provide on certain anthropological aspects of the sexual life of modern savages, but frankly, I'm beginning to worry about deleterious effects. You Americans, already so coarse, dearly love to be coarsened further. So much education is required here, so much more work to be done. I've often wondered, what if, in order to function in intercourse, it were necessary that a man's organ become, not hard, but soft—mushy, squishy, yucky soft. Think about it. The actual shape of the world would be radically altered. As in radical, getting back to the root."

"But I'm not directing the damn things," Perry argued. "I bring you the best, and there's not a particularly extensive choice."

"I know, I know"—when she touched his bare arm, the tissue glowed—"no personal criticisms intended. But the specific brand of eroticism you are repeatedly exposed to over there in your house of horrors is not conducive to developing sound attitudes."

"But my wallet is pumped."

"Oh yes, the great American fatality—damage others, damage yourself, what does it matter as long as the bank account grows fat? Bottom line, bottom line, it's all I hear, put your bottom on the bottom line. And so here we are in the one business where you can literally do just that. Do you remember, Perry, the first time you visited me?"

How could he forget? He had been driven out to The Rainbow Bridge as a joke by Eric, Rags's assistant, whom he met at the wedding of two individuals neither man actually knew, ushered into the sanctum sanctorum here to be greeted by a majestic woman in a sweeping fur cape sewn apparently from the white pelts of these abundantly underfoot cats. ("My little darlings!" she exclaimed later, shocked by the suspicion. "Why would I do something as vulgar as that?") She was the absolute personification of blondness, even her hair so theatrically pale it appeared as if the skin on her head had, under pressure, exploded outward into dramatic fibers that had been fashionably teased and moussed.

He stood before her like a private on parade.

"Are you a good sexer?" she asked.

He failed to comprehend. She repeated the question.

"Oh . . . uh, yeah . . . sure, I guess."

"Yes, you look like a good sexer."

"No complaints," he lied, dutifully.

"Take off your pants."

"Excuse me?"

"I'm afraid, Perry, I can only go on repeating myself for so long before I become bored, bored, bored. I don't wish to get unpleasant. I sense you want to remove your pants for me, so please, please do."

Even her eyebrows were blond. Perry did as he was told, inwardly cringing before the unembarrassed boldness of her stare. He hadn't known women possessed such weapons in their arsenals.

After a distressingly extended study, judgment was pronounced.

"Yes, you're someone we might be able to use, you look ordinary enough."

He was intrigued, he was broke, he was agreeable to busting his thespian cherry on a current production titled *Waiting for the Cable Guy,* but under the lights his brio wilted. A few days later he approached Freya with his candid camcorder proposal, she admired the depraved ingenuity, and every Friday for the past nine months he had been delivering the results of his "field project" to her bustling door.

Freya was a remarkable woman, her singular genius to realize the extraordinary transformative power of the video camera, "the most effective erotic toy yet devised," and its potential as a weapon of liberation. The official Cool Cat T-shirts displayed a picture of a camcorder above the motto IN HOC SIGNO VINCES. Her amazing success was based upon the methodically earned appreciation of an increasingly substantial portion of democracy's heroes, plain folks, your average jane and joe (may these referents be so forever inverted), who cheered her shimmy up the greased pole of the "business" from "anonymous hole"—typical remark of your typical wienie cameraman—in an early motel-room cumfest to the reigning years as headlined superstar of the highest-grossing series in the history of the adult video industry. (Perry, of course, owned a complete set in the latex-bound collector's edition.) So when she retired from active performing, she possessed a following of sufficient numbers that production money was easily available for the launch of her own videos, hot fun from "a woman's point of view," designed specifically for couples, men and women together, not just the usual bearded half of the sexual equation. Her goal of eliminating from the field stereotypical sex for arrested stereotypical men developed into a celebration of ordinary people, her fans, who were encouraged to buy, rent, borrow the equipment, and tape themselves, tape their friends, liberate the bedroom, liberate the block, for here was sex not only in the style your neighbors performed it, but sex as actually performed by your neighbors—the guerrilla punk aesthetic translated into the skin game—the cream of the amateur endeavor becoming enshrined in Freya's lucrative Home Spices line, a cavalcade of body types from the buffed to the porky, sexual attributes in every size and shape, a true portrait of America at play.

Of course, a smattering of these so-called "hand jobs" were ringers, scenes Freya had staged and shot as clandestine lessons in the Freya-approved joy-sharing method of equitable sex. Distribute the seeds and allow mimetic desire to take its course. The novice discovered, after an initial period of apprehension and embarrassment, that playing to the camera, to the spectator within a spectator within a spectator, that built-in audience inside every media child's head, released unexpected possibilities of delight. In the distorting mirror of the camcorder everyone was a star. See yourself as image, become the image you want to see. The inherent aphrodisiacal properties of technology had never been so robustly endorsed. Techniques improved, sexual and video. Testimony arrived from couples who claimed to be unable to make love without a camera present, others who were becoming aroused in electronics stores. Something momentous appeared to be happening behind the bedroom walls of the nation, something socially historic, was it any wonder young Perry wanted to hitch a ride on this stretch limo dash to the magic kingdom? The batch of sordid tapes he dropped like fresh kill at Freya's feet was his admission ticket to the enveloping nimbus of her fame and a gesture he knew, despite occasional criticisms, she prized, whether his offerings were processed into commercial fodder or stored upright in her private library of pleasures, these solid surrounding shelves of kissing, licking, moaning, and sighing—her gift to the marvelous country that had granted her adolescent winter dreams.

She regarded Perry with the look of a horsewoman sniffing a riding crop. "I want you behind a camera for me tonight. There's to be an event. Do you know Carl Dyne?"

No, he did not, and her description failed to distinguish him in Perry's mind from the pack of "lovable eccentrics" who swarmed over the property like confused lemmings.

"Tonight, my dear, Mr. Dyne's lifelong fantasy becomes, with our aid, realized in fact. We're crucifying him to the old oak out back."

"Real nails?"

"Oh, Perry, you're so evil. No, my little demon, he wishes to be secured by leather thongs, in the original manner, of course, and he wants the mean Roman centurions replaced by a nubile tribe of disrobed maidens, one of whom is required, during his prolonged agony, to be blowing him."

"Sounds like Mr. Dyne has too much time on his hands."

"No one has too much time, Perry, but then you're too bedewed to understand that yet. What there is too much of is boredom. And in boredom dwell the psychic mites." She showed him the sweet sickle of her smile, the one that opened him up from sternum to groin. "Don't let the icky mites get on you."

He mumbled out some adequate reply, she kept on speaking, the words barely registering on the vibrating cells of his mind as she guided him gracefully toward the door, her elegant hand brushing ever so delicately across his burning back, skin to skin, the intervening material of his shirt having cleverly dissolved, then the hand reached out for the gleaming doorknob and they were buried in a convulsive blast of party racket.

"You smell like celery," she shouted out over the noise. "Like clean rubber bands."

The door closed. He stood against the wall, savoring his sensations. He was positively luminous. He felt . . . *blond*, outside and in.

A red-haired wonder in a dragon-embroidered silk gown was saying, "Well, if I had a body part that changed size, I'd be obsessed with it, too."

"Enough to erect a shrine in your living room?"

"Isn't that Jack Nicholson?"

"So I waltz out in my tiny French maid's outfit with my tiny basket of cleansers and sponges and I have to yell as loud as I can into his left ear, 'No, no, Mr. Bertoni, I'm not here to do the floor, I'm here to do it *on* the floor.' "

The sweet bubble of Perry's mood evaporated in his hands. And before he could escape he was accosted by a short round man with a fake Germanic accent and the bizarre conviction they had already met.

" 'But I can't help myself,' " he whined asthmatically. " 'The terrible force driving me on!' " He paused, confident of a reaction.

"Yeah?" The weak smile on Perry's face hung there like an artificial ornament, precariously balanced.

"M," said the man. He waited. "I finally saw it, the movie you recommended."

"Oh sure. *M*." Perry searched the jostling heads in the immediate vicinity for a kindly buoy he could cling to.

" 'Who knows what it's like to be me?' " The man chuckled to himself. "Rather interesting little film, n'est-ce pas? This fascination with knives and little girls, well, it's the story of all us western civers, isn't it? We of the male persuasion. You declared it a masterwork, and now I also concur. Pity so few have seen it."

Perry interrupted, "Excuse me, but I don't know what the hell you are talking about." It was imperative that he reach the sanctuary of the buffet table as soon as possible. He launched himself into the mob.

"But how can you say that about Freya? For someone her age she looks so incredibly beautiful."

"Well, I hear that every night she rubs her crow's-feet with come."

"Oh really? Whose?"

Limping now in Perry's general direction came the ghastly Mr. Cyborg, clad in a silver bodysuit emphasizing the dangerously loose bolt of his hexagonally headed member. Perry pushed his way past a city councilman, an assistant fire chief, two schoolteachers, several other mid-level functionaries in local government who had risen high enough to believe they could do as they pleased but not so high that anyone would care, the sycophantic posturings of Jennifer Jumponher and Wendi Wantit, and into—at last!—the breathing space of the ample kitchen, where flushed couples were inspecting the drawers for amusing implements. Perry moved on through and out the back door.

The late western sky dispensed a gentle nonjudgmental flavor, the shade of the blue, the order of the clouds offering a completed look, the varnished surface of something thoroughly achieved. On the tennis court a giggling quartet was enjoying a sloppy game of doubles au naturel.

A required fixture of Freya's weekends was the solitary sobbing woman, her board position altering from week to week, but her presence clearly a necessity, the counterweight of pain against which the world's festivity was hung. Perry found her crouching beneath a mulberry bush at the corner of the house; he approached discreetly, uncertain whether to offer help or retire courteously; then he realized he knew her, not her name or her pleasures, nothing so elemental, but the bathos of her life story (doctored to the moment, he was sure), which had been inflicted on him for untold hours at an earlier party when, looking for a piece of spare rope, he stumbled upon her in the garage, weeping on the soft leather seat of Freya's Mercedes. She was a topless dancer at the Lariat Lounge, the bald fat owner a compulsive thief and degenerate lech, her boyfriend turned tricks and periodically beat her up, there was never enough money for drugs, she felt "funny" much of the time, her best friend stole her clothes—well, it went on and on, and, true or not, Perry couldn't believe a word, the tale had run out of gas, there was no more air in the tires. If bad storytelling was detrimental to your karmic health, living a bad story was a curse doubled. She'd get no dime in her cup from him.

Perry's objectives each visit to The Rainbow Bridge were three: (1) to share a private moment alone with Freya, (2) to score the vital stomachful of free food, (3) to score. He'd never batted worse than .666, but he'd also never been so behind this late in the game. He was therefore in no mood as he returned to the house, wending his ever-circuitous way toward the elusive yummy board, to be detained by the Jellicoe brothers, those matching male bookends to the Marguerita sisters, dual costars of the notorious and highly profitable *Twins on Twins*, "You'll not only be seeing double," declared *Vid-Eros*, the trade organ, "you'll be screwing double: a four-condom rating." Whatever modest charisma the camera loaned their leporine presence must have had a lien against it in the sallow unlensed flesh; Perry found the brothers arrogant, narcissistic, and plain silly, qualities of course not only abundant in their chosen career but positive benefits. The one with the diamond in his right incisor offered Perry a hit of Piracetem, a smart drug—it's new!—guaranteed to give your cerebrum an intelligence rush. Perry declined, believing this transaction the equivalent of buying prescription glasses from a blind man.

A woman with a blue face wandered past, holding a fishbowl of prophylactics and wearing a sign PRACTICE GLOVE LOVE.

Someone said: "And I was like, whoa, excuse me, but I don't want to be raped by orchids."

Suddenly Perry was seized by a girl who couldn't have been more than sixteen and delivered a full kiss, naughty tongue included, because he looked so much like that Hollywood actor, you know, and now she knew the thrill of kissing the original because all the similar features were located in roughly the same places, or something like that.

A startled woman with glittery strings of tinsel adorning her big salon-constructed hair rushed at Perry, threatening cassette-corder in hand.

"Senator Wilcox," she began breathlessly, "what are your views on unorthodox sexual practices?"

Gently, as if the machine might detonate, Perry pushed the cassette-corder away from his mouth. "I'm not John Wilcox," he explained.

"I haven't been elected yet, and I don't believe there exists such a thing as unorthodox sex."

"Thank you, senator," she replied briskly, punching the rewind button to check at once that this devastating sound bite had been duly captured.

"Never leave you alone, do they?" The old man had sidled up to Perry as if he'd be welcomed. He spoke in rasping confidential tones and he was wearing white silk evening gloves and an impressively authentic grass skirt. His large red-rimmed eyes appeared to have been too hastily inserted, the wrong size for their sockets.

"Didn't you hear what I just said? I'm not Senator Wilcox. I'm not candidate Wilcox."

"I understand. Listen, you can be who you want to be. Who am I to complain?"

"And after I divorced him," a passing voice explained, "he had a gelatin mold made in the shape of his cock and Lindsey asked him how many did it serve?"

"I'm not supposed to be here. This is not the party I was invited to."

"If you can imagine it, someone's done it."

"No, I don't want to see what lurks under the grass. I'm sure it's a very nice snake. Excuse me, I've got to take a leak."

Perry escaped down the busy corridor to the bathroom, where from behind a bolted door issued the squeaks and giggles of suppressed laughter but no response to his energetic knock. Frisky merrymakers danced deliriously by, the percentage of exposed skin increasing by the hour, designer people on designer drugs.

"So I asked him, did you ever hear of the sadhu in India who as young boys begin hanging weights on their penises until eventually the damn things get so elongated they have to carry them around in little baskets? Utterly useless for copulation, of course, but they walk around in a state of constant sexual stimulation. And so Todd says, 'Ah, the ideal American consumer.' "

"So Freya said, 'To hell with psychoanalysis, I've turned Freud on his head and given him a good blow job."

"So Hilary said, 'Now that I've got my clit pierced, I can't go to the grocery store without having an orgasm.' "

"So I said if he didn't have his finger up your ass, he couldn't possibly be a real Italian."

The Hula Man rounded the corner, skirt aflutter, bearing down on Perry with crazed determination. The rhythm of his hammering grew in urgency: "C'mon in there, open up!"

A young man in a bikini with a whistle around his neck cried, "Hey, Senator Wilcox, how's it hanging, bud?"

Bang, bang, bang, bang.

The door was cracked an inch, two inches, enough to reveal a pair of bloodred lips and one bold blue eye. "Can you operate a video camera?"

"Hell, yes."

The Hula Man was, incredibly, sashaying across the hall carpet, the grotesque spectacle of his creakily undulating hips clearing its own wide path.

The bathroom door yawned open and Perry was hauled inside. He found himself—holy adolescent fantasy!—packed into a close space with half a dozen frolicsome babes in various states of carefree deshabille, and though nudity was certainly no novelty to him, it was also no antique, his eyes couldn't seem to quit jumping around in his head, everything was breasts, butts, and porcelain. A bottle-blond Freya wannabe (legion was her number), nipples colored to resemble eyes, passed him an expensive video camera, saying, "We're making a scat tape, get in the tub."

He noted the perfectly ordinary bath, the trim Amazon with a ring in her nose holding the lid-sized sheet of Plexiglas, the circle of hushed expectancy, his own emotions on a muddled spin, impossible to disentangle the slightest guide to the truth of the moment. Is this how you're regarded in the final minutes before the previously friendly natives toss you into the pot?

"C'mon," he was urged from behind, poked in the ass by what he presumed was one sharp finger. "This is gonna be great, you're just the guy we've been waiting for."

"A gag for my boyfriend," explained the one with the ogling breasts. "Next week's his birthday."

"And he already has everything," added the amicable doorkeeper. "It's so difficult to be original anymore."

Perry commiserated. "I'll do my best." He climbed into the tub like the first brave man to go down in a submarine, assumed a relatively comfortable supine position, camcorder resting momentarily on his chest, a compulsive-obsessive vampire at peace in his sanitary, enameled coffin. The Plexiglas was laid over the top of the bathtub; the naked girlfriend clambered up. She squatted there above Perry's head as if magically suspended in pure space. He sighted up through the viewfinder and into the origin of the universe. "Ready?" she asked, glancing down into his anxious eye; he knew about the occasional lethal accident when this trick had been performed on a glass cocktail table. "When you are," he replied. What an indescribably peculiar sensation to find yourself flat on your back in a ceramic crib, bulging nipple eyes smiling benignly down, when abruptly, from the bearded mouth of the great torso face overhead, gushed a torrent of warm urine, exploding against the glass in a sparkling dance of the drops, bouncing like loose BBs over tile and tub and squealing onlookers, the noise terrific from Perry's position, the smell rich and strangely tender, Perry not knowing what to think, what to feel, this experience, like so many in recent months, unfolding in a realm beyond any moral categories he was capable of reckoning, he rode the vertigo ride and he was not unhappy, wavering neither hand nor eye, the year of professional camera work serving him in good stead here, down to the last clear droplet of this seemingly inexhaustible flow, when, as abruptly as it began, his willowy star leaped from her perch, lifted away the Plexiglas shield, streams and rivulets rolling off onto his clothes, "Thanks, dude," and grabbing the camcorder, she and her manic tribe were gone.

As Perry struggled to extricate himself from the tub, The Hula Man materialized in the open doorway, cast one long look upon the scene, and proclaimed loudly, "How can the man even begin to consider running for the presidency?"

Perry cleaned his shirt and pants as best he could with a wet washcloth. Who would notice the stains amongst this bedlam?

A pale mushroom-shaped man with a prodigious growth of body hair announced, "I haven't worn clothes in four days."

"Sylvia Plath once described the male genitalia as resembling a turkey neck with gizzards, but of course she was a poet."

"If you can imagine it, someone has done it."

"He said my love canal was polluted, so I told him his pole of muscle had termites."

Perry pushed his way through the promiscuous throng like a crazed commuter; he would be denied no longer.

Yes. Rising into view beyond the mountainous shoulder range of rude gluttons, the grand buffet spread, at last. He spied a hole in the defensive line and broke for daylight. He was in, toe to toe with the delicacies, his starving eye scanning the table fore to aft and back again, and failing to recognize a single edible tidbit. He started over, a slow pan, noting sizes, shapes, hues, registering each available odor. Fleshy tones seemed to predominate, dead sea creatures on ice, skinned, but not cooked. If fire, as Freya had once informed him, marked a crucial interaction between the human and the divine—of which cooked food was the symbol and celebration—then this raw medley indicated that tonight he and his fellow guests were on their own among the bare facts of one another.

He was preparing to sample the mound of pink goo he had concluded was probably salmon dip when, wheat cracker poised for the plunge, he noticed the pale curve of a discarded fingernail garnishing the peak of the rosy heap. Behind the punch bowl, a pool of iced blood he wished was doctored lingonberry juice but smelled instead of cold beets, he spied a neglected platter of thumb-sized sausages of Odin-knew-what ingredients that actually looked to have been at least walked past a warm oven. He resolved to risk a taste, had the speared brown thing halfway to his lips when the small unnoticed woman on his right spoke up. "You're not going to put that in your mouth, are you?"

"Well," he looked her over, dark hair, dark eyes, tight body beneath an I USED TO BE WHITE T-shirt, "as a matter of fact, yes, I am."

"But it's meat."

"Yeah?" Suspicions already mottling the pure plane of possibility.

"It's got meat *in* it."

"I put meat into my mouth all the time," he replied, popping the morsel between chomping teeth, and I bet you do, too, he wanted to add.

"I am Ula," she announced in a change of voice, apparently conceding the lost nutritional point.

"Yeah?" He wiped greasy fingers on his damp pant leg. "Pleased to meet you." Or had they already met? After a couple of visits you came to believe you knew, on some level, everyone in the room. "I am"— significant processing pause as he awaited a suitably august equivalent to emerge onto the screen—"Solander."

"Whenever I nibble on a piece of fruit or vegetable," she went on, "I can literally feel my organs being cleansed. A gentle flushing action that leaves me vibrant and refreshed. And not only the body but my soul, too, washed shiny and new. You are aware, I suppose, that you also ingest the soul of whatever creature you eat?"

"Sure, that's the point, isn't it—to cop the sinewy power of those big beefy beasts?"

"But the animal's soul, the state it's in by the time you gobble it down. Are you aware of the details of modern slaughtering techniques?"

"Enlighten me."

"This is serious, you know, life-and-death stuff."

"You're worried about the state of your soul and you come to a party like this?"

"I'm a big girl. There's more to life than food."

"An actress, right?" Unable to stop munching indiscriminately on the proffered goodies, Perry popped an innocent-looking cherry tomato into his mouth and immediately began gagging, as tastefully as possible, on the creamy paste within, pureed clam whose souls were obviously confused.

"You're so psychic," she was saying, sarcastically. "You must be a Scorpio."

"I'm a Druid." He managed to clear his throat with a foul sip of Bergenspritzen, "the bold new Ice Age flavor" distilled from melting glacial shelves.

"Oh, one of those."

She didn't know a Druid from a drawing board. "So," he asked, "have I seen you in anything?"

"Own a VCR?"

"You're a Cool Cat."

"*Warm Satin Nights, Valentine Fanny, Cowgirls in Leather Chaps.*

The rocking horse in the bunkhouse with the specially designed saddle horn. That was me up top."

"Nice adductors." He studied her for a moment. "Listen, a slight confession. I'm an actor, too, and I think we should consider working together."

"Well, Saul, I have a rule: no action with strangers, no exceptions. I need to know the guy, I want to like him, I want to make a sincere picture. I want to have fun."

"Good rule."

Her eyebrows moved into a wry lift. "You'd be surprised by the number who disagree."

"Civilian dicks."

"You got it—don't know what they want, don't want what they get."

"Look, I have this car—well, a variant species of car, but it putts me from place to place and—"

She was shaking her head. "Can't. Got a gig here tonight."

"Not the crucifixion?"

"Don't tell me, you're Judas Priest."

"I'm the cameraman."

"You said you were an actor."

"I do both. I'm ambidextrous. A wizard with the lens. I'll shoot you like a goddess."

"I hardly need your help to look good."

"You know that's not what I meant."

"I don't know anything about you, other than your gross eating habits, your ridiculous name, your lying tongue."

"After we wrap, I'll drive you home."

"Persistent little guy, aren't you? Like I said, there's certain information I require: birth date, hobbies, favorite Beatle, HIV test results."

"To go for a ride?"

"Especially to go for a ride. Who knows what borders we might be obliged to cross?"

"Well, I'm afraid I don't pack the necessary documentation."

"Your mistake."

It occurred to Perry that the only access he was likely to achieve to the treasures hidden beneath Ula's provocative T-shirt would be provided through the intercession of a rolling camera. Personal rejection was interrupted, however, by the arrival of Ula's roommate, Morag, who was cinched into a black Vampirella gown, her face a chalky cosmetic mask, her lips a deep nocturnal blue. Ignoring Perry, she whispered gravely into Ula's bowed ear.

"I'm needed," Ula said.

"Fire in the hold?"

"No, this time, I'm afraid, it's in somebody's pants and Morag and I have been delegated to extinguish the blaze." She leaned in close and for one dazzling moment Perry believed he was about to be accorded the consolation of a perfumed kiss instead of the comment, sotto voce, "Be careful in the john. I think you peed on yourself." Then she patted him on the back—good fellow—and slipped away.

He was reinspecting his trousers, spreading tented folds of material between his fingers, when he realized he was not alone in his attentions. Then his nostrils were assailed by the funk of smoldering bog.

"Lose something?" asked Rags, waving his black cigarette about for emphasis.

"No, no, minor party accident, spilled a cup of mead, that's all."

"Enjoying yourself?"

Perry wasn't sure whether he meant the evening's revelry or Perry's own hand-on-leg action. "Yes," he admitted.

"Ah." Rags's mouth snapped open as if about to catch a reward biscuit. "The irresistible banality of sex."

Perry, a mere supplicant here at the feet of higher wisdom, smiled wanly.

"I am referring of course to the ludicrous behavior you can observe in tiresome progress all about us."

Clearly, a lesson was about to be imparted. It was Perry's task to receive it. Eric, Rags's wingman, hovering in routine formation off the chief's port side, was staring at Perry with the supremely bored expression of a government agent indifferent to the fact that he will derive no pleasure whatsoever from beating the living crap out of you. He had never uttered a word to Perry again after initially bringing him to the house, introducing him to the Nordic cross-sex team. Freya and Elsie, Rags and Eric—in how many directions did the current flow, or were these potential linkages simply poses, another set of veils hung between themselves and the public's inquisitorial fixations? In either case, the implied message was the same, a crucial aspect of Freya's overall program of applying, if not a blowtorch, then at least a scented candle to the hard edges of gender identity in her time, in her adopted place—The Soft Revolution, a campaign more subversive, more revolutionary, and, she hoped, more lasting than guns in the streets. Nature rewarded the pliable, let us follow her guide. The pity was that so many of her adherents, like sullen Eric here, were about as pliable as glass tubing.

"Freya remains amused by the game," Rags said, his head a disembodied apparition speaking from within a cloud of smoke, "but the enchantment for me, I'm afraid, is growing thin, rather like the walls between worlds at this precarious season of the year. Perry, do you know about Samain?"

Perry did not.

"My favorite holiday. Our worlds are in torment, you see, this urgent clamorous asylum of the senses and that silent majestic Other realm, grinding perpetually against one another like great invisible tectonic plates, and as the sun declines, the barriers are attenuated, pared daily by knives of darkness, until wall is reduced to membrane and membrane to rupture and the dead are permitted to mingle freely among us and we, if we possess the knowledge and so choose, may pass through into the land of the dead. These are events for which the word 'truth' was coined. A culture which elects to inhabit a fun house of falsity will, not surprisingly, find it difficult to locate these actualities.

"This, of course, is what we attempt here at the Bridge, create an atmosphere where one truth, actual sex, can be exalted. But what do we get? This comic book sex you Americans seem to wallow in. It is your charm, I suppose, the ground for your material success, the reason you are inundated with immigrants. Who does not love a good fairy story? But you want to make a cartoon of everything: your movies, your clothes, your furniture, your books, your food, but especially your sex. Everything bright and tasty. But this is a dirty game you are playing with yourselves. This ideal of honesty and openness is a pathetic fraud. You pretend to be so innocent when none of you are and it is this charade that is genuinely pornographic.

"Back home in western Iceland there is a holy place called Helgafell. Today busloads of tourists are shuttled in and out—the view of the mountainous coast is spectacular—but one thousand years ago this outcropping of rock was recognized as the site of a door into the Other World. It was sacred ground to which one prayed, you dared not gaze upon the hill unwashed. What rituals were practiced there we can only imagine. One night, intoxicated with the sagacity of the young, Freya and I snuck out onto the rock and committed our first act of renegade sex, a raid on normality. We ceremoniously stripped to our skin and made love like animals into the teeth of the wind and the groan of the sea. Sex under these circumstances is thrilling beyond fantasy and you have to wonder, why is that so? The exaltation of your blood, your muscled flesh, elevates your being, offers it up, whatever creature it is that lies sleeping along the twists and turns of your nerves is awakened, comes vividly alive like the magnetic field pulsing about a high-voltage line, its yellow eyes slide open and it rouses itself to a howl that is answered by the elements, your dragon calls to the dragon of the natural world and receives a gorgeous reply. This was the reality our ancestors moved within and one still available to us today through any of three separate doors: sex, art, and murder. And each of these separate acts, curiously and appropriately enough, partakes of equal elements of the other two. I think Freya is resisting, but eventually she will arrive at the logical end of our ideas. For the true revelation of all our work, even these silly erotic videos, is this: we do not know who we are.

"Well, scary stuff, boys and girls, and the only answer to dread, as our ancestors well knew, is ritual, the placation of fright. Because when you're out there in the living dark and suddenly feel a proprietary paw laid across your rabbity heart, upon the bag of meat you believed was you, what choice but to bow down in prayer, put on the armor of nakedness, the shield of grace.

"Nonsensical mumbo jumbo to modern ears, I know, hip trendettes like ourselves who prefer to take our doses of fever and musk at the end of a long camera spoon. The emotions cathedrals were once built to house now seem to have fled to the dark sanctuaries of our hallowed multiplexes. A temporary relocation only, I'm afraid. Each passing year the viewing rooms—who could call them theaters anymore?— get tinier, the screens shrink, become less awesome, as we approach, in all aspects of life, the dimensions of TV. Like the lady said, 'it's the pictures that got small'; unfortunately, so did we. But then, make-believe can only carry us so far, right, Perry? That's why I'd like you here for my Samain gala. It'll be a mindblower. Are you one of the warriors, Perry, a true berserker?"

Rags smiled, his teeth as old and yellow as the artifacts in Freya's office.

Before Perry could formulate a suitable response, Elsie arrived with news the shoot was about to begin. Perry's services were required out back. Elsie and Eric glared at one another with the unforgivable enmity of aides-de-camp to rival generals in the same army.

"Remember, Perry," cautioned Rags, "here be dragons"—and he touched his crotch—"and here"—his head—"and here"—his heart.

What an evening. His sensibility felt embarked on a perilous voyage, internal gyro beginning a wobble premonitory of on-your-back illness or another, less comprehensible mode of mental deficit where your remaining wits (a slapstick posse of armed clowns) find it necessary to circle the wagons and start rationing the ammo. His mood was not lightened by his initial glimpse of tonight's star, who had groomed and costumed himself into a passable likeness of the standard Caucasian Christ with the shoulder-length chestnut tresses, the manicured beard, the brown eyes, the white robe, the leather sandals, the complete complement of Hollywood props. It was a role Mr. Dyne had been in training for since puberty, crawling between the bedraggled tomato plants in his indulgent parents' backyard garden, homemade cross lashed to his bleeding back, impressive crown of thorns digging into his scalp, a series of Polaroids memorializing the event now circulating among the rowdy and the randy gathered to witness the transfiguration of those crude rehearsals into an elaborate full-dress and somewhat revised version of the four Gospels.

On the patio, to Perry's surprise, stood a blazing grill the size of a billiard table, its bloody array of spitting meats attended by a sweaty oxlike man who had quit a promising career in pro wrestling to run security for Cool Cat Productions—Freya's fame, though quartered off the blaring midway, still of sufficient intensity to attract its share of dangerous bugs. This illustrious worthy, barbecue implements in tattooed hands, posed behind the crackling flames, smoke streaming over him in a constantly rising curtain, the image of Vulcan at his forge.

Ingewald, the dwarf, sat forlornly on the grass, vomiting noisily into a silver ice bucket. A fellow countryman of the Baldurssons, he roomed in a Spartan basement cell (no pictures, no plants, no windows) beneath The Rainbow Bridge. He spent his days reading empirical philosophy, his nights on the phone with relatives back in Reykjavík. He had appeared in more than two dozen videos and was beloved by sexers of every taste.

"I don't feel so good, Perry, I'm afraid I might do something bad."

"What are you talking about? You're incapable of giving a bad performance."

"I don't mean videos, asshole, I mean in real life."

"How bad?"

"Things, you know. My head's tight. I've lost breathing space. I wake up in tears."

"I felt like that once."

"Really? What'd you do?"

"Isn't it obvious? I killed myself."

Perry had to move smartly to avoid being splattered by a flung bucket of multicolored stomach chunks, simultaneously dodging other wet matter that happened to be flying through his air space from sources unknown. The earlier prevailing tone of controlled riot seemed to be balancing now on the edge of something worse. There were men wearing tube socks as penis sheaths and women with G-strings fashioned out of dental dams. There were fistfights in the hydrangea, orgasms among the croquet wickets. Freya was over by the picnic table, setting up the Last Supper scene, the participants in sundry intemperate states of mind, too busy clowning around with the hot dogs and the pickles to pay much attention, until Mr. Dyne, in a character-breaking outburst, began berating his apostles—the flux of unexpected obscenities positively exhilarating—for gum chewing, talking out of turn, and touching one another inappropriately. Freya handed Perry the camcorder and told him to shoot on his own initiative, the theme of this scene: food as sex and sacrament. Perry's main impression: John the Baptist had an extremely long tongue.

The rest of the evening proceeded at a hallucinatory pace.

The rosebushes along the western wall of the house served as the garden of Gethsemane where an ex–Bronco fullback betrayed Mr. Dyne with a highly enthusiastic kiss involving an exchange of bodily fluids Freya frowned upon, but endorsed by the hearty applause of deranged onlookers.

Pontius Pilate, a six-foot Valkyrie in drag (another rumored dalliance of Freya's shipped in from the homeland), ordered Mr. Dyne to suck her dusty toes, after which she whipped him with her hair.

An eruption of lawn sprinklers sent actors and audience scurrying for cover through the mist and the rainbows, head and leaf baptized alike. An enraged Freya demanded the identity of the prankster who had dared to ruin her scene, but there was no one within twenty yards of the faucet except an unconscious drunk with a condom for a hat.

Objects continued to disclose for Perry an unnerving shimmer even after the water had been turned off. Was this the herald of a lunacy the opening to which he had already observed in his viewfinder? He worried about fainting at an inopportune time.

"I feel funny," he complained to Freya. "I think there's drugs in the food."

Freya replied in the grand manner, "I serve no drug but that of love."

Elsie scrutinized him as if he were a particularly offensively dressed mannequin.

"Let's do it," Freya barked, like an honest-to-God American.

Banks of hard light mounted on tall poles had been repositioned about the picturesquely gnarled oak, a supporting character in its own right, high wattage carving an illuminated cave out of the solid opacity of the night, spectators gathered round like the crew at the site of an important archaeological dig, tense, subdued, primed for awe.

Freya called "Action!" and Ula emerged from the darkness, clad in flimsy raiment of diaphanous veils she shed singly, artistically (Elvis dispensing stage scarves in Vegas the operative comparison), slithering across the floodlit space toward the tingling tree, more alive now than it had ever appeared in naked day, where Mr. Dyne, his scrawny arms strapped to a pair of Y-shaped branches, eyes girlishly aflutter, feigned to yield his hairless body into the ecstatic admixture of bliss and pain of which he fancied heaven was justly composed. The mesmerized crowd attended in lickerish silence, Freya squatting on a root barely out of camera range, the jeweled irises of several crouched cats glittering down from the upper limbs, the incense of grilled meat wafting lazily over all. Perry zoomed in for the close-up. The sight of Ula's virtuosic mouth working Mr. Dyne's floppy crank with an ardor even the jaded might term "indelicate" introduced a potent dose of skittering ambivalence into Perry's jeopardized systems. In accordance with the dictum "Peer long enough into the camera and the camera will peer into you" he seemed to split into two distinct but identical organisms, sharing between them nonetheless, like yoked twins a common heart, one tattered shuttlecock of an ego being batted from this perceptual center to that in a brisk volley that left him confused as to which self was the original or indeed whether such quaint concepts as "originality" were even valid, in both the ontological and epistemological senses. It was all Perry could do to keep the camera steady and aimed in the proper direction.

At the climactic moment Mr. Dyne tossed his moist head back against the ragged bark and emitted a scream so exaggerated, so cinematically feminine, onlookers stared about in bewilderment, uncertain whether to laugh, applaud, or rush to his aid. His dimpled chin dropped to his chest, lolled lifelessly to one side, and there was silence.

"Is he dead?" someone asked.

Perry focused in on Ula, who gave the elided camera the startled-doe gaze of one caught in a crime she had momentarily forgotten was illegal, the blankness persisting for only a beat before she flashed the loosest grin of the night, blew the lens a soulful kiss, and scampered nimbly for the house. Perry stopped tape. Mr. Dyne had not yet stirred, much of his audience, grown quite bored with his wooden impersonation, his rubber member, were already deep in the wholesome embrace of one another, naked duos, trios, quartets even, in all combos, distributed across the sloping lawn, heavily engaged in (insert favorite sexual practice), versatile Freya striding anxiously amid the fun, directing Perry's laggard camera from one novel clinch to the next, herself pursued by the twinge of melancholy (none must ever know) such a feast sometimes raised in her, the spectacle of the multitudes screwing too near to the god's-eye view of the multitudes dying. Editing, however, was the great anodyne—there she could maintain the flow of arousal through time, her way of sticking it to death in the ass.

"The woman is an absolute witch," someone said.

"Triple X certainly," said someone else, "but is it politically correct?"

Perry at this point, incertitude as real as a disease to him, was stumbling around inside the notion that perhaps not everything he was beholding through his trusty camcorder was actually "out there." The last image he remembered framing as an objective fact was of a dignified gentleman in a Vandyke beard, latex gloves, and nothing else, hunched behind a juniper bush, furiously masturbating onto a slice of wheat bread.

Events assumed a hyperreal clarity.

He saw Satan himself, an electric charcoal starter in each taloned fist, chasing a big-bottomed nymph into the garage. He saw, under a picnic table, Eric and Elsie with artistic gravity, shaving one another's pubic hair. He saw Mr. Dyne raised from the dead and floating in bright radiance above the roof, from which elevation he tossed frozen pizzas to the starving flock. He saw Senator Wilcox running a slimy tongue into Ula's flushed ear.

He understood this was the vision of the mad, the prophets, where all is revealed as it is. He had been blessed.

He had no memory of the drive home, one minute hearkening with a drunk's elaborate attentiveness to Freya's postproduction critique ("blasphemy should be, I don't know, more droll"), the next minute scientifically inspecting the damage to a ratty green Ford Galaxie of antique love-bead-era vintage he had just reshaped attempting to squeeze into the last available space on the block. He thought about leaving a note under the Galaxie's wiper, thought about hunting through a trash can for a scrap of paper, thought about borrowing a pencil from a passing hooker, thought about printing the words in large block letters for easy comprehension, thought . . . Then he was upstairs, blundering about the reduced space of his room—its puny dimensions apparent for the first time—the lamp too bright, the TV too loud, trying to open the lid on a jar of Planters peanuts with a Phillips screwdriver, unseen fist banging on adjoining wall of unseen room, outside sirens, shots, shouts in the street, weekend noise, neighbors partying on.

Sockless, he was shuffling among his stale possessions, mumbling silly nonsense to himself, the harmless old inmate revered for his longevity in an institution where they died young and hard in various stages of ego deficit, pants around his ankles (it had become urgent that the horrible pressure on his abdomen be relieved), alternately exalted—the king of video space!—and debased—the same genetic worm boring through his father's software now begun its fatal work on him—searching aimlessly for an irretrievable odd or end among vast collection of same, unable to locate what he couldn't remember he was looking for, puttering about in a thoroughly disturbing and disengaged manner when he heard, firehouse dog alert, the fucking behind the wall. Determined to avoid the previous disaster—had that only been earlier today?—he attended to the Record button personally, observing his own human finger reaching out to depress the button manually. Numbers began their reassuring roll across the camcorder's timer. He looked into the viewfinder and saw: a naked white man, limbs and torso slashed with bold strokes of black paint, kneeling in liturgical fashion before a naked black woman with matching strokes of white paint, "Oh," she was moaning, "oh, Tommy, oh," and without further sound or movement her head burst into lurid flame, the fire standing straight up off her skull, arms lifting in useless spasms as if seeking to confirm by touch the unimaginable. Perry gasped, recoiling from the sight, and in his haste to increase the distance between himself and the image tripped in the tangle of his pants, crashing backward into a favorite table plucked from the Dumpster in the alley, ashtrays, beer cans, cassettes clattering across the hard rugless floor, where he landed on his back, a sharp bottle of vitamin B complex jabbing into his left kidney. He lay there for an indeterminate period, considering the dry riverbed system of plaster cracks, assessing the situation. His psychic temperature did seem a tad elevated this evening, retinae probably not responsible for the reports his brain was receiving. Slowly, to avoid further mishap, he crawled back over to the camcorder, lifted one unsteady eye up to the viewfinder and saw: another eye, monstrous and icy gray, looking back. Pure panic. It's mine, he reasoned, over the heaving clamor of heart and lungs, ordinary lens reflection. If he were truly insane, would his own hallucinations be studying him?—a conundrum best left unexplored for now. Cautious as a private under fire, Perry raised his throbbing head to the parapet, braced himself for a third peek. The room was empty! The special photographer's bulb burned on behind its stained saffron shade. From a framed field of coarse madder the stylized Siamese on the wall with the elongated body and triangular head continued to regard him through abandoned eyes. The thin plastic-sheathed mattress had been stripped of its pilfered hospital sheets. Room 512 was as devoid of life as a room could be. In the morning, should these symptoms persist, perhaps Perry ought to pay a call to the local human resource center for a low-income reality check. He turned then and noticed the open door he obviously had, in his befuddlement, neglected to close, let alone lock, the private idiocies, discomfitures of these last few hours on public exhibit for hallway creeps dragging their fungoid flesh to and from the reeking stall opposite the stairwell, how acute his embarrassment had his faculties been intact, when would this life ever mend? another inquest to be recycled into another day as suddenly he knew—the fine hairs of his neck so informed him—he was not alone, no, a shadow shared this space, his fetch perhaps, if a fetch slipped about in khaki trousers and painted feet, one such leg planted now at the edge of his frame solid as the trunk of the oldest beech, Go! screamed the hairs, the wind from the future playing over his nerves, and he wished, he wanted, but it was too late, he was too late, story of his life, as the long painted arm with the big big gun swung inevitably toward him, it was an illusion, he wasn't sure how it was done, but it touched his head, and then he knew he was falling, he knew precisely what was happening until the moment he didn't because EVERY-THING CHANGED.

Six

THE QUEEN OF DIAMONDS

HER dream name was Melissa. She lived in Chicago, or sleep's facsimile of that mythic city, under the haunted arrogance of its towers, in a shadowy winter light of alienated intimacy. A reluctant grownup, she preferred the loud garb of children, the bright frocks, the arbitrarily numbered oversized jerseys, loose jumpers with fuzzy animals embroidered on the bibs, her radiant red hair either pulled into a sleek ponytail or separated into cute girlish braids. She liked cheap jewelry, too, of the plastic, clunky variety, the weight of a dozen toy chains around her neck, arms rattling in bracelets from wrist to elbow. If a creep tried to get friendly, she'd kick him in the groin with her steel-capped lineman's boots. Goodness, this grocery store was large, bigger than a football stadium, miles of aisles, each strangely empty. No exit but the checkout lanes, and to pass through there you needed to make a purchase. There were guards in white masks. Her cart wobbled and squeaked and was almost impossible to steer. The bland piped-in music was driving her mad. Would this curse ever be lifted, or was it her fate, as the fabled Wandering Consumer, to trace these mocking aisles to the final decline and fall of Late-Stage Capitalism itself? Happily, she wouldn't have to wait, for there on the last shelf of the last aisle stood one forlorn can of fancy-cut green beans and she experienced a rush of relief positively erotic in intensity. Why? She hated green beans.

Late in the afternoon Jessie Horn awoke to the dreary realization that there now existed a possibility (not a certainty) she might (not would) dissolve into embarrassing tears during one of the night's numerous weddings. Well, she thought not. Last time she had cried hard enough to pickle a memory, Garrett was being led, bloodied and handcuffed, toward the waiting patrol car, her name a curse upon the night. Since then, her tender tissues had been scraped and cleaned and replaced with steel, and steel didn't leak. Pathos would have to take its place in line behind several other clamorous emotions. The face glaring back at her in the bathroom mirror was one she refused to acknowledge. And her hair was no dreamy red either but a horrid nest of peasant black she carried on her shoulders like a bundle of charred nettles. This was going to be a long day. She threw on a SAVE THE UNIVERSE T-shirt, a pair of jeans, and hurried out to pick up the kids.

Cammie, a tattered sheaf of fresh Crayola drawings in hand, was already patiently waiting outside Moe Dalitz Elementary; at Lucky Duck Daycare Jessie had to dash inside herself, scoop up one cranky Bas and flee, while simultaneously bestowing air kisses and gratitude upon the frazzled staff. Back in the car the children, ever alert to Mommy's moods, sat so unusually still, observing traffic, the passing phantasmagoria, Jessie wanted to stop right in the middle of the Strip and give them each a big hug. Weirder things had happened on this boulevard, but a public display of affection, an interruption of the mystic cash flow, would probably get her in real trouble. These days she was, as a practical survival mechanism, dedicated to the art of avoidance, her true goal the achievement of a state of personal invisibility. She wanted to be in attendance in life, she just didn't want anyone noticing her. Unfortunately, for reasons inexplicably arcane, the gaudiness of her own plumage being transparent to her, she was a person other people liked to look at. A crowd was not a warm solvent she could melt into but a crystallized field of bored anxious eyes. So amusement parks were not favorite places, but here she was on her way to Kid Kountry, a bloated monument to sensory redundance, price gouging, and group fun, because a promise was a promise and she had already reneged twice in the past two weeks.

For the children each visit was a ritual that must be performed in proper sequence or the magic was lost. First, a ride on the reduced-scale Union Pacific encircling the park and its celebrated attractions: the biggest video arcade in the Mojave, a grand circus tent containing three rings of nonstop acts, a miniature golf course depicting major events in the life of Elvis Presley (free game to all holes in one down the toilet bowl on the eighteenth), an enormous whale-shaped swimming pool from which every fifteen minutes spewed a geyser of water to drench the unwary and amuse everyone else, and a monitored recreation area consisting of sturdy reproductions of the world's wonders where children could build sand castles in the Coliseum, race up and down the steps of the Aztec Temple of the Sun, play hide-and-seek in Stonehenge, or tumble giddily down the crimson-coated throat of Hawaii's Kilauea volcano. Then it was off to the petting zoo for an extended session of touchy-feely-smelly with animals more commonly enjoyed in the kitchen and dining room than roaming at will about the house. Then forty-five minutes (renegotiated to an hour) feeding quarters into video games of exuberant violence, followed by ice cream cones from a vendor apparently dressed as a pimp, a stop at the batting cage for Cammie, who was already wondering why there were no girls on major league baseball teams, and a peek inside the big top to see if the killer klowns, Cammie's favorites, had been loosed yet upon an unsuspecting audience, but just past the entrance, lounging inside a cage air-conditioned so, the sign said, he would not get mad and break the bars, was a large male gorilla Bas took one look at and began to cry, a sign it was time to go. And through it all Jessie had not been unaware of the gray-haired, gray-faced man smoking a cigarette and leaning against the far rail as the train passed or the trio of jocks in matching shorts and UNLV caps waiting on line at the Devil's Drop or the two women with babies on the bench outside the rest room or the preening lifeguard with an abdominal scar or the bald-headed tourist in sunglasses who actually appeared to have taken her picture in front of his family or any of the several others she protected herself against through a willed act of psychic dislocation in which her body was rendered secretly unavailable for the fantasies, wishes, projections of strangers. Or so she hoped.

From the driveway Jessie could see through the plant-choked window Nikki fiddling around at the sink, but by the time she got the kids herded from car to house the kitchen was eerily empty. Okay. The mystery of the human relationship: a question with no answer?—tune in tomorrow.

For dinner Jessie made the children grilled cheese sandwiches, a request-night special, each prepared exactly the same way, cut into exactly the same pieces. She then settled into the chair between Cammie and Bas, mommy cop on break with a cup of coffee, the day's paper, her physical presence a barrier to further trouble as she attempted, for one minute, to lose herself down the caffeine chute amid titillating reports of catastrophes too distant to touch her life in any serious way.

"I don't want to go to Mamaw's," announced Cammie. "I want to go with you and get married."

"You're awfully young yet, honey." A respected Texas businessman had strangled his wife with her aerobics unitard and run off with his transsexual lover. The world in its course. "Who would you marry?"

"I want to marry Bas."

"No!" her brother shrieked. Whatever marriage was, he wanted no part of it.

"Yes!"

"No!"

"Yes!"

"No!"

Nikki appeared in the doorway, hair tied in her traditional impending-doom knot on top of her head. She said, with the determination of one who has carefully considered her position, "I'm getting a gun."

"Fine," Jessie replied, then, "That's enough!" to the children who were trying to get at one another with their fists.

"Maybe I can lift one of Pop's. He wouldn't miss it."

"Do what you have to do." She slapped the back of Cammie's hand and now it was Cammie's turn to cry.

"Well, I don't see why I have to be more worried about this situation than you."

"You don't. I can handle Garrett."

Nikki paused for a moment. "I'm getting two guns."

In the universe of the spirit every individual was a sun. Lovers and friends revolved in nearby orbits. Families gathered in constellations. Gravity impelled these bodies toward one another. Gravity was love and love was indeed grave. For if, more often than not, the music of the spheres resembled a howl of celestial feedback, that was because harmony was under eternal besiegement by evil centrifugal forces. The alignment of bodies in a pleasing and enduring pattern was devilishly difficult. A longtime stargazer, Jessie was still trying to read the proper signs, dodge the occasional space junk. Having weathered eclipse, asteroid showers, the shattering of worlds, she had learned the importance of keeping one eye acutely on the sky. And what exactly was it she was witnessing now: an ominous flaring in the heavens or a reflection on her lens?

"Oh, that's just your paranoia," Nikki had said last night. "Everything's the same as it ever was."

"That's what I'm afraid of," Jessie replied.

Why was it so damned impossible to love one good person cleanly, honestly, and have that love returned in kind without trial, without tragedy, without tears? When she died, she hoped all this would be made clear.

Tonight Cammie and Bas would get an extra kiss, an extra-tight hug, before being bundled off to Mamaw Odie's with favorite toys, pillows, individual security blankets essential for physical as well as emotional comfort since Mamaw's year-round air-conditioning was potent enough to chill a ham in the living room in the middle of July. Mamaw Odie was also the former Candy Cain, now retired, a highly popular masseuse at the Bucking Bronco Ranch in Nye County, six feet of lean woman in pink hot pants and white go-go boots, a specialist in the Venusian Love Burn and the Crème Spritzer, her trademark boast: "I can get any man, straight, drag, or fag, hard as a tent stake in less than a minute." When she quit the trade it was to marry a runty bowlegged deputy sheriff who flagged her for a speeding violation, "I got the ticket, and I got the man, as hetero a guy as any you'd want to meet," and five months later gave birth to Jessie, crouching, so she claimed, in a ditch like an Indian squaw out on the road to Bullhead City, a leather belt between her teeth. When Jessie was seven the deputy died of a heart attack while waiting in an optometrist's office for a new pair of prescription sunglasses. Everyone had always pretended he was really Jessie's father. Maybe he was.

"You got that Paiute blood in you," her mother said, "why you act the way you do."

"You're a racist, Odie," Jessie complained, "and a homophobe, too."

"I put up with you, don't I?" replied quick-witted Mom.

The kids loved Mamaw, her wide-screen TV, her weakness for sweets, her little dog, Shasta, who could count to ten, the "hootchie-cootchie" dance she did to make them laugh, and her new friend, Tito, who drank a bottle of beer, wiggled his ears, and stood on his head in his underwear. More entertainment, more nonnutritional treats, more customized coddling than you could get for cash at Kid Kountry. Their periodic complaints, the fidgeting, the dawdling, were really expressions of employee burnout, the nightly expedition to Odie's marking the third shift of an interminable day sister and brother had already come to understand was divided naturally into eight-hour segments only one of which was spent at home, useful indoctrination for future service workers of America. At least the security of Jessie's children was assured during these dark hours of maximum danger, no vacillating about firearms in this house, Mamaw had been locked and loaded since the Kennedy assassination.

Alone now, for the first time since waking, Jessie and Nikki sat inside the moving car stiffly as strangers of different tongues locked together in an iron cell, sullen fields of silence swelling aggressively at one another, each trying to trigger a lapse into defensive speech. A psychological experiment Jessie certainly had no patience for.

"No gunnysacking," she commanded. "Fair fight rules strictly enforced."

"They're my emotions, Jessie, I'll do with them as I please, thank you."

"Aha, a glint. C'mon, open up that Pandora's box, show us all your pretty treasure."

The car traveled on in its own sound, windows closed against an unseasonably early chill.

"When have I ever hidden the truth from you?" Nikki asked.

"Please. Sincerity is secrecy's other face. Truth in a suspicious mouth is still suspect."

Nikki waited a beat. "Go on. I don't want to miss a single one of these witty aphorisms. You've been reading behind my back."

Jessie breathed it in, breathed it out again. "Without me," she said, "you wouldn't have a problem like Garrett in your life."

"Sure, but I wouldn't have you, either. No one's clean, Jessie, we're always dropping baggage at one another's feet."

"Not all of it armed and dangerous."

"Well, as I said, I'm making moves to deal with that issue."

"Sometimes, Nikki, I think you look at me and see Garrett sitting here. I think some shit's been flung at the wrong target."

Shadows played tag across Nikki's impassive face. "I'm sorry you feel that way," she said. "I apologize. But I worry about things, I get tense."

"I'm worried, too," Jessie said. "About us."

"We're solid," Nikki assured her. "This ol' boat may rock a bit from time to time, but we ain't gonna drown."

Jessie dared the full strength of Nikki's gaze, she had weird green eyes from outer space few mortals could resist. "Truth?" she asked.

"Truth," Nikki pronounced emphatically. She waited then until the turn onto Fremont, into the naked incandescence of Glitter Gulch, the heart of a city at the heart of the country, their bleached faces exposed to immeasurable gales of cascading light, electric streams jeweling the skin, before inquiring, in all sincerity, "Who do you see when you look at me?"

Well. For Jessie, an intolerably complex question. Her "knowing" eye tended to get lost in people, in the ornate and patterned beauty of their strata and schist, in the transparent shapes time sculpted in the dark, the mesmerizing quirks, the harsh elegance, laminated canyons and smoky peaks testifying to the nova at the soul's core, the perpetual womb of images, the dance of savage possibility. Beneath such scrutiny proportions were onerous to maintain, the concept of a bounding wholeness relegated to triviality. The examined Other slipped out of focus, a certain ghostliness prevailed. The more you knew, the less stable the object of your knowledge. Mind haunted the world like a devouring demon. What did she see? She saw cracks and fissures and chinks. She saw her past rising up through the crust at her feet.

The Happy Chapel was a white, heart-shaped bungalow with heart-shaped windows and a heart-shaped door conveniently located north of the Strip directly across the boulevard from Stowe, Eyck, and DeKeeler, Bail Bonds. Out front on the green cement lawn a tiptoed Cupid, wings aflutter, squirted from pouty lips an eternal stream of blue-colored water into a marble pool deep in good-luck coins and casino chips. Ruby neon script said WEDDINGS in one window, OPEN in the other. Like the fountain, neither sign was ever turned off. Every inch of the interior (except the four chapel rooms, which were designed to individual motifs: Traditional, Grecian, Medieval, and Futuristic) had been decorated in some variant of red, exotic furnishings of silk, satin, velour, damask, and leather all dyed a mad fiery hue. Jessie worked in the left ventricle, The Bridal Shoppe, peddling rings, flowers, cakes, garters, intimate honeymoon apparel, and assorted local souvenirs of dubious taste, and renting gowns and tuxedos to anxious unprepared couples. In her duty heels and tight skirt and sucking on a cinnamon lollipop, she often referred to herself as Suzi Sugargram, your glazed Kewpie tart. She hated Valentine's Day with a passion.

Jessie toiled in "nuptials" because Nikki did, too, and Nikki was there because The Happy Chapel was owned and operated by her parents, Bud and Glenda Hardwick. Bud, or Reverend Pop as he was known to family and trusted friends, had been one of the true Vegas pioneers. Classified 4-F in 1942, having lost his trigger finger in a suspicious farming accident the year before, he had drifted out from Barstow to work at the magnesium plant in the Valley, making flares to help illuminate the American war effort. The hand his country had rejected was, nevertheless, sound enough to wield a hammer, and in the late forties he was part of the construction crews that built the Thunderbird and the Desert Inn. Money was flowing into the Nevada basin like water down a spout. Bud wanted some of it. He positioned himself in conspicuous places where he was eventually seen by Gus Golden of the Scheherazade, who hired him largely to follow Gus around and maintain a certain background presence, the missing finger contributing a useful defining note to intricate business negotiations. Prosperous for the first time in his life, suit pockets jingling, he married a local girl he met at an auto dealers' convention at the hotel, Glenda, Miss Atomic Blast of 1956. In 1957 Gus Golden was found in a trunk at the Trenton train station and Bud Hardwick found religion. It was a traumatic conversion: Jesus broke his life in two, tossed the first half into the fiery dumper. Bud staggered around penniless for several years, handing out Bibles to hell-bound tourists. Former business associates passed him on the street without a flicker of recognition, the old Bud was gone, it was as if the plasma of his identity had been abruptly extracted, exposed to a new type of light, then thoughtlessly reinstalled with the unprospected flats thrown into rough relief, familiar prominences reduced to background shadow. Thus was born Reverend Pop, an apostle in white shoes, green pants, and silver jacket, who smoked fifty Kools a day, sported a diamond cross-shaped pinkie ring, cursed like a private but wouldn't tolerate it in others, a tacit connoisseur of the visual splendor of big-breasted brides. He understood why, as a malnourished choleric five-year-old, he had been abandoned by his divorced mother to senile grandparents he barely knew—the way to the holy city was laid with bricks of pain. His ministry had been set by the Lord at the beginning of time. He would celebrate the sacrament of marriage in a desert of sin.

And so he had, but not without, on several occasions, endangering his own. Glenda, whose highest aspiration had always been nothing less than a spotlighted lead in the enchanted world of showgirldom, didn't know what to make of this access of religious fervor into their lives. When it was accompanied by an exodus of cash, she threatened to leave. Preaching was a loser's game, a break-even proposition at best, as far as she could determine, and she hadn't planned in her life on putting in time with losers. It rubbed off on you, she'd seen it happen again and again at the gaming tables. Losing was a virus you inoculated yourself against with a many-digited bankroll. Now suddenly she seemed to be getting sick and she was not happy. She cried, Bud prayed. Then she discovered she was pregnant, too—the virus was mutating—and, abducted by a mutinous heart, Glenda sailed off into the siren archipelago of serial affairs. Bud waited and prayed, a rock to come back to. Turned out the loose change she was able to gather on these extracurricular excursions amounted eventually to a pile large enough to trade in on the famous white bungalow where Bud and Glenda had been herding couples down the aisle now for more than thirty years, and if the smooth functioning of this matrimonial machine required certain emollients obtainable only in certain nondomestic locales, then Glenda's periodic absences were a demanding but vital sacrifice. Age had not changed Glenda so much as gently baked her; the skin was more creased and closer to the bone, but she retained her beauty, her animal spirits, her magnificent head of curly red hair that trembled like a charged helmet of metal shavings as she hustled impatiently about the chapel, charming her customers, badgering her employees, dosing each room with her trusty can of rose air freshener. Everyone said Nikki was just like Glenda, an accusation denied without much tact by mother and daughter alike, but both parents obviously loved their grownup wayward child—their only heir—and they liked Jessie, too.

The women had been granted complete operating supervision of the graveyard shift, Nikki out on reception, Jessie in back with the trinkets. Usually there was more than enough "action" to maintain that nice steady hum of profitable enterprise and engaged labor (in this case a fun-loving staff of organist, photographer, limo driver, and assorted on-duty ministers who tended, whenever the pace slackened, to gather in unproductive clumps about a beguiling pack of cards), so the boredom quotient remained relatively low. For Jessie the people were her entertainment, this unending procession filing past her counter two by two, nervous, awkward, the sense of exposure painfully acute, each hoping they were not going to get dumped overboard before reaching the Mount Ararat of nuptial bliss. Everyone knew the odds, you'd have better luck betting on the Super Bowl, yet still they came and Jessie loved them all, though her daily astonishment at many of these hopeful matches was a reflex she doubted she could ever lose. Her naïveté over the choices people made seemed virtually indestructible. What could this one possibly "see" in that one? Of what did this "seeing" consist? Important questions in her own life, complete enigmas in someone else's. The wisdom she had expected to gather at her listening post on eros's perimeter amounted so far to this: love is blind;

hope springs eternal; you can't judge a book by its cover; monkey see, monkey do; etc. Which could be, for all she knew, exactly the tacky guise wisdom would delight to clothe itself in.

What she knew she did have in place of a higher understanding was a storehouse of tales, anecdotes, snapshots, punch lines, and plaints from assorted humans at their most vulnerable and bizarre. The primitive force field generated by a bona fide wedding ceremony was of sufficient authority to dampen the apparent magnitude of a superstar. Of which The Happy Chapel had seen its share. Jacqui Best was married here (both times), as were Phil Jakes, Rhoda Darling, and the incomparable Tara, who arrived with her complete entourage of eighteen in two white stretch limos moments ahead of a frantic press convoy of at least a dozen trucks, vans, and rented cars, precipitating a traffic jam and near riot that lasted until long after the giddy bride and her eighteen-year-old bodybuilder groom had been whisked surreptitiously away in the backseat of Nikki's Hyundai, where their marriage vows were clumsily yet effectively consummated before reaching McCarran Airport.

But in a democratic enterprise such as this, fame mingled routinely with anonymity, and the memorable was a haphazard compound of the two, its greater portion proving to Jessie's satisfaction the absurdity of that oxymoronic phrase "the average person." There was, for instance, the obnoxious pig who, ten minutes before the ceremony, offered to ditch his shocked bride and marry Jessie instead. Or the Englishman with his arm in a cast and his right eye goggled behind a superfluous monocle who said he was getting coupled because "everyone dies, right?" as if the remark carried indisputable heft while the woman with him, dazed and silent, appeared woefully uncertain of her whereabouts. Or the busload of Korean tourists who pulled up unannounced one busy night, got married en masse, then couldn't stop joking about doing it all over again, as if the Vegas chapel experience were a variety of amusement park ride. Or the high roller with the low forehead and diamond-embedded incisors who tipped everyone in the place, including the next couple, one hundred dollars each. Or the legendary invasion of the pasta people, when an entire Hollywood movie crew, every collagen-glutted face and vacuumed gut bound to a different set of dietary restrictions, occupied the chapel for a diverting three days filming the key wedding scene of *In a Family's Way*, the offbeat romantic thriller about a young, handsome DEA agent who falls in love with the young, beautiful daughter of a Colombian drug lord and the wacky comedy of manners that ensues when the daughter, now pregnant, discovers that doting hubby was the murderer of her mother and brother in a previous bust and has recently been assigned to bring in her father, dead or alive. Every member of The Happy Chapel staff was in it, either playing themselves or posing as casual witnesses while Reverend Pop conducted the seasoned leads through their "I do's" over and over and over again. Surprise lesson for the uninitiated: infinite were the readings of a single line. Besides the Reverend, Jessie was the only other "civilian" assigned a speaking role; given the privilege of replying "Yes" to a passing question of Jason Ladue's, the young actor playing the DEA agent, she discovered at firsthand the swoops and echoes that can be contained within the ample space of a simple three-letter one-syllable word. She also discovered that up close the well-tended nap of Mr. Ladue's appearance offered evidence of wear completely absent from his big-screen image. When she finally viewed the finished product, on videocassette at a friend's house, having missed the theatrical release, as did perhaps most of the country, she was horrified to see personal physical defects magnified into inescapable lapses of moral will and presented without comment to a nation's critical regard: her hips were too wide, her hands too narrow, her nose too long, her thighs too thick, her eyebrows too light, and her hair . . . well, of course, her hair. At least her smile was pleasant, the toothy product of a Nikki-encouraged self-improvement plan to boost Jessie's hostess rating, her face in normal repose subject apparently to such hostile interpretation several clients had commented openly about it. Smile, damnit, you're in the hospitality business! So she had practiced, the obedient employee, at wedging blocks of consciousness up under those droopy facial muscles until now, whenever she was deliberately sharpening herself against her mood, as was often the case, the resulting persona could work to stunning effect. "You're the nicest young lady I've met in the entire state of Nevada," declared the nastiest, oldest widow in the country (she was eloping with her Albanian chauffeur) an instant after Jessie had realized how pretty the woman would look with her mouth stuffed full of mothballs and a wire coat hanger twisted around her short wattled neck. Viva, Las Vegas.

On the rare slow night, Jessie's attention might be arrested for un-tolled moments by the neon palm burning in her window. It was an amazingly detailed rendering, this animated tree of brittle tubing and electrified gas, renowned emblem of the Ishtar Gate, world's largest casino and hotel, sprouting from the night like a growth out of another, more vivid, more clever land where memories were diamonds and she was their queen: sweet doughy dimples on the back of Bas's jam-stained starfish hand . . . carving her name into Suzyn's basketball shoe with a dull X-acto blade . . . bottle of black Armored Slut nail polish cemented in its own goo to her desk top . . . Tappy the tattered sock kitten, button eyes and felt ears sacrificed in battle to one of his furrier relatives . . . dead purple corpse skin of the iris Hector gave her on the bus to Phoenix . . . Cammie's candy breath "I love you" tickling at her ear . . . winter storm in the Rockies, every separate flake falling at the same forty-five-degree angle, the same mesmeric rate . . . lipstick skulls on the mirror in the girls' locker room . . . the light on the lake the morning she lost her virginity, everything she was and was-to-be instantly apprehensible in the direct eloquence of sunfire on water . . . child's flecks of honest gold in Garrett's haunted eyes, ore for miners more intrepid than she . . . the broken emotions of a windup rabbit lying in cop-car shadow on the stubbled lawn . . . Nikki's naked body curled innocently into the protective cave of sleep . . . these glints shining through the black waste of her past with a cut clarity, a hard elegant persistence, domestic trivia yielding private significances as momentous as any public event, the day-to-day increments of the heart and the motion of the sky and the transit of the mountain and the voice of the sand—the cards you were dealt, the ones you played without complaint, you knew the gamble and you knew you could turn a winning hand.

Her first lover was a kid named Dow Webb who'd ridden in on Greyhound from St. Cloud, Minnesota, top of the world, age of twenty-one. His Uncle Early knew a guy who knew a guy. City was his for the asking. So was Jessie. She was impressed by his smile, his confidence, his chest. She was seventeen, running the streets at night with a pack of girls in an adults' play town with too little to occupy the restless and the underaged. They met one hot dangerous 3 a.m. out at the neon graveyard on Cameron Street, where Jessie and Luane and Suze (the Three Mousseketeers) and Dow and a pair of wire cutters were all attempting to breach the fence in quest of valuable sign junk. "I'm uh looking for an S," said Dow, wiggling his hands in his pockets, striking a pose no less effective for its obviousness. "Is that your initial?" Jessie asked. "Uh no actually uh I like the uh shape." She liked his, too.

Six weeks later they were living together in a trailer at the Anasazi Motor Court, eating macaroni out of chipped coffee mugs, screwing and squabbling under the omniscient eye of the manager, Mrs. Frank Lloyd, a diabetic with sad gray skin and a crippled terrier named Ralph who'd take an eager nip out of anyone foolish enough to try to pet him. Dow and Jessie's rent was always late, their electrical service often interrupted for nonpayment, but Mrs. Lloyd rarely complained; these kids were not only the children she'd never had, they were the best entertainment she'd enjoyed since *Three's Company* went into reruns.

During this period Jessie skipped from job to job, unable to maintain interest in activities she regarded as bankrupt to begin with. Life then was a hostile fluid you patrolled like a shark, never relaxing, never lingering, you had an important destination, as yet unknown, but ceaseless movement would steer you there. She worked variously as a waitress, a dog groomer, appropriately dressed attendant at the Bikini Fun Car Wash, telephone operator, telephone sales rep, tour guide at the Liberace Museum (the tears! the laughter! the opera buffa!— she quit in two days), until finally, on the recommendation of Lindsay Hoyle, who'd been in art class with her at Benny Binion High, she got hired as a brush technician at Lou Fox's Ars Maximus (formerly Monets for Monies). Inside a studio large as a railroad terminal she sat at an easel alongside ninety-nine other "brush techs," slapping out hotel room art at a modest assembly-line pace. Turned out Jessie had a special knack for knocking out Vermeers, an unexpected sensitivity to the poetry of objects, the psychology of light, the inherently transcendent nature of a quiet human space—qualities to soothe the weary traveler staggering back to his rented room in the dyspeptic dawn with eight clammy cents in his pants and no future, in this life or the next. Mr. Fox was impressed; he slipped her a bonus, he boosted his visits to her stool, where his hands, willful creatures that they were, began lightly stroking the downy cords of her neck, kneading the artist's cramp from her back. Jessie endured these horrid massages as long as she could—she really liked this job—but she could feel the swamp in his touch and understood that her boat would not be one rising with the tide. So eventually, regretfully, she gave notice earlier, for once, than she liked, but no big deal, she wanted to lie around the house, too.

For nearly a year the drill had been this: reel home from the wonderful world of work (ticket irrevocably stamped minimum-wage rides only) to find Dow lounging about in his underwear, attended by two or three of his grotty friends with ridiculous names like Badger, Six-Deck Vic, Moe the Mucker, names she had no interest whatsoever in attaching to the proper faces, they were his good buddies, not hers, obsessed devotees of The System, that ever-mutating, ever-iridescent path to blackjack's Holy Grail. The secret mechanics of The System were hopelessly intricate, its parlance—splitting, doubling down, hi-lo differential—an insider's code, but the mainspring seemed to involve a species of card counting, a task Jessie could hardly imagine Dow mastering since whatever stores of patience and concentration he had managed to haul down with him from the north country had been thoroughly consumed out here in the great southwestern fry pan of loss and disappointment. His mood had grown progressively reptilian, especially when the guys were gone and Jess was drafted into dealing to him, hand after hand of relentless beejay until her fingers were sore, her head throbbed under the glare of the kitchen fluorescent, the sickening slap of the cards punctuated by his high-pitched shrieks, "No, goddamnit! How many times I got to tell you, dealer stands on seventeen, always, always, always, you idiot!" And she thought, you don't know me, you don't know my secrets.

Yet there was a certain piece of her at the hard durable center—the last portion up the flue when any good American was cremated—that answered to Dow's challenge and the nature of his obsession. He attacked his game with a fervor suggesting the enormity of the stakes, more than mere money, for the entrancing beauty of Vegas consisted in the promise that here in the desert sand the problems of life could be not so much reduced as *clarified* into a simple mathematical knot, then quickly "solved" by the application of the appropriate theoretical blade. It was the rare Yankee-Doodle jill or johnny who escaped being touched by the poignant magic of such belief.

Hungry Dow had been searching for elements of The System since he was a little kid, running a casino complete with toy roulette wheel in the basement of his home in Minnesota, schooling other little kids in the valuable art of losing gracefully, painful previews of a future they would recognize too late. His own destiny, obvious even at this precocious age, was to win, whether by cheating ten-year-olds out of their lunch money or lying to his parents, what did it matter as long as debits were avoided. He was different, he experienced defeat physically, loss equivalent to a bullet to the chest, so when at last he achieved his boyhood dream of getting to Vegas and the city responded by employing his body for target practice, he died into rages only time and convalescence from the gaming tables could cure. Jessie usually left the trailer for Mother's house until optimism returned. That was the greatness of America, hope swam forever in the air before your eyes. And sometimes, just often enough to keep you hooked, faith was rewarded, like the afternoon Dow won $5,500, rushed home with the news, then proceeded to fuck Jessie for more than four straight hours without losing his hard-on. So she learned of the erotic radiance of money. "You know," he told her confidentially, "you can coast through this burg on a twenty-four-hour sex high." Perhaps. But that required you to keep winning and she didn't know any casino bugs who were cruising on anything stronger than desperation adrenaline. Gradually, without fanfare, it became the drug of choice in their house.

Money withdrew from their lives like the receding tide; silences lengthened; Dow's precious wooden carving of Ho Tei, the Chinese god of luck, was fondled, caressed, and rubbed with a tender devotion Jessie had never known. She kept expecting him to attack her; and though he fumed, he raged, verbal assaults sharp as claws on her flesh, he never laid a hand on her in anger or in love.

Time ran on without them, Dow at his cluttered table of soiled cards and useless charts, waiting for the Wheel to turn, Jessie at the bedroom window, studying the desert outside for clues. The desert neither waited nor hoped, it endured. The Lizard God remembered when rock flowed like a river, remembered when it would again, the passage between these events no more than the blink of one hooded implacable eye. This town is doomed, she thought, and we, its in-habitants.

And then one perfectly lucid morning she looked at this stranger she'd been sharing her life with for over a year and saw him for the first time and, unable to contain herself, such was the force of sheer astonishment, she blurted out, in all innocence, the fundamental question, "Who are you?"

In reply, Dow flung a full deck of cards into her open face, keen edges cutting at her forehead, her nose, her lips. She was too shocked to respond. Beneath the surface, where words ceaselessly arranged themselves into argument and rationalization, she understood that the Dow part of her life was finished. All that remained was for this truth to float to the top, turn its bloated belly to the light, for her to initiate the series of withdrawal actions that would end with her back in her old room down the hall from Mother, reliving the nightmares of her childhood (gargoyles on the bedposts, the lady machine in the closet with surgical instruments for hands, the trapdoor under the bed where clacking fingers lurked to drag her down to subterranean bondage as a zombie toxic worker in the polluted mills of the future), a headachy muddle of days spent fending off her mother's nagging ("the man held no chips, I could see it in his eyes"), the hideous advances of her mother's boyfriends, older, incontinent versions of Dow with bad skin tone and less brains. When she'd lifted enough bread from these besotted boyfriends' pockets to finance her getaway, she immediately fled into a new apartment, a new life.

She got a job as a dancing slave girl at Nero's Feast. In a week she was dating Spartacus. His real name was Garrett Pugh and he was handsome and kind and not without grand ambitions of his own, such as the realization of one hundred million dollars (a meager one million no longer seemed quite sufficient) by the age of thirty-five, the year his father unexpectedly died of a routine flu virus. The fact that Garrett was determined to amass this wad by one day operating his own casino endeared him instantly to Jessie—at last, a man working the right side of the tables. By day Garrett carried a spear through Nero's Feast; at night he attended classes at Tom and Jerry's Dealers School, tales out of which only confirmed Jessie's long-held suspicions: the first week was devoted to how customers cheat, the remaining five weeks to how to cheat the customers. Like Dow, he was rarely without a deck in his hands, and eventually Jessie learned not to flinch at the sound of cards being riffled. Trust, a wary but ultimately loyal dog, returned to take up residence inside her, glad to find the bed still warm, the bowl full. Garrett brought her back to the person she was when she first met Dow, and for that, she loved him. His eyes were a soulful brown, his lips the softest she'd ever kissed, she laughed a lot when he was around. They were married, coincidentally, at The Happy Chapel by Reverend Pop in a ceremony so brief their wedding pictures, she liked to joke, were a series of shots of an empty room. One month later she was pregnant with Cammie.

She was ill most of her term, shanghaied aboard this stormy voyage to the mysteriously distant land of motherhood. She carried an emergency paper bag with her wherever she went; Garrett massaged her back, kept her supplied with soda crackers, beef bouillon, and deep chocolate ice cream the few waking hours they managed to share each miserable day. Of course, once she showed, she was immediately fired from her job as dancing slave girl, her obvious condition too blatant a reminder of consequences in a town whose very existence depended upon the deferral of consequences until, that is, your accounts, financial, physical, and emotional, had been thoroughly cleared. At home with only herself and her basketball belly for company, she was bored. Television drove her mad, the noise and fever and folly of a casino without a payout—ever. She took to reading, between bouts of nausea, cheap paperback accounts of true crime, serial killers stalking the lonely down I-95, a satanic cult of teenage cannibals terrorizing Fresno, the crossdressing rapist of upper Broadway, stories with the same ambivalent allure of a reptile house, dread wound into hypnotic coils vibrant with meaning, even repulsion had its own particular message to impart. Secretly, she thrilled to the dissonance of violation, of accompanying, if only in the safety of her imagination, a fellow human being's reckless steps over the line, over all lines, into a quickening night of absolute freedom—or was such impunity before the law an enslavement more terrible than prison bars or meek obedience? She didn't know—but when miscellaneous body parts started washing up in her dreams, when anxious memories of pursuit through darkened rooms she'd never been in before haunted her days, she switched to reading tell-all celebrity biographies for fear the ugliness of the images crowding her head might begin infecting her baby's unborn brain. An irrational concern, but one whose truth she couldn't doubt as each burgeoning week of her pregnancy seemed to draw her deeper into the domain of magic.

The birth was an event of unspeakable proportions, a wild ride among significances memory couldn't recapture without damage: the cosmos was knotted in ligatures of pain; unravel the threads, liberate the stars whose blossoms promise ease from the agony of time; astounding the revelatory force of torment that carried her, teensy squeaking her, up and up, through ceiling and roof, out into space, out of space, to the cold chamber of the dark queen with the patchwork face of old nightmares who leaned from her throne to tell Jessie something she did not want to hear, and as the thin blue lips began to move, Jessie shrank back in horror, spinning down onto a point so dense the soul's implosion was averted only by a nova cry of life surfacing, and she opened her wondering eyes upon the holy puckered countenance of a new daughter, in whose glow the visions of her mad journey toward this sight began evaporating as cleanly as morning dew. Life is death's amnesia, she thought, and forgetfulness a grace to which we cling.

Now her moments were greedily absorbed by Cammie; nurturing a baby, she learned, required milk and her life—all of it. Distracted by diapers, feedings, fussings, timeless episodes of sheer adoration, Jessie lost track of her husband. She had no leisure to check his pulse, take his temperature, note the onset of disquieting symptoms. As far back as junior high school Garrett had devised for himself a master life plan, a secret timetable charting minimal rates of financial progression year by year to the precocious attainment of lusty tycoonship. Problem: the life was failing to keep pace with the plan. Garrett was fired from his first dealer's job for smiling too much, from his second for dropping a stack of nickel chips during a house rush. He rechecked his figures. An uncharacteristic testiness began to infect his manner. Rejected by several other casinos—paranoid visions of a deadly blacklisting nibbling at the edges of his mind—he was finally taken on at the Sand Dollar Saloon, a tacky grind joint for low-rolling tourists where the dealers dressed in fringed satin shirts, knotted bandannas, and ten-gallon hats.

Garrett loved playing cowboy. Once he put the costume on, the costume put him on: instant machismo in high-heeled lizard boots. He wore the outfit religiously, at work and at home, exploding into petty rages at the sight of an imagined stain. The pit boss was an unregenerate bastard, stewed in the cynicism of a lifetime back of the tables, ragging the help his sole remaining pleasure. "Vegas is a company town, kid, and you're the uninvited guest." He'd stand directly behind Garrett, exhaling warm shrimp breath down Garrett's neck, "Nerves, kid, it's all about nerves," flashing a skull's vacuous grin, berating him in front of the players for poor posture, improper dress, sloppy dealing, and other fictitious discourtesies. If a player walked with more than a few bills (the exact number varying in accordance with the pit boss's humor) he'd run Garrett through humiliating reps of breaking the deck, burning the top six, seven, eight cards, speed dealing (Garrett's technique only fair), and stripping (which he was lousy at). Then he might leave him in place anyway, through the next break or two, to work off his karmic debt, clear the atmosphere around the table so that the p.c. might be restored to its normal house heavy equilibrium. On Tuesdays and Thursdays Garrett was required to wear white socks, black only on the weekends, charms to counter the players' luck, fines for Garrett if he forgot. Frequently, on off days, Garrett would be unexpectedly called in to work a fourteen-hour shift; not a day passed without the threat of dismissal. When, finally, he assembled the audacity to ask, why are you treating me like this? the pit boss replied, "No reason, I just don't like you."

The first time Garrett hit Jessie, a hard slap to the cheek, he apologized immediately afterward. The baby had been crying for an hour, he was trying to eat breakfast at five in the afternoon, Jessie was complaining about his many moods, when suddenly he reached over and let her have it. Jessie was shocked, but she couldn't stay angry at anyone for long, especially not her husband; that face retained an absolving sweetness through all its weathers. And though welcome routine readministered its anesthetic throughout the house, there remained between them the dull throb of the vast unsaid.

Garrett took to carrying a copy of the life plan around with him, consulting it at inappropriate moments. He was scared; time was pulling away and his grip was weakening. A couple of drinks after work helped him to think, get centered into the quick of the issue. Then, without premeditation or regret, he found himself engaged in stealing from the casino, palming a chip here, a chip there. He bought himself a fancy gold watch exactly like the ones the players wore, and when Jessie questioned the expense, he hit her again. No apology. He sewed a modified magician's stash on a length of elastic up inside his sleeve, chips cupped in his hand vanished into his clothes faster than the eye could see, including, presumably, the electronic version hidden in the mirrored ceiling. He bought more gifts for himself: suits, jewelry, cameras, video gear, an occasional trinket or two for Jessie and the baby. She said nothing. The cowboy game had evolved, almost inevitably, into the abuse game, his tantrums as routine as a shrug, assimilated with daunting efficiency into the great apparatus of habit, nature's shock absorber, the trivial and the tremendous domesticated with cool equality. Repetition amounted to acceptance, on his part at least; home-front matters finally attaining a performance level he could get cozy with. For he was changing now, metabolism, psychology, the very patterns of thought, sloughing off that sickly loser's skin, moving up on his schedule, neutralizing the psychic assaults launched against him from every quarter, substituting beer for orange juice at breakfast. He was becoming the new man, immune, one who did as he pleased.

By now Jessie was pregnant with Bas, alone most of the day with Cammie and her reflections. As a girl she had heard her mother boast, "Every woman in this family can take a punch, and most have had to"—not a tradition she wished to perpetuate. From the vantage that motherhood had provided she could see that Garrett was simply another of the ubiquitous embryo-men who had swarmed around her life like roaches, roving canisters of unexpended ball juice, toxic to others, toxic to themselves, the lost boys who hadn't found, and never would find, any use to their lives, better off simply being managed by the big stick, big-daddy figures they seemed to be so desperately seeking —a role, unfortunately for her, completely absent from her repertoire.

It was after Garrett was arrested for drunk driving, and the scene that ensued in their bedroom, that Jessie began to imagine how she might kill him, a fantasy occupying the most pleasant moments of her day. As details accrued, picture quality sharpened, she understood how an imaginative act might be prelude and goad to its realization in actuality. She was scared by her own potential. What was worse, she could smell the decay on him, the house was contaminated by it, every room.

One hazy morning, Garrett sleeping off a binge, fully clothed body flung selfishly across their bed, the cessation of his snores an adequate warning, Jessie dressed her daughter, stuffed some clothes into a laundry bag, and left. There was a place for women like her, a nondescript house on a street of nondescript houses. In a month Garrett had found her. He pleaded and promised and she couldn't help herself, she went back, what the hell, she was sad, and lonely, too. The birth of his son, Bas, had a welcome sedative effect. Then, several weeks later, as Garrett prepared to leave work, he was met by the humorless representatives of casino security. When Jessie arrived to pick up her husband, a nice man in a gray suit and silver glasses explained the situation. She knew what was next. Back home she took what cash she could find, fat packets of it secreted throughout the apartment, and she took the car, another of his many recent extravagances, and she fled. One week of L.A. lunacy was enough to drive her back, to Mother's, despite the fear he'd be waiting for her there. But why should she twist her life about the tortured shape of him? And then, one dawn, there he was, standing out on the walk, a sheepish petitioner in the same wrinkled shirt and pants she'd last seen him wearing. "No comment," declared Mother, obviously angry, whether with her or with him was unclear. Jessie hesitated only a moment, then she unlocked the door and went out to meet her husband. His eyes were lidded, his complexion gray, apparently he hadn't slept in days. "You look good," she said. Keep the kids, he told her, keep the car, I'm sorry, I think of you always. He wouldn't discuss his legal affairs. He was frighteningly adult, so much so she experienced a perilous lifting in her chest not easy to suppress. She cared about him, she always would. They shook hands, they exchanged goodbyes, and as she watched him walk away down the empty street, she realized she felt sorrier for the both of them than she would have preferred.

She entered a period of high restlessness, beyond the possibility of placation, replaying old adolescent arguments with her mother, flirting outrageously with Mother's sympathetic boyfriends, losing her temper with the kids—an alarming development she defused by leaving the house. She buckled herself into the car and she drove, up I-15 to Moapa, down I-15 to Roach Lake, and back again, the loop she looked to hang herself on. A woman mad and alone in a dangerous machine at high speed. She liked the idea. Then, while chasing the sunset of one long and particularly melancholy day, the vanilla marbling in the sky going to raspberry red, holiday frosting dripping onto the stone jury of the mountains, she witnessed a remarkable sight: the flight of several thousand pounds of white Camaro through the clear liquor of a late desert afternoon, a movie image really, trailing the usual streamers of ragged unreality, the car some hundred yards ahead suddenly catapulting up out of a knot of braking traffic, flipping twice over with a dolphinlike incongruity, then slamming backward into the median gully in an explosion of dust and smoke and splintering glass. Jessie wasn't even aware she'd stopped until finding herself among a shocked group of other eyewitnesses, racing for the wreckage. The driver, a young woman, was still strapped to her seat, dangling upside down in her safety harness. She was unconscious, blood running freely from her honey blond hair. Jessie got one good glimpse of the face and immediately wished she hadn't. A man with a cellular phone dialed 911. A woman reached in through the shattered window, felt for a pulse. She looked up at Jessie, her dark eyes spirals to nowhere. "She's dead," she said.

"What?" Jessie asked. She had heard each word, separate and distinct, but there appeared to be a delay in comprehension.

"She's dead," the woman repeated. "Are you all right?"

A cool evening wind had sprung up, peppering their cheeks with sand. Out of the dusk the EMS van approached, a futile carnivalesque expression of color and noise.

The woman walked Jessie to her car, sat beside her as she began to cry, her body seized and shaken by something other, a release from levels so deep the fear would have been unendurable but for the tacit understanding that this woman, this stranger, would remain at her side until the crisis passed, however long it took. An hour later, no more tears to shed, her exhausted flesh a shell of shame and regret, what remained of her, spirit fragile as smoke, followed this woman home, where she was pampered, soothed by exotic teas, listened to attentively far into the night. Jessie liked her. Seemed they had met before, to Jessie's surprise, at Jessie's own wedding, where her new friend, an accomplished organist, had played at Garrett's request a solemn down-tempo rendition of "Light My Fire." The woman was Nikki.

A month later Jessie moved in.

She was changing so rapidly now, she fretted, only half jokingly, about the difficulty keeping up with herself. Actual molecules were being rearranged. She went about in wonder, muttering openly to herself, I am not me. Extraordinary. Waking up in bed beside the warm presence of another woman was an experience of such dislocating astonishments much solitude was required, silent tracts of it, to properly locate and sort her feelings, examine them for clues: what was the meaning of this confounding joy? She was like a child who has discovered ice cream and wants it every day, several times a day. Sure, she'd touched, even kissed, a girlfriend or two, but those were friend touches, friend kisses. How odd, though, how undeniably thrilling, to make sweet body love to your own sex, to know in the sand-papered tips of your soul the combination to the vault, to be wholly absorbed into the sensual treat of finding yourself, your complete self, in the living mirror of another's pleasure. Her hunger for Nikki was frightening; she'd revealed for the first time to anyone the emptiness of her life and been herself astounded by its size, the magnitude of its need. Each day was a relentless emptying-out, she thought, without the binding power of love.

Nikki, an unaffiliated sexual mystic, believed that love was the manifestation of the hereafter into the here and now, and that each time you made love, you did so literally—the rubbing of genitals warming the earth with the fires of heaven—as well as enlarged your future space in eternity.

"I want to be a wealthy angel," Nikki said. "I want to inhabit a mansion on paradise's north shore."

"I love you," Jessie declared. "I love the quality of your mind, I love the easy shape of your asymmetrical breasts."

Jessie refused to leave the bed for days at a time, and when she finally did, she shaved the hair from the right side of her head and dyed the remaining half platinum blond. One week she'd dress up like a prostitute, the next like a construction worker. The liberation from reproductive anxiety alone was exhilarating, how oppressively "natural" that weight had been. She wanted to run up to straights on the street, scream obscenities into their startled faces.

"You're out of control, girl," remarked an amused Nikki.

"Eat me," replied Jessie.

In the embattled privacy of their American home, they sampled freely from the smorgasbord of erotic practice, novelty the key factor in their choices. They were young and in love and rubber suits presented an irresistible turn-on. A serious flirtation with S/M ended in unintentional comedy, however, when Nikki, kneeling in oil and swimming inside a leather harness several sizes too large, collapsed in helpless laughter upon the ridiculously polished toe of the jackboot she'd just been rather brusquely ordered to kiss. Jessie, who'd been enjoying her role perhaps a bit too well, a cop's daughter after all, made an attempt at chastisement with a few lame strokes of her whip. Nikki shrieked in merriment, she sprawled on the floor, she wiped at her eyes. Thank God for the handcuffs. A touch of bondage, at least, proved to be pleasurably instructive for both.

One adventurous weekend they borrowed a pair of irons and a converter box from their friend Toby, the tattoo artist. She lived alone in a former storefront with a toothless black and white terrier named Rush and an evil emerald macaw whose entire vocabulary consisted of the phrases "I hate you," "Where's my money?" and "Are you looking at me?" The great unenlightened horde of the nontattooed Toby referred to contemptuously as "blanks." "You take a brand from my iron," she claimed, "and you learn real quick about the meaning of commitment. If everyone were properly inked, this'd be a nobler, more righteous country—a more beautiful one, too." Her particular specialty was Daliesque designs with a dice or playing-card motif. Her own right bicep sported a boldly realistic depiction of a slot machine, a trio of lemons up in the window—local equivalent of the notorious Born to Lose. Toby sent off her friends with a tube of Bacitracin, a box of bandages, and her blessing.

Jessie and Nikki began by practicing on a couple dozen grapefruit, inscribing shiny yellowy heads with a dense assortment of happy faces, hearts, roses, skulls, and clumsy unicorns that resembled rats with glandular problems. When all the rind was decorated, fruit flesh scarred for life, they started experimenting on one another, doodling on the body's scratch pad, the bottoms of the feet, the dead callused areas where the needles didn't hurt much and the marks would fade eventually with wear. Once human skin was broken, though, the mood was altered, the ante raised, something new entered the room. Probably it was Jessie who suggested moving the steel to higher ground, and it wasn't long before they were taking turns engraving their names with delicate hesitancy upon one another's trembling behinds. The spontaneous bout of lovemaking that followed was a revelation of animal heat.

"God," Jessie cried, "I never felt so horny."

"It's the chemicals," explained Nikki, "flooding our brains. From the wounds."

The sheets were a mess of blood and ink. Jessie fingered the fresh relief on her butt. "Now we own each other," she declared.

Nikki was examining herself in the mirror. "I think not," she said.

Most Saturdays they'd hop into Nikki's Jeep, drop the kids at Mother's, and head on out into the desert, through the red rock canyons, monuments to the plastic power of time, sandstone minarets and jagged archways, elongated shapes of fantastic animals, the rough busts of human heads, past the great Atlatl Rock carved with the hunting symbols of the ancient shamans who understood the rites of representation, how to ensnare the power of their prey within the inscription of the proper form, then down the seldom traveled spur road, the jeep trail, and off into the country, bouncing gleefully over the petrified tide of prehistoric seas, the hours free, the sky wide open, the day itself a living body with visible cords and vessels, a mountainous heart, genitals of light, to arrive in the secret place of true emptiness where the tourists rarely go. They left their clothes in the vehicle and, naked but for sturdy hiking boots, traversed the burning mesa, female *Wandervogel* of the new age, calling out fossil finds, the glint of possible precious metals, Jessie in fine Bogart rasp, " 'If ya know what's good for ya, ya won't monkey around with Fred C. Dobbs,' " scratching into a boulder pocked like a meteorite her own petroglyph, a stylized entwining of their initials, gift to the archaeologists of the twenty-second century. Hot and exhausted, they rested in the narrow shade of a Joshua tree, skin tones after weeks in the sun blending imperceptibly into earth tones, touch one, touch the other, hand, mouth, tongue.

"Super," sighed Nikki in the British accent she liked to affect whenever she was naked, and the shapeliness of her Madonna head, the liquid suggestiveness of her eyes, the entrancing movement of her lips as she spoke, were events equal in magnitude to their surroundings.

A chalky brown whiptail lizard darted furiously past, scaled quicksilver pouring down a rock.

"The truth," said Jessie, seriously.

Nikki laughed. "How could we honestly live anywhere else?"

And it was true. This country was special, not just because Jessie had been born out in it, but because it refined the senses, kept them keen. The body hummed like a receiver, intercepting messages beneath the noise of human traffic, down among the harmonic silences of spiders and scrub and soaring sandstone, whose baroque architecture often communicated directly with Jessie's heart, this primitive intimacy with the nonhuman a recognition of its continued existence deep inside her.

"If you ever wanted to kill somebody," Jessie mused, "this would be the place to do it."

Nikki made a face. "You possess the strangest mind of anyone I've ever known."

Then Jessie turned and whispered into her friend's ear, Nikki's brows arching in mock horror. "Sure your last name isn't James?" But she complied willingly enough, another act whose innocent energies she imagined nurturing the depleted earth, sex as good ecology, a psychic cloudburst. When they were done, they lay together on the rusty sand in the great blue basilica of this sovereign day.

"I love it out here," Jessie exclaimed. "I feel"—she searched for the precise descriptive—"rich."

She went on, "Eventually, you know, it will be revealed to tortoise and hare alike that the most significant moments in our lives are those in which we do nothing. What we do when we 'do nothing' is who we truly are."

Nikki opened an eye. "You're speaking in nonsensical proverbs."

"Why not? I'm in a desert, I'm having visions, I'm founding a religion."

"Great Goddess. Next, you'll be issuing commandments and praying for a penis."

"One commandment: Thou shalt keep thy hands to thyself—unless directed nicely otherwise." She wanted inside Nikki's eyes, but they had retired again behind closed lids, so Jessie addressed herself to the intervening wedge of cartilege, that perfect, perfectly memorized, retroussé nose. "Of course I've imagined life from the owner's end of a magical skin flute. What red-blooded girl hasn't? The key to the kingdom. The axis of the culture. The snake in the bedroom. Sure, let's get it on. And the bigger, the better."

A slow thin smile creased the mask of Nikki's face. "Okay," she confessed. "Me, too." Her gaze contained the amused acceptance of someone who had learned long ago to ride, without too frequent a spill, the beast of her own mind. "Fantasies can be fun, verdad? But TV ain't real life, neither. I remember the first time I ever heard of Freud and this penis envy nonsense. I was shocked. This is insight? This is science? The lack is not between our legs; it's in the male head. All I've ever experienced down there is a power, not an absence, a big bold beautiful power."

"And lust," offered Jessie.

"Of course."

"And spiritual apotheosis."

"Certainly."

"And the essence of womanhood pure and true, such as it is, now and forever, in the glory to come."

"In the glory to come, yes, most definitely."

And beyond the cozy campfire of their lives, Garrett, scenting their happiness, came prowling like a hungry wolf. He began calling again, on the phone, in person, at home, at work. He wanted Jess back. Without her, the days were stones dropping one at a time onto the exact center of his forehead, the nights a sabbat of demons only intently imagined acts of suicide could keep at bay. He understood he was being tried upon the spit of love, and that understanding was also his hope. People changed. Indeed they do, Jessie agreed. I don't know you. I don't know the person who once thought she knew you. She was sorry. So was he, the rage rising in him like mercury in a thermometer. He wanted the kids, then. No, she could keep the kids if he could watch her and Nikki in bed together. At which point Nikki called the cops, who, over the succeeding months, became a reluctant third party to this essentially unchanging dialogue. Once Jessie awoke to find Garrett in the kitchen making himself a grilled cheese sandwich. He left without resistance, silent as a ghost. The second time they found him in the house, piling furniture in the middle of the living room, two police officers were seriously injured during the administration of the municipal muscle necessary to pry Garrett from the premises. The children cried, Nikki cursed indiscriminately, and a significant portion of Jessie's privacy was rudely appropriated by the evening news, a sensation comparable to being washed in used bathwater. For weeks she was ashamed to be seen in public. Now, apparently, the devil was loose again, Toby claimed to have seen Garrett strolling down Sahara Avenue only two days ago—of course it was a friend, not the authorities, who passed on the warning—and Nikki was talking guns and Jessie was afraid, not so much of her ex as of herself and what she might do if he dared to cross her threshold for the third out. Why should the course of her time be determined by a man who used to walk around with come stains on his shirt?

Outside her window the sizzling emerald fronds of the neon palm seemed to stir slightly at the touch of night currents unsensed by its organic cousins. Sometimes, even gathered within the snug immediacies of Nikki and the kids, Jessie felt as if she were marooned on a desert island far from home. The burden of existence, her own, her family's, became an intolerable mystery, though it was obvious something significant and indefinable was working its way through their lives, through everybody's life, a sure push into incarnation from some distant unknown ground, a growth, an unfolding into a duty and a death—pleasant thoughts to accompany you down the long early morning hours. She wished she were a tree. Trees were her city's greatest lack. Trees provided oxygen and sanity.

Sometime after four the door of The Happy Chapel opened to admit a couple who might have passed for Ken and Barbie—a pair of real "blanks," as Toby would say. He, dressed in navy blue polo shirt, beige pants, looked like a golf pro; she, a bottle blonde in white leather miniskirt and matching jacket—her bridal outfit—resembled a Roller Derby queen. They had come directly from the county recorder's office, marriage license in hand, and they wanted The Works: flowers, live music, videotape, still photography, garter belt, etc.

"Guess how long we've known each other?" asked the woman. Her name was Kara. She was as excited as an adolescent on her first date. "Sixty-nine hours. Can you believe it, can you absolutely believe it?" She reached around and pinched her fiancé on the ass. When they kissed, it was like the indolent gluing together of shapeless organisms in a nature film on reproduction among lower life-forms.

"My mother's name was Jessie," said the man, reading it off her employee tag. "I'm Tom." His hand felt like a wire construct, a sculptor's armature. His eyes were washed out, full of bad weather and bad dreams.

"My first wedding," Kara explained, "was an absolute joke, such a piddling little thing, crammed into a deputy commissioner's office on Fourth Street. I was so embarrassed. Took about a minute and a half. About how long the marriage lasted, too."

"Well, I'm a marathon man myself," said Tom. "Should be able to squeeze at least a couple hours out of this one, don't you think?" He was speaking to Kara, but his smile followed Jessie around the room like a playful puppy eager for the pat of her hand upon his head, the private acknowledgment of a shared amusement. He emitted that peculiarly male air of affable assurance that lingered throughout her history like bad cologne. A man with a plan. She knew the type. Silently, she wished the bride good luck.

"Omigod, honey, look at the selection they have here!" exclaimed Kara, rushing over to glass counters ablaze with the stones and forged metal of several hundred unique wedding bands of which she seemed compelled to inspect each and every one, an interested Tom at her side, his proprietary hand never far from the cushioned appeal of her splendid behind, participants in a joint rapture over rather ordinary jewelry in which the fun was derived from regarding the trays Jessie set before them as containing priceless treasure from the burial chamber of a pharaonic tomb. Kara couldn't decide, each ring she tried on seemed more dazzling than the last.

"One month's salary," said Kara. "That's the usual rule of thumb, isn't it? How much do you make, anyway?"

Tom shrugged. He couldn't say exactly, his business was highly cyclical, all abrupt ups and downs.

"Now look here, mister, if you're going to start off this grand marriage by lying to me—"

"I never lie to my woman."

Her body softened, seemed to melt obligingly against his. "Now, what is it you sell again?" she asked in skeptically innocent tones.

"I sell America, babe. I sell pipe. Oil, gas, water. If you want it to go, call Puraflo."

Though Jessie clearly understood these facts were also meant for her delectation, she offered not a hint of response. In "hospitality," as in medicine, you learned to maintain a discreet distance from the "civilians"—the present-day multitude of the physically homeless, quite modest in number compared to the great unseen armies of the emotionally dispossessed.

"Isn't he just the most astonishing money-making beast?" blurted Kara. She clung to his arm with childlike persistence, as if at any moment he were about to levitate into the miraculous air.

"Pick a good one, babe," ordered Tom. "No sense in fussing over ducats on an occasion like this."

Kara pulled him down onto her face for another noisy prolonged kiss. Jessie rearranged the rings in her trays.

"I'm so happy," Kara declared, the blood up in her cheeks vivid as if she'd been slapped. "Is everyone this happy who comes in here?"

"We do tend to cater to smiley faces," confirmed Jessie, "but you'd certainly be a prime candidate for the queen of happy."

"That's 'cause I've got the king right here." She squeezed Tom's arm; helpless, they shared another kiss.

Jessie had seen it all before, the cuddling, the groping, the tonguing, appreciated her role as audience of one, a mirror to reflect the actors' desire back on the actors themselves, enhancing their pleasure, doubling their passion. Some of the exuberant folk she'd waited on in this shop would be more than thrilled to have a section of bleacher seats installed in their honeymoon suites. In a certain mood, who knew? she might also be so inclined.

At last, after a tedious scrutiny of the contents of all four jewelry cases, several false choices, Kara's quest for the perfect wedding ring ended with her selection of the Heavenly Light Diamonique cluster in fourteen-karat gold band—cheaper in price certainly than real diamond, but, to her eye at least, far surpassing in natural beauty.

"It makes my knuckles look younger," she declared.

Jessie, eager to get the gems out of sight before Kara could change her mind again, began hastily restacking the trays when her arm was suddenly, forcibly seized.

"Hey!" she cried, trying to wrest herself free from Tom's intimidating grip.

"Go ahead," Kara urged. "He's a genius at this."

Tom inverted her hand in his and gently unfolded her fist. "Such delicate fingers." He gazed with clinical regard into the weblike wrinkling of her palm. "Destiny's map. Always a remarkable sight. Well, no cause for alarm here. That's the longest lifeline I've ever seen."

"Longer than mine?" cried Kara, disappointed.

"You don't actually believe—" asked Jessie.

"Oh yeah," affirmed this Tom character. "The whole show's been prerecorded from the beginning, planted into our hides before we were even born."

Jessie searched his features for signs of irony. The signs were unclear. "Free will got erased, huh?"

He was stroking the flesh at the base of Jessie's thumb, the mound of Venus. "We're just the cattle of that dude in the big house on the hill—whoever, whatever, he or she is." He looked up. "Classic loveline you've got here. Obviously, you give as much as you receive."

"Lucky me. Those scales *are* blind, aren't they?"

"Tommy finds the love in everyone," Kara said, "so much love. I keep trying to tell him how naïve he is, but then, that's what makes him so sweet." She gave him an affectionate hug.

"I see a nimbus about you," he announced to Jessie, "bright and golden. Probably money, lots of money."

"Well, we are in Vegas."

"I see you on television, in the near future. Would that be something you're interested in?"

"I rarely watch it."

"Unconsciously, then. I think perhaps this is a desire you don't yet know you possess."

"Isn't he good?" asked Kara. "He's always discovering these precious little secrets in me which later turn out to be uncannily true."

"Yes," said Jessie. "I don't believe we've had a more perfectly matched couple in here in months."

Kara explained how it was the beauty of her hands that had brought them together, drawing Tom like an enchanted prince through the vulgar casino crowds.

"Women's hands," Tom exclaimed, shaking his head in wonder that such things should be.

Kara was a roulette dealer at the Silver Gulch. With the house percentage ranging from 5.26 to 11, depending on the bet, her game was not the most popular on the floor; unlike the busy beejay crew, the hectic stickmen in the craps pit, she could often be found standing idly behind her table, spinning the wheel, waiting for a player. When Tom began placing dollar chips on her layout, she barely glanced at his face, routinely marking him for just another grind—and an especially stupid one at that, chasing the number 22 over several dozen consecutive straight-up bets without a single hit. All he won was her. For Kara the years had built up inside an elevation from which she could at last see the road clear in both directions, and as her trip proceeded, she was liking the view less and less. The guy was clean, well groomed, fairly easy on the eyes, his superficial charm sliced by the prowling fin of an irresistible mischievousness, and—big and— he owned a roomy green Ford Galaxie whose nose was pointed resolutely out of town. She was estranged from her family, her first husband was in the joint, the second vanished on her, and—what the hell—she guessed she was simply a Woman Who Loved Bad Men.

The presiding minister that night was the Reverend Buster Mahoney, CPA, Gamblers Anonymous member, honorary Laughlin deputy sheriff, and a licensed graduate of the Elko Religious Farm, a combination monastic retreat, soul aerobics center, and diploma mill. Reverend Mahoney possessed a rather baggy, outsized personality out of which surprises were being continually dropped or inadvertently exposed. Introduced to Tom and Kara, he began telling tales from the lost L.A. years when he was "into" death, working the fringes of the discount funeral business—middle of a eulogy for a murdered drug dealer the deceased's beeper goes off, the mourners burst into laughter, Mahoney gets so flustered for the rest of the service he confuses this dearly departed's name with the one he buried two hours previous, and then sweats for days worrying what the insulted dealer's friends might do to him. In marriage, a more felicitous industry, he hadn't yet made a mistake. Minutes after meeting Tom, he was referring to him as Jerry.

For their ceremony Tom and Kara chose the Futuristic Chamber because the future, as Kara explained, quoting the mad Hollywood prophet, Criswell, from the infamous film *Plan 9 from Outer Space*, was "where you and I are going to spend the rest of our lives, whether we want to or not." The room was a closed cube of mirrors decorated with countless strings of running lights; survivors spoke of being sealed within a stark depopulated casino extended infinitely into space or of being trapped inside a bizarre video game, all the lasers aimed directly at you. The loud piped-in music was a medley of classic science fiction movie themes, the youngest at least two decades old, leaving the intrepid matrimonial voyager in an oddly disorienting limbo, the future and its background score having already come and gone, in some cases well before bride or groom had even been born. Reverend Mahoney, apple belly, fatty breasts, and all, zippered into a skintight crash suit, officiated as if from the bridge of the starship Enterprise; at his back, in place of mirrored glass, a solid wall of television monitors to magnify, reflect, and duplicate each nuptial twitch and jitter, an impressive technological supplement to the general atmosphere of anxiety and embarrassment.

The happy couple had composed their own vows, she declaring from memory in a clear voice rich with emotion her ardent fidelity to this stranger from the east, strange no more, an uncommon man deserving of greater happiness than she could provide, but nonetheless assured of finding in her company, as long as she was capable of drawing a breath, house advantage, sound money management, and all the love he would ever need—comped—while he, reading in halting rhythms from the scribbled sheet of hotel stationary in his quivering hand, pledged his strength to a fierce defense of their continued bliss, promised to honor the snowflake-special particularity that was Kara, to cherish the utter incorruptibility of her butterfly soul.

They exchanged "I do's," Reverend Mahoney broke into a hacking cough, the lights chased one another across the walls with accelerating speed, hidden loudspeakers vibrated to the amplified strains of the *Forbidden Planet* theme. When they kissed, a charge went round the room, a brief roseate glow upon the genitals of everyone present.

The new bride was ecstatic. "I got up this morning Kara Lamm," she announced, proudly. "Tonight I go to bed Mrs. Tom Hanna. No other woman in the whole country can make that statement." The miraculous budding of her face, renewed cheeks bright as the flesh of raw petals, ritual's signet pressed into living tissue for all to mark and know once again the vivifying power of ceremony, the repetition of right word and gesture opening a circuit in the aisle of time, eternity's proof in the turgor of the heart.

Tonight's organist, Mrs. Billie Hardwick, Nikki's great-aunt and childhood confidante, began to cry, but then she cried at every wedding, and she had attended several thousand.

Tom, before he left, made a point of kissing every woman in the chapel, including Jessie, slipping a bit of unexpected tongue into her mouth, hand straying ever so lightly across her ass.

"Gross," declared Nikki, glad to see them go.

"What do you give them?" asked Jessie.

"Are you kidding? There are no odds on the game that woman's playing. Where she's going, there are no winners. Mister Snake Eyes. She'll be lucky to escape with her shirt."

An hour later, dawn mustering a ragged world to attention outside her window, Jessie, conscientiously wiping the night's usual accumulation of smudges and prints from the glass counters, discovered the missing rings, a half dozen or so of the most expensive: the Shower of Gold, the Bird of Paradise, Crystal Blue Ecstasy, the Crown of Fire. She wanted to be mistaken, to have misplaced, miscounted the essentially interchangeable stock, but knew at once that no amount of wishful thinking, checking, rechecking the shelves, could erase the stubborn fact of loss gaping up at her from the mockingly vacant slots of the gem trays. There was no avoiding it. She'd been robbed. Nikki had to be told.

It did not go well.

Nikki glared at the evidence as if undiluted will were sufficient for the rematerialization of physical objects. "Pop will have an absolute shit fit," she said.

"I'm sorry."

She looked at Jessie as if she were a very young, very disappointing child. "How could you?"

"How could I what?" Jessie's voice rising on every syllable. "You act like I boosted the damn stones myself."

"Who was it? The Professor and Mary Ann, that loathsome couple who couldn't keep their hands off each other?"

"The woman's name was Kara. She was the only one who handled the rings."

"They were a team, obviously. His job was to distract you."

They exchanged one lengthy, mutually indignant look.

"Just what are you getting at? I show those crappy bands to dozens of couples every night. Anyone could have taken them. Who knows how long they've been gone? And frankly, I don't like the general tone of your remarks. If I'm to undergo an interrogation, then let's get some real cops in here."

"Great idea. Pop will be so pleased to have an official squad car pay a visit. Remember what happened when Roderigo dented the limo?"

"He'd fire me?" Jessie asked in disbelief.

"Why stop there? I'm the one who brought you into the business. No, we're just going to forget about this petty incident and pretend nothing has happened." She began arranging the remaining jewelry so as to minimize the appearance of a deficit.

"I'll pay for the missing merchandise. You can deduct payments from my monthly check."

"I don't believe I want to discuss this matter any further," said Nikki, and abruptly hurried from the room.

Jessie, dumbfounded, let her go, too dazed to open another round. She needed time and an undisturbed corner in which to assess her wounds, their seriousness, their motive, their intent. Was this unfortunate theft the issue or the issue before the issue? Had a wire been inadvertently tripped in the dreaded father-daughter territory, or had Jessie plunged haplessly down the rabbit hole of their life together, into the true history hidden away in these unexplored tunnels and warrens beneath the daily chitchat, the habitual sex—the subterranean lair of the wily human relationship: a dark maze of pop-up demons, fun house mirrors, spooky dead ends, multiple false bottoms. If only she could feel her children in her arms right now, this moment— sudden pangs of guilt at how few hours of the ever-shortening days she seemed to spend in their needy company. An incompetent bridal- shop drudge, she was a bad mother, too.

She perched on her stool behind the reprimanding silence of the cash register, counting off the minutes, the sole inebriated couple who stumbled in for nuptials and coffee at dawn perfunctorily attended to by a distant automaton on weak batteries. That absolute strangers could arbitrarily interpose themselves between you and those you loved was an intolerable horror. What Tom and Kara had done, while lifting a handful of relatively insignificant stones—if those were their real names, if indeed they were the actual perps—was a simultaneous ransacking of the contents of her heart. Absolute strangers. The com- mission of evil. For without trust the world became a howling waste of isolatoes, a postapocalypticscape of people, animals, trees, appar- ently untouched—only the living links between them totally obliter ated. The war was over and the monsters had won. In the bleak early morning light the neon palm out her window looked like a poorly sculpted cigar whose end had exploded.

Neither Nikki nor Jessie spoke a word in the car back or at home as they prepared for bed, passing one another in the hallway, entering, exiting rooms without a sound, emissaries from warring provinces mistakenly booked into the same frontier hotel. After an hour of toss- ing, turning, watching the cracks in the ceiling assume the hideous shapes of giant stinging insects, Jessie opened her mouth to insist dispassionately, "I didn't take those rings."

"I never said you had," Nikki replied at once, in a clear wakeful voice. "It was your job to make sure no one else did."

"Go ahead, speak your mind, don't hold back."

Nikki threw off the sheet and sat up in bed. "I wish there was a cigarette in this damn house. I can't believe we're having this discussion all over again. It seems to recur at monthly intervals, regardless of circumstances. What is it you want, Jessie, a notarized document testifying to my enduring faith? The problem's not with us, anyway.

This isn't the first instance of unpaid goods slipping past the door on your shift. There was a wedding gown a couple weeks ago, and some other miscellaneous shit over the last few months that Pop already knows about. He doesn't need an update on this latest incident."

Jessie was shocked. "Why didn't you tell me?"

"Wasn't that important. I knew it wasn't you despite what he might be thinking."

"Excuse me," said Jessie, angered by the overly protective, if not downright patronizing, attitude of Nikki's remarks—from the root *pater*, patriarchal, peter puffer, "but I wasn't aware your father's feelings were more important than mine."

"Unfair, Jessie, royally unfair. But then you always have to do whatever's necessary to win every argument, to have the last word, just as you have to control each vacation and spend the last dollar. My God, you even have to come first. I might as well be living with a man."

There was a moment then of charred silence in which Jessie simply stared at this creature she had taken for a lover. How could this be happening? Fooled yet again by that sly trickster—herself. She couldn't believe her abiding naïveté, the sheer bedrock intransigence of it, that, no matter how diamond-sharp the drill of the facts, seemed destined to remain embedded in her character to the final breakup and removal. Somehow, on the deepest, most profound levels, she had convinced herself she had finally arrived at a station of assured immunity from the plentiful and venomous relationship diseases, that the mere obstinate truth of loving someone of the same sex and weathering the abuse such outrageous heresy invariably provoked conferred a passionate unblemished love, a neurosis-free zone, in accordance with the natural economy of psychic checks and balances. What childishness. How little after all these years, all the long bitter accruing, the patient telling, of experience's bruises, how little of value she truly knew. The eternal innocent, perpetually amazed.

"I'm sorry," said Nikki, reaching out a propitiatory hand, but Jessie was up and through the door before she could be touched. She found refuge in the kids' room, on the edge of Cammie's bed, in the furry maternal softness of Mister Mac the talking bear, the sunny unambiguous cheer of the furnishings, an all-enveloping baking-bread aroma

of small children, the consolation of domestic detail, neglected crannies where grace dwelt, as crisis proved time and time again, the
moment when Garrett first struck her as tangibly present as the baby
blue rocking chair in which she sang Bas to sleep on nights of fear for
both mother and son. Was she to be required now, as penance for
what obscure unexpiated crimes, to endure once more the exquisitely
keen anguish of yet another separation? Already sobbing before she
knew she'd even begun, she simply let herself go, tears a sacrament,
purifying the mind, unshackling the rigidities of the flesh, life's salt
offering to life. A dream had told her she'd cry today, but she'd apparently misinterpreted the symbols.

Nikki began knocking softly at the door, tendering sweet words of
apology. Jessie wouldn't unbolt the lock. This was a private matter,
this washing of her soul, and she wasn't about to be interrupted until
crying stopped because crying was done. The little shirt of Bas's she
dried her face upon felt as blessed as any veronica. Beckoned mysteriously to the window, she gazed off, in the ascending sun, to where
gray mountains crystallized daily out of the clear blue solution of the
sky like ancient forms resolving themselves in the dark chamber of the
heart. And when the wrestling with shapes had concluded, one had
to rise and rise again. She thought of Nikki and the viridescent planets
of her eyes and the disarming crinkle of her smile and the untamed
cowlick at the crown of her head and how she sometimes smelled of
fresh french fries and Jessie thought: Nikki loved Bud loved Glenda
loved Roderigo. She thought: Jessie loved Bas loved Cammie loved
Mister Mac. And yes: Jessie loved Nikki loved Jessie. Love chains.
The true length of each connecting inevitably with another until a
single cardinal chain wound close about the riving globe to keep the
reckless pieces of it from skirring to the clamorous end of it. No one
could break a love chain. Not Tom or Kara or Garrett or Reverend
Pop or Mamaw Odie or mean Mr. Moses in the adjacent duplex or
the roving teen gay-bashers or the LVPD or the D.A. or the Family
Court or even Melissa. The stuff from which a love chain was forged
was guaranteed indestructible.

The truth.

N I G H T   O F   T H E   L O N G   P I G S

THEY left Sambir at dawn, the only white faces on an overloaded river taxi bound up-country for Tanjung Liang and the timber camps and scattered settlements beyond. The boat had filled quickly, and by the time the Copelands arrived, after a frantic last-minute bemo ride, clutching guardrails, their baggage, one another, through the narrowest, bumpiest, crookedest streets in town, they were lucky to claim a patch of space the size of a throw rug on the padded floor mats near the starboard side. Hung over, dehydrated, uncharacteristically grouchy, they decided not to speak until the urge for recriminations had passed. Around them every inch of deck was occupied, yet room continued to be found for late arrivals, whole families happily wedged into openings barely larger than a telephone booth, dozing babies dangled in beadwork carriers from hooks in the overhead beams. There were chickens in bamboo cages and a pair of ill-humored goats tethered to a red stanchion in the stern. Everyone, of every age and gender, was engaged in intense involvement with a cigarette, as if nicotine were some precious ingredient essential to well-being. The rows of hardwood benches were packed end to end with passengers who, like parishioners in their pews, faced uniformly front, obediently attentive to the muddled light emanating from the broken television set bolted to the forward bulkhead, Pastor Bob and his "World Wonder Hour" broadcasting live-on-tape from the Miracle Room of the Holydome in Corpus Christi, Texas, this morning's message: Dollars of Deliverance. The color on the screen had settled out into broad uneven bands of green, yellow, purple, the national flag of an alien planet superimposed upon the pastor's mesmerizingly piscine features. No one seemed to mind.

The harbor was swaddled in grainy fog, objects near and far standing about in random incongruity like icons in a dream. The bladed orange-streaked bow of a Malaysian freighter. The bulletlike dome of the town mosque, silver and wrinkled as if wrapped in aluminum foil. The red-tiled roof of the Hotel Happiness where brindle cats snoozed on the balconies and, like royalty, roamed through the rooms at will. The ghostly black sails of a passing prahu, sinister as shark fins. And downstream, visible through the murk at even this distance from the coast, the ragged gas flares of the refinery stacks of the Pertamina oil complex. The world in pieces at this uncertain hour.

With a sudden shriek of the boat's horn the deck shuddered to life and the long wooden pier began backing steadily away. They were off—up the Kutai River into the tangled mythical heart of Borneo.

Drake gave his wife's hand a squeeze.

"I love you," whispered Amanda, glancing over his shoulder to check that this modest exchange of affection had given no offense to a people whose custom permitted only public displays of same-sex tenderness. Pastor Bob continued to enchant his water-borne audience. The Bible is the book of business. God has a personal financial plan for each and every one of you. Let Jesus be your money manager. Lounging in studied insolence against the far rail, oblivious, apparently, to the promise of pennies from heaven, a small wiry man in baggy shorts, clean white shirt, and faded pink turban, a member of the crew, stared openly at Amanda from a cinnamon face so devoid of expression she felt herself reduced to thinghood, a peculiar irritating shape that happened temporarily to be obstructing his view of the greater private spectacle without. He was, like most of the crew, a Bugis from the neighboring island of Sulawesi, descendant of the notorious seafaring people whose piratical exploits so impressed their European prey that it was said their very name entered the language to frighten naughty children in the dark windy English night—be good or the boogeyman will get you.

"Where?" Drake's head went pivoting around. He couldn't tolerate such harassment and made a point of confronting perpetrators on the spot.

"Don't bother. He's gone already." The man's lithe, compact body unpeeling itself from the rail and scuttling rapidly aft, dragging his tail behind him. "He's been scoping us since we boarded." She knew now what was meant by the phrase "the Evil Eye," and wondered if evil was not a vacuum, the absence of connective tissue, psychic feelers drawn up so deep inside that the shell became the life, the power of blankness. A shiver ran through her shoulders. She grimaced. "Creepy," she said.

Drake continued to case the crowd. In his L.A. Dodgers cap and aviator sunglasses he looked like a baseball coach scouting the opposition. "Too damn early in the morning to be dealing with crap like this."

"Are you implying, then, that it would be okay later in the day, around two, three in the afternoon, perhaps?"

"Amanda."

"I was only asking."

Drake pushed back his cap and wiped his forehead with a black handkerchief. He was sweating already. "I don't know, hard to tell the perverts from the curious in this country. Who hasn't stared at us since we got off the plane in Jakarta? You want to be famous, you want the regard of the masses? Enjoy it."

"But these people aren't staring at us because they know who we are, they're staring because they don't. And I don't feel celebrated, I feel like a specimen on a slide."

"Hooray for Hollywood."

The boat chugged on, the racket of its unmuffled engines helping to clear a course through the harbor fog. The current sliding along the hull was gray and greasy as dishwater and it reeked of sweat and garbage and human waste—the insidious scent of expiring forms. They passed a huge Japanese tanker where a sleepy crewman, wiping his hair on a towel, peered down upon them with an expression of amused benevolence. They zigzagged between squat coal barges and drifting rafts heaped with pyramids of massive hardwood logs with the raw, shocked look of freshly cut timber. Along the bank now, emerging gradually out of the thinning mist, were the rows of ramshackle huts on spidery stilts and the houseboats with tattered washcloths for curtains and the hand sawmills and the floating docks, each with its moored semicircle of sleek longboats radiating outward like elliptical wooden petals. People had begun to gather on the muddy shore in broken file, mouths white with foam, vigorously brushing their teeth with river water.

"I have to admit," Amanda said, "that for the first time I am starting to entertain serious doubts."

"About coming here or getting famous?" asked Drake innocently.

"About marrying you, asshole." And her hands were up under his shirt, tickling his ribs.

"Watch it," he hissed, trying to hold back his laughter as he fended her off. "You're behaving like the Western barbarian you truly are."

She looked around. To her right two unsmiling men had interrupted their chess game to study this coarse foreigner. There were too many faces turned in her direction. She smiled cheerfully back, then snuggled down amid her gear, attempting to present as inconspicuous a target as possible. The burden of pale skin. That sordid history, too.

Drake hid behind the cover of his ubiquitous guidebook, *Indonesia Today*. " 'Among the Pekit of the upper Kutai,' " he read aloud, " 'death is not a natural event. It is caused only by magic or violence, and when a death occurs, it must be avenged or the spirit of the people will be diminished.' "

"Not now, Drake."

" 'Three days after dying, the confused soul eventually finds its way out of the labyrinth of the body, exiting the mouth in the shape of a local insect or bird.' "

"I'm tuning you out, mister." Amanda laid her arm like a compress over her eyes, hoping to lose, for a few blissful minutes, her particular place in time and space. Immediately she was assailed by a choppy montage of overlit travel footage. Vacationer's vertigo. Too much novelty in too brief a time under too little sleep. Each new dawn in this remarkable country initiated a fresh assault upon the frail fort of their assumptions, as if the Asian sun were a big mystical revolver firing copper-jacketed days into the unprotected wadding of their heads. In Jakarta they had seen a green mamba crawl out of a man's ear. Among dunes of red ash they had watched a twelve-year-old boy juggle volcanic rock above the undulating sea of clouds at the summit of Mount Merapi. On Bali they had been forced from the streets of Denpasar by a mob dancing to the whims of the monkey god. All the world's dreams, beliefs, spirits congregated here within the enchanted islands of Indonesia. The elements of the human unconsciousness occupied the landscape as visible objects. Power crackled from mind to mind and the earth itself was uneasy, groaning and rumbling in its chains, the prison of matter. She let it run. Eventually, this mad stuttering rush must fade, slow, come to rest upon the central image of this movie, her heart's newfound anchor, the great stone mandala of the Buddhist shrine of Borobudur, a mammoth manmade cosmic mountain rising dramatically from the Kedu plain on the island of Java (the exotic names of these hallucinatory isles—Bali, Sumatra, Maluku, Timor—the sensuous language of Occidental fantasy, of moonlit colonialism, of contemporary high-fashion fragrances). The shrine was constructed of seven stepped terraces, a base of four square topped by three round. Entering the east gate, symbolically swallowed by the gaping mouth of the kala, the monster head carved over the doorway, you turned left (demons lurked on the right) into a narrow passageway lined with bas-reliefs depicting narrative scenes from the Buddha's 550 lives, sermons in stone to draw the pilgrim toward enlightenment as you circumambulated the shrine through the constricting channels of the phenomenal world, rising terrace by terrace from the realm of forms suddenly, startlingly out onto the broad circular terraces at the summit, the revelation of the open sky, the liberating miracle of formlessness. Amanda had never been so affected by a monument, even though, mesmerized by the imposing physical presence of the place, she had, upon entering, stumbled on a step and badly scraped her right knee, the sentence "I tripped in the world of desire" instantly echoing through future dinner parties back in L.A. The intellectual and spiritual design of Borobudur exhibited an undeniably pleasing rigor. So the question posed by this shrine was doubly persistent: how did one break the tether of death? The prescription of the major Eastern religions seemed to be to pretend that you were already dead. Put crudely, death was the cessation of pretty pictures. Learn to disengage yourself from the film, and the heat of the senses could no longer burn; summon the courage to get up out of your seat and actually leave the theater, and you will have slipped the bonds of mortality. Buddha as the world's first spiritual escape artist. We have all been locked in the same box, he said. Now I will provide you with a duplicate key.

Under her, Amanda could feel the vibration of the deck, the sliding-forward movement of the keel, she could hear a baby crying, the murmur of incomprehensible conversation, the pages of Drake's book being periodically turned, the quiet tolling of a quiet day, when gradually, in the darkness, she became aware of the bellows of her chest opening and closing like a door swinging to and fro in an almost imperceptible wind, teasing her with glimpses of another darkness beyond the door, a darkness deep and luminous that pulsed gently to the measure of her heart, the careful spacing of her breaths, she controlled the door, she controlled the darkness, too, her darkness, her fear, her—progress toward nirvana abruptly blown by the scratch and pop of a cardboard match. Back in the world of pain and loss Drake was firing up his first *kretek* of the day.

"Those are evil," she said.

Drake glanced up from his book. She hadn't moved, but his wife's eyes had come open. How long had she been silently studying him? "I thought you were asleep."

"If you're going to start smoking again, why not stick to American brands, the good old tried-and-true domesticated cancer?"

Drake shrugged helplessly. "When in Rome." As he inhaled, the lighted tip of the cigarette crackled and sputtered, bits of exploding clove nuggets showering down upon Amanda.

"Ow! My blouse!" She sat bolt upright, brushing embers from the batik shirt she'd purchased not two days ago and was wearing now to impress any police officials they might encounter on their journey upriver. Drake had read that Indonesian civil servants were especially susceptible to fine attire.

"Go away," she said. "Before you have me in flames."

"Everyone else is smoking."

"Yes," she agreed, "and they all have holes in their clothes."

Drake struggled to his feet. "This ain't no veggie juice bar in Malibu."

"Go."

He went away, high-stepping gingerly among the arms, legs, torsos of his fellow passengers, muttering something cheap about smoking sections, low cholesterol, and alcohol-free drinks.

A shirtless child of three or four, clutching a half-eaten mangosteen in its slippery fist, was gazing at Amanda with the huge-eyed concentration of pure wonder. Without a thought, Amanda made a nasty face and stuck out her tongue. The child blinked, head jerking back as if struck, and, lunging for its mother, let out such a howl that everyone on the main deck must have turned around to stare. Yes, thought Amanda, it is I, the terrible white she-demon from over the seas. From her bag she pulled fat handfuls of typewritten paper to hold before her like a shield, damp tattered sections of a pirated manuscript copy of that hot new novel with cool attitude, *Wittgenstein's Jockstrap*, a dimly imagined tale of one vague young man's desperately vague quest for something or other, composed in a freeze-dried Europrose so devoid of nutrients even tears couldn't vivify it. Six-figure option to Pogo Pictures. Bernardo Scungilli slated to direct. Friends of Amanda's at GAM thought she would be "perfect" for the part of the earnest young English professor who serves as clumsy ventriloquist's dummy for the author's startlingly conventional views on any number of trendy topics. She also attends to our hero's less lofty needs. She's hip, she's urban, she gives good allegorical head.

After boring through half a page of deadwood, Amanda's attention began to drift. Her eye strayed surreptitiously over the crowded boat. She enjoyed looking at these people as long as they weren't looking back at her. She liked to try divining worlds from the grace of a gesture, the ebb of an expression, always aware, of course, of the ever-present danger of romanticizing our Third World brothers and sisters, but she

was a professional, this was her job to observe with scientific detach-
ment humanity in all its incarnations so that later, under footlights or
a Panaflex lens, she might mimic the truth with oracular accuracy.
So, no matter where she went, no matter what the circumstances, she
was always working, always gathering raw material. That, at least, was
the rationalization; maybe she was really nothing more than an unregenerate voyeur. In which case she had found her people.

Now, as if released from behind the insulation of the disintegrating
fog, the celebrated equatorial heat began to roll across the river in
great invisible waves. The unfettered sun turning the fine hairs of her
arms into spun gold as a dispiriting breeze lapped at her face like a
wet, lazy tongue. The shore slid past like pictures painted on a me-
chanical loop, the same melancholy scenery mile after slow mile,
every couple hundred yards the required pause at yet another floating
dock to board or unload passengers in a maddening replication of a
metropolitan bus route, all along the riverside the same happy people
standing in the same serried order, toothbrushes in hand, foam dripping
from their mouths, there was no jungle here, none, every green bough
and random sprig culled, cut, and shipped to Japan long ago for
chopsticks, in the wake of the machinery these open fields of coarse
weedy *lempang* grass, a depleted soil's surrender flag, vast uninteresting
expanses of secondary growth, a generic landscape, the depressing view
from the rear of an industrial park. The nagging wind nipped at the
stack of paper piled under her hand. Amanda watched for a moment,
then lifted her arm to allow a page, then another and another, half a
dozen at once, rise up into the wind and go flapping away over the
churning brown water. After a moment's hesitation, she withdrew
entirely the weight of her hand, let the wind take what it would. Like
a sudden flushing of doves, the remainder of the manuscript broke
into the air, tumbled helplessly about, settling in the furrowed turbulence behind like floating cobblestones to mark the trail home. An
elderly man nearby waggled a finger at Amanda, speaking sharply in
Malay. She apologized in respectful English.

Up on the roof, amid the strapped-down merchandise for village
stores upriver, the matching sets of lawn furniture, barbecue grills,
inflatable toys, the bags of plastic sandals, sun hats, boxes of canned
cocoa, laundry powder, and Duracell batteries, Drake had found smok-

ing refuge in a used obstetrical chair destined for a needy highland clinic. He was seated facing forward, feet propped up in the stirrups, watching this spectacular country advancing between his legs. So he missed the white flight of paper from the stern. He smoked a couple of *kreteks*, he took half a roll of photographs. The view was layered like a cake, in colors almost rich enough to eat, the sleek brown of the river still several miles wide at this point, dark and thick as gravy, teeming with traffic, the motorized longboats quick and buglike, the coal barges, the rafts heaped with yellowy rods of rattan cane, then the lurid green hills and, above, the sky virtually vibrating with blue fire. "The days are so bright here," Amanda complained, "my eyes hurt even behind these Ray-Bans." Of course, any day hurt with your system still dog-paddling through the alcohol of the night before. So far as Drake knew, it was not recommended that arduous jungle treks be begun on the morning of a hangover, but sometimes you had to forge your own path.

The evening had opened with the best intentions, an early dinner in the hotel restaurant, a brief stroll around the town of Sambir, and back to the hotel and to bed. But somehow, in the surprisingly over-crowded dining room, he and Amanda seemed to have been hijacked—there was no other term for it—by an older British couple at the adjoining table, the Harrelsons, Glen and Vivian, whose need for a touch of sympathetic company was distressingly overt. Drake had seen the scene often enough without wanting to play a part in it: dusky coconut culture serves as exotic backdrop for Anglo fantasies of global gaming and sexual derring-do under the rule that out in the non-Christian hinterlands there are no rules, no one is what he seems, and the congenial Welsh twosome you meet over rijsttafel in a restaurant whose wall murals depict a subtle range of lovemaking are, in actuality, ruthless agents of a foreign power who have selected you and your beautiful wife to play unwilling but critical roles in their horrid terrorist scheme. In fact, the Harrelsons were a pair of disillusioned tourists who had already done the up-country jaunt and were now, thankfully, on their way back to Aberystwyth. Art collectors of an eclectic adventurous sort, they had traveled far, endured much, in their search for genuine first-rate examples of Dayak beadwork, sculpture, textiles, and painting, and were departing "this mildewed thrift shop" with little more than a handful of locally mined diamonds purchased from a dealer in downtown Sambir for a price, they were willing to admit, less than half the going rate in London. The art, though once so highly valued throughout the world, had degenerated to the point of worth-lessness, "second-rate copies of copies, mass-produced, then artificially aged for gullible tourists." The Harrelsons were drowning their disappointment in Johnnie Walker Red and Bintang beer.

"But it sounds like the Dayak have simply adopted the lessons of the free enterprise system," said Amanda.

"And look what it's done to us," scoffed Mr. Harrelson, banging the bottom of his glass against the table.

"Save your money," advised Mrs. Harrelson in the tones of one whose recommendations were usually obeyed. Like a high-strung horse, she kept her lank strands of gray hair out of her face with nervous tosses of her head. She smoked one Player after another. "You will be trading a rather handsome sum of American dollars for the questionable privilege of viewing in situ dazed disorganized tribes in Western drag whose culture has been stripped and ravaged as thoroughly as the rain forest that once supported it."

"Do you know Indonesia's national motto?" asked Mr. Harrelson. He was bald and jowly and spoke in a loud voice that increased in volume with each drink. "*Bhinneka Tunggal Ika.* Sanskrit for 'Unity Through Diversity.' How absolutely preposterous. Unity at the Expense of Diversity might be more appropriate."

"At Lidung Payau," said Mrs. Harrelson, "we found in one of the tribal graveyards an effigy of a chain saw garnishing some poor elder's tomb."

"A rather witty gesture, don't you think?" asked Mr. Harrelson.

Mrs. Harrelson began shifting around in her chair. "Christianity is the chain saw of the spiritual world," she remarked with some heat.

"Well, I'm not much of a believer myself," offered Drake, "but—"

The woman went on. "It cuts the vitality right out of the soul. Then erects in the center of the wasteland it has made, the brutal sign of its triumph and occupation—a grotesque instrument of human torture, need I remind you?—and moves on like a horrid vampire in search of the warm life it requires to sustain its own deathlike existence."

Amanda burst into braying laughter. She couldn't help herself, she liked this odd woman.

"So the great art of a great people is irrevocably ruined, it's all garbage now. We've come too late." Mrs. Harrelson looked sadly into each of their eyes, to be certain they understood.

"And it's the same story everywhere," Mr. Harrelson declared. "The same process heading for the inevitable big showdown between Islam and Christianity. And it hardly matters who wins because in the end everyone everywhere will be subject to the one true god, working for the one true corporation, thinking the one true thought."

"And by then," Mrs. Harrelson said, "there'll only be one tree left. One bird. One flower. One dog. Horrifying."

"Disgusting," agreed Mr. Harrelson.

"Intolerable."

Mr. Harrelson leaned over, tapped Drake sharply on the knee. "You're not Greenpeace, are you? I understand there's a standing fat bonus among the native gendarmerie to anyone lucky enough to bag the pelt of one of those blue-eyed leaf freaks."

"Oh, Glen!" exclaimed Mrs. Harrelson.

"What a world, eh?" Mr. Harrelson examined the remaining contents of his glass, lost for a moment in the amber reflection. "Sound policy would have been to exterminate that awful white rajah set a century ago, the whole bloody *Lord Jim* crowd of them, stuck *their* overbred heads on cricket stakes out on the lawn of Government House."

"But, I wonder," said Amanda, "can you make a convincing argument for the case that each time a Westerner leaves home it's solely for purposes of greed or avarice?"

"Intentions, my dear girl, are so much pixie dust in this besotted life. Look to the ends. Look at the dripping record of our deeds."

"But isn't it conceivable that many people might wish to go abroad out of simple harmless curiosity, the pleasure of knowing what you didn't know before? It's only human."

"There are no harmless motives," said Mr. Harrelson.

"Curiosity is what killed the cat," said Mrs. Harrelson.

The discussion was obviously concluded. Mrs. Harrelson rummaged about in her rather large handbag for her wallet, which she opened and passed across the table to the Copelands. It was a glossy studio portrait of a pleasant young man in a British naval uniform, lips and cheeks garishly tinted by the photographer in processing.

"Our son," said Mrs. Harrelson. "Killed in his sleep aboard the *Ark Royal* during our Falklands misadventure. The Argentine missile hit amidships directly over his bunk."

"To maintain our claw upon every last scrap of worthless rock." Mr. Harrelson was drinking now straight from the Johnnie Walker bottle.

"Roger loved the navy," said his mother. "What were we to do?"

"I'm sorry," said Amanda.

"Go home," Mrs. Harrelson urged. "There's nothing more to see. Even out here. It's all soiled bank notes, television, and death."

Drake and Amanda fled the table at the first polite opportunity. Drunk, depressed, eager to drive the Harrelsons' odor from their nostrils, they ventured down to the waterfront and the notorious Hot Hot Disco, a long, loud building the size of a bowling alley and pulsing with music, bodies, and a sense of personal recklessness most communities preferred to keep well policed. Three steps inside and you knew in the roots of your scalp that under this spangled roof anything was possible. The place had the air of a frontier saloon where guns were checked at the door and the fraying fringes of the West found solace in unsafe sex and easy violence. The clientele, an inebriated mob of maenadic hookers and horny oil hands, was packed in so tightly that under the smoky black light it was difficult to notice at first that what appeared to be isolated outbreaks of highly energetic dancing was something else entirely. Hands were snaking with practiced anonymity in and out of sweat-damp clothes. Amanda was nearly stabbed in the eye with a lethal red fingernail attached to the end of some dragon lady's flailing arm. Onstage a quartet of skinny double-jointed Javanese was screeching its way through an enthusiastic, original interpretation of "That's All Right." The fat bartender was missing a thumb and a shirt. Amanda hadn't experienced a scene even remotely similar since her teenage bootwoman years as front fox for the all-girl cult band Angry Women Cleaning House. She and Drake found seats at a small wet table in the rear where they could sip their bottles of Bintang and observe as inconspicuously as possible. The flaring of a match at an adjacent table revealed the dark blue stain of a head-hunting tattoo decorating the throat of a Dayak man too young to have participated in the fabled ritual wars of his ancestors. He eyed the Americans through a series of perfect smoke rings, then spoke rapidly to the two girls in satin miniskirts who attended him. They all laughed.

Drake returned from an extended visit to the men's room to announce proudly, shouting into the amplified wind, "I just had a blow job on my way to the john."

"Male or female?" Amanda shouted back.

Drake leaned over, touched his wife's cheek with his lips.

They drank, they danced, they drank some more. Over and under the noise of the band, each number progressively indistinguishable from the last, other, more discordant sounds began insinuating themselves into the mix: the bright tinkle of breaking glass, here and there the screech of a protesting chair, the bark of a voice inescapably human in its intensity of outrage and threat. A bottle went sailing onto the stage. A trio of beefy Australians, sunburnt, drunk, in matching ten-gallon hats and powder blue western shirts, approached Amanda and asked her to dance. When she politely declined, they began chanting at her in a language that wasn't quite English.

"She's with me!" Drake shouted.

"I know," retorted the bland Aussie.

Drake pushed himself away from the table. All thought, all feeling, draining ruefully away. What was being given would be returned, no more, no less.

Abruptly, every light in the club was extinguished and the darkness was total. Someone screamed. The black wave of fear breaking over the room sent furniture toppling and tumblers flying. Invisible bodies began groping in blind panic for a way out. Drake seized Amanda by the hand and pushed on through the jostling crowd toward a promising patch of paler darkness from which flowed the wonderful scent of salt air and fish reek and petroleum waste in all its modern manifestations. Near the exit, traffic started to slow and thicken, skirting the fistfights that were erupting now with alarming rapidity, the familiar ozone-smell of impending riot harrying the revelers on. "This way!" shouted

Drake and, turning, was slugged in the mouth by a beautiful blond woman in a stunning red dress. Reeling backward in pained surprise, he probably would have taken a second hit had not Amanda, pushing determinedly from behind, propelled him past the commotion and out the narrow door into a false neon dawn and a stampeding horde of frantic taxi drivers who rushed them en masse, crying, "Where you go? Where you go?" The end of the century, the heart of the night, the well of the world.

"You okay?" he asked in the backseat safety of their hotel-bound cab as she hovered over him, trying to inspect the damage in the glare of oncoming lights.

"I'm fine." She touched a swell of angry skin over his cheek. "You'll live."

"The woman who hit me," said Drake, watching the driver's dark eyes flitting across the mirror, "I think she was a man."

When he woke the next morning, he found himself not in his bed, either at home or at the hotel, but sprawled in open air among the straps and stirrups of this bizarre chair, being baked in his epidermal jacket by a ruthless sun, dazed, headachy, oozing juice. He sat up amid a changed set, the greenery gone, replaced by an endlessly gliding progression of stubble and ash, black acres of unharvested soot, residue from the world's longest-running forest fire, the smoke heavy enough for months to alter flight paths in and out of Singapore. Darting about the river like minnows around an old bass were motorized longboats with neat cannonball piles fore and aft of astonishingly green squash and melons. Nothing he was looking at made any sense.

Down on the main deck he found Amanda among the suffocating crowd where he had left her, now studiously applying Tiger Balm to her latest collection of insect bites. "Your face," she remarked, "it looks like chicken tandoori."

"I fell asleep." He took the bottle of water from her hand and guzzled it down.

"I wanted to come searching, but somebody's got to guard our treasures."

Drake was staring beyond her, at the world outside the boat. "Strange shit," he muttered.

Amanda had her mirror out and was looking at her face as if to see it was still as she remembered. "I was beginning to feel abandoned here on the lido deck."

"Our pervert pal lurking around again?"

"No, thank God. Not that I noticed, anyway."

"Wonder where he went. The boat's not that big."

"Big enough for you to get lost in."

"I told you, I fell asleep. Up on the roof."

"I was thinking about you."

"Yeah? I was thinking about you, too."

They were looking at one another through their matching dark sunglasses.

"What you're thinking," he said, "is, I believe, a severe social faux pas, if not an outright felony, in these latitudes."

"Fuck the law. I wanna feel good."

This trip had certainly been a boon to their erotic life. In the last ten days they'd had more sex than in the previous ten months. Travel was indeed, as Drake liked to proclaim, an aphrodisiac. New scents, new tastes, new anatomies. They had barely closed the door of their first hotel room in Jakarta before they were stripping off their clammy, wrinkled airplane clothes and falling as one between cool, clean laundered-to-be-defiled sheets. The whole country was their bedroom; they got aroused within the ornate structures of Hindu candi; they stole kisses behind a pillar during the performance of a royal gamelan orchestra whose music (a dense, flowing pattern of percussive sound rising treelike out of low, deep rhythms, up through melody's swaying trunk into a twittering canopy of upper-register complexities) was said to confer immortality upon all who heard it, and yet, despite the care Drake and Amanda took to be circumspect in their behavior, even the least, most routine of their actions provided skit material for the ongoing show of Crazy White Foreigners, as Amanda was rudely reminded when she dared to engage the boat's "rest room," tiptoeing, roll of pink tissue in hand, across the crowded deck, apologies all around, to the cramped stall at the stern and the decaying wooden bench with a round hole a mere foot above the foaming current where she had barely settled herself down when a cluster of giggling children appeared beneath the insufficiently dangling blue terry cloth towel that pretended to be a curtain. Without a sense of humor, their hotel manager had tersely informed them, Indonesia will surely defeat you.

"Get away, you little brats!" Amanda screamed, lunging at her tormentors. It was like shooing flies. In an instant they were back again.

"At least fame in America doesn't entail intense curiosity about your toilet habits," she protested to Drake.

"Waaall," he drawled.

"Go away," she said, pushing at her husband. "Get out of here. You're the worst of the worst."

They passed a major timber camp, wide swaths of land stripped and bared, aprons of mud descending down to the riverbank, roar of diesel engines as the huge yellow machines continued chewing at the far fringes of the forest, the mouths of modern civilization eating away at the tasty wood, the plants, the insects, the birds, the mammals. The boat chugged on and by midday had entered upon the mirrored surface of a lake so clean, so still, it might have been a section of the sky itself fallen to earth here in the middle of the equatorial jungle. The shore was an impenetrable wall of vegetation, graceful nipa palm leaning out curiously over the glassy lake; the boat's progress attended by a chirping escort of freshwater dolphins romping deliriously in its wake. Country of perpetual wonder. The boat docked at a place called Tanjung Panjoy, an idyllic picture-postcard simulacrum of an authentic tribal village, the centerpiece on Jimmy Sung's Travel Tours into Primitive World, wealthy gangs of disoriented Westerners run up and down the river for a quick sampling of archaic man. The hotel manager had warned them, the Harrelsons had warned them, don't waste your time or your money on this Asian equivalent of a Potemkin village, pass on. The sole remaining longhouse, once home to more than twenty families, was now maintained as a profitable cultural museum and theater in which rather bored members of the Kenyah tribe dressed up in grandpa's colorful garb and pranced about for the cameras of paying visitors. Today's Kenyahs lived in separate buildings, neat secluded rows of boxlike suburban homes, one house one family, in accordance with the current government's coercive modernization campaign, full entrée into the high-tech, mass-consumption order of the future requiring the dismemberment of the social body into smaller and smaller pieces more and more dependent upon the structures of control. Community was systematically broken down into isolated individuals, and then the individuals themselves into contending fragments of confusion and desire, modular selves, interchangeable units for the new, interchangeable people of the masses' millennium. And as even the most rudimentary sense of wholeness was fading into extinction, the vitality of an entire culture was being processed for cash and entertainment. This late in our epoch, an old, old story. How deep into the interior did one have to press to escape the spectacle of such cannibalism?

They were standing at the rail, studying the painted bungalows with corrugated steel roofs, the sheltering palms, the vegetable gardens, the village actors in traditional dress wandering the tended dirt paths like costumed extras in Colonial Williamsburg, the souvenir stand sporting the traditional bright yellow Kodak sign, when drums began to sound from the direction of the longhouse. The 2 p.m. show was about to begin.

"Shall we go ashore for a howl and a dance?" asked Amanda.

" 'Never get out of the boat,' " replied Drake, and, at the sound of the famous fictional movie line echoing in the relevant air of this real place, they both laughed, the levels of self-consciousness attendant upon a contemporary journey like this were positively Piranesian in number and involution, the pertinent dialogue had already been spoken, the images already photographed, the unsullied, unscripted experience was practically extinct, and you were left to wander at best through a familiar maze of distorting mirrors—unless somewhere up ahead the living coils of this river carried one down and out of the fun house.

Amanda noticed the reflecting moon of a satellite dish rearing up over a distant rice barn. She wondered, "Do you think they have a telephone?"

"No," said Drake, "and even if they do, you're not using it."

"But you heard what Barry said," she persisted, Barry Stone being her agent at Global Artists Management, his loopy confidential voice penetrating twelve thousand miles of bristling static to burst at her ear during yesterday's obligatory phone check to her answering machine back home in L.A.: "Amanda, charmer, I know you're monitoring, so hold on to your coconut for this flash, just got a buzz from Ritchie Holderman, who says Trellis—you remember Trellis, Lemming's assistant?—she says that you are being seriously considered for a major role in *Dead End*, Lemming's epic about a senator who rapes and kills his own mother. You play a cop. I told Trellis that with your looks and your talent consideration couldn't last longer than five seconds, but no decision yet, you know Warner. Bring me a blowpipe. From the office window here—if I could even pry the damn thing open—I think I might be able to plant a poison dart in the Universal back lot. Okay, gotta go. Cheers to Drake. Keep your powder dry, you two—or whatever it is that shouldn't get wet."

"Yes," agreed Drake, "it's wonderful, you deserve the part, but there's nothing you can do about it from here, and until we get back there I don't want the business in my head. This trip is supposed to serve as sherbet, we're cleaning the palate for the next round."

"If this were Nebetz calling about your *Mr. Smith Goes to Pluto* project, the homilies would be running down a different track."

"Amanda."

"Yes?" she replied, the brightest girl in the class.

"So," said the boat's captain, who had come up unexpectedly behind them, "mister and missus are preparing to enjoy the opportunities of Tanjung Panjoy?"

"No," said Drake.

The captain laughed. He was a big man with a little head and a proud mouthful of gold teeth he couldn't cease displaying. "Everyone goes ashore at Tanjung Panjoy."

"We're not like everyone."

"Do they have a phone?" asked Amanda.

The captain laughed.

"We wish to go farther," explained Drake. "Where there are no phones."

"Ah," said the captain, "I understand. American headhunters." He laughed. "Want to go *ulu*."

"Yes," Drake agreed, "that's us."

"Okay," said the captain, "okay." As he turned to go, he flashed his strange passengers the peace sign.

"What does *ulu* mean?" Amanda asked.

"The end of the world. Funny, I think it means head, too."

"Do you suppose our friend takes a commission on each tourist he drops off at good ol' Tanjung Panjoy?"

"Every place on the planet is not run like Hollywood."

"True. Most are even worse."

The boat moved on, a big noise bullying its way upstream. In the afternoon the fierce eye of the sun clouded over and the sky turned gray, draining the color from the land, and without fanfare the rain began to fall in loud thick torrents and continued to fall without drama or variation for the next hour and the hour after that with the insistent doggedness of an event that, like it or not, had to be endured and brought to completion, like a fever or the phases of the moon. And, as Drake and Amanda soon discovered, it was an event requiring frequent repetition over the next several days and the impossibility, on an open boat like this, of avoiding the weather. This was their indoctrination into the dampness of exotic places; they would never be wholly dry again until they were back home in sunny California.

The boat moved on through a silvery curtain of rain that dimpled the river and rattled the roof, the obscure scenery so indistinguishable they might as well have been revolving in a blind circle. The Copelands tried hard to distract themselves, Drake with his guidebooks, his repositories of fun facts, assuming the role of color commentator on this trip, pleasure for him residing in the activity of seeing a thing, then reading about it, or reading, then glancing up to see what you have just read, the equation between word and object seemingly real and direct, knowledge was instantly practice, and vice versa. Amanda contented herself with a cheap paperback edition of *Paradise Lost*, one of those big, "deep," important books she had always meant to read, but in another life perhaps, the one she was inhabiting now too distracting to sustain an extended thought on any subject more elaborate than her career, its highways and byways, unless she physically removed herself from the systems, the culture, the peculiar heat and light supporting it. A country like Indonesia was supposed to be a relief. Time, in these quaint distant lands without clocks, was neither motion nor force but a static ground peopled with strange beings who wandered its contours in a metamorphosing dance of terrible beauty. According to Hindu legend, every thousand years a bird flies over the peaks of the Himalayas, trailing a scarf of silk in its beak. When the friction of silk upon stone has finally worn the mountains away, then one cosmic day shall have passed. Live within such a conception of time and you might be able to free yourself from the fetters of useless impatience. Why hurry? The present moment is a journey as rich and fabulous as any overseas excursion. Why pant on, lusting after your own death?

She realized she'd been reading the same eight verses over and over again. The construction of Hell was a process interminable. With melancholy pleasure she watched the rain, a virtual wringing out of the air, until abruptly, without a single cue, it simply stopped, as if the handle on the spigot had been smartly turned, and the clouds dissolved and the sky showed its skin, blue as Krishna's body, and the boat chugged on. Villages appeared with the easy regularity of telephone poles along a country road, each with its school, its clinic, its church, the progression of identical white crosses atop their steeples charting the course of the Light into the dank interior. The sun slipped westward and broke across the horizon's keen edge and spilled and the vault of heaven came open upon staggered banks of kindled treasure as between the halves of darkening land slid the boat, the river breaking from its bow in long slow aching waves of pure gold.

They slept fitfully that first night, fending off the careless arms and legs of their packed-in neighbors, experiencing more intimacy than they wished with strangers and none at all with each other. The second night the boat, for reasons as mysterious as most events on this trip, tied up at a nondescript dock in the middle of nowhere and Drake and Amanda dutifully followed their fellow travelers down a narrow path into the enveloping darkness and the surprise of a modest river town containing a *pengingapan*, lodgings for the night, a small three-dollar room in which, after bathing in a closed shed with a cement floor, ladling dubiously clean buckets of cold water over their lathered bodies, they could lie privately together on a cramped bed, listening to the scampering feet of small animals on the roof, the nagging unintelligible chatter of the Indonesian couple in the next room behind walls as thin as their mattress, the slow unwinding smoke of a mosquito coil curling and eddying in the soft light of a kerosene lamp. Without a word, they eased themselves into one another and proceeded to enjoy the sweetest, quietest, most intense, most prolonged coupling either had ever known. Voices babbled on behind the wall. Flying brown beetles buzzed and bumped against the ceiling. All of Borneo lay about them in the darkness. They began again. They felt like high school virgins.

In the morning it was back to the boat, the teeming deck, crying babies, restless children, engine spew, TV squawk, *kretek* fumes, the sun, the rain, the scenery, the books. "And fast by hanging in a golden chain/This pendant world, in bigness as a star/Of smallest magnitude close by the moon./Thither full fraught with mischievous revenge,/ Accursed, and in a cursed hour he hies."

Seven days.

At Long Duling, final stop on the languorous river-taxi route, *Indonesia Today* offered the practical suggestion that the adventuresome traveler seek out the services of one Pa Jutoh Den, combination headman, police official, and tour agent, whose sons were highly recommended as guides on any further jaunts into the wilderness up-country. He could be found in the distinctive small bungalow at the edge of the forest, the one with the carvings on the roof, parodies of Western men in exaggerated handlebar mustaches, Santa Claus beards, big white tombstone-sized grinning teeth. He seemed happy to see Drake and Amanda, greeted his new American visitors as if they'd already met under different circumstances. The interior of the house was cluttered from ceiling to floor with pictures, sculpture, bric-a-brac, of an outrageously Christian nature, the religion embraced with the enthusiastic fervor of a memorabilia collector. He was attired in a neat pressed beige uniform of the U.S. park ranger type. A brass nameplate on his chest read MR. DEN. His face was extremely wrinkled, as if it had been folded and refolded countless times over the years. He was cordial, correct, perfectly polite, but unsmiling. He asked to see their papers. Drake presented their passports and the impressively stamped and floridly signed letter of introduction he had obtained before departure from the Ministry of the Interior in Sambir (another handy guidebook tip). Mr. Den studied these documents in silence, glancing up now and then to study the documented. He said nothing. Apprehensions rising, Drake offered the chief his California driver's license and his American Express card. Then, his Pump and Glow health club membership, his Blockbuster Video card.

"I am not a stupid man," said Mr. Den.

"Oh no, I didn't think—"

"I see what you think." Mr. Den gathered up the cards and the letter and handed them back. "I knew you were coming. It's my job to know such things. My son has already agreed to guide you to the Apokayan."

"Thank you," replied Drake. "We certainly appreciate such kind consideration."

"Your English is excellent," observed Amanda.

A trace of a smile emerged from the creases on his face. "I have lived in Medford, Oregon, and San Jose, California, and Sacramento. Ten years. A long time. I left when my wife died. It's a confusing country."

"Tell us," said Drake. "And we're natives."

"Many interesting similarities between our two countries. Size, diversity, political turmoil."

"But you people are so religious," said Amanda. "Your beliefs seem so alive and urgent and meaningful."

"The spirits are with you, too," Mr. Den said. "All around. In the air, in the streets. You see them captured on your television screens."

"Yes," said Drake. "We pray to it daily."

The old man's eyes, dark as wet stones, rested their weight against Drake's pink face. "You don't know anything." He turned then to Amanda. "Why does this foolish man want to take you up this river to where you are not supposed to be?"

"We're trying to find a place we've never been," said Amanda, the cane of her chair squeaking beneath her shifting body.

"American houses are so big," said Mr. Den. "So many rooms. Such big yards, too. Do you have a dog?"

"Cats," said Amanda. "Two cats."

"I take it," said Drake impatiently, "you're not in favor of us proceeding upriver."

"I am not in favor; I am not against. My son will take good care of you. He understands what people like you want."

"And you don't?"

"No. It is you who don't understand."

Mr. Den insisted that they spend the night as his guests. The hot meal of rice and chicken was the best food they'd had since leaving Jakarta. At dinner they talked again about America. They discussed shopping malls, which Mr. Den occasionally missed, and pro football, of which he was particularly fond.

Drake and Amanda slept on rattan mats in the front room beneath the incriminating eyes of a hundred agonized Christs. Here was another reason they'd come so far—to brush up against an individual of Mr. Den's mismatched parts, dark strokes and slashes and spiky shadows with no discernible bottoms, "a cubist character," pronounced Drake, a man stubbornly unlike the Copelands or their friends. They were good Americans after all, they wanted to lose their entangling selves.

In the morning they were greeted at breakfast (bananas and sago paste, yum) by Mr. Den's eldest son. His name was Henry, a young affable man in his mid-twenties, lean, well buffed, with an interestingly piratical gleam. He was wearing a Garuda airline captain's hat and sucking an unlit corncob pipe. "No problem," he said, "no problem" in response to any doubt, request, concern, or passing observation. His sidekick, Jalong, who apparently understood no English whatsoever, simply grinned—constantly. The Copelands would get to know his perfect teeth quite well. Henry and Jalong were eager to begin the big trip.

"Right now?" asked Amanda.

"We load the boat, we go," said Henry.

"I like this guy's decisiveness," Drake declared. "Something new in our lives."

Their craft, a blue-painted longboat with a pair of huge sentinel eyes drawn on the bow and a trio of Johnson outboard motors bolted to the stern, was ready to depart in half an hour. As they roared away from the dock, a stolid Mr. Den waved goodbye as if he were in physical pain. The longboat skimmed over the surface of the river with such unaccustomed ease that Drake and Amanda, their exhilarated faces lifted into the cooling wind, grew drunk on the speed. Miles fled beneath them like panicked ghosts.

Thirteen sets of rapids.

The first stretch of white water came upon them with the suddenness of a traffic accident. The river seemed to have come apart before their startled eyes, broken rock protruding like bone from its wounds, gouts of foam spurting into the turbulent air. Henry, at the throttle, powered the boat up through the shifting whirlpools, maneuvering for position; he shouted something at Drake and Amanda that neither understood over the roar, but as he began gunning the outboards, it did seem advisable to secure a good grip on one's seat. Lining the boat up beneath the largest of the rapids, a thick horsetail of cascading current, he paused for a moment, the hull sliding about like a piece of ice on a grill; then, leaning forward like a determined jockey, he plunged ahead into the flood. The boat moved, hesitated, then, amid engine shriek and water thunder, simply stopped, the river running beneath its vibrating frame like the rushing rim of a wheel. For one awful instant they were suspended above disaster, the keel of the boat riding the force of the torrent like a reversed magnet, unloosed, unmoored, out of control, the sharp spray in their faces, Henry shouting out encouragement to the straining motors, grinning Jalong in the bow with a plastic bucket bailing like mad, the bouncing Copelands trying not to glance too often at one another with the blanched appeal of stricken airline passengers, the fragile longboat, as if responding to psychic entreaty, moved forward an inch, another inch, then, in one sweet dizzying lift, rose up and over the crest of the falls onto a slick moving sheet of unruffled stream, and they looked around at themselves and they laughed.

A mile and a half farther on and they did it all over again. It was like working your way back up the world's longest, meanest roller coaster. Even Henry's moves, as honed as any professional speedboater's, were not always equal to the wiles of the river. Sometimes a penalty had to be exacted before the proper slot could be revealed and the boat, struggling like a trapped fish high in the wild strength of a cataract, would be repelled by the springy web of some invisible force field in their path and down they would go, backward into the torrent, puckered fingers gripping the gunwales, trying to balance yourself on a bucking animal with no saddle, no reins. And Henry would have to reposition the boat for another attempt. Half a dozen times and more. Twice he gave up entirely and the boat had to be unloaded, physically carried to a point above the rapids, and then tediously reassembled. Neither American was permitted to assist. They sat together on a log, catching their breath.

"I feel like a geek," Drake said. "I'm not comfortable being waited on like this."

"You never complain at home," replied Amanda. A winsome smile for her helpmeet.

By dusk, when they arrived at a village of Henry's friends where the motorized longboat would be exchanged for poles and a dugout canoe, the Copelands were so exhausted they lay down on the floor of the first hut they were shown and toppled into an unillumined sleep, the ground continuing to move beneath them, flowing things, the grand stuff of the universe, and so missed dinner and the fine company of authentic indigenous folk, and woke in the dawn in their soiled clothes and congratulated themselves for having stayed the course. One word and the boat would have turned about in midstream. It was their gasoline, their food, their money.

"The worst is past," said Drake. "From now on we lounge about in the canoe, enjoying the views."

"What was so bad about yesterday?" Amanda asked.

He couldn't tell if she was kidding or not, so he pretended she was serious. "It's not every day one goes shooting the rapids."

"I thought it was fun."

"Right. Me, too. Wet, woozy, and ready to whoop. The great outdoors. You can't get this at home, without falling blind drunk into your swimming pool."

"How far are we?"

"I don't know. I lost the map in the drink."

After the rough-and-tumble of the rapids the serenity of the upper Kutai was a marvelous surprise—a gondola ride into the forest primeval, engine howl replaced by the delicate plash of dipping paddles, the increasingly lush landscape slipping past at a leisurely, civilized pace. Comfortably propped against the soft cushioning of his pack, Drake, binoculars in hand, scanned the bank for random signs of animal life. Drenched in sun block, a large straw hat shielding her face, Amanda entertained her husband with a running commentary on the passing scene in the unmistakable voice of Katharine Hepburn.

Henry and Jalong, rowing steadily, effortlessly, at either end of the boat, shouted out to one another over their heads, bemusement rich as moisture in the air. They were talking about them, but Drake and Amanda didn't care. In a spell of rare pleasure they were temporarily immune from critical regard.

The river twisted and turned, a lazy looping and unlooping back to the source, narrowing as it went, rank vegetation on either shore pressing down to water's edge and beyond, leaning reckless over the slow still tide, spidery branches reaching out to touch, link arms, sealing the world into one long wound tunnel through which drifted this odd little boat, its odder passengers, like a dead stick dropped by accident and flowing the wrong way up an undulating carpet of pollen and leaves and broken twigs where dragonflies cavorted in metals of acid green and blue. The light was muted here, of an aquarium clarity, and sounds were sharper, the air an intimate stew of sweat and rot, the collective scent of a million discarded tennis shoes. There could be no doubt, this was the jungle for sure, and they were inside it.

Ancient trunks and knotted vines, giant ferns and stippled foliage, the languid monotone of botanical patterning interrupted, at precisely the proper moment, by a sudden caesura in the greenery, bright orchids dazzling as summer clouds, flavored cups of epiphytic ice protruding from their beds of root growth thick as pubic hair up in the crotches of the stilted mangrove trees, or the swoop of incandescent plumage as a blue-throated flycatcher sailed out into the open river space and vanished, the eye barely registering its passage.

The whispers, the whistles, the shrieks, the calls of the forest life unseen.

Around a bend and the dappled air was alive with a soft cascading of pink and white, petals falling, floating, fluttering down like gentle shavings from improvements being made in heaven, a gift of beauty freely given in abundance whether there were minds to record and admire or not. Steeped to the nostrils in the rich fragrance of this flowery confetti, Drake and Amanda looked at each other in mutual astonishment, and for a moment every discomfort, every ache, every embarrassment was forgiven. Yes, this was a voyage into paradise. And, yes, it had been worth the expense and the exertion.

Midday they stopped at a clearing and shared a lunch of cold sticky rice and a can of oily sardines. It was near here, Henry informed them, that only a couple of months ago a previous boat was attacked by a king cobra who, swimming with amazing speed, caught up to the vessel and attempted to board. The snake was repelled by a brave Swiss tourist with a handy umbrella. Quite unusual. No one could explain it. Amanda stopped eating and directed her attention to the surrounding rocks. "Dum-dum, dum-dum, dum-dum," sang Drake, waving his fingers about melodramatically. "*Fangs,*" he said. "Just when you thought it was safe to paddle the rivers of Borneo."

In the afternoon they spotted their first mammal, a startled muntjac or barking deer who had come down to the water for a drink, fixed the intruders with a frozen stare, emitted a weird coughing sound, and bounded away. "There goes dinner," laughed Henry. They passed a gray monitor lizard lounging inconspicuously in the gray dry mud of the bank. "Very good also," said Henry. Amanda didn't know whether to believe him or not. Drake's guidebook-based attempts at bird identification were routinely corrected. "A picture is not a thing," Henry scoffed. Out of sight the shier species announced themselves in a cacophony of harsh inanimate noises—police whistles, stuttering car engines, ricocheting bullets, nightsticks on concrete—a regular *Naked City* soundtrack. Up ahead the river appeared to simply stop, running headlong into an impenetrable wall of woven jungle that shifted magically at their approach, a sorcerer's spirited veil, to disclose the widening cleft through which they might pass, marveling upward at the massed riot of vegetation balanced so delicately above their craning necks. They squeezed down aisles dark and tight as a sewer pipe, they wandered through high caverns of monumental dimensions boldly scooped out of forest stuff, they glided across heroic-landscape paintings in the grand style of the nineteenth century. Lengths of fraying liana dangled all around like abandoned theatrical cable from a long-since-vanished show. In the ear of his imagination Drake could hear the beat of muffled drums.

Late in the day they made camp in a clearing Henry and Jalong hacked from the underbrush with honed steel parangs. In half an hour they had created breathing room and a comfortable lean-to shelter with sturdy sapling floor conveniently elevated inches off the damp infested ground and carpeted in a spongy layer of tree bark. Dinner was rice, naturally, and a bony river fish Henry caught at dusk with a homemade hook and a hand-held string. The Copelands had begun already to fantasize about distant foods, Drake drooling over ice cream of the rich premium variety, huge heaping goblets of rum raisin and pralines 'n' cream, the greater the butterfat content the better, Amanda lost in a chocolate truffle reverie, thin sculpted shells of crème fraîche and gin and Grand Marnier and liquid cherries and raspberry puree, imagined tastes the sweetest.

Then Henry, sucking gravely on his dead pipe, began to tell them stories he had heard as a child from the great head-hunting days of the not so ancient past, when painted parties of six to seven hundred men in feathered war caps of braided rattan and coats of beaded honey-bear fur and armed with long horn-handled *mandau* blades and sharpened spears and shields of thick gumwood bearing the curiously gentle and childish face of the tree god framed by tufted rows of human hair, when these ecstatic, chanting warriors marched off on prolonged raiding expeditions into the perilous country over the mountains. It was a time when the spirit world was lucid and robust. Every decision, every act, was regulated by the songs, the flight patterns, the dreams, of the birds, those inspired messengers of the gods. The birds told them in which direction to travel, and when. The birds led them to the perimeter of the enemy village and at dawn directed their attack. The men rushed the compound, bellowing like maddened bulls. The enemy longhouses were immediately set ablaze, the fleeing villagers hunted down and slain and relieved of their heads, wherever they happened to fall. These precious trophies were then roasted, wrapped in palm leaves, and carried home in triumph to the acclamation of their waiting families. Such was the purpose of war. Little boys were given swords to hold and taught to strike at the fresh heads. The women danced with them, mimicking the actions of their men, sometimes in their frenzy biting at the dead lips and cheeks. The feasting and drinking lasted for days, and when the party finally ended, the new heads were suspended in nets with the old out on the longhouse veranda well above the reach of the snapping dogs. Everyone was happy for a very long time. Heads were the containers of divine power and, like magic seeds, once planted in the heart of a village, in the mud of the padis, conferred health, fertility, and prosperity upon each member of the tribe.

"But this practice," asked Amanda, "was outlawed many many years ago?"

"Oh yes," agreed Henry. "Officially, in my grandfather's time. No more war parties since. But sometime, you know, people get mad at one another."

"So now if it happens that an enemy is killed, this act is understood to be a murder, not a ritual?" Drake asked.

"Yes."

"And is the head ever taken?"

"Yes, but very rare. No one knows, not the government, not the police, not the missionary. Very rare. You must not discuss this topic with anyone please. Very sensitive area."

"I've read that in labor disputes a few years ago some timber and oil officials were killed and when the bodies were found there weren't any heads to go with them."

"Yes," said Henry simply. "Very sensitive area."

The Copelands were encamped upon the grounds of such events, experiencing frissons no television or movie screen could ever provide. Or so they liked to imagine. The darkness was their screen now, and it was filled with a multitude of strange eyes staring invisibly back at them. When Amanda needed "to go to the bathroom," as she so cutely put it, Drake accompanied her down to the river, brave man with a big flashlight. She stepped out of shorts and panties, waded into the warm black current, and squatted down, Indonesian-style, the roll of flapping paper held unsteadily overhead, light beam bobbing playfully about her—had she ever engaged in anything so ridiculous as this nerve-racking adventure in outdoor elimination?—anxiously swiveling to and fro, checking to see that no living creature had managed to sneak up from behind while simultaneously trying to avoid contact with samples of her own floating excrement.

After the cooking fire had burned down and the kerosene lanterns quenched, they experienced, from the illusory safety of their mosquito netting, the phenomenon of a natural darkness that was almost total but for the eerily glowing trunks of a few nearby trees smoldering with the soft fire of phosphorescent fungus, and they discovered that here, in this fecund climate, the night had a thousand tongues. Creatures chattered and squeaked and howled and buzzed and whooped and bawled in a never-ending racket of astonishing volume.

"It sounds," declared Amanda, "like a video game."

Drake turned toward his wife—even at this brief distance he couldn't actually see her—and said, "I wonder who's winning?"

As they lay there, attempting to gather whatever minutes of sleep they could against the demands of the coming day, bugs plopping like fallen nuts upon the netting, the hectic night life around them blended gradually into a gentle storm of vague static, the forgotten television in the next room that signed off the air while you fell asleep thinking of other things.

Drake's dream: his first shot in the director's chair and events could not be more disastrous, lights were popping, sets collapsing, lines being flubbed, actors late, actors missing, crew squabbling, execs complaining, funds withering, and in the middle of an elaborate take of a crucial scene the camera runs out of film. But this is his chance, maybe his only chance, to show the world, the industry, what he can do. He can't quit. So, hunched over the editing table, sweat dripping off his nose, paralyzed by the insight he hasn't a clue how to cut the film into a coherent piece of work, individual scenes like so many miscellaneous playing cards, he begins to wonder if the order of the deal would even matter. Would the audience notice? Would it even care? The questions swing above an abyss. The audience, too. He is the bridge maker. He must not fail. The film is in his hands, it's slippery, it slides apart, it can't be held, it's like a snake, it's in his hands.

They arose in the dank dawn out of a sleep without rest to quietly assume the previous day's languid positions in the boat, gazing speechlessly like sated connoisseurs upon mile after absolute mile of bursting, shrieking, pullulating redundancy, verdure without beginning or end, the moss-backed primordial crowded up against yesterday's tender birth, the same random elements combined, recombined in a ceaseless round of genesis and collapse. The scale of such vistas so great that their sense of themselves, the plain humanness aggrandizing every puny ego, lost its turgor, its shape, a goodly portion of its size. They were small and they were lonely, their solitude enlivened occasionally by the green cord of a tree snake dangling ominously near or the rare sight of a fleshy-nosed proboscis monkey bounding shyly away into the upper canopy. Then the jungle would resume its mood of poised tranquillity and the boat would pass on, the smoke from Drake's countless clove cigarettes hanging motionless in the stagnant air of its wake. Late in the day a huge rhinocerous hornbill came whu-whu-whupping on black leathery wings down over their heads, the totem bird of the forest people, conveying, even as they watched in startled wonder, a fresh soul to the far country of the dead and reminding Amanda, for no particular reason, of their interminable flight in from LAX, cramped hours, fetid thoughts in a whining aluminum tube to whose outer skin clung, in painted representation, Garuda, the mythical sun bird, capable of bearing Vishnu, Lord of the Sacrifice, from one world to the next quick as lightning. The national airline of Indonesia operated at more modest speeds. The blue curve of the Pacific extended into infinity. Back home Amanda had worked as a volunteer for the ecology group Groundswell, dedicated to raising funds and planetary consciousness. Until this trip she hadn't realized how big the planet actually was.

When the keel began scraping bottom, Henry declared the river leg of their journey ended. He and Jalong dragged the boat up into the deep grass and made camp for the night, again fashioning out of raw forest a snug little shelter with a watertight roof as easily as throwing up a pup tent. Neither man seemed to sweat or even breathe hard. After dinner (same, same) Amanda broke into a tin of Leeds & Palmer Country Tea Biscuits and offered them around.

"You opened those too soon," said Drake, taking two nevertheless. "Next week you'll be wanting them badly and they'll be soggy and damp."

"But I want them now. If I hadn't wanted them now, I wouldn't have opened them. And how do you know I don't want them more now than I would next week?"

"We're supposed to be pacing ourselves, remember?"

"Look, when my biscuits are gone, I'm not going to be filching your Fig Newtons—if that's what you're worried about."

"We've got to keep the big picture in focus, Amanda."

"Never lost it, Tuan Drake."

Amanda's dream: she is being pursued through the moonlit maze of a stone temple by a howling gang of yellow-fanged baboons. At their head a demon king with the inhuman features of a medieval gargoyle. She is caught, she is eaten alive, she is dead. The scene is briskly rewound and replayed. Again and again. She cannot wake herself up and make it stop. She sits up, she opens her eyes; she sees herself sitting up, opening her eyes; she sees herself seeing herself—the dark refractions of the sea of sleep.

In the morning they loaded their supplies onto their backs and moved single file out into the waiting jungle. From the shallow headwaters of the Kutai the land sloped severely upward. Less than halfway to the top and the Americans were feeling the grade in the burning muscles of their legs and the floppy bags of damp cotton that were their lungs. Drake paused to tie a bandanna about his dripping forehead, perfume to the black cloud of hungry gnats thronging in sync with his slightest movement. Amanda surprised herself by draining an entire bottle of water in one breathless gulp. "Wait-a-minute" vines tore at their clothes; rocks bruised clumsy knees and shins. At the summit Henry and Jalong went to work with their parangs and—presto!—a stand of young trees dropped dramatically away to reveal a spectacular "scenic view" of untouched rain forest rolling in deep green swells out to where clouds piled up like mountains of snow on the rim of the world. Over the valley hung a Laki Neho, a hawk, as if suspended from a string, planing in tight circles on motionless wings. Good sign, Henry assured them, now they would not have to turn back, to crouch at river's edge before their omen poles, waiting for crested spider-catcher to pass, east to west.

"Yeah," grumbled Drake, "I'll show you a lucky bird."

Henry and Jalong turned away to conceal their mirth.

Amanda wondered what folks in these parts did to amuse themselves in the days before dumb Westerners started volunteering to serve as stand-in clowns, fools, and jesters. She was leaning back against the slanted trunk of a dead tree, skeptical eye on the ruthless sun and this apparently impassable immensity before them being pelted so with hard light, and she couldn't help speculating whether that hawk might not be trying to tell them something else. Her attention was caught by movement closer to hand and she noticed that the ground near her feet, or at least the grasses, leaves, and bark chips covering it, seemed to be alive and heading in her direction.

"Drake," she called softly, not wishing to panic, cause undue alarm. She began backing away behind the tree trunk. "Draaake!"

He looked where she was pointing. "What the hell is that?" He leaned over, trying to decipher the meaning of this strange new phenomenon.

"Leeches," announced Henry, grinning as if they'd just discovered gold. "Very good friends. They like you."

"Sure, that's what they say at Global Artists, too."

Henry squatted down and began beating upon the undergrowth with the flat blade of his parang. "They already on you," he said nonchalantly.

"Where?" asked Amanda with some alarm, picking gingerly at her clothing. Then she saw the blood running down Jalong's leg. A quick search of her own person revealed several of the fat brown critters hanging like slimy ornaments from her terribly white calves and thighs and a cozy thick pair nestled against her stomach. Drake, who had attracted even more of the little suckers—one hardy fellow managing to squeeze its way through a boot eyelet for a hot meal in the hollow of his ankle—took pictures of this first close encounter with Borneo's wildlife. Neither he nor Amanda had felt a thing. Henry taught them how to scrape the parasites from their skins with the edges of their knives. Obviously, no one was going to be permitted to cross this forbidden territory without shedding some blood—an involuntary offering to the great forest itself—and an activity, loathsome at first, then merely irritating, that promptly became a regular habit of their day, thoughtless as brushing their teeth.

After everyone was rubbed down with tobacco juice (a trekker's tip provided by Henry, juice by an energetically chewing Jalong), rebuttoned, rebloused, and generally refreshed, they descended the ridge down a narrow winding trail into the submerged blue-green world of perpetual jungle twilight. The air was muggy enough to float in. In less than an hour the astonishing array of tropical life-forms, the knitted texture of an organic art, was reduced to the numbing reiteration of your own plodding feet, the complex orchestration of animal and insect sound condensed to the chuffing of your own breath in your own sea-throbbing ear. They tripped; they fell; they got up and struggled on without complaint—talking used up too much precious energy. Their bodies began to collect an impressive assortment of cuts, bites, stings, and scrapes. Their faces, as if coated in a protective layer of oil, were always slick with sweat, Amanda's hair in sodden ringlets to her chin. They crossed a rickety bridge of vine and bamboo, a fast tributary foaming yellow and brown beneath their tightwire steps. They waded through turgid streams of warm tea-colored water and crept down log trails slippery with moss. They floundered in mud thick as chocolate frosting, pungent as an open latrine, and then burst through the forest wall into an extraordinary clearing alive with light, simple strands of grass standing up like spun rarities ignited from within, and farther on an abandoned village, huts and barns long collapsed, only the gray bleached roofs left sitting flush on the overgrown ground, sprigs of fresh green sprouting here and there like ribbons on a dull suit. They came upon a flower in the middle of the wood, a massive scarlet eruption almost a meter in diameter, as if the forest floor had been incised and deliberately peeled back, exposing a raw ugly wound speckled with white poxlike scars and reeking of old meat. Buzzing flies of monstrous proportions clung to this flesh with an addict's avidity.

About two in the afternoon Henry said they should stop now and make camp. A bad storm was on its way.

Amanda looked up into a hopeless tangle of branches and foliage. "How does he know a storm is coming? I can't even see the sky."

"Because, you ignorant white lady," explained Drake in a ludicrous accent, "the sounds tell him, the sounds of his native homeland, the song of the furry and feathered creatures, the howls of the great monkeys."

"I'd punch you if I weren't so tired."

An hour later the dim light got dimmer, the tall shafts of the trees began to move like masts in a high gale, the leafy crowns swaying together in banded harmony, the moaning of limbs as wood rubbed against wood in the gathering dark. Henry and Jalong giggled nervously between themselves. "You hear," Henry explained in embarrassment, "the trees, they are having sex together." A ragged skirt of black cloud must have swept in low overhead, for down in their shelter it turned to night. Lightning began stabbing at the ground somewhere beyond their sight, the thunder loud in their ears like empty steel drums being rolled down a ramp. Bits of leaf and bark fell in gentle hail upon their roof, where they clung to the poles like desperate sailors as the rain descended abruptly in full force as if a trap door had been sprung and the equivalent of a mountain waterfall crashed down upon their heads. In thirty minutes it was over. No one moved. The forest dripped from every surface, noisily, steadily, on through the night and into the next dawn, when they awoke to swirling curtains of steam issuing from the earth and the chirping of tree frogs, the screeching of birds, the hooting of gibbons. Henry and Jalong were huddled in conference over a small pile of damp sticks, urging on the fire from their Bic lighters.

A groggy Amanda gazed askance upon the scene. Drake sat nearby, rousting nighttime squatters from his boots with a vigorous shake. "Where the hell are we?" she asked. "Skull Island?" She blew her nose, frowned at the result.

Drake was amused. "I hope Kong likes you," he said, "or we're screwed."

She ignored her husband. She was in need—of something, of anything. She hunted around for the Leeds & Palmer tin. Yes, damn him, the biscuits were slightly sodden, yet retaining more than sufficient flavor to transport her for a few delicious moments into a state where neither weariness nor discomfort could trouble her. Taste—the sense of the gods.

The day was downhill from there, as all the trails seemed to climb doggedly upward and even when the land lay apparently level and clear of snares it felt as slippery as a greasy kitchen floor. Their stamina, instead of strengthening with use, deteriorated by the hour. They had difficulty maintaining their balance; one would stumble and fall, then the other. Once, as Drake reached down to help his wife to her feet, she thought she detected something in his eyes. "I can take this as long as you can," she declared.

Drake was stone-faced. "I didn't say a word."

They paused for lunch in a cool glade beside a hill of black rock from which poured a dozen separate streams of white gushing water. Drake took a picture. Amanda flung herself upon an inviting bed of spongy ferns. "You know," she said, "I've forgotten what the sun even looks like." Silence. No one cared to comment. So what? Indifferent by now to the faint persistent aroma of organic rot, Amanda sprawled on her back, casual as any native, at the center of this cozy green cave. The massive gray columns of the ageless trees soared up around her into fantastic vaults of living tissue woven so fine that, in the tiny shivering spaces between, the broken light of day twinkled down at her in a flaring of prismatic color as if projected through the tall tracery of a stained glass window. Exactly. The ancestral scene every cathedral was designed to mimic, the home that will always be, deep in the spiraling wonderwork of the human gene, our lost link with the true paradise, the arboreal playground up in the bouncing boughs where divinities reside and delight in communing with their creatures. Had she any strength, Amanda might have attempted a shimmy up the nearest trunk for kicks. She heard Drake's voice, he was saying something to her, he was saying it again. She lifted her head. "What?" she cried. "What is it now?"

Jalong was pointing in her direction.

"He says you probably should not be lying in that particular spot," called Drake. "Fire ants."

"Holy Christ!" She leaped to her feet, brushing frantically at her clothes, finding nothing.

"A precaution," said Drake. "I don't believe we're in any immediate danger."

"Are they laughing? Are they laughing over there behind that tree? I'm not too tired or too weak to do something about that."

"Here," said Drake, extending an arm. "Forget about them." In his hand was a Fig Newton.

"Why, thank you. Whatever did I do to deserve this?"

"Do I need an excuse to act decent?"

She pretended to think for a moment. "Yes."

"I must love you," he said. "I'm immune to your insults."

She chewed thoughtfully on the Fig Newton. "Getting kinda soggy, aren't they?"

Henry called to them. With their knives he and Jalong had been prying a curious stone from the silt along the stream. He turned the mud-caked thing in his hands and all could see that it was a skull, small and discolored.

"Monkey?" asked Drake.

Henry shook his head. "Human," he said. "Human baby."

The bony hemisphere had been cracked open and the case once containing the world within the world was packed to the sockets with wet clay.

"How'd it get here?" asked Amanda.

Henry didn't know. Perhaps the child had been buried here, perhaps the remains had been washed downstream from another place long ago.

"That child was murdered," said Amanda. "Look at the size of the hole."

Henry shrugged. He squatted before them, washing the skull in the flowing water, and when he was finished, he ran a length of vine through the jagged hole in the cranium and out the foramen and wore the skull around his neck like an amulet. Protection that might come in handy further on in their journey.

Drake took a picture. "When in Rome," he said grimly.

"Why not?" asked Amanda.

That evening they pitched camp at the base of a looming mountain wall of gnarled limestone. At dusk they were startled from their wood gathering by a high whooshing sound as the rock face overhead splintered into thousands of dark brittle pieces sucked up and away in a towering vortex toward an invisible hole deep in the clear orange sky. A grottoful of chittering bats launched flapping on their nightly feed. Life up close on the food chain.

And later that night, long after the others had fallen asleep, the pale shaft of Drake's flashlight could still be glimpsed by curious nocturnal eyes, shifting fitfully over the pages of his remaining guidebook. Printed information had never seemed so vivid, so urgent, so necessary. " 'All the islands are permeated by the notion of *semangat*, or life force, inhabiting not only people, plants, animals, but sacred objects, villages, places, nations. The *semangat* of a human is concentrated in the head. The goal of life is to keep the positive and negative *semangat* around you in harmony. One way this can be achieved is through enhancement of your own *semangat* by, as certain tribes in Borneo, for instance, believed, taking the head of another. Blood, of course, is rich in *semangat* and was often used for anointings, for drinking, and, among the Makassarese of Sulawesi, as a solution in which royal

weapons were regularly bathed in order to keep them charged.' "
Amongst the wonder of words, the wonders beyond the word.

In the morning Amanda looked at herself in a mirror and screamed.
This was the longest she'd gone without an image check. Reacquain-
tance with herself, with what Borneo had done to her, was a shock.
She didn't speak to Drake for most of the day.

They labored up one ridge and down, and up and down another,
and on the third ascent before lunch encountered a jolly troop of
Australian girl scouts marching down the narrow path to the tune of
"Octopus's Garden." "Earning their merit badges in bush humping,"
mumbled Drake. Tremendously excited by the sight of friendly white
faces, they clustered around the Copelands, all speaking at once.
They'd hiked in from the coast up over the Muller Range and were
now headed back to the Kapuas for the boat ride to Pontianak and
the jet home. They were learning survival skills and they were bird-
watching (seventy-six different species so far) and they were bonding
with nature. Wasn't the environment absolutely marvelous? Weren't
the people super? The orangutans grand? Shake hands, Good luck,
and the girls disappeared, singing, into the trees, a hallucination of
wholesomeness, well-being, and irrepressible youth.

The deeper in they got, the more crowded the terrain. The jungle
was crawling with foot traffic. They ran into a team of polite Germans
under contract from their country's largest pharmaceutical firm, collecting plant samples in small plastic Baggies. A party of Kenyah passed
in single file, the leader nodding once and once only, their expressions
neutral, their eyes hooded but wary, not one word spoken between
strangers.

Then, late one night, a pair of gentle Dayaks stepped diffidently
into the bell-like glow of their cooking fire. They were carrying between
them an antique spinet, scarred and buckled and missing several keys.
They were returning home to Kalimantan from the oil fields of Sar-
awak, where they had gone for work more than six months ago. This
battered instrument the first purchase of their labor. The Copelands
shared their dinner and afterward watched through a mutable scrim
of woodsmoke one of these half-naked visitors pick out with dirty fingers
the notes of "Camptown Races" in a manner rousing enough to have
them all singing by the start of the second chorus. Again, the human

voice raised in song against the noise of the forest—a gesture of gathering import. And when they were finished, the last note ringing out into the hushed darkness, there was a pause and then from some wild wordless tongue the answer of a cry almost mortal in the gleaming nakedness of its anguish.

The sound haunted them into the light and along the same trail, past the same sights they'd seen yesterday or the day before or the day before that. Drake found himself humming, whistling nonsensically, fragments of melody from a time in his life when every song was new, a motley banner in the tumultuous air. Amanda told him to shut up. They had stopped on their midmorning break and she was squatting over her bag, searching for a spare bottle of calamine lotion. When he turned, he saw that the entire back of her damp blouse from neck to waist was covered in a rich swarm of salt-hungry butterflies, a soft breathing coat of such intense color it seemed about to erupt into fiery applause. He didn't speak. He didn't move. The moment a web of frail strands he didn't dare break. It was possible to believe that beauty was a reciprocal of love and that nature bore no wiles. Then his unknowing wife straightened up, the butterflies scattered like scraps of torn paper, and everything returned to how it was before—only different.

An hour later they found a message stick planted along the trail, the raw bark at its tip peeled back in thin strips and twisted into curlicues of local significance.

"Pekit," pronounced Henry. "Pass by here yesterday maybe. No game. Very hungry."

"Are they headed home?" asked Drake.

Henry nodded.

"How far is home?"

"Two, three days for them." Henry paused. "Four, five days for us."

Foot foot, foot foot, foot foot foot.

And it was they who moved, not the forest, working a treadmill of mud and slime and green sweat without respite or hope of progress, mind sunk complaisantly into body, a stone beneath the ripples and eddying of language. For hours no one daydreamed, no one experienced a conscious thought. Sun and air and space had all disappeared forever and the Copelands were simply these tiny tired pale creatures picking their way brainless as grubs across the tangled roots of the world.

Amanda was suffering from a more or less permanent headache, whether caused by heat or fatigue or unheard-of agents she did not know. Whatever the origins, this distracting pain had apparently come aboard as an obnoxious traveling buddy for the duration. Aspirin did no good at all. A single codeine tablet she popped as an experiment turned one morning's hike into the final leg of the world-class iron woman competition. Also, despite the frequent and generous application of numerous ointments and powders, some vital portion of her anatomy remained in perpetual itch. Her mood was less than congenial.

Drake never complained. Outwardly, he appeared to be managing the course, although he was certainly not about to tell anyone of the occasional words and phrases that had begun floating out of the woods on a wave obviously directed to his ear only. Once, perched on a flowering log, scraping leeches off his calf, he heard a clear distinct voice enunciating out of the massed foliage at his back, firmly, oh-so-quietly. "Help," it said. "Help me." Startled, he whirled around, but there was no one there. Later, on the trail, he heard the same voice again but speaking in tones of a lower register. "Bastard," it said. "Bastard, bastard." The voice, now established, returned at intervals at least once, sometimes several times a day, growing louder, bolder, expanding its vocabulary, as if someone malicious were following to taunt him from the jungle cover. He was too embarrassed to mention this phenomenon to Henry—probably a not uncommon trick of the senses in an alien environment—and he refused to confide in Amanda, certain she was already monitoring him carefully for incipient signs of physical and mental weakness. He tried not to worry too much; symptom or reality, the voice, like everything else in this bizarre creation, was prisoner to a life cycle of its own that would be played out to the end regardless of his wishes or defensive measures. Just another aggravation buzzing about his head with the gnats, the flies, the mosquitoes. Give the devil no due and he'll skulk off in frustration. Keep it centered. Maintain the harmony. Shoulder on.

Too exhausted at the end of the day to talk to one another, let alone read (black scratches on a white page seemed fantastic, meaningless, and absurd), they chewed on their rice and collapsed into feverish reveries of drawn tubs and sit-down toilets and soft mattresses in dark quiet rooms and air-conditioning, dozens of vents of sweet blessed air-conditioning, the apex of civilization.

"All right," Drake snapped suddenly out of a dead silence and apropos of nothing, "this trip was one fucking mistake, I'm sorry, I apologize, we'll never attempt anything like it ever again."

"What are you talking about?" asked Amanda, visibly irritated. "Who's complaining?"

Early one morning they rounded a bend in the never-ending trail and were confronted by a weathered post carved into figures of hideous shape, the slaves of the dead; their long protruding tongues and even longer erections were hung with clumps of wilted plants and banana peels and crushed eggshells and pig and chicken bones and handfuls of other unidentifiable moldering rubbish—a *hampatong* placed at the approach to every village in order to frighten off evil spirits. Farther up the trail several unsmiling children were gathered, peering anxiously back at the tall birdlike strangers.

"Long Buwong," announced Henry.

They followed the trail into a bright sun-struck clearing where waited a silent gathering of the Pekit people, their mahogany faces fixed in stiff identical grins of such exaggerated peculiarity as to fall without the parameters of social decoding. In the surrounding shade stood a pair of active longhouses on piles at least fifteen feet high, each structure decorated in a flowing skein of interlocking spirals and curls, organic shapes, the living geometry of trees and leaves and vines amid which peeked here and there the same singularly human face of a blandly cheerful disposition. Pigs rooted and dozed in the dark mire beneath. Chickens wandered freely. A couple of hairless dogs, glued together in mid-coitus, struggled squealing into the underbrush. A young man in a Raiders cap and a black T-shirt displaying a jawless skull above the flaming logo BURNING SORE began making his way through the crowd.

"I do believe," Amanda confided quietly to her husband, "that we have entered the enchanted world beyond irony."

"Sure," agreed Drake, "but what's gonna take its place?"

The young man stepped confidently forward, shook each of their hands with great vigor, and stepped back again, all the while grinning with lunatic intensity. There followed an uncomfortable pause which the young man finally interrupted to announce in excellent English, "My father is coming." Then he stepped back again.

"Well," Amanda declared, "these are certainly a handsome people."

"I think they like us," said Drake.

The children watched them from behind their parents' legs. Most of the villagers were dressed in Western-style casual wear, baggy shorts and oversized T-shirts, though a few of the women were wrapped in beautiful sarongs of an ornate and abstract design. The pause lengthened. Then Amanda called to Jalong to bring her the green bag. She unzipped the side pocket and pulled out an armful of white T-shirts promoting her recent film *Cyberpsycho City of the Dead, Part II.* The screaming woman with the drill bit exiting her chest, "That's me," she said. In minutes every resident of the longhouse from toothless grandmas to wobbling toddlers was dressed in the outrageous shirt, whether it fit or not, a few dangling well below the wearer's knees.

Then, as if in response to some subtle cue, the excited crowd began to part, opening a path for a wizened little man with wrinkled and tattooed limbs and a wrinkled and tattooed face, the traditional pierced and stretched earlobes, one of which was torn, the pink strands dangling like stale taffy off the side of his little head. He was wearing a military-issue olive drab shirt and an elegant leopard-skin cap adorned with shells and gold coins and black and white hornbill feathers. He was also wearing the widest, thickest pair of black-framed glasses Drake had ever seen. "Look," he blurted, "it's Swifty Lazar."

This was Tama Usong, chief of the Pekit. Up close and magnified by huge lenses, his eyeballs revealed not a speck of white but sat in their sockets like a pair of transparent eggs filled with some mysterious fluid the rich dark hue of tobacco juice. With his son translating, he welcomed the visitors to his village, apologizing for the unforgivable lack of proper ceremony, but promising amends before the evening was through. He led them away from the crowd, past another wooden pole, bleached by the elements and sculpted by human hands and driven into the ground at the very center of the clearing, the axle upon which prisoners of war were once tied and sacrificed in an hours-long ritual of systematic bloodletting because without blood, the visible flow of life nutrients, the things of this world would vanish out of time.

They climbed like clumsy apes a notched wooden ladder up onto the wide veranda of the chief's longhouse. The walls and overhead beams hung with rattan mats and fishing nets were white with rice dust and the loose planks of the floor (no evidence of a single nail) clattered and shifted beneath their feet. The longhouse was partitioned into more than a dozen apartments, though many were empty and untended, daylight pouring through the holes in the rotted wood. The chief's rooms were located in the sturdy middle, a gloomy Spartan space reeking of smoke and animal grease and the musky, not unpleasant scent of the human at close quarters. The chief's possessions were few: an arrangement of artfully woven floor mats, a couple of spears, a tall blowgun leaning in the corner, several painted shields, a few baskets, an exquisite Chinese vase embellished with fierce gold dragons, and, incredibly, hanging at eye level on the otherwise bare wall, a trio of framed pictures, the official government photograph of President Suharto, the standard lithograph of a thorn-crowned and teary Jesus, and, in the elevated place of honor in between, a black and white glossy of a smirking Jack Nicholson.

"My God," exclaimed Drake, "this damn photo is actually signed."

"You're joking." Amanda moved in to read the inscription: "To Papa Usong, the Granddaddy of the hunt, Your pal, Jack."

"The chief here is blowing us away," said Drake.

The son nodded enthusiastically. "Tuan Jack is our good friend."

"Of course," muttered Amanda, wryly, "Jack is everybody's friend."

Seemed that the famous movie actor had personally visited the village many years back and had on many occasions since sent letters and gifts. Except for a guide and two porters he had arrived completely alone, a solitary wanderer who preferred visiting the noble places of the earth without the distractions of an entourage. He was a great explorer. He had danced for the Pekit people, an occasion still remembered with fondness by all who witnessed it. One day he would return and there would be such celebration as to exceed the week-long harvest festival. Were Drake and Amanda friends of Tuan Jack, also?

"Unfortunately, no," admitted Drake, "but maybe if the chief here could arrange a private head-to-head, there's this screenplay I've been working on for six years now . . ."

"We've shared the same makeup person," said Amanda.

The chief's wife emerged from a back room, carrying a teakwood tray of dainty white teacups filled to the rim with a black oily-looking brew. She radiated a daffy hospitality, beaming away at her guests, every tooth in her head stained with betel nut. Everyone was happy; the village hadn't received any visitors since the Swedish ski team came through six months ago on some sort of off-season training exercise. The chief's wife was wearing a bright yellow sarong and a length of stereo cable wrapped around her waist for a belt.

Amanda took a sip of the suspicious-smelling, lukewarm liquid. "Interesting," she said.

Drake shrugged his shoulders, lifting his brows in quizzical confusion. He stared into his cup, hoping to recognize the drink before he had to take another sip. He couldn't; he did. He still couldn't quite place the bizarre taste. "Would you please inquire of the chief," he asked the son, "as courteously as possible, just what it is we have been enjoying so enthusiastically in our cups here."

"Coca-Cola," said the son. No translation necessary.

The chief's face lit up with pleasure. "Coca-Cola," he repeated, proudly. He and his wife always tried to keep on hand a few old bottles for their Western guests. Everyone seemed to enjoy this medicine so much.

"Thank you," said Drake, solemnly. "We are indeed honored."

He offered a toast to the chief, who returned the compliment, declaring his sunburnt company "warriors of the trek," who had braved and suffered so much to travel so far to have found themselves in this simple settlement amid the maze of the big, big woods.

The chief then led his guests out onto the veranda, where the ever-inquisitive Drake asked about the heads. Weren't the rafters usually trimmed with dozens of cured heads?

The chief chuckled. All sold, long ago, for much cash to people like you. Too bad. We need money now, also.

Before Drake could ask another question, Amanda began tugging on his arm. "It's time, Mr. Curiosity, for your afternoon nap, you know how you get without those extra two hours of rest."

The chief showed them to a set of rooms exactly like his, dark, rank, and empty. The floorboards were bowed and cracked and through the rather wide spaces between they could see the bare ground underneath the longhouse, the mottled backs of the pigs nestled together in the cozy, rejuvenating mud. The chief gave them a lock and a key for the shiny fresh hasp on their door. The village was changing. People go away now to coast and come back with new ideas. Not how it used to be.

"Yes," said Amanda, "same story in our country."

The chief was surprised.

"Oh yes," she went on, "our people too go to coast, come back with new ideas. They either end up in jail or on the big screen."

Drake smiled, threw out his arms. "Look at us."

The chief embraced each in turn, speaking solemnly into their ears as he did so.

"He's giving you his personal blessing," translated the son. "He hopes your dance will be successful."

"Why, thank you," Amanda said, "what a poetic way of putting it. Honey, give him something nice."

"Oh, yes. Right." Drake rummaged around in one of his sweat-stained bags. He handed the chief two cartons of unopened Marlboros.

"More," urged Amanda. "God, you are so cheap. Give him the bottle, too."

Drake hesitated. "But I was saving that in case we got in some real trouble."

"How do you know that isn't the situation right now?"

"Oh, all right," he said with jagged impatience, and when he turned around again it was to present to the delighted chief the fifth of Johnnie Walker with all the ceremony of an officious wine steward.

"Look how happy he is," said Amanda.

"Well, let's hope he doesn't get too happy and then blame us for it."

As soon as they were alone they spread out their bedding upon the rough uneven planks and hung their mosquito netting and crawled inside and immediately fell into realms of sleep so profound as to be uninhabited by even the rarest, most monstrous dreamlife, and when soft-spoken Henry came at dusk to awaken them for the evening's festivities they rose up in confusion, unable for several scary seconds to place themselves or their whereabouts within the mystical circle of reason. Their muscles felt tenderized; they were too aware of their bones.

"Big excitement," Henry announced, barely able to contain himself. "Special treat for special visitors from Hollywood, U.S. of A. You are to come now."

They staggered to their feet, looked at one another and laughed, and they followed Henry down the veranda and into a large meeting room filled with villagers who sat on the floor in long neat rows. A pall of cigarette smoke already hung from the overhead beams like sheeting of blue gauze. The chief welcomed the Copelands with fussy animation, showing them to their seats of honor up front upon a gorgeous piece of tapestry displaying an ancient motif of interlocking dragon-dogs. At the head of the room stood an altar of some sort above which was mounted a ferocious hornbill mask. In a grave ritualistic manner compounded of equal parts of the priestly and the theatrical, the chief removed the black and gold covering cloth to reveal a wooden stand containing a twenty-six-inch Sony Trinitron and Philips (Dutch influence never far from this former colony) VCR. From a leather pouch lying on a shelf under the machines the chief produced, again with no small measure of formality, a single videocassette. From outside the longhouse came the husky cough and subsequent roar of an electric generator being cranked into action. The chief popped the cassette into the recorder. The crowd quieted; the television flickered awake. The camera was in motion, a traveling shot, tracing in distorted close-up the ominous bends and curves of a dark blue bas-relief, actually caressing the sinuous forms of—was it lettering of some kind, the title of the picture? Or was it, yes, omigod—the bat sign. Amanda and Drake turned in unison to stare at one another in openmouthed shock. Holy Incongruity! In the middle of a Pekit longhouse in the middle of a Stone Age village in the middle of an equatorial rain forest in the middle of mythic Borneo they were about to sit among a tribe of former headhunters and watch a video of *Batman*.

Though they had obviously seen the film numerous times, the Pekit attended to the dark flow of cartoon brutality with the intense concern of a graduate seminar on modern cinema. Then Nicholson appeared and the crowd went wild. The ensuing chorus of whoops, cackles, and verbal exclamations never fading entirely away but burbling on as a secondary background track, ready to flare full force the moment their man reentered a scene. And when Nicholson made his first entrance in complete Joker regalia, several of the Pekit men got so excited they leaped to their feet and started stamping deliriously upon the floor. For the Joker was the very image of the pale-faced demon who wandered alone through the forest, stealing Pekit blood by night to sell in glass jars to the white men on the coast. But the Joker was also their good friend Jack, who had tamed the demon by assuming its guise. This was their favorite film, their only film. And when, at picture's end, the bat signal shone reassuringly moonlike in the evening sky over troubled Gotham City, the audience broke into a mad ovation. Theirs was a culture that had not yet forgotten the necessity of tending to the sky and the divine matters astronomical, meteorological, and ornithological therein.

The chief stood up and the room immediately quieted. He began to tell a story. He spoke of the time when he was young and the red-chested trogons always crossed the river in the proper direction and one day he became quite ill and fell into a powerful trance and flew himself faster, higher than any bird up over the roof of the trees to a cave atop Mount Liangpran where he battled from dusk to dawn with the ferocious soul of an Iban village. And on the following day the Pekit won a great victory over that hated village and the warriors returned with more heads than anyone had ever seen and the Pekit were happy and prosperous for a long time after.

Then a second man with a deep voice and a spoon instead of a boar's tusk or tiger's fang inserted in his upper ear hole rose in place to relate the famous tale of the talking frog who lived in the pig wallow at the beginning of time and whispered to the ancestors the news that when one member of the tribe fell sick, all would fall sick, and the rice and the palm and the mango would wither and die, but that there was a remedy for such evil—the taking of human heads. Without fresh heads, everyone would die. So the ancestors followed the frog's advice and the Pekit thrived. How fortunate that in the days when the sun was young, frogs could talk!

This story reminded a third man of the garrulous head captured in battle and brought back to the village to be kept in holy sanctuary within the main longhouse, where it was bathed and caressed and engaged in social conversation and tenderly nurtured with daily offerings of food and drink and—every skull's special favorite—tobacco. For years it proved to be a good friend to the Pekit, chattering away like a pet cockatoo, all its advice thoroughly sound. Then suddenly the head fell silent, refused to speak despite long sessions of gentle coaxing. Mounds of nice fruit and vegetables and sticky rice were piled high before it. The Pekit prayed and danced and sang; thinking it might be lonely, they surrounded their friend with other heads. Nothing worked. The *padis* festered. The pig and deer fled from the forest. The people sickened and died. The few who remained gathered their belongings and moved over the hills into a distant valley where they built a new longhouse, planted new fields, and the first head taken in the first battle spoke to them and said that what they had done was good. So the Pekit learned the wisdom of moving frequently, before the spirit of each place died.

The story had altered the nature of the room as the audience, lapsing into sullen silence, contemplated the present-day implications of its truth.

The chief clapped his hands sharply twice, then called on Drake to restore the cheer. It was the funny Westerner's turn to make a fool of himself.

Drake, dependably nervous before any assembly larger than a comfortable two—a potentially fatal career flaw he'd been undergoing weekly hypnosis to try to correct—didn't know where to begin. Then he realized he could take advantage of the situation by visualizing this fascinated congregation of feathered and tattooed Pekit as a boardroom of skeptical movie execs; he could practice his pitch. So he began to tell the story of a fearsome man of chrome who traveled backward from the time not yet come to kill a woman who would give birth to the boy destined to lead the revolt against the machines. That was as far as he got. The Pekit broke into huddles of animated discussion. Several had already seen that picture and were filling in the details for their friends.

Then Amanda asked for her turn and threw the gathering into complete consternation. Women danced; women sang; they did not speak, not even the beautiful white missus from the land of many stars. Amanda insisted. The Pekit elders conferred heatedly in a corner until eventually the ethics of harmony and hospitality prevailed over prior objections. The American woman could say what she liked. Never one to shrink from a theatrical challenge, Amanda seized center stage with the authority of an inveterate ham, shooting bold darts into each Indonesian face curious enough to meet her gaze, daring her audience to interrupt her. She performed for them a vision of a tribe of brave hunters who set sail in an iron boat upon the river of time; they drift out past the jeweled stars to worlds beyond imagining in search of metals rarer than gold. What they find is a demonic shape-shifting dragon who lays siege to the boat, slaughtering the hunters one by one until all that remains is a lone woman who, after a round of harrowing battles, defeats the dragon and sets the boat on a course for home. Amanda saluted her entranced listeners and sat down. There was a moment of startled silence, then the room exploded into raucous laughter. A preposterous tale. A woman warrior? How big was this dragon? How fast? How many claws? How long was her blowgun? Upon such considerations whole philosophies have been erected. And as the discourse turned metaphysical, the mood soured.

"And you criticize me for innocently questioning the chief," said Drake. "Look at how the women are staring at you. Why don't you start signing up volunteers for an action committee?"

"Just shut up," said Amanda. "Won't hurt them to hear a different kind of story now and then."

"It's not them I was worried about."

Social disaster, if not worse, was averted by the timely arrival of dinner, pork and breadfruit and bamboo shoots and rice in sufficient quantities to feed a party twice this size, carried in steaming from the kitchens in the separate structure behind the longhouse. Then the endless bowls of *tuak*, rice wine one was expected to consume in a single swallow. After a couple of bowls, everyone was smiling. The spirit of congeniality had been restored. Now the real party could begin. The village orchestra, seated neatly along the far wall, started to play upon a variety of exotic instruments, oddly shaped drums and flutes and gongs and animal horns, infectious tunes that demanded physical accompaniment, so, one by one, as the bowls of *tuak* went around that company (one sip tasting tart and cidery, the next smooth as cream), each rose to take a turn dancing before the others, dances solemn, dances humorous, dances in imitation of the wild boar or the rhinocerous hornbill, dances in lengthy reenactment of the hunt, the women displaying an amusing fondness for exaggerated vaudevillian impressions of the pomposities of their men. The chief's son in the Burning Sore T-shirt presented an inspired parody of the Copelands' arrival, Drake's multifarious vanities punctured with consummate skill, the stiff-backed carriage, the oh-so-casual one-hand-in-the-pocket stance that couldn't quite conceal the basic underlying nervousness, the impatient supercilious look he often assumed when trying to listen to someone else talk for a change. The Pekit howled with delight; Amanda, too. The boy had even whitened his face with rice paste, enlarged his nose with a piece of folded paper, and greased his hair with pig fat to comb it straight back from his forehead. A pair of borrowed sunglasses completed the look: L.A. headhunter ultra cool.

Without waiting to be asked, Amanda leaped to her feet and started scooting energetically across the floor, cocking her head at intervals, emitting an abrupt "Beep-beep" from the corner of her mouth. Nothing would do but that this tough crowd be given a professional re-creation of classic moments from Warner Brothers' Road Runner cartoons. She barreled along the desert highway, dodging busses, cars, giant boulders launched by her archenemy, Wile E. Coyote. When she blew up the hapless wolf with a primo stick of dynamite, the Pekit squealed with pleasure. It was only when she sat back down again to thunderous applause, having fully redeemed herself with that exhibition of outrageous witlessness, that she realized how horribly drunk she truly was.

Drake, without any initiative on his part, had become hazardously involved in a disparate tussle with the potent *tuak*, a drinking contest with a young man of bottomless capacities, another of the chief's fine sons (how large exactly was the royal brood?), the contest quickly attaining the delicate point where honor and pride, etc., etc., dictated that Drake not lose, American manhood before the bar of an entire Dayak village, even as his inner gyros went swinging level with the slippery surface of the wine he was lifting cautiously as a ticking bomb to his benumbed lips. His opponent's gloating face near and far was bulging and swaying like a painted balloon, as were, he noted with a detached scientific precision, the lines and angles of the room. How could he ever have gotten so wasted so quickly? Now a young girl appeared before him, a girl with golden skin, as beautiful a girl as any that ever was, a kind girl who helped him out of his sticky shirt, his pants, too, an excellent measure considering the mounting stuffiness of these close quarters, soft caramel limbs coaxing him out onto the floor, where, stripped to a tattered pair of black boxer shorts, drums thudding eloquently in liturgical cadence, he embarked on a hunt for the great prey. A trail opened before him, the jungle of signs as clear as a book. In the blue predawn haze he crept upon the unwary enemy. He waited, gauging the transcendent moment to strike. Then, all at once, he was in motion, charging, shrieking, wielding the blade of his sweet *mandau* with a lover's zeal. He danced as he had never danced before. Heads tumbled around him like cabbages. He deposited his trophies at the feet of the girl. He went to his knees, he bowed. The Pekit, who initially believed he was imitating a mating rooster, clapped and cheered, impressed by the uncanny accuracy of his moves. Then, as the drums continued to sound, the girl helped him up and the song of the Pekit embraced the night as her silken hands sought his face, his head, his hair, stroking at his chest, his legs, his drenched skin blazing beneath her touch, all he had to do was think it and her hands completed it—was this real? was he dreaming?—but when he opened his eyes he found himself in a strange bed with a strange leg thrown across his thigh. He eased himself out from under his snoring companion and looked about the room. He recognized nothing. His shirt, his pants, his underwear, were gone. On the floor he found a loincloth one of the men had worn last night as a dance costume; he wrapped it around himself as best he could and staggered through the open door.

Outside, the milky light was as bright, as loud, as the milky wine. The veranda was littered with slumbering bodies sprawled about in every conceivable attitude like discarded mannequins. Carefully, he went tiptoeing his way among this minefield of contorted limbs. At the end of the veranda he stood gazing outward, one clammy hand clutching the rail, the other gripping his sodden penis, weaving somewhat unsteadily while attempting to christen the yelping dogs below with the ropy arc of his urine. He found Amanda among the fallen, her head hanging halfway off the edge of the veranda, where she had crawled sometime during the boisterous interminable night, the planks of the floor actually inclining uphill all the way, head changing size with each breath, body bathed in a foul sweat, and quite relieved when the real vomiting finally began, then alarmed when it wouldn't stop, emptiness emptying itself, muscles quaking, tears running freely from her burning eyes, she could hear the pigs under the longhouse rooting excitedly among the unexpected treasures of her stomach, and then nothing until the chimerical voice of her husband, his familiar hand on her shoulder, raising her into his arms, and back to the room with their stuff in it, and when next the lids of her eyes became unglued, Drake was standing over her stark naked but for a filthy scrap of Pekit cloth.

"Good God," she managed to croak, the parts of her mouth dry and thick. She looked up again. "Good fucking God."

"How you feeling?"

She squinted up at him. "You're too chunky to wear that," she mumbled. "Too pale, too."

Drake looked down at himself. "I like it. I'm keeping it on. For the duration of our stay."

She forced herself up onto her elbows. Drake's sallow, somewhat flabby flesh offered an aspect of nakedness lamentably more naked than that of their equally bared hosts. For, despite nautilus machines and morning jogs, Drake's body did not adapt well to the unaccommodated state, the cast of his skin was dull, the motion of his muscles graceless: thoughts you did not share with the one you loved.

"Our hosts," she observed, "are all on their way to Oz. You're on the way back."

"Yes, but I think I've found my movie."

She sighed. "What?" she asked.

"Me. Us. The story of what's happened here on our vacation through time."

"Do me a favor."

"Of course, my cannibal queen."

"Ask around, see if they've got some sort of magical root for a hangover, and bring it to me, quick."

He stood there pinching his waist and hips. "How can you say I'm fat? Where?"

"The root," she croaked. "Get it. Fast."

His ridiculous bare feet went thumping away down the veranda. From one of her nearby bags she pulled a half-empty quart of Evian water which she drained greedily. Once all the bottled water was gone, so was she. Fixing a limit on their village stay was a good first step on the road to sobriety. She lay still on her back, massaging her bruised eyeballs, against which beat the ragged surf of her polluted blood. A couple of months steeping herself in the poisons of this place and her whites would match the chief's. Drinking was a serious occupation among these people, a matter of confronting whatever was washed free. She had no memory of last night's festivities, other than a nagging suspicion that unwanted bowls of that vile *tuak* had been forcibly poured down her gullet once she was too fried to protest, precious shreds of her consciousness offered up raw to the leering rice goddess. The ugliest cat in the creation wandered in and began rubbing its ratty colorless fur against her hips. The beast had no tail, no ears, and no teeth and the sound of its meow was little more than a thin querulous creak. Its gemmed eyes rested upon her with the severe indifference of a stone effigy. It knows my mind, she thought. It is not a cat.

Drake returned in the company of Henry and a solemn old woman half-naked with cracked shrunken paps and a head of coarse hair tangled down to her waist. She carried herself with a remote professional air and the backs of her wrinkled hands were covered in a strange geometry of tattoos, fine parallel lines and spirals intertwining and congruent triangles and circles within circles. The *belian* of the village, Henry explained, the shaman.

She squatted beside Amanda, in swift succession palpating her forehead, her arms, her hands, her thighs, her feet. From a shabby beaded bag she extracted a single white egg which she proceeded to rub over Amanda's face and skull, crooning all the while in low guttural tones what sounded remarkably like a child's lullaby. The held egg traveled slowly down the left side of Amanda's body, then slowly up the right side. When she was finished, the *belian* raised the egg into the air above her head as if in blessing, the chanting increasing in volume and tempo, and then, in a sudden flourish, she brought the egg down sharply onto the edge of a porcelain plate at her feet. Out of the cracked shell slid the white, the yolk, a curled tuft of human hair, an orange pebble, a black feather, and a U.S. buffalo-head nickel. The *belian* scrutinized this riddling mess with scowling intensity. She remained silent for a long while. At last she sat back, hands on her knees, and she spoke, in a voice brown and ancient, its unruly syllables echoing back to spare uncluttered things, to beginnings.

How simple and few the chess pieces of the soul, thought Drake, much impressed by the potent gravity of the ritual, a tree, a snake, a bird, a mountain, a cave, a bear. The elements of everyone's story, the game time plays with human lives.

"*Belian* say," Henry translated, "problem of American lady is not with *tuak*. American lady sick from too much movie. Not good. Movies are visions sick people have before they die."

Amanda let out an ambiguous moan and covered her eyes with her arm.

"Okay," said Drake, "I can buy that. What about making them?"

"*Belian* say if American lady not healed in two days, then she sacrifice chicken and fly away into spirit world, find American lady's lost soul."

"Now, that's something I'd pay to see right now," said Drake. "How much for the chicken?"

"Please," said Amanda, without moving her arm, "thank her effusively for me. I'm feeling much better already." She had no memory of ever before experiencing such a sharpened focus of another's attention. The accompanying sadness like a wind sweeping through her. Suddenly she sat up and reached for her bag. She pressed into the *belian's* creased palm a brand-new tube of Neosporin. "For the sores on her legs," she said to Henry. "Tell her."

The *belian* accepted this gift with a dignified nod and, rising, with plate in hand, announced that she must go now down to the river to drown in its cleansing current the evil pictures she had extracted from the American lady's confused body. Her hard black eyes coldly afire with the sights she'd seen on ecstatic voyages to the country of madness and the dead, eyes which heralded the grim fact: honesty is fearful and the fearful is marrow and pith of the spirit. No wonder the woman lived alone in a detached room at the far uninhabited end of the longhouse. Hers were eyes that would never go out, in darkness or in death.

"So," began Drake, as soon as they were alone, seating himself cross-legged beside his ailing wife, "how do you feel, really?"

"Really, I feel much better."

"That's great. You know, I had a hunch this might work. She didn't want to come, of course, she's suspicious of folks like us."

"And what kind of folks are we?"

"The burn-the-trees, poison-the-well, fuck-the-kids, there-isn't-an-egg-big-enough-to-soak-up-all-the-evil kind, I suppose."

"I thought she was nice."

"An indifferent country doctor running her routine on a paying patient."

"How much did you pay?"

"Never you mind. What's important is, the treatment worked."

"Yes."

He was silent for so long she believed he'd left the room when his voice surprised her, saying, "I thought I'd go out today with the camera, you know, snap some candids of the archaic life. You think you'd be all right here alone for a while?"

"Yes, yes, I'm fine, go on, go and get your pictures."

"Well, it is research, you know."

"I said I'd be fine."

"Sure?"

"Drake," she said, realizing later, even as he went, her pallid Tarzan with a Nikon around his neck, that, no, she was not better, remained in fact exactly as she had felt upon arising, that is, thoroughly drained, bruised, hollowed out, the miserable thumping in her skull relentless as a clock.

She lay motionless on the hard floor, a wet towel folded over her forehead. In the sounds of the village around her, the barking dogs, the hammering, the ceaseless weaving of human speech, human laughter, she could hear the noise of L.A., of her home.

After an hour, unable to sleep, she wiped her face and wandered out onto the veranda. A circle of Pekit women was busy husking rice, pounding the grain in wooden containers with large clubs. As they worked, they looked over at her, they talked among themselves, they looked back at her, they giggled merrily. With a wan smile she descended the trembling ladder log to the "village green." Some naked children were dragging a sick monkey around the funerary pole on a string. There were no adults to be seen. She followed a path through a pleasant stand of cool trees and out into the baking rice fields, where she discovered her husband posing various Pekit farmers in the knee-deep paddy. His skin was the color of a baboon's ass.

"Had enough?" she called from the shade of a sheltering tree.

Drake turned around and waved. He looked like a scalded baby who'd outgrown his diaper. Heat was rising off the field as if from a sheet of exposed metal. They worked the crop, these Pekit men and women, bowed at the waist as if in obeisance to the green shoots their gnarled hands so tenderly fondled. A killing labor with scant return, subsistence level year-round: what the children fled, growing up and one by one drifting down to the lights, the cash, of the coast. How could it be otherwise? The peopled night and the forest of the spirit in exchange for outboard engines and athletic shoes and television sets. How could it be otherwise?

Clutching the camera upside down like a turtle or some rare object he had found in the mud, Drake waded over to the grassy ground where Amanda stood waiting, brushing the hair out of her mouth.

He smiled. "I didn't expect you out so soon in the midday sun."

She shrugged. "I was bored."

"Sorcery," he said. "Proven reliable in nine out of ten university studies in combating the effects of hearty partying."

"You didn't answer my question."

"Yes, ma'am, I am through." He looked down in mock amusement at this awkward seminude body he happened to be momentarily occupying. "Believe I most definitely got more than a touch of a burn out here today."

"I mean it, Drake, I'm ready to signal for the flight out."

She might as easily have slapped him across the cheek for the look of genuine shock now hanging off his face. "But we just got here," he protested. He was beginning to wave his long arms around in the generally ineffectual way he always did whenever they began an argument he thought he might not win. "We just got here *yesterday*, for God's sake."

"Yes, and excuse me for having lost count of all the yesterdays prior to that. But at this point they've blended together into one excruciatingly long day of which tomorrow and any other tomorrows we spend in this rancid sink of a country will only be needless copies. I'm tired, Drake, my head hurts, my feet stink, I want to go home."

"But I thought the *belian*—"

"I want to eat something that doesn't taste or smell of fish, I want to sit on a cold toilet seat, I want to talk on the telephone for three uninterrupted hours."

As she spoke, Drake's expression underwent a minute tightening. "Well, I'm afraid we can't depart just yet."

"Why not?"

"I've put in for permission to go out on a tribal pig hunt."

The argument continued, over dinner, and well into the night. The Pekit, sensing private difficulty, left the visitors to themselves. At last, long after the rest of the village had fallen asleep, Drake admitted to his wife, as they sat in their room glaring at one another over a sputtering lamp of tree resin, that he simply wanted to kill something in the Stone Age manner before he left forever the Stone Age life. How about this relationship? answered Amanda. Of course, Drake couldn't explain such a compulsion, it was silly, it was disgusting, it was a demand of the irrational, but when craziness was feasible and didn't hurt anyone (except the pig, Amanda pointed out), why shouldn't said demands be acted upon? Besides, the experience could also be reasonably chalked up in the research column, plus they'd spent a hell of a lot of money and a lot of sweat to reach this potentially lucrative ground (so why not take full advantage?), and furthermore, Jack had gone on a pig hunt, too. His need eventually wore her down, and when Amanda finally relented they celebrated by sharing the last Fig Newton, passing it back and forth like a joint, and he vowed that once the village council approved his request, the morning after the hunt they could pack their bags and go.

Negotiations with tribal elders turned out to be as delicate and convoluted as bargaining with production executives, and for remarkably similar reasons. The Pekit were a people whose cultural life was centered upon the nuances of the wind, their ability to read accurately the whispers of the prevailing mood. Mood was their compass, their guide, the barometer of their existence and of the elliptical shadow where the here and now overlapped with the over there of the spirit world. An inability to gauge the correct mood left one in ignorance of primal matters, exiled from the truth, and stranded on the trail to loneliness, lunacy, and hunger. Since mood consisted of a collective sense of attendant presences, seen and unseen, the ideal tactic in a tribal society was to maintain a mutually agreeable level of harmony, a genial atmosphere among all members, or a psychic debt could be incurred. And the more that was owed to you, spiritually and emotionally, the richer you were. Drake's presence on a hunt and his offer of financial reimbursement for the privilege had to be considered in this complex uncertain light. Also, since a successful hunt depended on a successful interpretation of jungle signs, the fear was that Drake, a virtual repository of Western nervousness, inelegance (of mind and body), and general insensitivity, would shatter the mood, scatter the prey. That, after all, was what the West was all about: charging in, clearing out—by gun, by bulldozer, by unritualized anxiety. So Drake's case was not a simple affair; the decision would require time, deliberation, and favorable augury. Drake was sympathetic to these concerns, he understood he was on trial, so he would wait without complaint, prove himself a capable guy by hanging out, doing whatever was asked of him for as long as it took to get an affirmative reply— the virtue of patience winning over Pekit doubts.

Six days.

Amanda's mood growing more dour with every sunset. In the morning, awakened by the encompassing sounds of communal contentment, she'd lie there on the threshold of yet another radiant day and think, I am in paradise, yes, so why am I so blue? But, try as she might, the pressure of her perceptions couldn't be long resisted: amid the extravagant unreal splendor of the land, the versatile beauty of the people, life, the mingy getting and spending of it, remained terribly obdurate (a dismaying reminder of her own hopeless enthrallment to the principle that the allure of comfort draws us on); the demands of tribal society upon the concept of individualism were of a rigor sufficient to submerge the burgeoning ego in a welter of social and spiritual necessities, there was no secret self in the commonly understood Western sense of the term, private space equaled public space and vice versa; and, over and above all these concerns, hovered the brute monotony of the Edenic condition, the same duties, the same food, the same jokes, the same sky, a mindless routine so psychically enervating no wonder the Pekit were so involved in the various dramas of the spirit world—it was their theater, their soap opera, and no wonder all visitors were compelled to perform before the assembled village—the need for novelty, for entertainment, of even the crudest brand, was universal and inextinguishable.

One night, lying patiently on the floor mat beside her husband, waiting for sleep to claim her, she experienced a vision, she saw herself from faraway, from a remarkable vantage out in deep space, from God's veranda, and she saw the world on which she lived, saw it whole for the first time, a transit stop on eternity's commuter line, the flux of fresh souls arriving, and in unbroken unnumbered succession the freed souls of the dead streaming off the planet like pollen from the head of a flower. She caught herself with a start as she began to fall helplessly through herself. Her heart going like mad. So far from home. She reached out in the dark to touch Drake's chest, its reassuring rise and fall. The world still functioned as it should, by the standard terms, all normal in the engine room, on this predestined course to what unvarying end? And outside, through the cracks between the splayed planks of the moldering wall, she could see the blackened ham of night studded with star cloves.

A discussion one evening after dinner (rice and rice with rice on it) did little to improve Amanda's humor. She discovered the chief was more depressed than she was.

A tree, he explained, is a picture of the cosmos. The cosmos exists in the shape of a tree, as does God, as does man. The flights of birds are the thoughts of God. That is why man wears feathers on his head.

The forest is man's life, but those who go away from the forest forget that this is so. When they return, the trees are always in their way and they become angry. This is when the cutting begins. They think to make life easy, but they do not understand there is no extinction. The trees and the plants and the birds and the animals that disappear from our shadow world go to take up residence in the spirit world but horribly transformed into demons, angry and vengeful. So as the great trees fall before the blades of the bulldozer, they sprout again in the night of the soul that grows darker and darker, more impenetrable, more mysterious, more evil.

Because once all the trees are gone, there will be no way to get back to God. Then there will be no God.

Drake gave the chief his Dodgers cap and a pack of clove cigarettes. He seemed immeasurably cheered.

The days passed like stones down a bottomless well.

One afternoon, as Henry was instructing Drake in the preparation of blowgun-dart poison from the boiled bark of the upas tree, Drake casually asked him if he had a *palang*.

Henry was shocked. "Where did you hear of such things?"

"In a book."

"Books are filled with much nonsense. Ancient practices to thrill tourists. Like the heads we're all supposed to have strung up like party decorations."

Drake kept looking at him, his face as serious as he could make it. "Only reason I asked, I been thinking of getting one for myself."

Henry's eyes were cool and brown, the shape of his thought flitting through like afternoon shadows on a glassy pond. When he spoke again, it was with a different voice from the one he normally used with Drake. "I don't have such a device myself, but many of the men of this village do. Many men along these rivers. Jalong wears one. But I believe this, too, is a dying practice among our people. Why would a rich American like you want a *palang*? Do your women demand them, too?"

Drake was amused. "No, no," he said, "at least not yet. To be frank, I have no idea why I am so fascinated. I'd never even heard of a *palang* until I read about them in a guidebook and from that moment I've never been able to get the notion out of my head. I suppose it's like a kid hearing about hang gliding or fire eating for the first time and knowing instantly, intuitively, that that's something he's one day gonna have to try regardless of what anyone thinks. You're helpless, you're out of control, you might as well go ahead and get it over with before your nerves give out and plunge you down into something worse."

Henry listened respectfully. "I think maybe you were born into wrong tribe. Come," he said, rising to his feet, "I take you to *palang* man."

His name was Pak Mofung and Drake thought he recognized that mischievous moon-faced grin from the first-night welcoming party. A small energetic man, he was tremendously excited by this unexpected guest. That an esteemed Westerner should voluntarily choose to visit his apartment (the neatest in the village, Drake couldn't help observing) was an extraordinary compliment. He reminded Drake of the manager of a fast food restaurant. And when he heard the reason for the call, he seized both of Drake's hands together and began pumping them vigorously. It would be an honor to perform this special operation upon Mr. Copeland, the first American he had ever so attended. And certainly for such a noble subject he would be glad to work for free, but did Mr. Copeland happen to have anything for him? Drake handed over his sunglasses on the spot and sent Henry back to the room for the last carton of Marlboros. Pak Mofung was thrilled. And when would his good friend like to have this procedure done? Now? He clapped his hands in delight.

He motioned Drake to a well-worn stool. "Please, please, sit, sit." He disappeared behind an aqua shower curtain into a back room and returned a moment later with a first aid tin filled with strangely configured shapes of wood and metal. He measured the length of the first joint of Drake's right thumb with a broken piece of a child's ruler. "Good," he pronounced. He rooted around in the parts box, muttering to himself like a lonely tinker. Fists clenched, he came around to stand before Drake. "Now, Mr. Copeland, now is the time when I am so sorry to ask you to please undress yourself."

"Sure," said Drake, "don't know how we could do this otherwise." He slid off the stool, tugged once at his loincloth, and he was naked.

"Please," said Pak Mofung, indicating the table where he had arranged a folded towel for Drake to sit on. In one hand he clutched a stubby section of bamboo, in the other a thin, highly polished nail. He seated himself on the stool between Drake's open legs. "Excuse me, please." He leaned forward, reaching for Drake's penis, and as he did so, the limp organ shrank visibly in size, recoiling from his touch, retreating up into Drake's body like the wrinkled head of a frightened turtle. Pak Mofung giggled. "Look, he want to get away from me so bad!" He giggled again. A rare man who truly enjoyed his work. After much tugging and twisting, he finally got the bamboo piece over the penis with the guide holes on the end accurately aligned. He held up the shiny nail. "Are you ready, Mr. Copeland?"

"I guess," said Drake, the feathery edges of a creeping panic beginning to envelop his body. Do I really want to do this? Do I? DO I?

"Is there a bird or animal you like in a special way?"

"I guess," said Drake, the image of a shaggy black-maned buffalo flashing into consciousness; why, he did not know.

"Do you see your friend?" Pak Mofung had positioned the sharpened tip of the nail at one of the guide-hole openings.

"Do it," urged Drake. He took a breath and gripped the edge of the table. A bolt of rawest lightning leaped across the crackling flesh of his glans and out to the rim of the knowable. He went up into the air, he came back down again.

"Done!" cried the glad *palang* man. "Look, no blood!"

The inflexible ends of the penetrating nail extended in glittering absurdity from either side of the bamboo tubing like a sword plunged through a locked box into a magician's willing assistant. Except that this was no trick. From the shyly protruding tip of Drake's penis blood began to well thickly and fall in starburst drops upon the immaculate floor.

"Okay," Pak Mofung admitted. "Maybe a little blood. But no pain, eh?" He seized one of Drake's knees, shook it like a dice cup. "How you like?"

Drake wasn't sure. He felt dazed, as if he'd been involved in a terrible accident and managed to crawl from the wreckage relatively unscathed. He looked down at himself.

"I like it," he said at last. "I like how it looks."

Pak Mofung nodded happily. "Now wife love you much."

Drake smiled. "My wife already loves me."

"Never too much, Mr. Copeland, never too much." Then his laughter abruptly ceased and he resumed his serious mask. "Now, Mr. Copeland, I'm afraid I have confession to make to you."

"Yes?" Drake braced himself.

"All out of best *palangs*, no more bone or brass wire or outboard motor cotter pin. But I make something very special for you, Mr. Copeland, very special."

From the clattering odds and ends in his first aid tin he plucked a tarnished ballpoint-pen refill. He tested it on the palm of his hand. It was empty. With a pair of pliers he twisted off about an inch and a half's worth of metal barrel which he then coated with a yellowish goo scooped out of an antique shoe-polish container. Working quickly, dexterously, he removed the nail, the bamboo sheath, and slipped the ready-made pen *palang* through the weeping hole in Drake's penis. He finished off the job by slathering the entire organ with slimy gobs of the same medicinal goo, "to keep your spear from getting sick and falling off, ha ha ha." In America, Pak Mofung advised, Drake should replace his fine ballpoint with high-quality U.S. *palang* of gold and diamond, like the one the president wears. President's wife must be one happy lady. Yes, Drake agreed, she certainly was. And Drake promised to do what he could to spread *palang* pleasure throughout the fifty states. Before he would shake hands goodbye, Pak Mofung had to try on his new sunglasses. Did he look like a movie star? Yes, said Drake, he did, and he took a picture to prove it.

"I always knew you were nutty enough to do something like this," said Amanda, gazing in candid fascination upon her newly adorned man, "but I was never sure you actually would. It looks bad; does it hurt?"

"Oh no, not at all. In fact, it's rather invigorating."

"Yeah? Let's see what you say after you take your first pee. The Vaseline glop—I assume that's some sort of healing ointment."

"Yes."

"You're not going to get infected and lose it, are you?"

"Some have died," he admitted. "Casualties on the long march toward erotic utopia."

She couldn't take her eyes off it. "Penis jewelry," she exclaimed. "What an ingenious people. When can we try it out?"

"Pak Mofung said two months, but I don't know if I can wait that long."

"Me either."

"They say that once you've had the operation, you won't ever go back. They say sensation for both partners is multiplied beyond description."

"You're a man of many parts, Drake."

"All equally lovable, I hope."

"I hope so, too."

That night, as if the piercing implement had been a rod of flint striking volatile sparks from a hard covert place within, Drake found himself unable to sleep, the tinder of his mind nicely fuzzed, high on the new-sprung chemicals of his own body, restless fingers straying irrepressibly downward to touch in ever-recurring wonder the swollen actuality of his wounded self. He felt launched, flung into space among the brave, the foolhardy, the mad, warped by the physics of desire into shapes antic and fabulous, the transmuted population of the coming world.

That night he wanted fervently to act as the vessel for what the Pekit called a "good dream," a linked succession of well-cast, spankingly paced, brightly lit images rendered with such conviction its graphic unfolding is experienced as a major waking event, an exact embodiment of real life but for the nagging apprehension that every object, every deed, is saturated in significance, for Drake personally, for the village and all its inhabitants, too. For if he could convey valuable info to the Pekit from the other side, how could they resist inducting him into the sacred friendship of the tribe? But, too jacked on his throbbing *palang* to enter the grace of a profound descent, he spent fitful hours drifting in an imaginary dugout on the current of his breath into the twilight country at the borders of consciousness, ending eventually amid a haunted grove of ironwood trees festooned with hundreds of dismembered arms and legs dangling like gaudy ornaments in all the colors of corruption from frazzled ropes of human hair, this grotesque mobile swinging silently in the soupy green light of the forest, blood dropping in a scattered singsong rhythm upon the outstretched leaves, the tumbled logs, the swaying ferns, the befouled beds of sodden moss. Wedged into the crotch of every branch was a human head, eyes distended in extravagant expressions of perpetual shock, as if the trees themselves had bred this outlandish fruit for a peek upon the world and been unexpectedly appalled by what they beheld. And the question that had been ever turning in Drake's mind found a stop: no, head-hunting was not evil, but a resolutely moral practice undertaken on specific occasions and for specific reasons which focused and contained the murderous impulses of the tribe within a ceremony of devoted attention. No, head-hunting was not evil; it was a form of prayer. Evil was a rampant thing that loped along the ground and sped through the air, a homeless hankering thing in search of companionship, a faithful friend. And when it came to find you, it would indeed come as a friend. Then, in order to restore your balance, your personal harmony, you'd have to take a head. You'd have to. Or find yourself, your family, your people consumed by evil. And then, you too might find yourself accoutered in a belt of cured skin with a knobby kneecap buckle.

Sometime before dawn the chief's son with the BURNING SORE T-shirt crept into the Copelands' room and touched Drake softly on the shoulder. Drake sat up, instantly alert. Not a signal was given, not a word spoken. Drake grabbed his jungle boots and his driest socks and his camera and followed the chief's son out onto the veranda, where a silent group of Pekit men was gathered with their spears and blowpipes and sheathed *mandau* blades. The mangy dogs milled skittishly about their tattooed legs. The chief looked at Drake, looked into him, and turned majestically away, the meaning of his gestures as clouded as Drake had always found them. A man Drake had never talked to, therefore never noticed, handed him a sturdy well-balanced spear. Drake's sensitized fingers closed around the shaft, the bumps, the nicks, the worn bald patches, the untellable history of the wood. Drake nodded gravely and shook the man's hand. The man smiled, half his teeth gone, the others broken and discolored stubs.

They filed quietly out of the village, the eager dogs trotting on ahead, down the dirt trail winding along the foaming yellow river, mile upon mile, Drake as elated as a little boy on his first trip to Disney World. He liked the casual manner with which he'd been notified of his acceptance on this hunt, the cool attitude implying both "Of course you were expected to come" and "Be grateful you've been so chosen." The forest was alive, vibrant with the tones he could recognize but not identify. Critters. Life. Even the muscleless plants seemed to reach out to him with green spatulate hands. This was it, despite the early chill, the random scratches appearing on his unprotected arms and legs, this was existence at its most effervescent, the real thing, walking the edge on a genuine Borneo pig hunt.

Nothing much happened all morning. They hiked far down the river to a favorite pig wallow off the trail where the dogs sniffed and snorted and snapped at one another, utterly unable to follow out a single trackable spoor. They went on, the frustrated hounds breaking into spells of inexplicable barking no one could hush. They spied a rare orangutan high up in the knotted bough of a dying fig tree, its sad human face peering stoically down at its hairless cousins, the famous "man of the forest," who knows how to talk but won't for fear of being put to work. One of the men moved forward into a crouch, lifting the enormous blowpipe to his mouth. The first dart hissed away into the leaves and the gentle russet-haired creature was gone before a second could be tried. For Drake the morning passed in an elevated druglike state of private bemusement, shuttling endlessly between ex-hilaration and dolor as fluently as stepping from sun to shadow and back again. The Pekit didn't talk much to one another. The mood, reading the mood. They stopped once to snack on folded banana-leaf packets of cold rice. The bland taste of the grain burst upon his tongue like a handful of liquor-filled candies. Not once this day had he directed a single thought toward himself. For several blessed hours he had forgotten totally who or what he was, an episode of longed-for amnesia that could only be interpreted as an act of grace. Now. Now he was truly on vacation.

Suddenly, from far up the trail, the nervous song of the jungle was silenced by the ferocious yelping of the dogs. All the men immediately sprinted off, Drake stumbling along behind at a brisk grandfatherly trot. When he caught up, he found men and dogs surrounding an immense thicket of thorny brush that shook and squealed like something possessed. The Pekit shouted out instructions to one another as they maneuvered themselves around the trapped boar. The noise of the dogs was as loud as stone being broken on stone. Occasionally one of the delirious animals would quit nipping at a nearby doggy ear and go tearing off into the living brush, only to return a moment later howling like some creature newly released from hell. The clump of thorns rattled and shook.

"Are you sure that's a pig in there?" Drake called out.

No one bothered to answer him. The man who had given Drake the spear remained close by his side, apparently his appointed guardian for the hunt. Wild pigs were dangerous beasts, particularly when cor-nered. Mean, ugly, and quick, they came equipped with a nasty pair of razorous tusks. Guidebook facts for the curious traveler. Drake grasped his spear and held it at the ready, or what he imagined would be a good defensive posture.

From inside the quaking bush came a yelp of canine pain and then an awful tearing clattering sound as out from his lair, in a panicked blind charge, bolted an angry black pig as big as a small buffalo, followed in close pursuit by a shrieking horde of Pekit men, their spears carried on the run like jousting lances. Even as they rushed on in jagged concert, one of these spears was abruptly raised and darted quick as a whaler's harpoon into the frightened animal's spotted flank. The pig let out a human scream and dashed off up the trail, dragging the heavy bouncing shaft behind. Incited to greater frenzy by this first hit, the Pekit sprinted away, howling in demonic unison and shaking their weapons.

The pig did not get far. A second, then a third strike crippled his rear legs, and when Drake rushed up in a sweaty pant, unable to speak, the wheezing animal was lying on its side in a bloody patch of flattened grass, its wounded body trembling feebly as if laid across a block of ice, curds of dirty foam bubbling up between its convulsing jaws, the hard round buttons of its eyes already fixed on some happier land. It smelled of blood and excrement and the corroded brassiness of carnal fear. The chief looked at Drake and gestured impatiently, speaking tersely to his son.

"He want you to stick it, too," explained the son.

All the Pekit were looking at Drake. Instinctively he knew that he dare not pause, dare not reflect, he must avoid the snares of thought, he must step up with bold decisiveness, the hefty spear gripped firmly in both hands, he must jab the keen tip deep into the sacramental flesh of this living beast—like so!—and he could instantly feel the throbbing quickness of life traveling up the shaft into his clenched fists like the not unpleasurable tingle of a low-grade current and down he pushed with an unaccustomed and profound ferocity and the spear shuddered to his shoulders and abruptly the power went out. The Pekit made jokes among themselves and patted Drake on the back. The pink Hollywood boy had been deemed capable at last. But there, on the ground before him, was this death, absolute, irrevocable, a potent mess. A sense of contagion stained the air. Drake didn't know what to think or what to feel; he was exhilarated, he was disgusted; he was thrilled, he was repelled—simultaneously—his emotions locked in such a maddening contention of equally measured opposites, honesty declared he could affirm neither one nor the other, and within this paralyzing space of dark infinite confusion, a murder twisting on its axis, Drake was struck by the dread that perhaps all this inner churning and collision marked a site whose magic had been irresistibly beckoning him since childhood. Points where the magnets pulled alike in all directions defined a human border, the pattern cast by this equilibrium of force tracing out the faintest suggestion of a shape, of being perhaps, and the invisible orders ranged in trackless silence beyond. But if this were a foundation, a potential dwelling place, what a feast of intimations and curses for brooding eternity. A towering rage passed over Drake like the shadow of a great wing, whelming in an instant conjecture, ambiguity, the tendrils of independent sensation. His hands shook and to make them stop he slammed the blunt end of his spear into the ground. He had frightened himself and he wanted to leave this jungle—but not before recording for one last time the evidence of his pilgrim's progress through the back lot of the known world. He handed the camera to the chief's son, showed him where to look, where to press, and though he couldn't quite bring himself to pose with booted foot triumphantly astride the fallen pig's haunch, he did, in waterlogged Timberlands and grubby loincloth, assume a self-consciously casual stance beside the dead creature, spear at ease, attempting to project onto the film the least dimension of the complexity he was experiencing at the moment, but seeming, he was quite sure, the compleat itinerant idiot.

The chief's son frowned, lowered the camera from his eye. He couldn't see anything through the viewfinder. The fungus, which had been proliferating inside the lens barrel since their arrival, irising steadily in, had concluded its work. The lens was completely blocked.

"And that's why we don't have a single picture of the crowning event," Amanda was explaining to their friends, the Burkes, over an elaborate dinner of Indonesian cuisine (*tempe* and *krupuk* and vegetable salad with sambal sauce and grilled carp and chicken baked in spiced coconut cream and, of course, the ubiquitous *nasi goreng*, or fried rice) back home in Brentwood, California, U.S. of A. The tablecloth was a shimmering hand-drawn batik of red, blue, and gold in the famous Cirebon "rain cloud" motif, symbol of mystical energy. On the wall were mounted a pair of *wayang* (shadow) puppets of carved buffalo hide, Siva, the Lord of Sleep, and Kali, the Power of Time. In the background, providing appropriate aural atmosphere, played a cassette recording of the gamelan orchestra, "Drifting in Smiles," a liquid tapestry of metallic sound stirred by foreign rhythms quaint and oddly melancholy.

"Screw the pictures," cried Jayce, "I want to see Drake's *palang*."

"Did it hurt?" asked Brandon.

"No more than getting it caught in your zipper," said Drake. "I thought of God and country, and did my duty."

"Does it work?" Jayce asked.

"We haven't dared try yet," said Amanda. "He's still knitting."

"A piece of metal up inside me," mused Jayce, "I don't know. What if it falls off?"

"Straight lines that shameless shouldn't be permitted to go parading about in public," muttered Drake leeringly, tapping an imaginary cigar, "and neither should you, my dear, if you know what I mean."

"Stop it, Drake," she said, pushing him away. "I'm afraid you're simply going to have to show me this bizarre ornament. I have such a poor imagination."

"See, she's already measuring me for one," said Brandon.

"Private viewings for a small fee in the bedroom after dessert," Drake said.

"I don't eat dessert."

"Oh, you're gonna love this," Amanda assured her. "A tropical delicacy."

"What happened to you two out there?" Jayce was genuinely puzzled and disturbed. "I can't believe you're even the same people."

"We're not," replied Amanda, genially. "Who wants coffee?"

"As a matter of fact," joked Drake, "we brought back these giant pods for you we found out in the forest . . ."

"You haven't mutilated your body with some exotic practice, have you, Amanda?"

"Show her the tattoo," Drake urged.

"No, you didn't!"

The Copelands laughed.

"Well, Jesus," said Jayce, "at this point I'd think you two capable of just about anything."

"You know," said Brandon, "you don't have to travel halfway around the globe to get your organs pierced. There's a shop down on Santa Monica Boulevard that'll do it, male or female, thirty bucks a hole."

"And how would you know about such things?" asked Jayce.

Her husband shrugged. "I keep my ear to the ground."

"One world, one culture," proclaimed Drake.

"And to think," said Jayce, "you survive this grueling trek through darkest Borneo to return in time for the worst earthquake in years."

"Yes," said Amanda. "We were in the grocery store and I thought I was having a delayed reaction to the trip—a total nervous breakdown."

"I had mine while we were there," said Drake.

"Yes, he did, and it hasn't stopped yet. You should have seen him in Vons."

After weeks of roughing it in Jungle World, they discovered the innate preposterousness of the modern American supermarket, its extravagant realities inducing in each of them a crazed infectious state of uncontrollable giddiness. Halfway down the first aisle and they were pulling items at random off the shelves, thrusting the gaudy absurd packaging into one another's demented faces.

"Shoestring potatoes!" Amanda screamed. "Vacuum-packed!" And—crash!—into the basket went the can.

"Cheese balls," answered Drake. "No cholesterol!" Crash!

They were naughty children on a sugar spree. The notion of gratification a hilarious joke. The more highly processed the product, the less its nutritional value, the greater their amusement, the keener their need. They quickly filled two carts with good ol' American junk food and were being not so subtly stalked by an unamused assistant store manager whose gleaming bald head, Drake decided, would make a stunning addition to the contemporary look of their living room, up on the mantel perhaps, somewhere between the laser clock and the soapstone hand grenade, when the floor turned to Jell-O and cartons of milk began tumbling out of the dairy case.

"I couldn't move," said Amanda. "People were shouting, running for the door, I couldn't move. I thought my springs had sprung."

"The lights were swaying," Drake continued, "ceiling tiles bouncing off our heads, pickle jars exploding at our feet, I thought I was gonna die."

"We were in bed asleep," said Jayce, "and I couldn't understand why Brandon kept shaking and shaking me."

"I was already up and racing for the doorway."

"Nice guy, huh? The heroic gentleman."

" 'Earthquake!' I screamed, 'Let's go!' You knew the drill, Jayce. I assumed you were right behind me."

"One more like that," Jayce declared, "and I'm gone to Oregon."

"That's what you said after the one before this."

"What would you do in Oregon, anyway?" asked Amanda. "The fresh air would make you sick, the trees would give you the creeps, the people would bore you."

"She's right, Jayce," said Brandon. "You can't avoid your birthright. You're a child of pollution and the business. You know you wouldn't be happy anywhere else."

Jayce took a sip of the deer penis wine, momentarily forgetting what she was drinking. "But I'm not happy here," she said.

"Yes, you are," said Brandon, "but you think you're not. We're all happy here, aren't we, Drake?"

"Mega-happy!"

"Let me see the bottle," Jayce demanded. "This stuff ain't half bad."

"Daddy would never permit us to move, anyway," said Brandon. "Let his princess out of his sight? I don't think so. He's got plans for the littlest heir."

"He's got plans for you, too, doesn't he?" asked Drake.

"I hope so, buddy, I sincerely hope so."

After carefully examining the label, Jayce held the wine bottle up to the light, peering intently into its murky depths. "Is this anything like mescal, except instead of a worm at the bottom of the bottle, there's something else you have to swallow?"

"If there is, baby, I know we can count on you to find it."

"Brandon!" said Amanda sharply.

Jayce poured herself another glass. "Oh, leave him alone. He's just jealous because I got another part while you were gone."

"Jayce, that's wonderful," said Amanda, glancing across the table at Drake.

"No big deal. The remake of *Breathless*. Very small role, folks, and I emphasize the word 'small.' "

"Didn't Orion already do a remake of that?" Drake asked.

"Of course," said Brandon, "and we're going to keep on making it until we get it right."

"And Godard was simply mimicking those old Monogram Studios gangster pictures to begin with, so even the original is a copy." An idea Drake found extremely amusing.

"Cud chewing," snorted Brandon in disgust. "That's the whole process today."

"Who do you play?" Amanda asked.

"A cop," said Jayce.

Now everyone laughed.

"It's a new character Daddy had added to the script to showcase his princess," said Brandon.

"He did not!"

"I'm afraid he did."

"How would you know?"

"Rusty Iacobelli."

"Rusty Iacobelli is a slimy shitass."

"He got it from Caleb."

"Caleb! The worst. He'd set his own mother on fire to tell stories about how funny she looked trying to put it out."

"Maybe so, but he hears what's going on."

"He hears what he wants to hear."

"Now, people," cautioned Drake, "let's watch our stress levels here."

"Anyway," said Amanda, "congratulations. I think that's wonderful about the part."

"Thank you," said Jayce. "It's a move in the right direction."

"Remember her first role," asked Brandon, "when she was a flesh-eating cockroach."

"A nimryx," corrected Jayce. "From the planet Torus. I was the queen. And what are you giggling at?" she asked Drake. "Mister Assistant Director on Lampshades from Hell or whatever the fuck it was."

"*Specks on a Looking Glass*. It's a cult classic."

"For what cult?"

"All right, everybody—dessert," Amanda announced, carrying in from the kitchen a stylish bamboo tray containing two coconut-sized gourds with impressively thorny husks. "*Durian*," she said, placing the tray before them. "The national fruit of Indonesia."

Drake showed them how to find the seam without getting pricked and how to wedge the blade of the knife in until the shell split cleanly open. Inside, nestled among the twin compartments of a white Styrofoam-like pod, were a pair of gelatinous gray lobes resembling diseased kidneys or the separated hemispheres of an unfurrowed brain.

Jayce drew back, wrinkling her nose in revulsion. "It smells like kerosene."

"You have to work your way past the odor," explained Drake the connoisseur, "to get at the feast of flavor within."

Jayce looked dubious.

"It smells like rancid milk," said Brandon.

"Just hold your nose," urged Amanda, "and pop a piece."

Drake, already chewing heartily on a large gummy section, made encouraging faces at his guests.

"I don't know about this," complained Brandon, his own obscene morsel slipping twice from his fingers before he finally got it safely maneuvered in between his lips. "Oysters without the half shell." He chewed and grimaced and chewed, working his way through a variety of curious expressions. "Strange," he said, "it tastes like"—he paused to consider—"it tastes like soap . . . no, hair cream or . . . or beets or bananas, no, more like onion . . . and tapioca. Fascinating, the taste keeps getting away from me."

"Isn't it great," Amanda said. "It's almost whatever you want it to be."

"The complete Indonesian experience inside one candy shell," Drake declared. "The beautiful, the ugly, the ordinary, the bizarre, the sweet, the sour, simultaneously assaulting your senses."

Brandon reached for another piece. "You know," he said in surprise, "this shit ain't half bad once you get used to it."

"Many Indonesians find it rather addicting," said Amanda. "I think it's the chameleonlike character of the fruit."

"All right, you guys," said Jayce. She made a grand show of biting into the tiniest sample and immediately spit it out into her hand. "Gross!" she exclaimed, chugging from her water glass, then deliberately wiping her tongue with her napkin. "Mayonnaise and bad tuna," she said.

"Okay, then, how about a nice hot cup of civet cat coffee?" suggested Amanda.

"Every precious bean guaranteed having passed through the alimentary canal of said feline," explained Drake. "Promotes health and longevity, too."

"You're not the same people," Jayce insisted again. "In fact, I don't know if Westerners, or anyone else for that matter, should be permitted to visit that loony island."

"It's thirteen thousand islands," said Drake. "It's more islands than there are stars in the heavens—or on the Warner back lot."

"And loony, every one."

"But there's a loony place for everybody," argued Amanda. "Even you, Jayce. Some special cuckoo spot waiting to take your measurements."

"Everyone knows Jayce's measurements," said Brandon. "They've been printed in Vogue."

Amanda smiled and raised her wineglass to her lips and, glancing up, saw to her astonishment a strange man standing in the bright frame of the kitchen doorway, a presence so incongruous and unexpected he seemed to have stepped catlike through a tear in the very air itself. The boogeyman, she thought.

It was Drake who first noticed the odd expression on his wife's face. Then he saw the man, too. He looked like a shoe salesman at the mall. The stranger was wearing a blue polo shirt and khaki pants. He was holding a gun in his right hand.

"Who are you?" Drake demanded, rising out of his chair.

Jayce froze.

Brandon twisted around in his seat to see what was happening, then tried to move back, out of the line of fire.

"Sit!" ordered the man, waving the barrel impatiently about. "Now, the secret words for tonight's game are composure, obedience, and cash."

Jayce's eyes had grown large and unnaturally bright, as if trying hard to see in the dark.

"Tommy!" It was a woman's voice coming from the back door. "I can't find the duct tape. Where'd you say it was?"

"Under the seat!" the man yelled. "The passenger's side!" Then, with a half smile, to the stunned people gathered around the dining room table, "If I have to go out there myself . . ."

"What cash I have is in my wallet," said Drake.

"On the table," Tommy ordered. "You, too." He tugged at the hair on the back of Brandon's head. "And, ladies, your purses, please."

"I don't have a purse," said Amanda, controlling her voice as best she could. The intruder's eyes were as hard and gray as sun-bleached pebbles.

"Wallet?"

"It's in the kitchen."

"Tell me where."

"On a hook with the keys beside the telephone."

Tommy nodded. "Everyone empty their pockets, too. Quickly."

No one spoke or dared to trade a glance. They began making small cairns of change, keys, combs, handkerchiefs, breath mints, etc., on the tablecloth in front of them, and when they were finished, they sat before these modest offerings, their hands in their laps, like chastened schoolchildren.

"Well, well," said Tommy, smirking at the vial of crack cocaine lying atop Brandon's quarters. "Beam me up, Scotty. The ol' Enterprise is hovering over all of us these days, I guess, the anointed and the damned."

No one said a word.

"And I suppose you don't have a purse, either," he asked Jayce sarcastically.

"In the living room."

"I possess many talents, my dear, but I'm afraid mind reading is not among them."

"Beside the white chair."

"I do hope there's some pleasant surprises in your respective wallets, folks," he said in an exaggerated drawl, "because from here it looks like a rather pathetic accumulation so far."

The back door slammed. They heard the woman's voice before they saw her haggard face peering inquisitively over Tommy's shoulder. "Pretty people," she said. Her dyed-blond hair had begun to grow out months ago and hung now, in dull unwashed strands half-blond, half-black, along thin cheeks caked with makeup that couldn't quite disguise the rampant acne. She was wearing torn jeans and a sleeveless black T-shirt. She noted the disappointing piles of change. "Is that all?" she asked.

"Tape their wrists together. Their ankles. Tight."

"I'm sorry," said Drake, "but this is all the money we have on hand. We just returned from a trip overseas."

"What are you going to do?" asked Brandon.

"Tape their mouths, too," said Tommy.

"Please," implored Jayce. "I won't be able to breathe. I've got a sinus condition."

"Tape hers first."

"Hey," said the woman. "It's you, it's Tara Toye. Look, Tommy, look who it is, Tara Toye."

"I'm not Tara."

"Yes, you are."

"My name is Jayce Starling."

"Are you sure?" the woman circled her in a crouch, examining her features from various angles.

"Who's Tara Toye?" asked Tommy.

"Oh, you know. She was in that flick about the cop . . . you know, the rebel cop with the black partner."

"I'm not her," insisted Jayce.

"You are, too."

"Please, you can examine my Actors Equity card."

The woman moved in for a final close-up inspection. She smelled of smoke and garlic and auto exhaust. "Okay, so maybe you're not. Amazing resemblance, though. You could be her twin. So, what have you been in?" But before Jayce could reply, the woman turned to her partner. "Tommy, I can't tear this fucking tape. I need some scissors or something."

"Scissors," demanded Tommy.

"Second drawer from the left by the refrigerator," said Amanda.

The woman went back into the kitchen.

Tommy pointed the gun at their uneaten dessert. "What the hell is that?"

For several long seconds no one spoke. "*Durian*," Drake said.

"Looks like a puddle of snot. That the latest among jaded trendettes like yourselves? There a special spoon for scooping it up, too?"

The woman returned, nervously clacking open and shut a large pair of yellow-handled shears.

"What are you going to do to us?" asked Brandon.

"Beats me," Tommy shrugged. "What do you think you deserve?"

"More than a visit from you," snapped Drake.

Tommy smiled. "Well, yeah, but you got it anyway, didn't you? Life's rotten with modest surprises. I know mine has been."

They sat quietly and allowed the woman to tape them up. From behind sealed mouths their frightened eyes sought the touch of one another, a lifetime of unspoken messages in those darting gazes.

Tommy turned up the wall rheostat. The room became as bright as a photographer's studio. "That's nice," he said, approvingly, then to the woman, "Turn on the lights in the living room, turn on all the lights. I can barely see a thing in here and I like seeing how other folks live. It's like visiting zoos."

"Hey," called the woman, "you should see the TV they got. Projection. Stereo sound."

"Certainly," said Tommy, "they're state-of-the-art people, they got all the right stuff." He was moving from chair to chair, rummaging through their heaped belongings, pocketing the paper money. "Twenty-three stinking bucks," he said, turning Brandon's wallet inside out. "I know you think you're oh-so-cool not carrying any green, but what happens when someone like me shows up who is in great need? What will you do? What *will* you do?" He took his time studying Brandon's driver's license. "Thirty-four?" he exclaimed in mock incredulity. "You're thirty-four? Coulda fooled me, buddy. You look at least forty. Better start eating right. Try to relax. Get more sleep." He slipped the license into his hip pocket. "Maybe we'll go over to your place after we're finished here, make a night of it, house party 'til dawn."

As Tommy rounded the table to where Drake sat waiting, Amanda suddenly jumped up, mouth, hands still taped, and bolted for the kitchen.

"Kara!" Tommy shouted, lunging back to cut her off, his outstretched hand just missing her canted shoulder as she passed. She never made it to the back door. He brought her down hard with a full flying tackle that sprained her back and caused something in her nose to go crack. "Stupid," he hissed at her ear. "Ver-y stu-pid." The heavy tip of the gun barrel tapping against her skull on each separate syllable.

Kara raced in, breathless, her fingers clutching an array of jewelry, gold chains, bracelets, earrings. She looked shocked. "What happened?"

"You stupid bitch! I said tight." Tommy tugged in disgust at the loose pieces of gray tape dangling from Amanda's ankles.

"It was tight," Kara protested. She couldn't believe what had happened.

"I'll show you tight, and I'll show you on you." He pushed himself off Amanda's body and slowly got to his feet.

Amanda's eyes had filled from the blow to her nose and now her tears were running out before her onto the nice gilt-patterned linoleum. This is my kitchen, she kept thinking, this is my house.

"Now stay here and watch her," ordered Tommy. "Can you handle that? Can you manage that one simple task?"

"Don't worry about it," said Kara.

"Well, I do, honey dearest, I truly do."

Tommy returned to the dining room. A gathering of eyes upon him like anxious birds ready to kite. "Don't look at me," he said, raising his arm as if to whip the gun barrel across Drake's face. One by one he snipped their ankle tape with the scissors and led them singly through the house, one hostage to a room, where he pushed them roughly down and retaped their feet. Tight. Brandon sprawled across the king-size mattress in the master bedroom, Drake on the twin bed in the guest room, Jayce on the rug in a utility room containing a sewing machine, an ironing board, an Exercycle positioned in front of a television set.

When he returned to the kitchen, Kara was sitting on the floor beside the bound Amanda, licking a Fudgsicle and kindly explaining to her helpless captive how all that she and Tommy needed or wanted was their money (they were operating under the duress of an unanticipated but temporary shortage) and when they had the funds, they would leave. Nothing personal. Their house had been chosen entirely at random.

"Okay, hero, let's go." Tommy heaved Amanda to her feet, walked her out into the living room. He looked around, then guided her over behind the couch, shoved her brusquely onto the floor. "I don't want to look at you anymore." When he retaped her ankles, he pushed up her pant legs so that the tape adhered to her bare skin. When he finished, he patted her familiarly on the ass, promising, "I'll be back."

Amanda lay there like a trussed animal, immobile, docile, as scared as she'd ever been, especially when they began calling each other "Tommy" and "Kara." She hoped those names were aliases. She stared at the fine weave of the rug and listened to the sounds of the intruders moving through the house. She heard furniture being overturned, drawers flung against walls, glass breaking. She didn't feel human or even real, she felt like an object, a thing. She started to gag on the tape.

When Tommy and Kara were through, they settled onto the couch to assess the situation.

"Eighty-six fucking dollars," complained Tommy.

"There's the TVs," suggested Kara. "They got a shitload of TVs, stereos, VCRs. Plenty of clothes. There's a big goddamn TV in every room. Every one."

"Crap," declared Tommy. "What would we do with that fucking crap?" And he was up on his feet, pacing the floor. At the end of his turn, Amanda could see his shoes. Expensive Nike Cross Trainers.

"I could use some clothes."

"Then take them!" he snapped. "What the fuck do I care?"

"Let's go, Tommy. If eighty-six dollars is all there is, that's all there is."

The man paced.

"I want to go, Tommy," said the woman. "I've had enough of this place. I've had enough of you."

The man's footsteps moved away to the other side of the room and off down the hallway. The woman sat on the couch. She lit a cigarette.

Suddenly, from inside the house, there was a pop. It was the loudest sound Amanda had ever heard. "Tommy!" shrieked the woman. She leaped off the couch and out of the room.

Amanda imagined the flash. She imagined the short explosion of light and that was all. The rest was unimaginable.

The woman kept screaming Tommy's name, then, "Oh my god! Tommy! Jesus hell, what did you do! Are you crazy! No, Tommy, don't, please don't." There came the furious sound of a second pop. "Oh shit, oh my god, this isn't what you said. This isn't what you said at all. Oh fuck, oh fuck, oh fuck."

The man's voice was quiet, remarkably calm. "I want you to do one."

"No I can't no please don't make me Tommy." She sounded as if she were crying.

"Stop it now," said the man. "Open my pants."

"What?"

"Open my pants. Now!"

"Please Tommy don't make me."

"Feel with your hand."

"I don't want—"

"Do it!"

"It's wet. You're wet."

"Yes. I want you to share in this experience. I want you to feel what I feel, know what I know. This is important. I want you to do this for me."

"But I can't oh my god I can't do it Tommy don't don't."

"Stop now, stop and think. Would I ask you to do something I didn't believe you could do?"

"No but—"

"I'm here, I'm with you every step of the way. We're a team, and after tonight no couple will have ever been any closer."

"I don't know I don't . . ."

And their voices trailed away as they moved down the hallway toward another room.

Amanda was alive, she was still alive, and this was life, knowing this. She could hear her heart kicking against the confining walls of her chest. She could feel in her nostrils the wind of her breath rushing out and back. She could see the terrified mouse that was her mind running round and round, searching for an exit. Then came the sound of the third pop and the footsteps heading back down the hall as from the stereo speakers the gamelan orchestra played deliriously on, nothing pleasing or placid about that discordant noise now, its bronze vagaries conducting sense down fun house steps into the randomness of hell. Death is not a natural event. It is caused only by magic or violence . . . It had always been a formidable achievement to acknowledge that you, personally, as a body, as a consciousness, were someday to have an end, unthinkable to comprehend that that day might be this one. But for now, for this particular chiming now, Amanda was alive and anything was possible, she could see, she could hear, she could feel the advancing numbness of fettered hands and feet, under her the rock finality of the floor, the urgent pressure of its absolute otherness, and she could endure in all its strident simultaneity the madness of consciousness, whole worlds flaring and gone like sparks in a void; the beauty, the horror, pasteboard categories masking the all-inclusive something that was upon her now, though there was even time to wonder, in a singularly incurious manner, after the police had come and gone and the medical examiner had removed the duct tape from her lips forever, would her departing soul emerge from the chrysalis of her mouth in the shape of a rare enamelled insect or as a fabulous bird on rainbow wings?

Eight

THIS IS NOT AN EXIT

SHIRTLESS and hipshot, the man leaned in idle solitude upon the rail, gazing fixedly out to sea, out to the edge where the world stopped and the clean sheet of blue sky was stained with the faintest discoloration, a careless smudge of charcoal that seemed to suggest that somewhere over the horizon there was fire upon the water. Then the smoke, if that was what it was, simply vanished as if it had never been, leaving nothing to look at but a stale rerun of the same old sea, the mirthless folly of the waves in perpetual curling and planing up and down the deserted beach. It was December, though unseasonably warm, the air streaming with bright surfaces, broken-bitted, a steady, dry rain of clear light. The day seemed like an arrangement set in miniature inside a crystal ornament. Behind the man, the sliding glass door stood wide open, a thin white curtain flapping intermittently in the Pacific breeze. The waves broke. The man did not move.

Inside the house a well-proportioned woman wearing only a pair of black bikini bottoms descended the spiral staircase into a living room whose aggressive decor, southwestern antiseptic, was defiled by a single dissonant note: the vulgar design of the magazine cover lying carelessly atop her polished glass cocktail table. She scooped up the November issue of *Guns & Ammo* and paused for a moment to study the slumped shape of the man lounging alone out on the deck. Beyond Will's head she could see a gracefully ugly gray pelican hovering nearly motionless in the wind before plunging, beak first, into the heaving green swells. Everywhere the currents, seen and unseen. The man did not move. The woman went on briskly into the kitchen, returning almost immediately with a handful of red grapes. She passed behind the man without speaking and took the stairs stealthily, two at a time.

Sometime later the man came back inside, closed and locked the door. He went to the bottom of the staircase, listened for a few seconds, then called abruptly up. "Tia!" he called. He waited a moment and called again. When there was still no response, he mounted the stairs heavily, one at a time.

He found her sitting up in bed, rubbing self-tanning cream over her breasts, an open book spread casually across her lap. "Oh," she exclaimed, looking up in surprise, "I didn't know you were in the house."

He remained motionless in the doorway, a huge presence filling a frame. "I called your name—twice."

She continued rubbing. "I'm sorry, I guess I was lost in this daffy book."

He came forward into the room. "The Bible?"

"I know, don't laugh. But have you ever read it? Stranger than you could even imagine."

He sat down on the bed beside her. "I didn't even know there was one in the house. Are we permitted to own a copy in this county?"

"Hector was talking about the Old Testament yesterday at work."

"Hector knows how to read?"

And then her lively eyes, dark and shiny as beetle shells, so attentive to the movement and moods of him, blinked once and abruptly went out, as if an unknown hand had reached in out of nowhere and simply snapped the switch. She seemed to be reading again, but the cold words on the page were nothing more than noises in her head to mask her thinking. One sure lesson she had learned from her years among the men was to always hold some portion of herself in reserve, the transparency of womanhood in this insidiously surveillant society requiring here and there certain opaque gaps in order to maintain even minimal standards of sanity. And, strangely enough, it didn't seem to matter exactly what part of her life she withheld, what memories, what emotions, what daily episodes, so much as that *something* that was hers and hers alone be kept secret from the man she was living with. After all, that was what they did, that's how they'd protected themselves for all these years. Tia had already outdistanced three tolerable husbands, the last a disappointed film producer whose naked body had been discovered by a passing neighbor dangling from a yellow boat cord beneath the rear deck. He was the one who'd left her with the cute son, Todd; the fancy house; and the money to purchase her own business, The Babylon Gardens, nursery to the stars, which she'd operated with great success both financial and personal, having met there many fun boyfriends and now Will Johnson, her fourth husband. He'd shown up one busy morning in response to the HELP WANTED sign in the window. He looked healthy and "interesting" and certainly strong enough to haul bags of manure on his broad shoulders, which he did with brisk efficiency and dispatch for several "interesting" months until finally he just moved into the famous house on Valhalla Drive. He hadn't worked since. And now he wasn't going to get to hear Hector's fascinating religious theories that had sent her leafing curiously through these queer pages: of how the Bible was most likely a literary con job that employed words as vestments to desexualize, to denature, to disremember the origins of Christianity, the origins of all theological belief; that under the grand guise of revelation Holy Scripture hawked amnesia and obscurity; that all beginnings were mired in pain and blood and beneath every church was buried an executioner's knife. We are descended from kings, Hector's father had told him, a people who did not shrink from the truth of the Sun Stone. Hector was working for Tia by day and attending law school at night. He and Will had never gotten along. Like repels like. So now here she was on her one day off, trying to locate this bizarre story of Abraham and Isaac in an unfamiliar text without a damn index, and not only was she not about to ask for Will's help, she wasn't even going to tell him about it.

"I think you're jealous," she said.

"Who, me?" His eyebrows knotted in boyish perplexity over those innocent gray velvet irises. "I don't get jealous."

"That's not what you were admitting so sweetly the other night at dinner."

"I must have been drunk. Besides, what does it matter? I'm a different person in every room of this house."

She had casually cupped one breast in the palm of her hand as if to weigh it. "Do you think this nipple is larger than the other one?"

"Yes," he replied impatiently, "and you're gonna need expensive and painful surgery to get it corrected."

"Well, perfection is costly," she said, staring down at herself, "but then, so is ugliness."

"You're already perfect."

"I'm getting there."

"Maybe I should have something done, too," he said, pulling at the image of his face in the mirror on the far wall, "plump up these cheekbones, straighten out this nose."

"Please. You'd probably end up looking like Boris Karloff in that awful movie you like."

"*The Raven.*"

"Yes, and after that sadist finishes operating on his face—"

"Bela Lugosi."

"—doesn't he lock him in a room full of mirrors where he goes mad from his reflections?"

"Would you still love me?"

"We'd have to cover your scars or only make love in the dark."

"I could wear a paper bag over my head."

"Or a leather mask," she mused. "That might be fun. Everyone's doing it."

"Then, by all means. We wouldn't want to be caught with our pants down in an unfashionable pose, for Christ's sake. What would the sex police think?"

"You're so cruel," she said, handing him the greasy bottle of lotion and shifting around to present her exposed back. "That must be why I love you."

Later, when Todd awoke from his afternoon nap and immediately began crying for his mother, Tia sent Will to deal with him. Todd was a nervous child whose need for reassurance was constant and exhausting. Every man who came into his mother's harried life, for any duration whatever, he simply referred to as "Dad." Fatherhood to the boy was neither a physical presence nor a biological fact but a concept of slippery, dubious quality, a role that could be, and was, played by a whole troupe of itinerant actors of varying shapes and sizes and odors and theatrical ability. He seemed to like Will, though; he responded well to his particular performance.

Will gathered up the boy and carried him down the winding stairs and through the spotless room and down the salt-seasoned back steps to the soft brown undulating beach. Todd liked to play tag with the surf, running along with arms outstretched a tiny step or two ahead of the slick sheets of cold foamy water. An oil tanker sat on the bumpy horizon like a toy silhouette pasted to a slate board. They found the petrified carcass of a dead gull half buried in the damp sand, its tail feathers stripped and torn, ridges of smooth bone showing through the left wing and shoulder. They dug birdie a decent grave and covered him over and blessed his soul and planted at his head a clumsy cross twisted out of a shredded Popsicle stick.

Afterward, the boy sat quietly in Will's lap, pale forehead wrinkled in furious thought. Then he said, "Kids don't ever die, do they, Dad?" Will looked down into his stepson's clear blue guileless eyes. "No, Todd," he answered, "they never do."

When Tia joined them, she was wearing sunglasses and her wide-shouldered Joan Crawford bathrobe. She inspected the fresh grave with the dignified sorrow of a general contemplating her losses. "Poor birdie," she said.

"He flew away home," muttered Will, leaning back to toss a small pebble out into the surf.

"Let's talk about something else," said Tia brightly. "Let's see who can race down to the old pier and back." And she was off, clots of wet sand flying from beneath her toes, playfully pacing herself just out of Todd's reach until his frantic laughter eventually gave way to cries of complaint, then anger, and when he at last stopped, refusing the diminishing delights of this stupid game, so did Tia, and she leaned down and took his soft warm hand in hers and together they walked on side by side, mother and son. Slowly, Will rose from his seat in the sand, brushed off the back of his pants, and followed after. In the rich light of the declining sun they appeared as figures of gold risen up out of the sea to adorn for too brief an interval the unrefined blandness of the air.

Years ago in that section of the beach had once stood a long wooden pier that time and tide had reduced to a broken row of ruined pilings, barnacled, algae-furred, jutting haphazardly above the swell like ancient menhirs in a rolling field. They watched the ocean lift and fall, measuring itself against these rotting shafts. Todd chased after the ubiquitous sandpipers strutting along the beach like a convention of unemployed waiters.

"You'll never guess who dropped in to buy a Christmas tree yesterday," said Tia. She could feel a shift in mood approaching and she wanted to deflect it.

"Even if you tell me," answered Will, "I probably still won't know."

"Evan Fontanelle."

He stared blankly.

"The director," she explained impatiently. *"Interstate Inferno, Blue Veins, Schweitzer!"*

"Never saw 'em."

"His mother was the actress Chana Dander, who shot her husband with a hunting rifle right in the middle of the living room right in front of the son. He was six at the time."

"Was that his father?"

"No, of course not, his father is Lars Thorwald, the head of Flagstone Films."

"I assume he got a good tree."

"Our very best."

"That's nice. Everyone likes a good tree this time of year."

They were down on their knees, drawing with sticks in the sand (he a cubist-style dog with Xs for eyes, she a larger-than-life finely detailed rose), when she casually announced, without a glance in his direction, "I feel that Si's been around quite a bit lately."

Will continued to sketch. His dog had developed a piggy corkscrew tail. "Did you call Ghostbusters?"

"He heard that, too."

"Well, and what's he gonna do about it—get together with a couple of his spook friends and go 'Boo!' outside my window?"

"You can be sure that wherever Si is, he's made the right connections. Si couldn't tolerate civilian status of any kind. So go ahead, rub him the wrong way and you're coming back as a toad or a cockroach."

"And how do you know that wouldn't be better than . . . than this?" He gestured vaguely about the scenery with his stick.

She stood and scuffed at her drawing with her foot. Then she turned and called for Todd. When she looked back at Will, he was standing there not three feet from her with the strangest expression, balanced so precisely between mirth and anger it was impossible to read. When the aliens landed, these were the faces they would wear and earthlings would be powerless to interpret their meaning. "Stop it," she said. "You're scaring me." Men, she had learned, wanted to be the hierarchs of their lives. They were not. Even so, none of the ones she had met wished to entertain seriously the notion of ghosts, the fact that they were real, they haunted, they hovered, transparent space swarmed with them, their presence so intimately familiar because many of them were us, the shades of our former lives. "Sometimes I think you're composed of more gross matter than anyone I've ever met."

"Outside of California," he replied, "I'm normal."

What could she do? The crinkle in his smile was a boon of the universe. They strolled together back to the house, and as the sun ponderously, majestically, sank, they settled down in the warm dunes to watch, a happy family enjoying the quiet close of a leisurely day, the lambent air, the slow flaming of the sky, the insistence of the waves slapping a ragged rhythm against the shore.

And later, after dinner, when it was time for sleep, they separated and retired to separate rooms, private people who respected one another's privacy.

Will lay sprawled across his unkempt mattress, staring at the television with the look of someone who had placed a bet he can't afford on a number he's certain cannot win, the remote riding his breaths up and down his bare chest. He rarely watched anything more than a few minutes before leaping channels. Around and around the carnival dial. What was the point in lingering? It was always the same: bodies, guns, cars, and food. Around the dial around the clock. The vague unappeasable itch that worked without respite under his skin seemed to believe it could find what it was seeking somewhere on that magical screen. But, typically, the more he watched, the more restless he became. He was helpless to stop. The same futile routine day after day, night after night. Click, click, click. He wanted to see something he hadn't seen before.

Sometime before dawn he must have slept, but he couldn't be sure.

In the empty kitchen of the empty house he sat at the breakfast table spooning in a bowl of fortified oats and staring at the color portable on the counter. It was a Tweety and Sylvester cartoon. "He don't know me very well, do he?" said the clever bird. Nothing, nothing, nothing, nothing, nothing. He drank a beer, then another. The ocean rolled and crashed.

Out in the garage he removed the board with the old license plates nailed to it—Illinois, Colorado, Nevada—and from the niche in the wall drew out a battered leather briefcase which he carried over to the Intrepid, the spare car Tia allowed him to drive, and flung into the seat beside him. Time to get to work. Out of the house and onto the road, a solitary in his cage, he joined the other solitaries locked and buckled into their cages, hundreds, thousands of them, all streaming determinedly along in a credible masquerade of purpose and conviction. How many understood, as he did, the true function of the car as a secret device for finding yourself?

He drove south along the coast road, the sea on his right playing peekaboo with him at the bends and curves, the city ahead lying obscured in the splendid yellow smoke of its own wastes. Every minute or two he reached out to change the radio station. Every pop tune was a monotonous fraud; every voice bellowing through the megaphone of a morning talk show issued from the mouth of an idiot. He wanted to hear something he hadn't heard before. Sometimes he imagined he could even feel the media microwaves bombarding his skin, as if he were being literally baked by encoded clichés. Here was the not so otherworldly source of Tia's intuitions about ghosts; indeed, we *were* surrounded and we had no wagons to put in a circle or any effective exorcists to fend off the assault. But these disagreeable thoughts, he well understood, were merely that—thoughts—the fleeting vagaries of an unstable moment; later in the day he would welcome the contrary opinion. This life was a merry-go-round in which you passed through the same thoughts, the same feelings, over and over again until you died. He reached out to switch radio stations. Who at this unfocused hour of the morning could bear the synthesized corn of the title track from a movie about a famous Top 40 singer who witnesses a murder and after an hour and a half of harrowing contrivance ends up sucking the nightstick of the glamour-boy detective assigned to protect her? He watched his hand move toward the dial, he glanced back at the road, he watched his hand, and then, without warning, he was invaded by a sensation, it began like an injection of black dye at the base of his spine and it rose swiftly up his back and spread, darkly hooded, out over the top of his head. Who was he? What was his name? Where was he now? Because it had happened before (everything had happened before), he knew enough to ignore the questions and stay with the car, maintain control of the machinery, because when a moment splintered like this into a million riddles, every ? was a doorway into another world, and the experienced traveler kept a firm hand on the wheel, secure in the knowledge that eventually he would catch up with himself. Even as a child, he had been subject to such irruptions, accepted their normality, and had come to see these "gaps" as the holes in the sieve of personality through which something important but undefined was being systematically strained.

In the city there were a dozen or so places that made up his city, the stops on his daily rounds. Since his mood, and often his behavior, seemed to vary so from one location to the next, he needed to visit at least three or four of these places in order to feel like a semiwhole person by nightfall, as if his being lay scattered in pieces about the town and required fresh recollection every morning.

The Adonis Health and Racquet Club was situated at the end of an asphalt drive winding in a graceful S curve through an artificial landscape of manicured shrubbery and gently rolling fairway grass. The building itself resembled one of those suspiciously low-key corporate headquarters defacing suburbs from coast to coast in the popular defensive architectural style of contemporary nondescript.

"Good morning, Mr. Talbot," said Jeremy, the boy at the front desk, above his curly-haired head the club's motto in lurid rainbow script: DESIGN YOUR SELF!

He walked on by with a curt nod. The guy with the permanent smile on his face was not a guy to be trusted. He went straight to the locker room, changed into his standard uniform of Northwestern T-shirt and USC shorts, and strolled on out to the weight room to begin his daily circuit. Toning citadel to the stars, the Adonis was crowded at every hour of the day and night. Will ignored his conditioning peers, including the famous woman on the treadmill muttering metronomically to herself, "I am fat, I am fat, I am fat, fat, fat," and went immediately to work, moving methodically from one gleaming machine to the next, carefully exercising each major muscle group in turn, watching himself in the mirrors, he enjoyed looking at himself, it was like watching someone else, squeezing the sweat from his body like juice from a lemon, day by day flushing the impurities from his soul. He was clarifying himself, he was becoming. He was always aware of his body now, its center of gravity, its stride, its stance. It was this awareness, in fact, that had finally liberated him from the prison of "normal" life.

In the shower afterward, a man with too little to look at noticed the seven blue dots arranged in parallel series on the white inside of his upper left arm and inquired if they were tattoos.

"Birthmark," said Johnson. "My lucky stars." He rubbed at the skin vigorously. "Itches when it gets wet."

"How odd," said the man. "They're perfectly symmetrical. I thought nature abhorred a straight line."

"That's a vacuum." Johnson turned off the water and grabbed his towel. "Excuse me."

"Why, yes, I believe you're correct. I was never any good at biology, anyway." He hurried to keep up, following Johnson back to his locker. "Now, what have I seen you in? Wait—don't tell me, you were the renegade cop in *Renegade*?

"No."

"The crippled ballplayer in *Diamond in the Rough?*"

"Afraid not."

"The alien prison warden in *Condemned Planet?*"

"No, look—"

"One of the prisoners? One of the scary monsters?"

"Who do you think I am?"

"Why, Ridley Webb, of course."

"If I give you an autograph, will you go away?"

"Listen, I didn't mean to bother you, Mr. Webb, and I wouldn't want you to interpret our little exchange here as the product of an intrusion. I'm not that kind of person."

"You have a piece of paper?"

The man looked down helplessly at his dripping, towel-wrapped body. "Well, I . . . ."

From inside his locker Johnson withdrew a felt-tip pen and a soiled one-dollar bill. Hastily he scribbled a signature across George Washington's placid face and handed it to his astonished fan.

"I don't know what to say," he said, examining the note front and back like a cashier checking for counterfeits. "I've seen all your films, but this"—waving the bill in the air—"this is just so like you. Thank you"—offering a moist hand—"thank you very much."

"My pleasure," said Johnson, "but don't let this get around, if you know what I mean, I'm solvent for now, and I'd like to stay that way."

"Hey, that's good. Always the joker, eh, Mr. Webb?"

"I find it's the easiest way to go. And now, if you'll excuse me, I'm gone."

Out in the parking lot, Johnson, in an expensive red wig, sat in his car, the briefcase full of hairpieces, cosmetics, and prosthetic devices open on the seat beside him. He was trying to adjust a matching red mustache in his rearview mirror. His skill in applying disguises did not seem to be improving with experience. He found it difficult to judge what looked most real. Finally, when his patience was spent and he'd convinced himself he could pass as a red-haired, red-bearded kind of guy, he cranked up the car and drove on over to a downtown block of several used and rare bookshops. He parked and put on a pair of sunglasses, a set of false uppers, and a cowboy hat that was lying on the backseat. The first store was owned and operated by a pair of burly twins who both happened to be present, so he walked right back out again.

In the second store, Gemstone Books and Rarities, he found a small young woman sitting all alone at a big desk. She was reading a paperback copy of *The Idiot*.

"Pardon me," he asked in a ludicrously affected voice, "but do you happen to have a *Ben-Hur* 1860 third edition?"

"The third edition?" she repeated, with the dreamy disoriented quality of someone surfacing from a dangerously long dive. "I don't know," she said. "I'll have to check."

"With the erratum on page 123," he added.

She typed into the computer on the desk before her. "We have a first," she said, shaking her head, "but, nope, no third. I'm sorry."

"I thought so," said Johnson. "How about the Chevalier Audobon 1840?"

She typed. "No listing," she said, looking up at this odd man with an open, pert expression as if eager to see how she could be further diverted. "That last title," she asked, "what kind of book is it?"

He leaned toward her confidentially. "To tell you the truth, I don't honestly know. They're Christmas gifts for my parents. I'm working off a list." He waved a scrap of paper apologetically in her face.

"They must be serious collectors."

"The house is full of books from the attic to the basement, if that's what you mean."

"Sounds like a wonderful home to be raised in."

"Oh, of course it was—and they gave me a precious gift, a lifelong love of reading."

"You're a lucky man."

"Yes, I suppose I am."

"Of course, my life here is relatively narrow, I only come into contact with people who read. Sometimes it's easy to forget there's that whole horrifying world of illiterate couch potatoes just right outside these walls."

"The Kartoon Kultur, yes, difficult, though, to avoid its vile contamination."

Then the phone rang and she took a call about a book that required her to search through the computer file. Johnson wandered the aisles, glancing at titles and listening to the soft modulations of her voice. Unlike people, books were so quiet. Through the spaces between the shelves he stared unseen back at Ms. Antiquarian, the impassive lenses of his eyes registering the special light and shape of her without judgment or editing. When your look went out in secret without possibility

of being returned, you were at that moment nobody and there was
safety in that state and a certain measure of contentment, but also the
ever-present danger of a forgetting deep and prolonged, permanent
losses beyond resuscitation, the person who goes in is not necessarily
the same one who comes out. Under his quivering nose swam the
names of hundreds of authors, too many—who were they all, this
garish spectacle of ranked identities?—and suddenly the great black
snake began climbing the naked tree of his spine and he had to get
out of this tiny shop and he had to do it now, hurrying past whoever
she was before she could hang up the phone and utter a word, any
word, the word that spoke the end.

As soon as he was back in his own car, he was fine again. He
understood himself, he knew how to handle such breaks in the trans-
mission. He felt hungry now, and he needed a drink, so he drove over
to The Smoking Mirror on Wilshire for lunch, best burritos in town
(this month at least), and stood coolly at the bar, nursing a glass of
"Precious Water," the house specialty, a bizarre concoction of tequila
and red mystery juice, and eyeing on the wall this grotesquely sculp-
tured face with a mammoth dog's tongue hanging lasciviously from
its grinning mouth. He was waiting for the wheel to turn. He would
remain in place until the press of human bodies, the noise, the smell,
the plain animal heat, became absolutely unendurable. He sipped his
drink and listened to the conversations around him. The chatter of
presumptuous parrots. He noticed the fingers clutching the bar, long,
elegant, expertly manicured, before he even heard the voice. "Skull-
crusher," it said, and there was something special in its tone that caused
him to glance over, but she had already turned away and all he could
see was a dark river of gleaming hair flowing down a well-dressed back.

"Excuse me," he asked, "but I have a rather curious request which
I hope you won't mind indulging."

She turned back, studied him skeptically for a moment, before the
harsh set of her features softened a notch, as if some air had been let
out of an overinflated balloon. She had dark eyes and thick eyebrows
and a thin mouth too wide for her face. She waited for him to continue.

"Would you allow me to examine your hands?" He smiled easily,
as if embarrassed by his own question.

"This isn't some new perversion going around, is it?"

His gaze went directly into hers. "No, no, not at all." He extended his own pliant hand. "I'm sorry. The name's Lyle. I'm a sculptor. I specialize in hands. Heads and hands."

"Oh, so you're not a pervert, you're a professional." The remark amused her.

"I've never heard it put so succinctly."

"I don't like to beat around the bush."

"Well, fancy that, neither do I."

The bartender arrived with her drink, a parasol-crowned, skull-shaped mug of pink foam.

"Here, let me get that," offered Johnson.

"Sorry," she said, "I don't allow strangers to buy me drinks."

"Good policy," he agreed. "The roads are fraught with marauders."

She took a sip through her straw, watching the movement of his face. "You know, I thought you wanted to read my palm. I had an old boyfriend once who went around doing that to every woman he met. He was an asshole."

"Yes, well, I'm a professional, don't forget. I deal in visions, not prophecy. Visions and Things, that's the name of my gallery."

She laughed. "Why do I have this eerie feeling that everything you're telling me you're just making up as you go along?"

"Isn't that what we're all doing? C'mon now, let me see."

"Oh, what the hell." She stretched out her arm as if to show off a ring. "Are you gonna immortalize it, me and my hand?"

"Stranger things have happened." He cradled her hand in his, scrutinizing it like a jeweler, top and bottom. "Beautiful," he declared. "The fingers of a musician."

She laughed again. "I'm afraid the only keyboard I've ever played is a Macintosh." She tried to pull away but his grip held firm.

"You don't encounter symmetries of this perfection that often. I could really do something marvelous with these."

Finally he released her. She looked at her own hands as if she'd just noticed them for the first time. "Well, Lyle, I don't want to tell you your business, being a professional and all, but frankly, I can't see it. If these aren't the broken-nailed mitts of a glorified keypunch . . ."

"Please, you do yourself a disservice. And your profile, too, you know, is quite interesting."

"Yeah?"

"Very Roman."

"Well, I eat a lot of pasta, so that probably accounts for it."

"It's all in the proportions. Millimeters, really. Beauty, you know, a matter of fractions."

"Carla," called another woman, squeezing her way through the crowd. "Our table is ready."

"Okay, I'll be there in a sec."

The woman, who might have passed for Carla's cousin, stood before Johnson and openly looked him up and down. She gave no sign of what she had seen. "In the corner," she said, "by the window."

"All right, give me a minute." Carla began gathering up her purse, her drink.

"Carla," said Johnson. "What a lovely name."

"Yeah, it woulda been Charles if I was a boy. Well, it's been fun chatting with you—I'm sorry, what was your name again?"

"Lyle," he said. "Lyle Coyote."

"Right." She laughed and shook his hand. "Of Visions and Things."

"Listen, let me give you my number." He jotted some figures down on a wet napkin. "I'd be honored if you'd consider allowing me to do your head and hands sometime."

"Why, thank you, Lyle, it's very flattering, I'll keep it in mind."

"I mean it, I think we could do beautiful work together."

"Nice meeting you," she said.

He watched her slip away into the dining room. He finished his "Precious Water" in one long swallow and shouldered his way out the door and into the parking lot. From the front seat of his car he had a clear view of the entrance, all the different people coming and going like shapes on a screen. Sometimes, especially when he was in his car, he imagined that he could see behind himself, too, that his head was equal in compass to the full horizon 360 degrees around and the sky was the polished concavity of his skull and that everything he could see or think possessed equivalent reality and the people scurrying about so industriously through the city of his mind were merely ideas that could be explicated, adapted, or refuted.

When at last she emerged from the restaurant, in the protective company of her female friends, he left his car as if in a trance and came toward her across the wide expanse of black pavement as if she were the only living thing on a deserted planet. At the unexpected sight of him her smile vanished and she spoke hurriedly to her companions, who all turned now in unison to see for themselves this man they'd already heard much about at lunch.

"Carla," he called, flashing his teeth, Mr. Geniality radiating a youthful frat-boy charm. "Hi. I'm sorry to interrupt, but could I possibly talk to you for a minute?"

She and the friends traded wary looks.

"It's important. Please." He seemed the most reasonable of men.

"Go on," said Carla to her hesitating companions. "A couple minutes. I'll be fine."

"We'll be right here," said the one who had come for her at the bar. "Over by the car."

Carla looked at Johnson now as if she'd known him longer than the five minutes they'd already shared. "I've got to get back to work."

"That's okay. So do I." He took her by the arm and led her away from the busy entrance, around the corner, where the foot traffic was less pronounced. "Please forgive me for bothering you again, but I simply couldn't allow this chance to pass without seeing you again."

She looked at him without expression, without even blinking her eyes.

"I don't know about you, but something rare happened a while ago back in there."

She waited, she would let him speak before revealing a single thought, a single emotion.

"Did you feel that sensation when we first moved toward each other at the bar, not just physically, although that was surely there, but something secret and special, moving invisibly together until it went click! loud and solid like pieces of a puzzle falling simultaneously into the exact right places at exactly the right time. Did you feel that, the tumblers dropping in a lock?"

She looked directly into the holes of his eyes for the space of one measured beat. "I gotta go," she said, bending her head and taking a step to pass him.

He reached out for her. "You won't have this opportunity again, maybe ever."

"No," she said, looking him again in the face, "I guess I won't."

He watched her step around him in an unexpected elaboration and around the corner and back to the car where her friends huddled in a vigilant group and listened to her report. He could see them begin to laugh. They were all looking at him now. Then Carla turned and called out. "Your mustache," she shouted, "I think it needs more glue."

He reached up and felt along his upper lip, where the adhesive had begun to peel away and the strip of false hair was lifting off the skin like a caterpillar on the move. Then he couldn't remember what happened between that moment, stuck out there in the middle of the cackling parking lot, feeling his face like a fool, and the moment later, out on the Santa Monica Freeway, having chased and caught up to their car; he was beginning to pass, to run it off the road, when he looked over and saw, in the driver's seat, a lone, startled man in a black mustache and a security guard's uniform. Who was *he* masquerading as?

His day was ruined now. There was nothing to do but drift around until the churning stopped. When he looked into other cars, he saw people like himself. This was L.A. Everyone was on patrol. Eventually he found himself meandering down the smooth familiar curves of Valhalla Drive. Where else was there to go?

Then, rounding the last turn before home, he was stopped by the startling chaos before him that blocked the road and transformed his dull backwater neighborhood into the scene of a natural disaster: there were trucks and cars and monster RVs and a couple of open semitrailers and a ragtag army of intent good-looking people of all ages in baggy shorts and baseball caps, many clutching hand walkie-talkies as if the hard gray rectangles were bricks of precious metal, all moving earnestly among the tables loaded with good-looking food, the folding chairs, the cables, the light stands, with a self-important arrogance, an air of imperviousness, of brute inevitability, because, goddamn it, they were members of a goddamn movie crew.

Johnson parked his car and, before he could even unbuckle his seat belt, noticed the tall thin man with rounded shoulders and a golfer's tan give him a dramatic shrug and head in his direction—a neighbor he recognized from early morning walks on the beach. "What could I do?" called the neighbor. Bright camera lights burned in his front window. Through his open door moved an army of grips, electricians, and other assorted etceteras. A set of dolly tracks ran down the edge of his driveway into the street. "They offered a lot of money," he explained. "It's a Rudy Lobo film."

"You could have said no."

"It was a *lot* of money."

"Oh," said Johnson with a sarcastic shift in his voice, "then, in that case, you had no choice." He clapped his neighbor on the back. "Dawn of the Dollar Zombies," he proclaimed, cheerfully. "Never fear, you are not alone."

"Now, look," said the man whose name Johnson had never known, had no desire to know, "I was planning on notifying the neighborhood, but this all happened rather suddenly. They weren't supposed to begin shooting for two weeks."

"And how long are they staying?"

"Three days."

Johnson continued to stare at him.

"Five days, tops."

"And how do I get home during all this fun?"

"Between takes," said the man. "They allow cars through then. They're not unreasonable people. Actually, most of the time you can come and go as you please. But it's pretty fascinating, I have to admit, to watch all these folks scurrying about doing mostly nothing or standing around doing even less."

"Quiet please!" shouted a young woman through a battery-powered loudspeaker. She had a stopwatch around her neck and a walkie-talkie in her other hand. "Rolling," she said.

"And—action," ordered someone else in a quiet unamplified voice.

Everyone hushed then, turned expectantly in the same direction like sheep grazing in a field. There followed a long-drawn-out moment of held breath in which nothing happened. And continued to happen. But no one moved, no one breathed. Suddenly, the now-closed front door crashed open and a frantic man in a torn T-shirt and jeans came charging out and across the sloping lawn. He was pursued by a woman with disheveled hair and blood on her face. She was waving a gun in the air as she ran. They fled down into the street, the camera moving on its tracks with them. The woman shouted something, then she fired the gun once, and the man pitched face forward onto the pavement. No one moved. No one breathed. "Cut!" shouted the unamplified male voice. He was seated in a folding chair with his glasses pushed up onto his pink forehead. He looked like a trial attorney having a bad day.

Then from out of the crowd of spectators came the knowing, eternally nasal adolescent voice of the true cineast: "Quite reminiscent of the famous final scene in *The Killers*, 1964. Remember: 'Lady, I don't have the time,' says Lee Marvin, gut-shot himself, then he plugs that bitch Angie Dickinson with a gun sporting a silencer the size of a tin can, staggers out of the nice suburban home, spits a gob of blood on the drive, and falls dead on the sidewalk, his briefcase pops open and all the money he's been after goes flying up into the wind, which, of course, is reminiscent itself of the final scene in *The Treasure of the Sierra Madre*. Very pretty. Great movie. It was also, incidentally, the last picture Ronald Reagan made before going into politics. He played an evil crook. No comment."

The camera was hauled back up the tracks, the actors huddled with the director, then went back inside the house. After a while someone yelled "Rolling," and the front door crashed open, and etc., etc. And again. And again. And to those watching from behind the barricades there appeared to be no significant change from one repetition to the next.

"Maybe they should have him shoot her," suggested Johnson.

"Maybe they should try making a movie with no shooting at all," said someone else.

"They did," cracked Johnson. "It's called *Fantasia*."

As the fifth take was being readied, a member of the crew in a black satin bomber jacket with the title *The Bonfire of the Vanities* emblazoned on the back strolled over to where Johnson and his neighbor were observing with amused concern a trio of harried makeup artists applying additional coats of blood to the already gore-stained face of one grimacing actress. Loftily, he informed Johnson that the First A.D. wished to see him.

"What's that?" asked Johnson. "The year Christ was born or a new rock group?"

"Follow me."

The First A.D. turned out to be a skinny, pretentious kid in his late twenties with the title of assistant director. At a glance Johnson could see he'd fucked both of the attractive young women with whistles and other silver doodads hanging fetchingly from their slender necks and who hovered attentively about the A.D.'s chair like the ladies-in-waiting they indeed were. In the magical enterprise of contemporary movie-making even the least acolyte at the very bottom of the end credit roll was touched and redeemed and illumined by the dazzling wand of media technology, everyone was a knight.

"I've been watching you," the First A.D. said.

"Yeah?"

"Yeah. You got an interesting face. You hold yourself in interesting ways." He looked up at his girls and their shiny obedient heads nodded in agreement.

Johnson said nothing. He waited to see what was next. The A.D. was staring at him as if it was his turn to produce a response. He stared back. "Look," the A.D. said at last, "how'd you like to be in pictures?"

Johnson was silent, waiting politely to see if there was more. There wasn't. "You gonna make me a star?"

The assistant director glanced up yet again to check that his assistants were enjoying this little exchange as much as he was. "No, not exactly—but, hey, who knows, everything in this industry's a crap shoot, who knows how far you could go? I want to talk to Brian about it"—another telling glance—"but I think you might be just right for our next project. You've got the look. Ever done any acting before?"

Johnson caught one of the girls studying him on the sly. He smiled. "Just the normal day-to-day stuff," he said.

"Yes, the Actors Studio of life. We get some of our best people from there. Well, listen, here's the deal. It's called *Blunted*. Cop picture. Elite multicultural squad of specially trained officers infiltrates an international gang of drug dealers and professional assassins. Bang, boom, bong. Public can't get enough. As I said, I like the way you carry yourself. I'd like you to read for us."

"As a cop or a thug?"

The A.D. laughed. "And a sense of humor, too. That's great. You have a number where you can be reached?"

"Here," said Johnson, pulling out his wallet, "let me give you my card."

"Great," said the A.D., accepting it. "So, Mr. Talbot," he said, reading the name off. "It's Larry, is it?" The two men shook hands. "And you're in insurance?"

"Sure am, got a minute?"

"Ha," he said, pointing at Johnson as he turned toward his audience. "This guy. He's great. So, listen, we'll be in touch." They shook hands again.

Johnson winked. "See you at the movies."

After the next take, they lifted away one of the blue sawhorses and waved his car through. He crept past the double rows of parked vehicles, the tangle of film equipment, as if drawn by a chain at theme park speed past an animated spectacle he'd put down money and purchased a ticket to see with his own eyes. He continued on down the empty street, easing gently into his own driveway, where he parked. He sat inside his car and stared up at his house. He'd never really looked at it before. And now that he did, it looked like somebody else's. He had the odd impression that the fancy gray exterior was only a façade one board thick and that when you finally left your car and turned the key in the lock of the front door and passed through the door you'd find yourself still outside, facing the windy expanse of the open sea. Instead, he found, as he always had, the geometric patterning of the Navaho rug, the side table loaded with yesterday's mail, and the elegantly tortured shape of the cypress tree rising up through bright architectural space three floors toward the skylight built into the roof, its twisted branches and trunk the effect, over the years, of the psychic storms within. Even without the knowledge that Tia's car had not yet returned he would have known at once the house was empty. He could smell it, the cold still absence of animal life. He went through all the rooms and in none of them did he feel safe. He got a beer from the refrigerator and went upstairs and stretched out on his bed. He switched on the television. Dick Powell and Claire Trevor were battling badness in stark black and white. "I want to go dance in the foam," declared Powell, "I hear the banshees calling."

Sometimes, despite the alluring, unflagging flow of images, the surface tension would be broken for an instant, by an especially obnoxious commercial perhaps, or an overripe cliché, and he would discover himself slipping down inside himself, below decks, into a complex of passageways of no clear design or intent, gray steel corridors, some no wider than the average auto tire, snaking up, down, and through fantastic tiers of cabins, holds, bays, compartments, some of which communicated with the bridge and some of which did not, and there the hatches were bolted and access denied to all, even he who roamed the tunnels like a fugitive expecting to find—what? The missing charts? The classified cargo? A big scaly monster? Or bastard versions of himself running amok through the equipment? And other people? Well, other people were the doll-like figures who lived among the stick furniture on the lower levels. It was a solid ship, built to last, the message of its construction inhering to each impeccable rivet: your service here, like that of those who came before and those who will come after, is temporary duty only and can be terminated arbitrarily without warning. You hoped you had embarked on the correct mission.

At the raucous sounds of their entrance, Todd's shrill cries, Tia's singsong scolding, echoing up through the hollow interior of the house, he flicked off the set and drained his beer bottle and went downstairs to greet his nice family.

He found Tia in the kitchen, cutting an apple into slices for Todd. He came up from behind, startling her, and she turned, the knife in her hand missing his chest by inches. "My God, you scared me," she said. Gently, he removed the blade from her fist and laid it neatly upon the counter as if restoring a museum relic to its proper case. Then he took her in his arms and kissed her, his hands slipping down her back to knead with slow, suggestive purpose the plump cheeks of her ass. When they stopped, she looked up at him with eyes that touched his face like stroking fingers. "Yes," she said, murmuring then against his chest, "that's what I like. That's why men should sit home all day, elevating their testosterone levels. My God, the way Si worked, what that lunatic industry did to him—he took phone calls sitting on the crapper—and on those rare occasions his body surprised him by managing to produce the gift of an erection, we celebrated, we did a goddamn May dance around it."

Will pulled himself away. "Listen, do you think it would be possible to spend more than five minutes together without mentioning that man? No wonder you sense his presence, you blurt out his name in every other sentence."

"Well, you know what my reply to that would be."

"Yes, I do, and here's my rebuttal." They kissed again for quite a long while, and even as he felt her hand moving against the crotch of his pants, he was faraway, thinking of how a name was a prison, too, binding you to a place even after you were dead and he thought: I don't belong here.

Later that night, after Todd had been fed and read to and tucked safely into bed, they "made love" in their usual manner, employing a number of devices to heighten their enjoyment, several of them stamped as authentic state property. Sex acquired an informative extra edge when you were utterly free to pretend that you were stark raving mad, the thrill of ecstatic liberation you were able to achieve blindfolded, strapped naked to the bed, a rubber gag muffling your cries so as to avoid waking the child, was positively otherworldly. "I love you," whispered Will, "I've always loved you, you are my goddess." He could smell the pine in her hair and then he came in a convulsive chain of brief explosions, as if something were being forcibly, almost painfully, yanked from his body.

Afterward, in the solitude of her room, lying contentedly atop the mussed sheets, Tia perused the pages of her secret scrapbook, a complete collection of photographs of the genitals of all the men she had ever slept with. The pictures relaxed her, prepared her for sleep as effectively as any drug. The act of looking without restriction at another's organs fulfilled a need she couldn't satisfy in any other way; pornography was generally too coarse and exploitative and penises were hardly ever revealed except when erect, in their maximum size. The lack of normal genital display was eroding the mental health of the society. We were being denied an important human birthright. On such reflections she passed into the warm waters of the dream.

And in Johnson's room the television set burned on all through the night. Earlier in the evening, in a dangerous moment of sexual abandonment, he had imagined that he was a different person and so was Tia and he had almost called out to her by a different name. The loss of control, however temporary, frightened him, and incidents like this seemed to be accumulating of their own accord. When you lost track of the names in your life, you relinquished contact with the reality of that life. It was a subject he had pondered in many a lonely room much like this one. A name was like a seed dropped into the saturated solution of time about which the shape of its letters, the sounds of its vowels, coalesced a particular, a unique identity, the fated actuality of a life. Change your name, though, and you change your reality. Events will begin falling into new, previously unthinkable patterns. Was that the meaning of this near-verbal slip, a message from the interior to refashion the design? He frowned at the television, waving the remote impatiently at it as if attempting to discipline a dog with a stick.

The next morning he scrapped his usual schedule and drove directly over to Le Gun Club, target range to the stars, a stop he wouldn't normally make for two more days. He liked the people there, and he liked the noise and the smell of powder. Names weren't a problem here, nobody used any. It was a members-only establishment for the financial and cultural elite of the city to pop some caps as other folk might drop in at the local range to hit a couple of buckets of balls. The woman on the other side of the wall in the Armani jacket and yellow shooting goggles was blasting away at her target with a Smith & Wesson 49, shredding paper. Will had two guns with him, a Sphinx AT-2000 and a Sig Sauer, both having once belonged to Si, who had bought the weapons, fired each once, and then locked them away in his closet. Why he'd decided to go out at the end of a rope was a mystery to Johnson. A bullet seemed so painlessly quick and certain. He started with the Sphinx, immediately placing six rounds into the target's B zone. Had cardboard been flesh he would have effectively demolished someone's exposed head. He enjoyed standing there in a two-fisted grip, exploding bits of metal toward a printed representation of a human body. Eye merged with mind merged with target in a deliberate and necessary yielding of self which was neither scary nor disorienting. He felt confident. He felt calm. The stresses of the last few days forgotten. Now he could go home and take a nap.

He remembered to go around the long way and enter Valhalla Drive from the north side so as to avoid that movie mess. He was a block from his house when he saw at last what he'd been expecting to see for too many months to count and he realized at the instant of perception that he'd always known, not in his consciousness, but in some deeper, truer way down in the blood because body knowledge was old, older than mind, it knew the marsh and the log and the meaning of the log and the crocodile dozing atop the log: parked in the driveway next to Tia's BMW was a strange car, a strange blue Tracer. Will immediately backed up and parked far enough down the street so that Tia probably wouldn't notice him. Then he sat and he waited. His mind was running on again and he tried to ignore it, the words forming and reforming and coming back at him no matter how often they were dispersed, circling around and buzzing his head like black predatory birds with the persistence of a truth that couldn't be fended off. He would not allow himself to hear in his ear what the letters were spelling out in his head, the sheer outrageousness of thought. He kept shifting around in his seat. He couldn't get comfortable. He couldn't keep still. Between the houses he could see the ocean, all that racket and agitation, a big heaving shape assembled out of boundlessly multiplying nervous little shapes.

An hour later he watched a man emerge from the house, his house. He removed the binoculars from the briefcase on the seat and focused in. Tia stood in the doorway, the good hostess to the end. The man, the stranger, stood beside his Tracer, jingling his keys in his hand. He was young, of course, and fit, a generic California boy with no distinguishing characteristics whatsoever, who seemed to be receiving with intent gratitude every valuable syllable dropping from Tia's mouth. Will watched: the animated movement of her lips, the immediate response of his, that old Ping-Pong game in which there were no losers. Then the lips stopped and Tia's hand went up in a friendly wave and the strange man climbed into the strange blue car and drove away.

Johnson waited until he had passed before starting his engine and pulling out after him. He was not angry. He was not unhappy. He was concentrated. There were no other vehicles but the boxy blue shape weaving about before his eyes and connected as if by an invisible cable to the front fender of his own car. Up and down, over and through, the twisting concrete spaghetti of the Greater L.A. freeway system, all the way out to Long Beach and a secluded singles apartment complex called the Sol y Sombra Courts.

Johnson followed the Tracer into the parking lot and, from a discreet distance, watched the strange man emerge from his car, lock it, and stroll casually down the shaded walk, one hand in his pocket, to turn in at a door like any other door and fumble with his keys and finally disappear into an apartment like any other apartment. From his seat in the Intrepid Will stared at the door. It was a door like any other door. He looked to the left, he looked to the right. The parking lot was empty. He looked back at the door. There was a brass number on the door. With his binoculars he could read the number. The number was 42. He got out of the car.

On the way home he stopped at Vons to pick up some avocados—he felt like guacamole—and while lingering near the produce counter he noticed a curious willowy woman in gray sweats, squeezing the plump cassava melons, one by one. He edged toward her. He smiled. "Your hands," he began . . .

When he returned at last to the sanctuary of his own house, he found Tia upstairs, giving Todd a bath. "Where have you been?" she asked. Her face drawn, her voice flat.

"Christmas shopping," answered Johnson. "Don't look in the car."

Todd stood up in the tub, pink and sleek, stubby penis protruding from beneath his belly like the plastic valve on an inflatable toy. "Look, Daddy!" he cried. "Look at me!" Hands tucked up in his armpits, he began flapping his elbows as if they were wings. He made a harsh squawking noise with his mouth and deliberately flopped back into the tub, splashing soapy water up against the wall, onto the floor, and over his mother. "Todd!" she cried, wiping blindly at her eyes. "Todd, sit!" The boy continued to giggle, watching Will for his reaction. Tia looked up. "He's been like this all day"—she turned to grab her son and shake him as she spoke—"and he's going to hurt himself."

"Do what Mommy says," urged Johnson. "She's a good mommy." He bestowed smiles like blessings to these supplicants at his feet.

"He's excited," she explained. "Santa came to playschool this afternoon."

"He did!?" asked Johnson with mock excitement.

Todd nodded his head solemnly.

"Did he have a red suit and a big white beard?"

Todd's eyes grew large with memory. "Yes!" he exclaimed.

"And did he go 'Ho-ho-ho'?"

"No!" cried Todd. "He FARTED!" The last word screamed out as he collapsed down into his suds in an exaggerated fit of helpless merriment.

"It was after lunch," explained Tia with a half-suppressed smile. "Santa had a little problem."

"It's the kids," said Will, "who keep us honest."

She looked up at him. "How are you doing?"

"Good," he said, "I'm good."

Tia began soaping Todd's back. "I had one of the guys from work out to the house this afternoon."

"Yeah?" asked Johnson blandly. "Who?"

"New man. You don't know him. Anyway, he's interested in buying that awful heap of yours."

"Really? But it doesn't run."

"It's his hobby. He likes fixing up old wrecks."

Will looked at the mirrors. They were all steamed up. "But I've had that car for years. There's sentimental value in those sprung seats and rusted chrome."

Tia smiled. "I know." She and Will had made love in its roomy interior like a couple of randy kids shortly after they met, in the deserted after-hours parking lot of the Gardens. "But I'm tired of it sitting out there in the garage, taking up space. Wouldn't it be wonderful to be able to park both cars inside?"

He thought for a moment, then abruptly turned to go. "We'll talk about it."

"I want that green monster out of my garage," she said.

"Daddy!" cried Todd from his sloppy tub of warm water. "I love you!"

Johnson went downstairs and out onto the beach. The surf seemed louder in the dark. A wind from out there in the salt night pressed softly, insistently against the contours of his face as if measuring him for a mask. It was pleasant to feel a force moving invisibly *at* him for a change and to know, more or less, the nature of its strength and the order of its interest in him. Each individual life seemed to serve merely as a culture for the incubation of mystery. And as the organism aged, the mysteries proliferated, whole colonies of them black as the spaces between the stars, and as numerous. The darkness that gobbled you up.

After a while he heard behind him the sound of approaching feet hissing through the sand, then felt the touch of Tia's hand upon his back.

"Beautiful," she asked, "isn't it?"

The moon, low and incandescent, had laid a shimmering bar of silver across the water, a highway of light.

Johnson stared up into its huge mottled eye. "Say cheese," he proclaimed. "It's like the aperture is wide open and it's about to snap our picture."

She leaned her head against his shoulder. "Such a romantic."

"There aren't many of us left."

There was a silence, then she said, "Why do you always act as though you're under surveillance? No one's watching you, Will. You're free to do as you please."

"Someone's always watching."

"Well, if that 'someone' is meant to refer to me, maybe we've got a problem."

He patted her hand. "No problem."

"Because most folks would regard my attentions as an aspect of love."

He made a contemptuous snorting noise. "Most folks."

"Please, Will, don't start."

"I never start. I only finish."

She waited until the turbulence of his words was carried off by the wind. Then she asked, "Is something wrong?"

"No."

"You haven't seemed like yourself lately."

"Really? Who have I seemed like?"

She didn't answer. She turned without a word and headed back up the beach toward the house.

He watched the twinkling lights of a freighter far out to sea moving so slowly they seemed to be not moving at all and he wondered what sort of ship it was and where it was from and where it would be tomorrow at this time and where he would be, too.

Back in his room he settled into bed with a bottle of Moosehead and his remote. He went channel-surfing. He was trying hard not to think, to remain clean by hosing himself off in the daily data stream. There were thoughts up in brain heaven anxious to be born; he could detect their clamor. There were shapes pressing at the elastic borders of this three-dimensional world; he could feel their pain. In the next moment, at any moment, anything you could possibly imagine could be rendered as fact.

He seemed at one point to wake up out of a shroud of befuddlement. All right, call it sleep. He shuffled to the bathroom. As he stood there splattering piss into the bowl, his vagrant eyes found themselves in the mirror over the sink and mind saw itself confronting a face it could not remember. Whose was this? Could it actually be his, the revealed vision of a self he'd burned down a life in sacrifice to, or just another pagan image? Where was the glass to show him that truth? He picked up a tube of Tia's lipstick—there seemed to be one beside every mirror—and he wrote upon his forehead in crude letters that read correctly in their reflection but backward on his skin the single word BOGUS.

He left his room and on bare feet padded silently down the carpeted hallway to Tia's door. His fingers, tuned to a professional thief's sensitivity, closed deftly around the brass knob of her door and soundlessly turned the cylinder in the plate like the numbered dial of a vault. He eased himself into the room and stopped, still as a mannequin in the cool blue light of the gaping moon. The dark air was alive with the presence of her, the heat and scent of a breathing animal. He did not move. Gradually, as his eyes adjusted, the image of her rose clearly into view. She was lying asleep in the bed he knew so well, her body at a forty-five-degree angle across the mattress, the pale shafts of her legs protruding like lengths of sculpted wood from beneath the covers, and in the theater of his mind he saw her eyes as dark unwinking stones set in an oval of colorless clay. He watched her for a long while. She did not move. The obscurity under the sheet. The awful toil of time and earth and the sinewy motion of the planets locked inside the design like coiled snakes.

He stepped to the open closet, his hand moving among the sleek garments that hung there like the blade of a precision machine. The hand stopped to caress a dangling fold of skinlike texture and this he drew from its hanger and, without a backward look, left the room as quietly as he had come, closing the door softly behind him.

It was a black satin dress, a favorite of Tia's she had once worn, during her life with Si, to a grand old-time Hollywood party at Steven Spielberg's house. Back in his room Will stripped off his clothes and pulled on the dress. He stood before the mirror, studying himself like someone uncertain whether to make a purchase. He sat in a chair, he lay on the bed, he walked about the room. He didn't know what he was doing. He roamed the house, upstairs and down, even making a brief appearance en costume beside Todd's bed. It seemed crucial that he visit each room, debut his new persona before the assembled objects of each individual space, submit its unique aura to the history of the house. He was feeling so jacked, not sexually, but how he did when he couldn't find anything to watch on TV. Things moved in his body quick as darting fish, and he understood these things had not necessarily originated exclusively inside him, but had hatched elsewhere and slipped hungry and unseen through the prolific air.

Sometime in the early morning he returned downstairs, and beneath the shocking light of the kitchen he cut his finger while slicing a lemon for a vodka and tonic. The sight of his own blood infuriated him. This feeble flowering of the flesh. He let the tap water run chilly and smooth over the wound until it flowed sweet and clear. He sat at the kitchen table, nursing his drink, trying to avoid in the big picture window the matching reflection of himself sitting suspended in black space over the cries and explosions of the unchanging sea.

When he finished his drink, he went down the stairs and out to the garage and felt his way in total night around the polished contours of Tia's BMW over to his ruined car, the original vehicle, the one he had arrived in so long ago. He unzipped the dress, allowed it to fall whispering into a soft puddle at his feet, and, with barely a sound, opened the door on the driver's side and climbed in. Naked he sat, hands on the wheel of the Galaxie 500, staring through the windshield into the darkness ahead. He was at the controls of himself then, up on the bridge in the captain's chair. He reached under the seat for the reassuring touch of the Glock 19, and, yes, it was still there, the Old Baptizer, it had not abandoned him, he could see the gun's sorcerous shape through the nerves of his fingers. All the bonds of a life, the swelling clusters of knot upon impossible knot, severed instantly! in the blink of a trigger. The arena cleared, except for a disagreeable stain in the sand, and you could begin anew. Reborn in a bolt of lightning and a whiff of sulphur. The chambers of the heart, the conduits of thought scoured pure and wholesome as an innocent babe's.

But then everything got complicated again and you had to do it over and the intervals between doing kept getting smaller. All he wanted now was to come to a stop, but even here, in the dank confinement of this garage, the Galaxie was moving on beneath him. Beyond the windscreen the darkness that had appeared to be so inflexible, so monolithic, was moving, too, it teemed, it swarmed with minute specks of light, just as the fires of the day danced with specks of dark, and now it was all he could see, this nervous ballet between ground and being, the eternity of noise rushing trapped between channels. There was no self, there was no identity, there was no grand ship to conduct you harmlessly through the uncharted night. There was no you. There was only the Viewer, slumped forever in his sour seat, the bald shells of his eyes boiling in pictures, a biblical flood of them, all saturated tones and deep focus, not one life-size, and the hands applauding, always applauding, palms abraded to an open fretwork of gristle and bone, the ruined teeth fixed in a yellowy smile that will not diminish, that will not fade, he's happy, he's being entertained.